MW01227276

Death By Fire

S.C. MUIR

Copyright © 2022 by S.C. Muir.

All rights reserved.

No portion of this book may be reproduced in any form without written permission
from the publisher or author, except as permitted by U.S. copyright law.

To everyone who believed in me.

PRONUNCIATION GUIDE

Mari: **Mar**-ee

Yu'güe: You-**gway**

Morana: More-**ahn**-uh

Zahir: Za-**here**

Reina: Ray-**ee**-nuh

Amí: Uh-**me**

Brahn: Br-**ahn**

Lovíth: Low-**veeth**

Orcian: **Or**-see-in

Anya: **Ahn**-yuh

Taryn: **Tare**-in

Illan: Ee-**lahn**

Ryker: **Rye**-kur

Maura: **More**-uh

Kiernan: **Kere**-nin

Hanan: Huh-**naan**

Rodrick: **Rah**-drick

Please be advised that this book contains graphic descriptions of the following common triggers: violence, fire, blood, death, memory loss, murder, kidnapping, and PTSD.

This book also references the following common triggers: violence against queer folks, homophobia, and emotional abuse from a parent.

If you would like to know if this book contains something specific, you can email my team at authorscmuir@gmail.com

CHAPTER ONE

MARI

The fresh snow crunched under Mari's boots as she ducked behind a boulder. She could see her breath in wisps as she calmed her racing heart. The trek up the mountain had been an arduous one, nearly causing her to turn around. The snow always made it hard for her to hike, and her feet kept sliding along the soft ground.

Mari watched as the white fox lay down on the snow and turned its face to the bright sun. She would have done the same thing were she not waiting for the perfect moment to strike. As her family's main huntress, it was her job to bring back any game she could find. In Yu'güe, there were three moon cycles of the year that the mountains were impassable from the snow. Mari and her mother would spend weeks collecting any meat they could to store for the harsh weather. The snowy season was already beginning, but Mari needed one last trip to the mountain.

The Yanhua Mountains were the one place she could find solace and solitude. The high snow capped peaks, when viewed from the ground, appeared to scratch the sky. From where Mari crouched, she could just make out her village. The homes of Yu'güe stood in the valley of the mountains, forming a circle of protection, keeping away intruders. For thousands of years, no one had traveled off, or onto, the island.

The fox Mari watched stirred, standing up and shaking its pure white coat free of snow. If Mari hadn't seen it lay down, the fox would have blended in perfectly with the ground. Just as the fox took its first steps away, Mari raised her left arm, palm facing the creature, and fingers bent slightly inward. She took a deep breath and snapped her hand into a fist, yanking her arm backwards. The fox collapsed to the ground in a heap as its soul flew from its body towards Mari. The translucent soul looked exactly like the fox she had just killed, and it stood at her feet, wagging its tail.

"Thank you for giving your life for us." Mari kneeled down and pressed her forehead on that of the fox's soul, closing her eyes. The tingling in her head sent electric sparks up and down her spine and when she opened her eyes, the soul had dissipated, but Mari felt it in her bones. With every animal she killed, she gained a soul to her arsenal if she was ever in danger and needed a protector.

Mari stood and made her way to the fox. Kneeling beside the carcass, she rested her backpack on her knee to pull out the wooden sled. She unfolded it from its small square into a large rectangle. The light brown sled had wide carved holes on the sides to hold the animal down as she dragged it back to her home. At the front end, a fraying rope was tied, the end of it knotted into a makeshift handle.

With little effort, Mari secured the fox onto the sled, strapping it into place. She had to slide off her wool gloves, and in the brief minutes she needed to tie the ropes, her fingers stung from the cold air. Once satisfied with her knots, she shoved her gloves back on and rubbed her hands together. Sliding her backpack back over her shoulders, she grabbed the handle of the end rope, and began her trek down the mountain.

On more than one occasion down the slope, the sled started going too fast, overtaking her. The one time she lost her grip, she dove forward, landing in the snow with a soft thud, just grasping the edge of the sled. Mari breathed a sigh of relief as she got a better grip and took the rope handle back, tying it around her waist so the sled couldn't run away.

Mari took out a dried piece of meat from her pocket and snacked on it as she walked. The dried meat her family kept in storage for the colder moon cycles and her hunting trips tasted better than cooked meat to her. While her mother detested it, Mari loved it.

As she ate her snack and trekked down the mountain, her eyes remained trained on her village, becoming larger with every step. She could just make out people walking between houses, skinning animals, and cooking their evening meals. Her small village of just one hundred people was close knit. No one had a private life because when someone did something exciting, everyone knew about it. This was Mari's favorite thing about Yu'güe; she considered everyone a member of her family.

Ever since Mari was little, she'd known to go to Liana for clothing and that her favorite form of payment was a good story. Eri would exchange pain medicine for a discussion on books he'd read. She would talk to Elder Suzanne about her grand-children when she needed a new pair of laces for her boots. Elder Myron would watch any of the children for a hot drink and pleasant conversation.

Mari's parents were the head of Yu'güe's council, and the people came to them—and now Mari—with concerns and ideas for their clan. Perán and Melinde had been chosen to lead the council nearly ten years ago and had accepted the role with honor. Being a leader in Yu'güe was not without hardships, but Mari's parents took them in stride and even asked Mari about her thoughts. For the first ten years of her life, Mari had been training to become the next leader of Yu'güe's council. Her father would read to her the meeting notes the scribe had taken and reassure her she was going to be a great leader.

But all of that changed when her brother passed.

Just days after Mari's tenth birthday, her older brother, Hanan, ran away from Yu'güe. He had been engaged to the princess of Orcian, of the Water Mages, even though he had love for anoth-er. When he told their father he did not wish to continue with this marriage, their resulting fight could have leveled houses. The same night he ran away, he had died.

On the way down the mountain, Mari stopped at Hanan's resting place. His body lay at the base of a collection of boulders that Mari visited every time she went hunting. She slid the sled to a stop and crouched down, placing her palm on the large gray stone. Mari leaned forward and pressed her forehead to the rock.

"I miss you, Hanan." Tears pricked at the edges of her eyes. Eleven years later and his death still hung heavy on her heart. "Father was wrong; you were not a disgrace."

The fear of being seen was the only thing that pulled Mari back to her feet to complete her journey. She risked a glance over her shoulder as the boulder fell out of view. Suddenly, she was five years old again. Hanan had taken her on a walk to the water so she could see it for the first time. He'd brought a few smooth rocks to skip on the clear blue sea, even though all she could do was make a satisfying plop as the stone plunged to the bottom. Mari had been completely awed by the snowy shore and the bright blue water lapping against the snow. Her eyes had nearly bugged out of her head as she'd stared at the still expanse in front of her. She'd immediately thrown a rock into the water, but instead of making a splash, it had hit a water bird directly on her head. The animal had squawked loudly and sped up the shore towards Mari, chasing her angrily. Hanan had tried to help but was laughing too hard to shoo the large black bird away. Mari had spent hours crying, but Hanan had got her to stop by offering her the last of his dried meat.

Mari's heart felt like it was covered in stone as she wiped the tears from her eyes. The last thing she wanted was for her parents to see her crying. Now, as the future princess of Brahn, she had to be strong all the time. Once Hanan had passed, Mari's father had secured a marriage between her and Prince Zahir, the next ruler of the Fire Mages. Where Hanan's marriage to Orcian's princess was questionable at best, Mari's betrothal was met with outrage.

Thousands of years ago, the four mage clans lived together. The Death Mages were hunters and protectors, keeping dangers outside their world. The Water Mages were builders, constructing homes and businesses for everyone. The Life Mages took care of medicinal needs, healing those who were injured or sick. The Fire Mages cooked and supplied food sources for the mages. All four clans had lived in the city, Brahn, that was now reserved only for the Fire Mages. They had married and interacted with each other, with some people able to use two types of magic; these people were called Dual Mages.

Dual Mages had unimaginable power. Death/Water Mages could create full tidal waves filled with the souls of those they had killed. Fire/Life Mages could create living beings from flame that could hunt for the mages and were used in life threatening situations. Dual Mages had been extremely common before the clans split, at least as far as Mari knew.

One woman, Morana, had been a Life/Death mage. She'd begun to use her magic in ways that went against everything the clans stood for. Instead of using her Death magic to hunt animals, she murdered the other mages, intending to rule over the four clans. With every human soul she took, she extended her life by one year. The Life Mages already had double the life span of the other mages, so it did not take long for her to become almost immortal. Her army of human souls was used to intimidate and control others.

Morana was eventually taken down by the Death Mages. Only using their magic for killing animals, Morana went against their very core beliefs. She was slaughtered by one of Mari's ancestors. The Death and Life mages were so ashamed of what Morana had become that they isolated themselves, so as to never let anything like that happen again. Slowly, the four clans became independent, and all dual mages were wiped from existence as time passed. Now that Mari was in a betrothal where she could give birth to a Dual Mage, her clan, as well as Brahn, were terrified.

Mari, too, did not love this plan. She feared giving birth to another Morana. Her father did everything to convince her she would not raise a murdering mage, but she was doubtful. What was to say she would not create the next Morana if no one was sure how she became so delusional?

By the time Mari arrived back at her home, her mother was already waiting to take the fox out back to bleed it. She stood outside, arms crossed, and her lips pursed. Her long, dark brown hair was bundled up into the hood of her jacket and her long fingers were hidden inside a pair of black gloves.

"Where have you been?" she asked, watching Mari untie the fox from the sled. Her voice was as cold as ice.

"Hunting," Mari said. Her fingers undid the knots efficiently and she began to drag the fox behind the house.

"Leave it. Your father wants to speak with you."

Mari nodded and handed her kill over to her mother without another word. Her heart thrummed in her chest at what her father would speak with her about. As soon as Mari was inside the warm house, she shed her thick layers and undid the laces of her boots. She found her father sitting cross-legged on the floor by the roaring fire. In the shadow of the flame, Mari realized for the first time that the wrinkles in his forehead had gotten deeper, his bald head nearly reflective in the firelight. His snow-white complexion and small circular nose mirrored her own.

"Mother said you needed to speak with me," Mari said as she sat across from her father, legs tucked beneath her. She pulled her shoulders back and looked him in the face, hiding the fear rising in her chest.

"We leave for Brahn in three days' time. You will be packed and ready to go at dawn." Peran's voice was hard as stone.

"Three days?" Mari couldn't help the outburst from her mouth. "Why have I been given very little warning?"

"What should you need warning for? Everything you need is in Brahn. You are to bring only personal items you wish to have." He turned his gaze back to the fire and poked at the burning wood with a long metal stick.

"How can you expect me to get ready to leave my home in just three days? I want to say goodbye to our people. I cannot do everything by then."

"You will do as you're told." Peran narrowed his eyes. "Unless you want to end up like your brother." He nearly spat the last word.

Mari flinched and prayed to the Gods her father didn't notice. While Peran had never said it directly, he had hinted to Mari that *he* was Hanan's killer. "Yes, Father. I will begin to get my things together."

Mari trudged to her bedroom, the weight of what was to come heavy on her heart.

CHAPTER TWO

ZAHIR

Zahir's footsteps were soft as he glided through the shadows of the city. He held the black hood tight around his chin, begging his white hair to remain hidden; in the shining moonlight, anyone would notice it. He moved silently, peering out from behind corners before he made his next step. He had mastered this way of navigating the inner city of Brahn; after all, a prince had to explore his own city.

Zahir had wandered through Brahn at least once a moon cycle since he was twelve years old. Now, at twenty-five, he didn't even notice the restaurants and taverns pulling patrons in with the overwhelming smells of spices and stews. He blocked out the clinking of glasses and raucous laughter that filled the streets late at night. He did notice, however, how as he went deeper into the heart of the city, the cracked windowpanes and the rats scuttling around his ankles. The streetlights changed from torches to natural moonlight and he relished in the silence that contrasted the loud streets. It was in these areas he knew it was less likely he would be seen.

Three days into the moon cycle, Zahir and his friends would drink at the smallest tavern in Brahn. On this night, the bar would close its doors, only to open them for the high prince and his guests. Zahir had never asked them to do this, but they insisted. Even if being the tavern where the prince drank would make them the most popular establishment in the city, they had expressed their desire to keep Zahir's secret. So, each moon cycle, he would walk into a nearly empty bar, save for the table with his closest friends.

Which was why Zahir was confused when he saw only Reina sitting at their usual table. Her long black hair was tied up with gold ribbons that she kept moving out of her face, her dark brown skin matching her equally brown eyes. Out of all his friends, Zahir liked Reina the best. She never just told Zahir what he wanted to hear like everyone else in his life did. He appreciated her honesty and loyalty, and the fact she was engaged to one of his royal guards meant he saw her around often.

"Where is everyone else?" Zahir asked, sliding into the seat across from Reina. He took a quick glance around and lowered his hood, exposing his face, with it his golden skin and white hair.

"I don't know. This is very unlike them," Reina said. She held up two fingers to the barkeep, who nodded and began making their drinks. The group had a specific drink order that never changed.

"What could have possibly held them up? Rodrick is not on duty tonight, and Kiernan should have been out of his father's shop hours ago." A sudden panic rode through him. What if the rebels had gotten to his friends on their way here? Since Zahir's betrothal to the Yu'güe princess was announced, there had been increased turmoil in Brahn. His people were terrified of a marriage between a Fire and Death Mage. They screamed for change, begged for it to be stopped, and often turned to violence as a means to protest. Over the past several moon cycles, as the wedding drew closer, the rebels had begun to burn homes and shops in the city, costing Zahir's people their jobs and sometimes their lives. He was becoming increasingly frustrated, especially since his father, King Ryker, had been fighting their violence with threats.

Every night the city burned, the king issued a new decree. At first, it started with enacting a curfew: everyone had to be in their homes from sundown to sunup. When this did nothing to quell the violence, Ryker began restricting the flow of goods to parts of the city. It started with luxury items, like metals for jewelry. After that, he instituted more restrictions, including things like fruit, fabric for clothing, and firewood. Without these items, Zahir noticed the clothing people wore became more tattered, their expressions angrier.

Zahir had tried to speak out against his father, but Ryker was simply angered and would not listen to advice from his son, who was 'not yet ready to assume the throne'. Every time Zahir told Ryker that what he was doing was wrong, he watched his father go from annoyed to furious and had, on several occasions, been thrown out of council meetings. On days like that, he wished there was something he could do for his people. During one moon cycle, he found food and clothing and moved them out of the palace to distribute them to the city. When Ryker found out, Zahir was kept away from his council meetings for a full two moon cycles.

"How are things at the palace?" Reina asked after their drinks were set on the table.

Zahir took a long sip of his drink before he answered. "My father's memory is getting worse."

"Oh, no. What happened this time?"

"He can't seem to remember what he has done to keep the rebels at bay. He keeps saying strange things, like how I'm different from my siblings, or how my mother is too good for him. I don't remember the last time he even addressed Roan by name. He keeps calling him 'my boy.'"

"Gods, how is Roan handling it?"

Zahir sighed. "I don't know. He's only nine, so he may not even notice."

Ryker's memory had been slipping for several years, but since the rebel attacks had increased, it seemed it was going faster. He had trouble remembering the names of his guards and advisors. He forgot about meetings he was required to attend, forcing Zahir to go in his place. Ryker struggled to remember what day it was, or how many moon cycles had passed since something happened. Most recently, he forgot Roan's ninth birthday. Zahir's brother had been devastated when his father had failed to attend the festivities.

"How are you holding up?" Reina asked, taking a drink.

"It's... not easy." Zahir leaned forward on his elbows and rested the heel of his right hand on his cheek. "I don't like seeing him like this. And there is nothing I can do to help."

Reina offered Zahir a soft smile. "If there is anything I can do, tell me. My father is a tradesman; he may be able to smuggle medicine from Lovíth."

"We have tried." Zahir sighed. "They check all cargo before departure."

"Wow, and I thought the Death Mages were cold."

Reina's contagious laugh pulled a chuckle out of Zahir. While he found the joke funny, he couldn't help but wonder if his future bride would be cold and distant, like Yu'güe's landscape. While his marriage had been arranged for a decade, he had learned about Princess Mari of Yu'güe through the yearly letters they exchanged. He had discovered her role as a huntress, her favorite food, and what Yu'güe was like; the way that Mari described it, Zahir could almost picture the snowy mountains that rose above her village.

In the time he had spent reading about the Death Mages, he could not find one single passage about their personality, other than that they were peaceful. He knew his wife would be a pacifist. He knew she could kill people in an instant, and had learned that they ate their dead, instead of giving them a proper funeral. He'd been told they could raise the dead, if their bodies had been eaten by the mage. Zahir had also read that they could speak to the souls they had killed and ask for advice on their life troubles. He wasn't sure whether he believed that, because if he were asking for advice, what would a dead mage know about current affairs?

Zahir tilted the rest of his drink into his mouth and stood up abruptly. "I should be heading back. With the rebel attacks, I should not have come tonight. If the others come, will you tell them I'm sorry?"

With Reina's agreement, Zahir slid his hair back into the hood and slipped it over his head. He wrapped his cloak around his broad frame and stepped out into the chilly night air. The moisture in the air was so low that Brahn's scorching day temperatures turned into cold evenings. Going outside at night was nearly unbearable without a light outer layer, whereas during the day, any extra fabric was too much. Zahir liked the night; there was something comforting about his cloak wrapped tightly around his body.

While Ryker had enforced curfews, there were still people out wandering hours past sundown. His plan was not well enforced as there were not nearly enough guards to patrol the city and corral people into their homes, which the people had quickly surmised. The bright flames that lit the street cast an eerie glow on the pavement and he evaded them as he walked, knowing this path to the palace was rarely ever policed.

Which was why Zahir was surprised when he saw two of his father's guards pulling a cowering child and her mother out of their home. The little girl couldn't have been taller than his waist, and her mother's wide eyes were filled with terror. The woman pleaded with the guards, insisting they hadn't done anything wrong. Tears ran down her cheeks as she held her trembling hands clasped in front of her chest.

The two guards stabbed both the woman and the child in the stomach and Zahir jumped out from his hiding spot, engulfing his entire body with bright orange flames, tackling one of the men. A blood curdling scream escaped the man's lips as Zahir burned the man alive, his knees pressing into the man's groin. When the other attacker tried to pull Zahir off his compatriot, he simply hauled the other man to him and watched as the skin charred under his fists. One thing Zahir knew, that the rest of the city didn't, was that the guards Ryker sent into the city were not mages. If anyone in Brahn wanted to fight against them, their magic would char their mortal skin.

It was the first time Zahir had smelled burning flesh. He desperately wanted to pull his hand away from the second man to cover his nose, but he knew that the life of the woman and child beside him depended on his action. The mother comforted her daughter, telling her everything would be all right, as she clutched her own bleeding stomach. Zahir rolled off the guards and extinguished his body as he kicked their burning corpses away from them.

He kneeled down beside the young girl and removed his hood. "You are okay, little one. The High Prince is here to help you."

"Your Majesty," her mother said with a shuddering gasp. "Those were your own men."

"And they were doing wrong," Zahir said as he examined the little girl's wound. The knife was buried to the hilt, and Zahir knew that if he pulled it out, the wound would only be worse. "Can you walk?" He looked at the mother, eyes pleading.

"I am unsure."

When she tried to stand, Zahir shot to his feet and pulled her up. She screamed in pain, but was able to stand on her own, one hand holding onto the knife in her stomach and the other pressed against the wall of her home.

Zahir scooped the little girl up in his arms. "We're going to the palace. We are nearly there already. Around this corner is the closest entrance. Can you walk that far?"

The woman nodded, sweat beading on her pale face. Her blonde hair was beginning to stick to the sweat on her forehead. Even Zahir was unsure he would have the strength to walk after just being stabbed.

Zahir led the woman around the corner to the palace. The small door was nearly invisible in the dark, but Zahir could find it with his eyes closed. Holding the girl tight in his arms, he kicked three times on the door, signaling to the guard stationed behind it that it was, in fact, a member of the royal family. The one guard who knew Zahir had been leaving the palace swung the door open, and their eyes widened with horror.

"Ren, I need you to help me get these two to the hospital wing." Zahir rushed inside and the guard immediately slammed the door and wrapped an arm around the woman's waist to help her walk.

"What in the Gods' names happened?" Ren asked as they moved through the unlit labyrinth of the palace undergrounds.

"Two of our own guards attacked them. They were dragged right out of their house and assaulted."

"Do you think they went... rogue?" Ren lowered their voice as they spoke, not wanting anyone to overhear them insinuating that their own guards had turned to the rebel cause.

"I must speak with my father immediately." Zahir panted as he jogged up the stairs. He kicked open the door with the toe of his boot, flooding the stairwell with torchlight from the hospital wing.

"My!" the older woman sitting in a chair knitting said as she dropped her needles. "Get her on the bed, now." Zahir laid the girl down and wiped the tears from her cheeks. "You will be okay. Amí is the best medic in all of Brahn. What is your name?"

The girl sniffled as she watched Amí scurrying around, collecting supplies to heal her wounds. "Marabelle."

"Marabelle, you are braver than any warrior I have ever met." Zahir kneeled beside the girl and held her hand tightly in his. Out of the corner of his eyes, he watched Ren lay the mother down on another cot, holding their hands around the knife so Amí could pull it out. The woman screamed, and Ren pressed hard on her stomach with a towel, trying to keep the blood from pouring out.

"Mom!" Marabelle shrieked, trying to sit up, but falling back down immediately, clutching her wound.

"Look at me, sweetheart." Zahir smiled, trying to get the girl's attention as Amí began to clean and suture her mother's wound. "You are going to be a warrior one day; I just know it. You remind me of Prince Roan. Do you know him?" When the girl nodded

20

slowly, stars in her eyes, Zahir continued. "You are brave and strong like he is in the face of struggle. You care deeply for your mother, who will be fine."

Zahir's distraction was ended by Amí hurrying over to Marabelle's bed and grabbing the hilt of the knife. Zahir placed his hands around the wound and watched Amí pull the knife out. Zahir pressed on the child's stomach as he waited for Amí to clean and suture her wounds. Within seconds, Marabelle had fainted. Thankfully, the cleaning and stitching took mere minutes, then Zahir was able to wash the blood from his hands.

"Please send a message if their condition changes. And do not tell *anyone* who they are... They were attacked by palace guards." Zahir instructed before he rushed out of the hospital wing and towards the council chambers. He knew Ryker had a late night meeting this evening and he needed an explanation.

As Zahir swung open the large wooden door of the advisory chambers, he found his father, sitting at the head of a large table, shooting daggers out of his eyes at the interruption. Zahir held his head high as he approached the table, aware that every person in the room was staring at him in utter confusion.

He slammed his hands down on the edge of the table and said with confidence, "Will you please inform me why two of your guards attacked a woman and her child in the streets of our city this evening?"

Ryker leaned forward, his elbows on the table and hands clasped neatly in front of his chest. Despite the late hour, his stark white hair was perfectly groomed, not a single strand out of place. His bright gold eyes shone in the torchlight, and Zahir could have sworn there were actual flames there.

"I sent them to dispose of any rebel sympathizers." Ryker's voice was cold and Zahir could feel his heart freeze over.

"The girl is a child. She's Roan's age. How could you possibly think that she was a rebel sympathizer?"

"No one is innocent, Zahir. You must learn your place if you are to be our next king," Ryker said, his even tone boiling the anger in Zahir's veins.

"You are slaughtering women and children! How many have you had murdered?" Zahir spat at his father, his own white hair spilling out from behind his shoulders and over his chest as he leaned forward on his hands. "How could you kill your own people?"

"You will speak to me with respect and you will not question my methods. These rebel attacks are getting out of hand."

"There are other ways of dealing with them. There is no need to slaughter innocent people." Zahir could have sworn he would have been dead if looks could kill.

"You will get nowhere if you let others walk all over you." The hint of a smile played at the corner of Ryker's lips, and Zahir stood up straight and turned back to the door.

Zahir clenched his hands into fists, flames sneaking out between his fingers. If his magic could hurt his father, he would have challenged him to a fight right there in front of every advisor. Ryker would have beaten him in a fight, regardless, and Zahir was too angry to remember all his years of training.

"Oh, Zahir?" Ryker said as he grabbed the door handle. Zahir paused and turned his head so he could see his father's smiling face out of the corner of his eye. "Your wedding has been moved up. You will be married in a fortnight."

As if the night could not have gotten worse, Zahir's anger battled with fear as he slammed the door behind him, blowing out every torch in the hallway.

CHAPTER THREE

MARI

Mari stared into the mirror, desperately trying to find her round, snow-pale face under the layers of makeup. The bronze color painted on her eyelids accentuated the bright green of her eyes and the blush pink stain on her lips was already wearing off as she absentmindedly licked her lips. Her usually tangled reddish brown hair pulled at her scalp in an intricate updo that she thought resembled her mother's hairstyle. Somehow, the makeup had made her cheekbones look much more prominent than normal; it almost appeared that her cheeks were sunken in.

She stood from her seat before the mirror and took several steps back. The white dress hung tightly to the curves of her hips and emphasized her chest. While her arms and back were almost completely exposed, the floor-length gown pooled around her feet. It was a stark contrast to her usual hunting clothing, and she had to admit that she did look beautiful.

A quiet knock on the door had Mari straightening and folding her hands in front of her stomach. "Please enter." Her voice was commanding and even, a tone she had been practicing through years of training.

"Mari?" The door creaked open to reveal her short, plump mother in a navy-blue gown that swung against her shins. Her silky brown hair was tied in a knot on the crown of her head, not unlike Mari's. Her heels clicked against the wood floor of the dressing room as she approached. "You look radiant." She rubbed her hands up and down Mari's arms, beaming.

Mari forced herself to smile. "Thank you, Mother. Is it time?"

"It is. How are you feeling, baby?"

She took a shaking breath. "I am nervous."

"You should know that your father would not marry you to someone he did not think was a good fit."

It took everything in Mari's power not to scoff. Since she was ten years old, her father had told her she would be married to the Fire Prince by the time she was twenty-one. It was simply a fact, and not something that was up for discussion. The one time she had asked why, her father had given her the answer that it was simply her duty: that if her clan, Yu'güe, and the fire clan, Brahn, were to begin peace negotiations after millennia, it was up to her to marry the prince. Her father had told her for years that she would end up just like her "disgrace of a brother" if she refused to enter this marriage. Going from a huntress to a princess was never a dream of Mari's. If she could have lived her whole life hunting in the snowy mountains of her home, she would have had everything she wanted. She wanted a peaceful life, not one in a royal court. But any life was a better alternative than death.

Mari nodded and took one last cursory look in the mirror before following her mother out of the room. The stone guest house that the royal family of Brahn had put her up in was on the other side of the city. It was at least double the size of her home back in Yu'güe, and ten times as lavish. The six bedrooms were adorned with paintings and fur rugs, and the mattresses were stuffed with bird feathers. There was a bathing room for every bedroom, and the relaxation space had several soft seats and a fireplace that was always blazing hot. The kitchen was stocked with utensils Mari had never seen before, and the chef who worked in the guest house was able to recreate dishes from her homeland. Even though they weren't as good as when her mother made them, Mari couldn't help but feel homesick every time she ate.

Her home, or rather her parent's home, had been a wood cabin with two bedrooms and only one bathing room. It was not adorned with paintings and fur rugs. There was no fireplace that never died. The mattresses were filled with straw that poked through the sheets every so often, stabbing Mari in her thighs. The cold air seeped through the cracks and Mari always found herself wearing her fur coats and wrapping a soft blanket around her shoulders. She would heat a cup of tea only after building a fire in the fireplace, where her mother would boil their soup each freezing night.

The one thing Mari knew she would enjoy was the blazing heat of Brahn. Her whole life, she never experienced temperatures where she could leave her home without at least two shirts and a jacket. But here, she was walking to a horse drawn carriage in a thin white dress and high heeled shoes and she actually felt a little warm.

Mari turned her face to the sun, closing her eyes to feel the warmth scorch her skin. She could only pause for a second before her mother ushered her towards the cobblestone streets and the open carriage that awaited her. Ten men clad in black armor stood around the carriage, swords slung around their hips. Mari ignored the urge to fidget with her dress. She had been warned that rebel attacks were commonplace in Brahn and therefore she was to be escorted by guards at all times.

Mari stumbled in her high heeled shoes as they slipped into the cracks in the street and her mother grasped her elbow, eyes widening in horror.

"I am fine, Mother." Mari shook out of her mother's grip and pulled her shoulders back to continue on her walk.

Once she was seated on a plush red velvet seat, her mother and father climbed in, sitting across from her. Her father's bald head looked shinier, and redder, in the sunlight of Brahn. The sharp angles of his face and eyebrows always made him look angry, despite the smile spreading across his lips. He rested a hand on his protruding stomach, unbuttoning his black coat so it didn't stretch tightly across his torso. In the three days they had been here, her father had barely been at the guest house. He was constantly meeting with the king and his servants to ensure everything was set for her wedding at the palace. The dark bags under his eyes were evidence of the late nights he spent outside the house. Mari was lucky that her own dark circles were covered by makeup, as she, too, hadn't slept since arriving in Brahn.

Her father scratched at the gray beard that was perfectly trimmed for the first time in Mari's life. He asked as he gestured to the three-story buildings lining the road, "This clan is beautiful, is it not?"

"I have yet to see much, but I am sure if it is anything like the guest house, it is marvelous." Mari spoke in an even tone that she hoped hid her trepidation. In just a few short hours, she would be free of her father's threats. She could only hope that Prince Zahir was kind; from the yearly letters they exchanged, he seemed like he would be.

Once a year since she was ten, Mari and Zahir sent letters about their lives, as was required by their parents. It was used as a means to know their families and clan happenings, so there was less to learn just before their marriage. Mari had kept each of Zahir's letters in a small box beneath her bed, but her father had not let her bring them to Brahn. Those letters had given her just the slightest insight into Zahir's personality. He loved his mother and little brother, Roan. His sister, Anya, and her roommate, Taryn, tormented him growing up, to where he and Anya no longer had a relationship. He had seemed distressed when he wrote to Mari an entire letter about his father's memory loss and what that meant for him and his family.

Mari was pulled out of her thoughts as she spied the residential buildings in the lower circle of Brahn. The one story brick homes had windows with large cracks in them and Mari couldn't believe how just one street away were such fanciful homes. The men and women here wore plain outfits of a tight shirt that exposed their muscular or thin arms and a pair of flowing pants that cinched around their ankles. They did not stop to watch her go by; they were walking the streets, glancing in her direction every so often. Mari wrung her hands in her lap as she tried to tear her eyes away from the glaring expressions of the people.

It was soon they reached a small-town center, bustling with people. The hubbub was almost overwhelming. Sellers had their doors wide open, bells jingling as customers walked in. People were chatting and laughing loudly. Mari wanted to laugh along with them. She glanced at clothing displays in the windows showing off gorgeous gowns and clean-cut suits. A small stone sided bakery had a cake painted on its sign and the smells wafted over to the carriage; Mari sighed and tried to memorize the name of the bakery, wanting to visit in the future.

The one thing that caught her eye the most was a familiar looking man in the town square, holding hands with another man. He was fair skinned and thin, his high cheekbones the most prominent feature on his face. One of them briefly caught her eye and waved. When she waved back, the other man turned around and widened his eyes. This man looked strikingly similar to Hanan. By the time Mari had shaken her head, the pair of men were gone, as if they were never there to begin with. She must have been daydreaming, the wish of having Hanan there on her wedding day heavy on her mind. There was nothing she would have wanted more.

"Is everything all right, Mari?" her father asked, matter-of-factly.

"Yes, Father. As we get closer to the palace, I find myself becoming more nervous." Mari knew she couldn't outright lie to her father, but a lie of omission was a completely different story. Any mention of her brother would ruin the rest of the carriage ride.

"That is understandable. This is a big change in your life, and you are moving far from home. You must remember we are only a boat trip away."

Mari nearly laughed; she couldn't believe her father thought the tumultuous journey here was nothing. She had been ill for the entire trip, the boat rocking wildly through the ocean waves. Yu'güe was isolated, on an island much further south than the rest of the clans. The Fire and Water Mages shared a land mass, with Brahn taking the east and Orcian, the west. Water Mages felt called to the western waters and built their civilization there. Life Mages had set up their clan north of Brahn and Orcian, on an island called Lovíth, which was only a two-day trek from Brahn.

"I will visit as soon as I am able." Mari set her sights on her mother. "Do you have any advice for me?"

"The key to a successful marriage is to make sure both you and your husband are happy," she said. "Do not worry about the little things; focus on what your husband likes to do and what he likes to eat. The other things, like learning to live together, will fall into place. When your father and I were married, your grandmother told me it's more important to know the personality of who you are married to, not their habits."

Mari could feel herself relax a little. She had been most terrified that her lifestyle would not be compatible with the prince's. She had spent her days learning to hunt and skin animals, and had learned how to cook warm stews and clean her house. Mari had never learned how to sit by and let someone do anything for her. From the age of ten, she had been helping to provide for her family. If the court etiquette lessons she had been given over the last few years had taught her anything, it was that she would do none of that again.

Mari had learned that she was expected to take care of very little once she was married to the prince. She would simply attend events, plan lavish balls, and provide heirs to the throne. None of it sounded appealing. She didn't want to schmooze with aristocrats, and had no desire to be dressed in fluffy ball gowns, dancing in front of hundreds of people. She had never wanted children, but now there was simply nothing she could do.

As they reached the outskirts of the upper sector of the city, the homes were several stories high, with slanting roofs that pitched inward. Lining the large rectangular windows were stones that looked strikingly similar to the gray cobblestones of the street. The stones looked to be haphazardly bound with a white paste. Mari's eyes were immediately drawn to the baskets of flowers lining several of the windows on the higher floors. Vibrant orange and pink flowers were blossoming over the rim and their long leafy stems intertwined as they crept toward the edges of the window.

Mari sighed contently at the sight of the flower beds. In Yu'güe, the ice and snow that covered their entire valley allowed no vegetation to grow. Six miles away, on the coast, several mosses grew. These were the only green plants on the entire island. Growing on small rocks, they were soft and used in medicine. Some were used to treat cuts and scrapes, while others were used to stop a fever or cough. Most were heated in water and the ill drank the broth, and only one was eaten raw. Mari shuddered every time she thought about the one fever she'd had as a child and had to eat worwor. The moss had stuck to the roof of her mouth and the spaces between her teeth. She had emptied her stomach not even ten minutes after eating it.

Citizens lined the streets in vibrant red and orange clothing, waving and throwing blood red flowers into her lap. Their long stems had little thorns on them that stabbed the pads of Mari's fingers when she picked them up. It had startled her at first that a flower could be so dangerous, but she figured that if these people were throwing them at her, how unsafe could they be?

The women wore their hair in long, sweeping waves to their hips that swayed when they walked. Their vibrant dresses cinched around their thin waists and the long sleeves fell loosely around their slim arms, clasping at their wrists. The colors on their lips and eyes resembled Mari's own makeup, and she realized it must be a style in the clan. The men lining the streets wore long, dark, loose pants that latched around their ankles. Their button up shirts were loose and flowed in the wind. To Mari, everyone looked relaxed and happy.

The carriage made a sudden left turn, throwing Mari from her thoughts and back to the city. Her eyes scanned the faces of the people lining the streets as the ride came to an end. The crowd was thicker here and Mari could barely make out the individual faces of the masses. The one thing she noticed was groups of women huddled together and giggling, with bright smiles on their ruby colored lips.

Mari jerked forward in her seat as the carriage came to a hard stop at the base of the palace steps. She sighed and waited for her father to exit first. The long white dress hid her dragging feet as she stepped down the stairs and onto the cobblestones. She had to keep her chin from dropping when she turned her gaze up to the palace.

Standing at the top of several hundred stairs was a massive palace that caved inward at the center. The red stone walls were trimmed with gold accents that gave it a look of pure elegance. A tall tower was erected at the center of the building that came to a gold point at the top. Mari had to crane her neck to take in its full height.

Mari's father gently grasped her elbow and gave a slight tug as he walked forward. Allowing herself to be dragged up the wide, gray stone stairs, the train of her gown trailed behind her, sliding up the smooth steps. The blood pounding in her ears and the clop of her heels on the ground were the only sounds that filled the still air.

The nervous feeling suffocated Mari as the panic rose in her throat. For a second, she wondered if she had simply stopped breathing, and inhaled deeply, but the air that filled her lungs did not calm her thrumming heart.

As she neared the apex of the stairs, her eyes fell on the prince dressed in his black ceremonial robe. The letters she'd received had not prepared her for his devastatingly handsome face. His gold eyes reflecting the sunlight matched his sun-kissed skin beautifully. His white hair was pressed onto his forehead by the crooked gold crown on his head, and Mari slid her eyes over the sharp angles of his jaw and watched the closed-lipped smile appear on his face as she drew her eyes up to meet his.

Mari's heart stopped as her father let go of her, ushering her into the open arms of Prince Zahir.

Chapter Four

Zahir

Zahir stared blankly into the mirror as he slowly buttoned his black shirt, rolling up the sleeves to expose his forearms. His gold eyes shone in the flickering candlelight and his usually bound white hair fell in waves over his shoulders. A single braid rested uncomfortably against his left ear and he had to keep himself from toying with it; it had taken him hours to get right. The square angles of his face were always more prominent when his hair framed his jaw.

As he slid a long, gossamer black robe onto his shoulders, he jolted, heart skipping a beat, at the sound of a knock at the door. He'd asked to be left alone until it was time for the wedding; he knew it couldn't possibly be time to go. Cinching the robe around his waist with a velvet strap, he walked barefoot to answer the door, the hardwood floors creaking under his weight.

"Zahir?" a high-pitched voice asked from the hallway as another knock came.

A warm smile slid onto Zahir's lips as he opened the door to his nine-year-old brother, Roan. "Hi, little man. What are you doing here?" He picked Roan up under his arms and swung him around in the air.

"My glasses," Roan said in between bursts of laughter as his square-framed spectacles fell to the floor. "I need my glasses. And you are going to mess up my hair."

Zahir chuckled as he placed Roan on his bed and picked up the glasses that had clattered to the ground. He placed them on the bridge of Roan's nose and gave his brother's dark brown hair a good tousling. "At least your hair is easier to fix than mine. Look at what mother made me do." Zahir pulled at the braid, eliciting a giggle from Roan.

"Are you excited about your wedding?" Roan asked as Zahir dropped onto the bed beside him.

Zahir took a deep breath before answering. "Honestly, I am nervous." When Roan asked why, he continued. "I worry that we will not get along. Do you remember what it was like when Taryn moved into the palace with Anya?"

Roan nodded gravely, his eyes widening. Three years prior, Zahir's sister, Anya, had discovered her Twin Flame. These people were said to be born from one soul and when they encountered each other, their Fire Magic was enhanced, and they became unstoppable. Twin Flames were extremely rare and if someone was lucky enough to find their partner, it was nearly impossible to ignore the tie between their magic. Taryn had moved into the palace almost immediately after they discovered their connection, which was a complete nightmare. Anya and Taryn had never gotten along well in school and hated each other with a burning passion. When Taryn had joined the family, it had been non-stop fighting and screaming through all hours of the night. Training sessions were impossible and Zahir was constantly caught in the crossfire, dodging flames as they stormed through the palace grounds.

"Is that going to happen again? I still have nightmares from when they melted my toys." Roan crossed his arms and pouted, remembering when Anya almost burned down the entire palace.

"Of course not, little man," Zahir said, putting a comforting hand on Roan's shoulder. "I will do everything I can to make sure we are civil with each other."

Roan nodded. "You are good at talking. You always calm me down when I feel too many things."

"I am always happy to help, Roan. That will not change, even when I am married." Zahir smiled at his brother, his heart warming at the knowledge that his brother loved him so much.

"Do you promise? Will we still play together? Will you still read to me when I can't sleep?"

"Of course." Zahir kissed the top of Roan's head. "Nothing is going to change. Just try not to walk into my bedroom naked anymore."

Roan laughed, smiling widely up at Zahir, and pushed his glasses up the bridge of his nose. "Maybe my new sister will do things with me, too. I can't wait to show her the library."

"I am sure she would love that." Zahir hoped he wasn't lying through his teeth to his brother. He had spent many nights lying awake, trying to picture what she might look like. What her voice would sound like. While Zahir thought he had an idea of who she was—a selfless, warm woman—he desperately desired to know more.

"Are you almost done getting dressed?" Roan asked, pushing his hair out of his eyes. He looked just like Zahir, with his wide gold eyes and square jaw that was still covered by a layer of baby fat.

Zahir looked down at himself. His black shirt was tucked neatly into his straight legged black pants. The black robe around him was falling off his shoulders, the velvet tie loosening the longer he sat. His bare feet scraped against the wood floor as he swung his legs forward. "I still have much to do. Do you mind if I find you later? I need to finish getting ready."

"Okay." Roan sighed, lowering his eyes in disappointment as he stood. "I love you, Zahir."

"I love you too, little man." He smiled at his brother as he padded out of the room and slid the door closed behind him.

Zahir sighed as he leaned forward, pressing his elbows into his knees and hands into his forehead. His mind raced with a million thoughts about what his wedding meant. In Brahn, an heir only took power away from their living parent in dire circumstances. In Zahir's case, his father's memory was beginning to slip. He had begun asking the same questions repeatedly and could never seem to remember what the answer was. Then, he'd started to have trouble with his problem solving and thus couldn't come up with any solutions to Brahn's struggles. His mood had also begun to change slowly. He was usually a very calm and levelheaded man, but Zahir had noticed that his father was becoming easily angered. The medics had seen this memory lapse happen in people in the lower sectors of Brahn, but even they were unsure what it really was.

Zahir wondered if he would need to assume the throne earlier than intended. The thought of becoming king was something that both excited and terrified him. On the one hand, he had been training for this transition for nearly fifteen years. On the other hand, his father had not been well received after his coronation due to the state of the clan. Zahir wondered if his citizens would think he would follow in his father's footsteps.

Zahir's panic rose in his chest and his heart beat wildly against his rib cage. All he wanted was to be a king that his clan would approve of and look to for guidance. Insurgents had been trying to take over the city and overthrow his father for nearly ten years but had never been treated as a credible threat, as they had never penetrated the palace walls. While they were slaughtering innocents, King Ryker had been sequestered away in the palace, safe behind locked doors and hundreds of guards. Zahir hadn't meant to resent his father for this, but after watching a child get attacked in the streets, he couldn't help but feel angry.

A memory bubbled to the surface. Just yesterday, Amí had come to Zahir to tell him that both the woman and child he had rescued were safe and on the mend. She had moved them to the servant's quarters to ensure they were not found. The relief that had flooded him was incomparable to anything he had ever felt.

As an airy voice filled his ears, a shudder ran through Zahir's body. "What is *wrong* with you?"

He would know the voice of his sister, Anya, anywhere.

Slowly, he lifted his head and met her icy stare. "It is not the time, Anya."

Anya's eyebrows slanted inward as she squinted at her brother. Every angle of her face was sharp, giving her a permanent, glowering expression. Her high cheekbones nearly broke out of her skin and her cheeks appeared sunken in with all the makeup she had applied. Her ruby red lips were the color of blood, standing out against her smooth tanned skin, and her auburn eyes glowed in the flickering candlelight. Her long black hair was pulled up into a knot on the top of her head, framed by her shining gold tiara. Two long clumps of hair fell down her face, resting on top of those sharp cheekbones.

Anya pushed the sleeves of her gold dress up to expose her forearms as she glided into the room. Her bare feet made no noise against the wood and she found her way in front of the mirror. She pursed her lips at her reflection. "I look like a doll."

"What do you want, Anya?" Zahir sighed. His sister rarely ever visited his rooms, but when she did, it was always unpleasant.

"I just wanted to wish you luck on your wedding day. I am sure you will need it." Anya tucked her free lengths of hair behind her ears.

Zahir stood and tightened the belt around his waist. He folded his arms over his chest and walked behind Anya, staring into her icy glare through the mirror. "You have not wished me luck on anything in my entire life. Why now?"

Anya laughed. "Am I not allowed to wish my little brother luck? What has our world come to?"

"Please leave me alone, Anya. I need to prepare for my wedding." Zahir narrowed his eyes at his sister.

"I wonder what your wife will be like. I cannot wait to befriend her and tell her *everything* about you." Anya straightened and leveled her gaze at Zahir. "You want her to know everything, don't you?"

Zahir's heart rate picked up. "What do you want?"

"Renounce your status as heir." A sly smile piqued at the corners of Anya's lips as she whipped around to face him. "Tell Father you do not wish to be king and that you think that I, his eldest, should be. You are the first heir in history who is not the first-born child of a king. How do you think the clan will react to that? Do you not think they will denounce you?"

Zahir felt his heart drop to his feet. "You will *never* be queen, Anya. Father named me heir twelve years after you were born. Do you not think he would have named you earlier if he wanted you to rule? Even he knows you would burn Brahn to the ground."

Anya's hands ignited in orange flames as she balled them into fists at her side. "You will never be a righteous king. You will never do what the clan needs. Your wife will force our people to overthrow you. Do you think they want a Death Mage ruling alongside you?"

Zahir knew his clan did not want his marriage to occur. The rebel attacks were proof of that. But Ryker would not call off the marriage because 'reuniting the clans was more important than some innocuous insurgents'. No one had interacted with the Death Mages since they migrated halfway around the world to the southernmost point of the sea. Even Brahn, who traded regularly with Orcian, had never communicated with Yu'güe. That is, until Zahir and Mari's marriage was arranged. The general consensus was that the Death Mages were biding their time until they could wage war on the other three clans. Zahir had never truly believed that rumor, but there certainly was something in the back of his mind yelling at him to protest his marriage. His father, however, was certain that it would only help Zahir as king.

"After centuries, we are uniting clans. Mages will be free to travel between clans again and migrate as they please. If you knew the first thing about our clan, you would know isolation has not been kind to mages. The sharing of information has halted, and no new techniques have been invented since we sequestered ourselves. Back in the Golden Age, we could learn how magic worked for other mages; but now, we only have stories. This is a *good thing*, Anya. If you cannot see that, then I am glad that Father named me heir." Zahir shook his head.

"You will regret this, Zahir. You and I both know you have no place on the throne." Anya pulled her shoulders back and raised her chin as she made her way towards the door. Her parting words echoed through the room. "I can't *wait* to see how many of our people your demon wife eats."

The door slammed shut and Zahir was left alone again with Anya's words ringing in his ears. He believed beyond any doubt that he would be the best king Brahn had ever had. He wanted no glory, no fame. He only wanted to be a king his citizens could be proud of. Zahir desired to do everything for his people, always putting their interests above his own. Coming from the palace of luxury, he knew he had a lot to learn about the poor sectors of the city and was willing to put in the work to hear what support they needed. He also knew that there was no way to please every person, but as long as his actions as king helped those who needed it, that would be enough.

Zahir cinched the belt around his waist one final time before picking up his gold crown from the table beside his mirror and placing it firmly onto his head. His eyes matched his crown beautifully and seemed to even make them glow. Squaring his shoulders, he pushed strands of hair out of his face.

"You are being married, Zahir. You can do this." Zahir smiled at himself in the mirror. Although it didn't quite reach his eyes, he thought he still looked happy. "There is nothing to fear. She is just another person. Make sure you make her feel comfortable. You can do this."

While Zahir had read and reread the letters Mari had sent him over the years, his hands still shook. He had read about her fruitful hunting season, and the ones that were not as bountiful. He had learned about her brother, who had passed shortly before their betrothal. The first three years of letters were filled with stories of her brother, who she clearly loved very much. She never mentioned how he died, but Zahir was not going to pry into the life of someone he barely knew. Although he had learned many things about Mari over the years, it still felt like he barely knew her. He had taken the time to craft his letters, explaining the family dynamic she would come into and describing his home, but he never received that information from Mari. He had so many questions.

Zahir took a long, deep breath before he turned on his heel and strode out the door. Two palace guards were waiting for him, their hands clasped behind their backs and their silver armor glinting in the candlelight. They waited for him to pass before following behind in perfect step. Torches lined the halls, casting orange light and dark shadows across the walls and, as they turned right at the end of the hall, Zahir saw his mother and father waiting.

King Ryker stood, holding Queen Maura's hand, running his thumb against her knuckles. Maura dabbed at her eyes with a cloth as she watched her son walk towards them. Ryker's muscled body was hidden behind a similar outfit to Zahir's, his ceremonial robes red instead of black. Maura's bright red silky gown swept the ground, spreading out from her hips in a bell shape, her midnight black hair landing in thin curtains around her narrow face.

Zahir had always thought he looked more like his mother than his father. He shared her gold eyes and her petite nose. His long silver hair matched his fathers, as was customary for a king and his heir, and he also had his father's strong, square jaw.

"Oh, Zahir," Maura said, wiping another tear from her eye. "You look radiant, baby."

Zahir kissed his mother's cheek, careful not to mess up the makeup he was sure had taken hours to put on. "Thank you, Mother. You are beautiful, as always."

Ryker put his hand on his shoulder. "You are ready for this, Zahir." Ryker offered a closed lip smile, their argument still fresh.

"Thank you, Father." Zahir smiled at his mother before leading his parents down the hall, away from the bedchambers, and towards the main area of the palace.

The hallways were lined with bright, always-burning torches that cast eerie shadows around the corners. Paintings of the royal families, the streets of Brahn, and the sunsets from the mountain tops were hung on the walls. There was one painting of Zahir, Anya, and Roan that always caught his attention. It had been commissioned shortly after Zahir was named heir, right after he had dyed his hair silver. Some of the dye had clung to his forehead and his baby fat was still around his jaw. Roan's glasses were crooked from when he'd run face first into a tree in the gardens. Anya hadn't stopped glowering for days, and that permanent scowl still sat on her face years later.

But the painting hadn't captured any of that. The three of them appeared the very definition of royalty. Zahir's hair looked like it was meant to be silver and not that it had been freshly dyed. His jaw looked perfectly square, as if he were a man and not still a child. Anya's features were plain, hiding any evidence of the glare; if Zahir squinted, she almost looked proud of him. Roan looked like the most well-behaved child; his hair was not a mess as it usually was, his glasses sat perfectly straight, and he was looking forward. Zahir was always impressed that the artist had painted things that were clearly not there.

Zahir took a long, deep breath as he stopped to face the palace doors. The entryway of the palace was the most ornate room in the building, as his father wanted to show off his wealth to visitors. The black rugs matched the maroon walls perfectly. The paintings of each king since Brahn's formation were hung around the room in succession, ending with Ryker. The style had changed over the years, from more traditional portraits in armor to more informal ones with the kings in their ceremonial robes.

The doors swung open, the bright light from the burning hot sun assaulting Zahir's vision. He tried desperately to keep his eyes wide as they adjusted to the change. The cheering voices from his people rose up to greet him as he stepped over the threshold and he looked out over the steep staircase to see a large crowd of people screaming excitedly at the top of their lungs. From the apex of the stairs, he could see most of the city, the red roofs of buildings glimmering under the sun's rays. The heat from the sun didn't bother him as much as it had when he was a child, especially as the breeze was brushing his hair away from the back of his sweating neck. Zahir raised a hand to greet his people and the cheers only deafened him.

Zahir walked slowly over to the edge of the staircase where his uncle Illan stood, his long graying hair tied back with a band to expose his round, red face, brown eyes, and fluffy white beard. The long white coat he wore dragged along the ground and barely buttoned over his large stomach, exposing the white buttoned up shirt and pants that cinched at his ankles. Zahir wouldn't have wanted anyone else other than the man who had trained him in politics and magic his whole life to officiate his wedding. At times, Zahir felt closer to his uncle than his own father.

"How are you feeling, Zahir?"

He tightened his shaking hands around the sleeves of his robes. "I will not lie, Uncle. I am quite nervous."

"You are going to be a wonderful husband and king. Of that, I have no doubts." Illan offered a toothy grin to his nephew.

"Thank you." Zahir turned his head to the bottom of the stairs just in time to see his bride, Mari, step out from her carriage. She slowly made her way up the stairs, looking everywhere but at the top. Zahir willed her to look at him, if only to see if she was just as nervous as he was.

As she and her father reached the top of the stairs, Zahir's heart stopped in his chest. The white gown she wore hung around her hips, showing off her beautiful curves. Her pale skin was almost reflective, as if she had never seen the sun before, and the bright green of her eyes reminded Zahir of the trees just after it rained. As their eyes met, Zahir could see the nerves on her face, and a wave of comfort ran through him that he was not the only fearful one.

Zahir reached out to Mari as her father handed her off to him at the top of the stairs.

CHAPTER FIVE

MARI

P rince Zahir took Mari's hands in his and squeezed ever so slightly. His palms were warm to the touch, and she could see the slight beading of sweat above his brow.

"We are gathered here today, in the sight of the Gods, and these witnesses, to unite the bonds of marriage. High Prince Zahir of Brahn and Princess Mari of Yu'güe. If it your desire to take the vows which will unite you at this time, please respond, 'it is.'"

Mari parted her lips to correct the officiant, a large bellied man dressed in white robes, for she was not a princess, but decided it best to keep silent. While her parents were the council's leaders, they were not a king and queen.

Zahir and Mari looked at one another and paused before answering simultaneously, "It is."

Mari broke away from Zahir's gaze and focused instead on the white facial hair of the officiant.

"Do you, High Prince Zahir, take Princess Mari to be your equal in marriage? To treat her with nothing but respect, to help her in times of peril, to never believe yourself to be above her?"

Zahir never took his eyes from Mari's face. She wondered if he felt any apprehension about marrying a woman he had never met. Was he merely playing a part for his people?

"She will be my equal," his voice rang out, slicing through the wind like a knife.

"Do you, Princess Mari, take High Prince Zahir to be your equal in marriage? To treat him with nothing but respect, to help him in times of peril, to be his equal?" The officiant's tone became filled with excitement.

Mari slowly turned her head to her husband-to-be and felt panic rise in the back of her throat. It took everything in her power to speak, "He will be my equal."

"Prince Zahir, please take the ring you have selected for Princess Mari. As you place it on her finger, repeat, 'With this ring, I give you my heart.'"

Zahir took the ring from the officiant and pulled Mari's hand up so he could place a beautiful gold band on her left ring finger. He slid it on delicately, as if he feared breaking her. "With this ring, I give you my heart." He spoke quietly, in a volume that Mari wondered if only she was meant to hear.

"Princess Mari, please take the ring you have selected for Prince Zahir. As you place it on his finger, repeat, 'With this ring, I give you my heart.'"

Mari took the ring with a shaking hand and began lifting Zahir's right hand. Zahir stopped her and raised his left hand for her. Mari felt a blush creep up on her cheeks as she quickly slid the ring on his finger. "With this ring, I give you my heart." Her voice was steady, unlike the rest of her body.

The officiant raised his arms high into the air. "I now pronounce you husband and wife. You may kiss your bride."

Mari felt her body tense as Zahir looked from her eyes to her lips and back again before leaning in to dust his lips against hers, gripping her hands tighter than before. Mari returned the kiss as excited cheers filled her ears.

When the pair broke apart, they locked eyes for a moment and blushed at the realization that their first kiss had been in front of hundreds of people. Zahir let go of her hand, holding her right tightly, as he led her back towards the palace where people dressed in gowns and soldiers in armor lined the halls, throwing yellow petals over them.

They were whisked through the palace by four guards armed to the teeth to a parlor, where two steaming cups of tea rested on a small wooden table. Two cushions had been placed at either end of the table for the newlywed couple.

Once settled on their cushions, Mari and Zahir sat silently until the servants and guards left them alone. Mari blew on her tea, waiting for her betrothed to speak. Growing up, she had learned it was best to wait until someone spoke to her—a rule she absolutely loathed following.

"How is your tea?" Zahir asked Mari as she took a sip.

She swallowed quickly, hot tea burning her throat on the way down. "Lovely. Lavender is my favorite. Do you like lavender tea, Prince Zahir?"

Mari wanted to smack herself. Going into this, she knew their first interaction was going to be uncomfortable, but never in a million lifetimes could she have guessed that it would be a conversation about lavender tea.

"It's not my favorite. I much prefer jasmine." Zahir laughed as Mari nearly choked on her drink. His laugh was soft, like the wind blowing through leaves. "There is also no need for titles. We are married, after all."

"Zahir, then," Mari said. Her cheeks warmed as she watched a warm smile spread across Zahir's face. "Is it always this hot outside?" Mari had felt sweat dripping down her forehead, and she hoped her makeup wasn't running down her face. It had taken hours to get it right.

"For the next moon cycle or so, it will be. After that, it cools off, especially at night. The air dries out a bit for a few moon cycles and it gets cold when the sun is below the horizon. The palace is always kept cool, so there is no need to worry about the heat inside." Zahir's voice was formal, like he was reading out of a book. Mari hoped he would relax as they got to know each other more; she did not like the idea of keeping on her professional façade for the rest of her life.

"That is good to hear. It's quite the change from Yu'güe. At this time of year, we are usually running out of the food stockpiles we gather before the heavy snow. In a moon cycle or two it warms up, and it is easier to hunt." Mari wondered if there were animals in the forests on the outskirts of the city she could hunt, and hoped that she would be allowed to, even if there are guards present. The idea of being locked up like a prisoner was not in her plans.

"I have never seen snow. Can you tell me about it?" Zahir leaned forward on the table, resting his chin in his hands, like a child.

Mari smiled as a memory surfaced. "Right before it snows, the clouds in the usually bright blue sky become dark. There is a certain smell in the air that I can't describe with words other than it's almost crisp. When it falls, it coats the ground lightly first. The dirt gets covered with white and then slowly, there is nothing but a field of white. When I look out of the window, I can see it blowing around in wisps, landing and creating piles. The tops of the mountains are covered in white throughout the year, even if there is very little snow on the ground." Mari hadn't realized that her voice had gotten softer as she spoke, but Zahir had leaned even closer and was staring at her with a soft smile and slightly widened eyes.

"That sounds beautiful. I would love to visit one day to experience that. You speak fondly of your home."

"I love Yu'güe very much. But I have never been anywhere else. This is my first time leaving our island. Have you traveled outside of Brahn?"

As Zahir opened his mouth to respond, the royal guards returned to the room, whisking the couple away again. Mari's heart rate increased, and she could feel the heat radiating from Zahir. She refused to look anywhere but at her feet, desperately praying that she wouldn't trip over herself.

The royal guards pushed a set of doors open and the couple strode into a large ballroom. Arms linked, Zahir whispered it was time for their first dance. Mari's eyes widened at the beautiful decoration of the room. Long wooden tables lined the ballroom, with tall vases of red and purple flowers flowing over the edges. A square of wooden floor peeked out at the center of the room from the edges of bright red rugs. The polished floor shone under the sun's rays, the glass ceiling revealing a bright blue cloudless sky that lit up the room, eliminating the need for torches.

Smiling guests lined the hall, applauding loudly for the new-lyweds. The women wore brightly colored gowns that hung loosely around their bodies and swayed around their shins as they moved. The suits the men wore were stark black, as if to not draw attention away from the women. Mari wondered if that was a customary thing in Brahn, wanting to know more about how fashion was determined here. In Yu'güe, fashion was not on anyone's mind. The only thing that mattered was staying warm in the bitter cold.

The applause died down and Mari tried to ignore all the pairs of eyes, watching her every move. She and Zahir took their place at the center of the room, waiting for the soft sound of music to begin. Once the notes floated through the ballroom, they locked eyes and moved closer to one another. Zahir placed his hand on her lower back, her hand on his shoulder, and their free hands met.

"Zahir," Mari whispered, looking nervously around the room. "Everyone is staring at us."

A smile lit up the prince's face. Leaning in close, Zahir whispered, "I hadn't noticed."

As the dance progressed, Mari began to forget the hundreds of people watching her. She never let her eyes wander from Zahir's as he danced her through the room expertly, spinning her in fast, dizzying circles. Her lips parted in a smile as colors blurred in her vision and her silky dress swept around her legs. She almost forgot that this was the first time she had met Zahir. He held her with confidence, as if they had practiced this dance together a hundred times.

When the song ended, applause filled Mari's ears and she couldn't help but smile at Zahir. He placed a kiss on her cheek, and she blushed, pulling away. Mari was never one to be the center of attention, so this day was forcing her out of her comfort zone.

Many hours, and many glasses of champagne later, they were led to their bedroom. It was larger than she could have imagined, and she gaped in awe at the beautiful suite that overlooked the gardens. There was a separate dressing room for each of them, and a large bed sat in the center of the room, made up with black sheets and blankets draping over the sides. Dark wood columns held an even darker canopy over the bed, casting shadows on the floor from the moonlight shining through the balcony doors.

The moonlight made it hard to see out of the glass doors, but Mari could make out a few trees and the edge of a pond that shimmered in the light. A small balcony was attached to their room with a round table and two metal chairs that left enough room to stand on either side against a wrought iron railing.

"Do you like it?"

Mari spun around to face him. "It's beautiful. I never could have imagined such a gorgeous room."

"Your wardrobe has some items in it. I had some dresses sewn for you. I also purchased some athletic clothing, if you wanted to train. When we have a chance, we can get you whatever you are missing." Zahir lifted a finger and pointed to the dressing room to the left.

"Thank you. That was very kind of you." She began walking towards the dressing room. "I'm going to change into something more comfortable."

Closing the door behind her, she leaned back against it, taking everything in. She was a princess of Brahn, a world completely unlike her own, and married to a prince. She couldn't believe how much her life had changed in a few short hours. Coming from a nation where she lived in a small house, a palace was quite the change. It would take her weeks to get used to the temperature and customs, but she was willing to put in the effort. Her parents had made it clear that she was to do whatever she needed to please her husband, while making sure to take things slow.

Mari ran a hand along the four dresses in her closet, the silk sliding between her fingers. The dresses were different styles of ball gowns, all sweeping the floor. She noticed that they all had a little gold stylistic addition to the bodice. One of them looked like it had gold vines and leaves snaking around the front and back of the dress to the point where it flared out. Another had a candle, the symbol of Brahn, stitched above the left breast.

A floor length mirror awaited her at the end of the room. Mari spun around in her white gown, admiring herself. The gown hung tightly around her hips and accentuated her chest, so different from her usual hunting outfits. She had never worn a dress before arriving in Brahn, where she had lived in sundresses and sandals for a couple of days. She knew that the beautiful clothing was one thing that would not take her long to get used to. Slowly, she peeled the wedding gown off and hung it carefully, making sure not to tear it. Mari knew she would never wear it again, but she still wanted to preserve its beauty.

As she wiped the makeup from her face at her corner vanity, the realization hit her that Zahir could be expecting sex. A wave of panic washed over her. She had never been intimate with a man before. Her parents had told her to take things slow and make sure she was comfortable, but her mother had pulled her into the living room while her father was out and had explained how to please her husband on their wedding night. Mari's face had turned bright red and she'd refused to look at her mother as she described how to satisfy a man. She had not wished to know what her parents did behind closed doors, and she did not have any desire to have sex with a man she barely knew. She hoped that if she declined sex that Zahir would be accepting. Growing up, there had been men who had hurt girls she knew if they refused to do what they asked.

Slipping on a gossamer nightgown, Mari headed back into her bedroom, expecting to see Zahir waiting for her. To her surprise, he was still in his dressing room. Mari wondered what had held him up. He wasn't the one caked in makeup and a priceless dress.

Mari wandered over to the left side of the bed and slid under the covers, adjusting the pillows so she could lean against the headboard comfortably. She pulled the blanket over her stomach and twiddled her thumbs, waiting for Zahir to join her.

Before long, he emerged from his dressing room in nothing but a pair of loose black bottoms that flowed around his shins. Staring at his chiseled torso, a blush crept up her cheeks. She suddenly felt very overdressed. Noticing Mari's staring, Zahir averted his gaze while he sat on the edge of the bed.

"I, uh, want to let you know that I'm not expecting us to be... intimate." Zahir's voice was quiet and he looked at Mari as he waited for her to say something.

"Oh, okay," Mari said, mentally berating herself for her response. "Thank you."

"We have our whole lives to do... *that*. I think we should actually get to know one another first."

"I want that too." Mari covered her mouth as she yawned. "Maybe we can start tomorrow? I'm absolutely exhausted from the wedding."

Zahir nodded as he rubbed his eyes with his palms. "Me too. I hate parties. I can sleep on the floor if it would make you more comfortable."

"No, it's okay. It's just sleeping." There was a part of her that wanted him to sleep on the floor, but she did not feel right about it. She was in his home, after all.

Mari nestled her head into her pillow as Zahir slid into the bed beside her, turning away from her. She stared at the ceiling, wondering what tomorrow would bring in this new life.

Chapter Six

Mari

Mari had to admit that seeing Zahir leaning against the railing of the balcony, half-naked and looking out at the gardens, was not the worst sight to wake up to. The sun reflected off the ridges in his muscled arms and back and steam poured out of the cup in his hand as he blew on whatever was inside. The small cup looked like it was made for a child in his large hands.

Zahir turned around when Mari groaned and rolled over in bed. "There is tea if you want," he offered as she glanced at the cart in the center of the room holding a teapot, cups, and a few small pastries.

Mari sat up instantly, brushing her fingers hastily through her hair. Every morning, it looked like her hair had been tousled in the wind for hours. She could not even begin to imagine how it looked when she had been tossing and turning all night until sleep finally took her. "Thank you."

Mari poured herself a cup and joined Zahir on the balcony. She looked out at the flowers and trees that decorated the grounds, knowing she would never grow tired of the view. The bright orange and pink flowers reminded her of sunrises back home and the green of the trees was a similar color to her own eyes. In the distance, mountains rose high above the horizon and their peaks were hidden behind wispy white clouds. Mari doubted that they rose high enough to have snow at their peaks. Taking a sip of her tea as she gazed at the landscape, she nearly choked, realizing it had gone cold.

"Is it not warm?" Zahir asked, turning to face her. He leaned his left hip against the black railing, his bound white hair swaying behind him. Mari noticed how his jaw jutted out more when his hair was pulled back, making him appear older.

"Not quite." She coughed.

"Here." Zahir took the cup from her and soon, her tea was steaming as if it were freshly poured. "Is that better?" he asked, handing the tea back.

Mari smiled as she sipped her now steaming tea. "Much. Thank you for that. Your magic is so subtle."

Zahir shrugged. "It can be. I have been training my whole life to be able to do little things like that. When our magic first presents itself, it is nearly uncontrollable and flares if we are upset or angry. I am able to control it by controlling my emotions and my breathing."

"That is very interesting. Do you train your magic often?"

"Every day. My uncle has been my trainer since I was a child. He has helped me hone my skills and use it to help me, rather than destroy the grass." Zahir let out a little laugh, and Mari wondered if he was thinking of a certain memory.

"So, you're a Death Mage," Zahir said after Mari did not respond for a minute, "That's interesting."

"What kind of horror stories do they tell you about us?" Mari knew that Death Mages were not loved in the world. There were terrible misconceptions that they brought upon death and destruction; she had always wondered what lies the other clans had heard about their way of life.

Zahir refused to meet her eyes as he answered. "If I am being completely honest, nothing good. We may have learned that you eat your dead?"

"*That* is what you learned? I never knew why the Death Mages have such a bad reputation." Mari smiled sweetly. "We only eat the dead children."

"Excuse me?"

Mari laughed, setting her empty cup down on the metal table. "You should see your face. I am just kidding; we aren't cannibals."

Zahir let out a breathy laugh, rubbing the back of his neck, and she wondered if she had chosen the wrong time to try and introduce some humor.

"Of course, I knew you were joking. How does your magic work? I haven't been able to find many descriptions of it."

"Do you want me to show you?" she asked. When Zahir nodded, she raised an arm and looked out to the gardens, searching for a small creature. She heard the chirping of a bird and immediately flinched, her arm pulling back ever so slightly. Mari took a steadying breath and waited for the chirping bird to take flight.

Without warning, the bright yellow bird darted from a tree into the bright blue sky and Mari didn't hesitate before she clenched her fist and drew her hand backwards. The bird immediately plummeted to the ground, but the almost translucent soul floated in place. Mari pulled the soul closer to her and even though she knew it could not hurt her, she could feel her heart pounding in her chest as it drew near. Mari let the bird's soul lightly touch her forehead and she thanked it for its life. The familiar feeling of electricity shot down her spine and she pushed the bird's soul away from her, letting it fly around the garden. She watched it fly as she moved her hand in a fluid figure eight. The bird flew between the trees, soaring up towards the bright blue sky, and back down to the balcony where it disappeared when Mari closed her fist once again.

A loud scream erupted from the ground below and Mari looked down to see a blonde woman in a plain brown dress drop the basket of fruit she was holding, widened eyes trained on Mari. The woman fell to her knees with her hands clutched to her chest. Mari couldn't hear what she was saying, but she saw the woman's lips moving rapidly. Mari wasn't sure if her pale face was just her skin tone, or fear from watching Mari use her magic.

"Oh, now I feel bad. She didn't know what I was doing," Mari said as she turned to Zahir to see his eyes wide and mouth slightly agape. She heard him mutter something to himself that sounded a lot like *we are going to have some fucked up children*, but she didn't think that could have been right. When she asked Zahir what he said, he cleared his throat.

"I, uh, said, remind me to never disagree with you." Zahir rubbed the back of his head and stared at the bird carcass on the ground. The woman below hurriedly gathered up the fruit before racing back inside the palace.

"My magic is really the only weapon I have," Mari said, looking down at her hands. "I saw your guards all carry swords; is that because of the recent rebel attacks?"

"No, they have always carried them. We have taken on more guards since the attacks, though. While they rarely reach the palace, we don't want to take any chances, especially with my father's memory loss." Zahir's voice was even, as if he were talking about a stranger, not his own father.

"I was sorry to hear about that," Mari said, remembering the letter a few years prior where Zahir had told her that his father had begun to forget little things easily, like what he'd had for a meal. "Is there any hope he will recover his memory?"

"Our medics don't think so. There are medicines in Lovíth, but they refuse to trade with us."

"I should think so. We don't trade with any other clan," Mari said, confused. Yu'güe had not even spoken with another clan since Hanan's betrothal.

"We trade very often with Orcian. We send goods back and forth every four moon cycles," Zahir said, as if it were obvious.

"You *what*?" Mari slowly raised her eyebrows and her dry lips parted. "Yu'güe has been isolated for thousands of years because of what... happened. We have never received help from another clan. How could you trade with Orcian?"

Zahir put his tea down on the wide balcony railing. "It isn't up to me, Mari. To my knowledge, we haven't stopped trading with them."

"I can't believe this." Mari crossed her arms and placed them beside Zahir's cup. "Here, I thought we were beginning interclan relations after thousands of years just to find out that they never stopped for you."

"I want trade to open between all four clans," he said, lightly placing his hand on Mari's lower back. She flinched at the touch but realized she actually liked the warmth of Zahir's hand on her back. "Afterall, isn't that the point of our marriage?"

Mari sighed. "That, and to give birth to a dual mage. Do you ever worry that we might give birth to another Morana?"

Zahir physically recoiled at the casual mention of Morana's name, rubbing a hand down his face and gripping the railing. "Sometimes," he said, his voice quiet. "I wonder if she was nurtured to be evil, or if the combination of magic did something to her mind."

"Legend has it, her parents were just as surprised as anyone else," Mari said with a sigh. "I noticed how your people don't seem too enthusiastic about our marriage. Some are, but I saw many who seemed to want nothing to do with me."

"I am not going to lie; the rebel attacks picked up closer to our wedding. Just two nights ago, I rescued a woman and her child from being killed," Zahir said, his eyes trained on his feet.

"Thank the Gods you were there." Mari stood up and untwisted her arms to reach for Zahir's hand. The feeling of his hand in hers sent a tingling sensation up her arm and a blush crept onto her cheeks as she realized that, while she had corresponded with Zahir for ten years, she didn't really know him. Mari slowly pulled her hand away and clutched it to her chest.

"If I hadn't been trained in combat since I was a child, I would have been useless." Zahir smiled at her. "I'd be willing to teach you some hand-to-hand combat if you would like. We have a training room in the palace."

Mari's eyes lit up with excitement. "I would love that. I remember you wrote about a library in the palace?" She had pleasant memories of curling up in her bed under her fluffy blanket and looking out the window as the snow fell, reading a book about her clan. She wanted to learn everything about her world. There was no corner she didn't want to look behind.

"We have books that cover the history of all of the clans. They are mostly about Brahn's history and success stories, but there is a little something on each clan."

"That's so exciting. I can't wait to dig through the shelves." Mari wistfully thought of all the tomes she would get to read in the coming years. "What do you like to do?"

"I train a lot, mostly melee and general mage training. I spend a lot of my time now in meetings, though. Once my father fell ill, he sent me and my uncle in his place. We report back to him and he tells us what he wishes to be done." Zahir shrugged. "It's nothing glamorous, but I'll probably be in meetings for most of the weeks to come. Definitely after my coronation."

"When is the coronation?" Mari asked, not sure it was appropriate.

"When my father is no longer fit to rule." Zahir took a shuddering breath. "Our advisors think it should be any day now, but I think he will hold onto the throne as long as possible. His memory is fading, and he does not always make the... best decisions, but he can still hold a pen. I think my uncle is hesitant to remove him because it would be like admitting defeat."

"I'm so sorry about your father."

"Thank you." Zahir stared into his cup as if it were the most interesting thing in the world before suddenly straightening and taking a deep breath as a knock on the door made him turn his head. "Duty calls."

"Do you have meetings today?" Mari asked, hoping she would not be left alone for the whole day.

"Unfortunately. I wish we had more time this morning to spend together, but my schedule is a bit full. We will have dinner with my family tonight. I can have a couple of servants show you around the palace today, if you would like?"

Zahir hurried into his dressing room and reappeared shortly in shining black armor. His hair was pinned down onto his forehead by a red-jeweled crown, different to the one he wore at their wedding.

Mari gave Zahir a small wave as he disappeared out of view. For the first time since her wedding had been announced, she was alone. There were no servants bustling about, getting her ready for appearances, gown fittings, or lessons. There were no neighbors wanting to hear her excitement about becoming the Brahn princess and seeing the world. Her parents were no longer dictating every move of her life. She was alone in her bedroom, drinking a second cup of tea and taking bites out of a delectable cream filled pastry, while looking out at beautiful lilies and trees. She felt calm for the first time in several moon cycles.

Once her teacup was empty, and her fingers shook from the caffeine, Mari dragged herself to the closet and slipped on a black dress with gold lace covering the bodice and sleeves. The lace train of the dress danced along the floor as Mari twirled around, the gold insignia of Brahn, a lit candle that never melted, emblazoned above her heart. She gasped when she realized the back of the dress revealed half of her body; exposing her curves was never her first choice. Women in Brahn, from what Mari remembered from the carriage ride, were much more petite than those in Yu'güe. She decided that if it were not appropriate, the dress never would have been commissioned.

Perfectly on cue, Mari stepped out of the dressing room and was greeted by two female servants, standing at perfect attention. Without speaking, they led her from the room and down the winding halls of the palace. The halls were adorned with paintings of the royal family and tapestries with intricate designs. Bright torches lit the halls, casting shadows everywhere Mari looked.

She was taken through the entirety of her new home and she gawked at the ballroom where she and Zahir had danced, decorated now with long tables, velvet chairs, and floral arrangements. Black and gold curtains fell from the ceiling, and she stood to watch a few artists with paint splattered clothing create art on the curtains. She couldn't make out any of the paintings, but the servants informed her they were working on scenes from her wedding. Mari put a hand to her chest and thanked the artists for their work and let them know she was excited to see everything.

She was shown how to get to the kitchens if she ever needed something to eat between meals, the doors to the gardens for when she wanted some fresh air, and the medical wing if she wanted medicine for anything. While there, an older woman told her to be careful spending time outside, as the sun's scorching rays could burn her pale skin. Mari had never heard of someone having a burn from the sun, but made a note in the back of her mind to be careful with her time outside.

The next stop on the tour was a huge training room. It was a long space, floored with concrete, and lined with various weapons. Mari ran her hand along the hilts of some of the swords before picking up a blade and swinging it blindly through the air. She had never been trained in swordsmanship, but she'd always wanted to learn. If there were ever a time she couldn't use her magic, she would be completely defenseless.

"May I practice for a few minutes?" Mari asked her servants, hefting the sword up to place it back on the wall. She took their silence as approval and made her way to the center of the room.

Taking a deep breath, Mari pulled her arms up, her hands rounded like she was holding two bowls. She closed her eyes and brought to mind the images of animals she had killed. The last fox seemed to float to the forefront of her mind as Mari pushed her hands away from her body, palms twisting to face the wall across from her. Wisps of cold snow danced across her fingertips as the fox's soul materialized on the ground in front of her. It turned to face Mari, its blinking eyes waiting for instruction.

Mari heard the two servants gasp and she turned to face them, the fox padding up beside her. They were watching her, eyes wide, their hands covering their mouths. Mari sighed, ashamed she had terrified two more people with her magic.

"There's nothing to be afraid of; he won't hurt you." She bent down and put a hand on the fox's back as if she were going to pet it. "He's not real. I am a huntress and we only kill animals for food."

To show them, Mari smoothly twisted her wrist in a figure eight motion and the fox pranced in a circle around her, coming to a stop as soon as she halted her hand. Mari put her hand out toward the servants to invite them closer, but instead, they both took several steps back.

"I'm not going to hurt you," Mari said, sadness thick in her words. "I would never hurt another person."

"Your magic is beautiful," a female voice rang out.

Mari lifted her gaze but saw no one besides her servants. A small brunette girl with smooth umber brown skin poked her head out from behind one of the pillars.

"Thank you." Mari smiled.

The girl walked over to Mari, careful to avoid any of the ice that was slowly starting to melt. Her black top and tights exposed her midriff and ankles. "I'm Taryn." Her short brown hair was cut in a bob that ended at the sharp edge of her chin. It made her look serious, even though her wide hazel eyes were lit up with excitement.

"Mari."

"Oh, I know who *you* are, of course. You are Zahir's wife." Taryn wrapped her arms around Mari's neck, pulling her into a tight hug. "We are going to be such good friends."

"You are Princess Anya's twin flame, correct? I'm sorry, I met so many people at the wedding it has been hard to keep names straight." Mari smiled at Taryn, who seemed to have no fear of her, or the ghost fox at her feet.

Taryn bent down and put her hand on the fox's forehead, not realizing it would pass right through. When she tried again, she hovered her hand there and the fox nuzzled its head up through her hand. "I am. He's beautiful. How long are you able to call on their souls? And where do they come from?"

"I can call on them forever. They are a part of me; with every soul I take, I gain another in my arsenal to use if I ever need it, which I don't anticipate." Mari said, thankful that Taryn wasn't scared.

"Anne, Rylie, come here. There's nothing to be afraid of. This little guy is such a cutie," Taryn said and Mari watched as the servants came three steps closer but refused to get within ten feet of the fox. "Would you like to join me for something to eat? I haven't eaten since breakfast and I am absolutely famished."

As if on cue, Mari's stomach growled very loudly, and she laughed. "That would be lovely, Taryn. Lead the way."

Mari clenched her hand into a fist and pulled the fox back into her. The familiar electricity filled her veins, and she let out an involuntary shiver before she followed Taryn and the servants out of the training room.

"Can you explain what twin flames actually are? Zahir mentioned it without any explanation," Mari said as Taryn slowed her stride, so they were walking side by side.

"We are pairings of mages that amplify each other's magic when we fight side by side. We realized we were paired because we were both in the dueling club at school. Anya went to a fancy private institution with the advisors' daughters, whereas I was in a small class across the city. Our schools would fight against each other to practice our magic. Women are able to be soldiers, but we do not receive the same training when we are younger, which makes it harder to become one. There are certain standards and a lot of times, we just cannot keep up. I really wanted to be a soldier. Schools have started to introduce dueling clubs to prepare us better.

"Anyway, we were paired up to spar and something just... clicked. I felt this magnetic pull towards Anya, and when we fought, it looked more like we were dancing rather than fighting. We both felt angrier as we fought, and our flames nearly got out of hand. Our instructors did not stop us because they were in such awe of our magic. After that fight, it was obvious we were twin flames."

Mari had trouble keeping up with the speed of Taryn's words; they fell out of her mouth like a waterfall. "Wow, I would love an amplifier like that. That sounds amazing. I would love to watch you two train one day."

"You are welcome to watch us any time. We train every other day at sundown. You should find a time to train with Illan; he is very knowledgeable. I think you will like him. He is very kind. He hasn't used his magic in years after an attack on the palace where he had to save King Ryker. Illan is one of my favorite people here, other than Roan, of course. Have you met Roan yet? He's just the cutest little kid."

Mari found it hard to keep up with Taryn's constant changing of topics. How the conversation went from training to Zahir's younger brother was beyond Mari's comprehension. "I met him briefly at the wedding. He was really tired though, so I didn't really get to talk to him."

Mari remembered the little boy who looked exactly like Zahir with his head down on a table, eyes fluttering closed as the music and dancing went on around him. He had been dressed in a small robe and black pants that looked similar to Zahir's. Mari had never been good around children, but if they would go to sleep as easy as Roan, she could handle them.

Taryn opened the doors to reveal a large kitchen that had stoves and ovens lining the counters along the walls. In the center of the room was an empty table that was almost as long as the entire kitchen back home. The smells overwhelmed her, but she couldn't figure out what they were. She could smell cooking meat and she recognized some of the spices, like thyme and oregano, that her chef in the guest house had introduced her to. But most of them were novel to her nose.

Taryn pranced over to a cabinet that, when she opened it, cold air smacked Mari in the face. "What is that?"

"A cold room. Do you not have these in Yu'güe? We store perishable food in these, so it doesn't go bad. We fill them with ice every few days and some kind of material keeps the cold from seeping out. I don't know the science behind it, but I sure do like using this thing." Taryn pulled out a metal tray wrapped in a cloth and shut the door quickly.

"We build sheds outside of our homes and keep our food in there. The weather is so cold that we don't need any kind of insulation," Mari said, watching as Taryn uncovered a large tray of sliced red meat. "What is that?"

"Cow. Have you ever had it?" Taryn asked, pulling several slices off with her fingers and sliding it into a pan. Taryn walked over to the range and lit a small fire in her hand that she pushed onto the stove. Mari watched in awe as the flames moved from her hand to the metal surface. Taryn placed the pan on the range, much to the protest of Anne and Riley, who insisted they should fetch one of the chefs.

"Do you tend to cook your own food often?" Mari asked, surprised that even after living in the palace for years, Taryn did things for herself.

"All the time. My family owned a restaurant in the town square, and I helped them out there after school. My parents taught me how to cook and I really loved creating my own recipes." Taryn smiled wistfully when she talked about her home. "We didn't have chefs or maids to clean up after us, so I'm used to doing everything myself. It's strange to come here and have someone to do all of your chores for you. I cook and clean for myself all the time. I shop for my own clothing. I don't love being waited on. Did you have servants in Yu'güe?"

Mari couldn't help the soft smile that spread across her face as she listened to Taryn. "No, I did everything for myself, too. I hunted for my family, my mother cooked, and my father cleaned. The first time I had someone other than my mother cook for me was when I came here, and we had a chef in our guest house. He was very nice and made delicious food, but it wasn't the same. I want to do things for myself here too."

"You might have a harder time as the princess, soon to be queen. I don't think many here will allow you to do things yourself. It's a high honor to serve the king and queen. I had to argue my way into doing things for myself here, and it's only 'allowed' because I have no title. Sure, I am Anya's Twin Flame, but I'm not her romantic partner." Taryn cut off suddenly and pulled the pan off the flame, sliding the warmed meat onto a plate she had pulled from a cabinet.

The smells of the meat were familiar to Mari. She could place the scent of butter and pepper, but there was one more spice she knew she had eaten but couldn't remember its name. Mari followed Taryn's lead and picked up a slice of the cow with her fingers and slid it into her mouth. Mari let out a moan as the flavors danced on her tongue; this cow made the dried meat at home that she loved so much taste like nothing. As soon as she swallowed, Mari immediately ate another piece.

"This is absolutely delicious. I think this might just be the best thing I have ever eaten." Mari sighed. "If this was what being a princess is like, I'm going to enjoy this."

Taryn laughed as she finished another piece of their snack. "Have you met Anya yet? She has been saying for a week that she is so excited to meet you."

"Not really. I spoke to her briefly at the wedding, but I don't think that really counts." Mari recalled speaking with Anya at her wedding, but it was such a blur. She remembered bits and pieces of their conversation, but it was simply small talk. It was hard to have a meaningful conversation with several hundred people in one night.

"I think you two will get along. I don't see how you couldn't."

"I hope so. I'm having dinner with everyone tonight, which I'm actually a little nervous about," Mari said, sheepishly. "I'm not really sure what to expect. I have been taught all of your customs, but I still worry I'm going to mess them up."

Taryn laughed. "I remember what that was like. Before I moved in here, I had so many lessons from Illan and other tutors to prepare me for court life. I lived in the poorer sectors of the city and did not know a single thing about being semi-royalty. I had to learn how to eat with all the different utensils and how to bow correctly to King Ryker. I remember there was one day that I was reciting all the different courses of meals and how to eat them, but I kept forgetting that there were four courses before the entrée, not three. It was horrible learning all of that. I'll also be there tonight, so that's one less person you have to worry about meeting."

"Thank you, Taryn. I'm glad we had a chance to talk. I still have a lot to learn here and I'm glad to have met a friend." Mari smiled.

"It's been so lovely meeting you. I should go bathe. I will see you later, though." Taryn skipped out of the room, her hair bouncing around her shoulders.

As Taryn disappeared from view, Mari expressed to Anne and Riley that she was absolutely dying to see the library. Inside the enormous wooden doors, the library was filled with various scrolls and books describing Fire Mage techniques and the history of Brahn. Mari knew she would spend most of her time there. The servants showed her the part of the library that held the history of Yu'güe. There was one small shelf that held a few scrolls in an ancient language even she didn't recognize, and three tomes of the government, laws, and customs of Yu'güe.

She pulled a book off the shelf titled *The Dark Ages* and wondered if it was a book about Morana's atrocities. When she flipped open the dusty cover, she knew immediately that it was.

In the days preceding the Dark Ages, there lived mages who could wield two types of magic. There was only one mage, however, who could use opposite abilities. Morana was the first Death/Life mage to ever live past childhood. It has been said that the magic cancelled out and harmed the body.

As Morana approached adulthood, she was said to have receded from her family, refusing to exit her rooms or see anyone who called on her. It was then that bodies were found in the city square, covered in ice. It was obvious that it was the work of a Death Mage. Weeks passed before anyone called on Morana.

She began slaughtering mages in the masses. Instead of fighting her, everyone cowered. No one wanted to be the one to oppose Morana.

Nearly a full moon cycle later, did the first titanium weapon exist. A Fire Mage, Briaxia, forged the weapon in her shop after cutting herself with the metal and losing her ability to call fire to her hands. As Morana *became more powerful, Briaxia was forging the weapon that was Morana's demise.*

Mari shut the book closed with a loud thud and nearly threw it back on the shelf. A shiver ran down her spine at the thought of being cut with a titanium blade. After Morana's death, titanium blades were forged by the hundreds to slay any mage whose magic seemed too strong. She couldn't imagine how horrendous it must feel to lose her magic.

Running her fingers along the spines of some old books as she walked, she peered at the dust coating the tips of her fingers and wondered why these books had not been touched for so long. If she had lived in a place with an expansive library, there would be no book left untouched.

When Anne and Riley informed her it was time to freshen up for her dinner with the king and queen, Mari looked up in surprise, her eyes heavy and her limbs sore from being still for so long. She wasn't sure how she had spent so many hours looking through the books, but as she trudged out of the room, her heart was heavy with disappointment at being pulled away from the beautiful library so soon.

CHAPTER SEVEN

MARI

Mari was surprised to see Zahir waiting on their bed as she emerged from the bathroom. She had taken a long, relaxing bath after the library to calm her nerves about meeting the rest of Zahir's family.

Pulling the towel tighter around her body, a blush crept up on her face. "Have you been waiting long?"

"Just a few minutes." Zahir stared intensely at Mari's face, as if he were trying desperately to not look any lower.

"Let me put on a fresh dress. I'll just be a moment." Mari hurried into her dressing room and slammed the door behind her. Her rapid breaths and racing heart made her let out a soft laugh. She had not been expecting Zahir to see her in nothing but a towel so early in their relationship.

Mari took a minute to select a black dress that looked like it had gold vines and leaves snaking around the front and back of the dress to the point where it flared out around her ankles.

She twirled around in a mirror and loved how it accentuated her chest and her auburn hair stood out against the gold. While she missed wearing pants, this dress was so beautiful that she was okay with one more day without her usual clothing.

Mari watched Zahir's eyes obviously trail up and down her body as she emerged, causing heat to rise on her face.

"Come, I don't want us to be late for dinner." Zahir held his arm out, and Mari took it, linking her fingers together around his arm. She could feel the definition in his muscles and nearly swooned. "You look really... nice."

Redness deepened on her cheeks. "Thank you?"

"No, it's a good thing." Zahir put a hand to his forehead. "I apologize. I am not well versed in *this*." He waved a hand between the two of them.

"You can't tell me you have never had a woman on your arm." Mari looked at him, suspicious that someone so handsome and regal would not have at least been intimate with a woman.

"I wouldn't consider anything I have done to be as formal as this. I knew I was to be married, so it couldn't be anything real."

Mari felt Zahir's words hit her right in the gut. She too had been with someone, despite knowing it would never be real. "I see." She paused. "Is there anything I should know before we go to this dinner?"

"Don't talk to my father unless he speaks to you first. Bow upon entering the room. Wait for him to eat before you do." Zahir lowered his voice. "As long as you do not question him or say anything polarizing, it should be fine."

Mari's mouth was dry, her throat aching. She suddenly felt like she had rocks in her stomach, and she wasn't sure she would even be able to eat. "Good to know."

Zahir paused before opening the large doors before him. "Just follow my lead."

Mari followed Zahir through the doors and into a large dining room. A wooden table was set in the center, surrounded by eight high backed chairs. High King Ryker sat at the head of the table with Princess Anya to his right, the queen at the other end. Prince Roan sat beside the queen, watching Mari with wide eyes. Taryn sat between Anya and Roan and waved at Mari as she came closer. The king and princess both wore sour expressions as they watched Mari and Zahir enter. Mari had never seen the high king up close, and now, without the distraction of her wedding, she realized how large of a man he was.

Zahir bowed to his father, hands clasped together before his chest, and Mari followed suit. She watched Zahir out of the corner of her eye and when he pulled up, she lingered for just another second. Zahir took the seat next to his father, with Mari sitting beside him, an empty chair to her left. The young boy with dark green eyes was seated diagonally to her left across from her. The first thing that Mari noticed about the royal family was that Zahir and his father were the only ones with long silver hair. The rest of them had dark brown, almost black hair. The queen's gold eyes matched Zahir's perfectly, and her stark black hair hung limply around her face, pulling attention from her wide smile. Princess Anya's dour expression accentuated the sharp angles of her cheekbones and nose; her face a thinner version of the king's.

"Congratulations on your marriage." King Ryker raised a glass to his son and daughter-in-law. "Maura and I are thrilled to welcome you into our home."

"Thank you, High King Ryker. It is an honor to be a part of your family." Mari felt Zahir grab her hand under the table, and as he gave it a reassuring squeeze, her heart fluttered at the contact and she squeezed his hand back.

A coy smile played on the king's lips as Anya spoke, "I'm so excited to *finally* have a sister. It sure took Zahir long enough to marry." Her voice was sultry and intoxicating, and it pulled Mari in to listen to her. "I can't wait to spend time with you."

"I am excited as well. I spent some time with Taryn today, and she thinks we will get along very well," Mari said with a smile.

"Her magic is amazing," Taryn gushed. "She moved the soul of a fox around the training room. It was beautiful."

"You can control dead things?" Anya asked, her nose crinkling. "That sounds disgusting."

Mari was taken aback by Anya's sudden flip in tone. "Well, I can control its soul, not its body."

"Still, you play with dead things." Anya took a long sip of her wine.

"What can you do with these souls?" Maura asked, offering Mari a warm smile.

"If we find ourselves under an attack, we can call upon them for protection. They can pass through other living things and essentially turn them to ice. I have used them occasionally in my hunting just to practice," Mari explained.

"How interesting." Ryker leaned forward on the table. "I would love to watch you use your abilities one day."

"Can I see too?" Roan asked; so excited by the prospect, he dropped his spoon on the floor.

"My little warrior, pick up your spoon," Maura said softly.

Roan's eyes seemed to light up. He bent down to pick up his spoon and locked eyes with Mari as he sat up. "I'm going to be a warrior when I grow up."

Mari nodded her head and smiled. "You will be an excellent warrior, Roan. I bet you could beat me in a fight already."

Roan flexed his non-existent muscles. "I am pretty strong."

"He's only nine, but he is excelling in training for his age," Zahir whispered, picking up his wine glass and swirling the red liquid. "It's remarkable."

"He truly is my son." The king said, raising his glass once more. "Now, let us dine."

The rest of the meal was full of empty silence interspersed with shallow dialogue. The dinner, however, was exquisite. Mari had never tasted such delicious foods. Zahir told her what everything was as she was served. A beet and kale salad with a red berry dressing. Trout roasted in rosemary and thyme with a creamy butter sauce. Roasted potatoes with onion and garlic. While Mari had not heard of these spices, the flavors danced on her tongue and she knew that the food in Brahn would be much better than that in Yu'güe.

As the family swallowed their last bites of a chocolate dessert that Mari adored, she felt Zahir couldn't get her out of there faster. Without so much as a hasty goodbye, she was dragged from the room by her wrist, being told not to look back. It wasn't until they were back in their bedroom that Zahir said a word.

"I know you want to get along well with my family, but my sister is... unpredictable," Zahir said as he ran a hand through his hair. Several strands had fallen over his eyes and his brow was furrowed. "I worry that she is going to do something to harm you."

"She seemed very pleasant at dinner. Would it be a bad thing if I tried to have a relationship with your sister?"

"Anya believes she is the rightful heir to the throne because she is the eldest. She is not married and does not wish to be. Anya has been trying to undermine me for years to get her hands on the throne. My father can change his heir, but it doesn't look good. With his memory going downhill, I worry that he truly will change his mind if Anya is persuasive enough." The creases on Zahir's forehead showed Mari just how concerned he was about this possibility.

"Do you really think she would do that through me? What would I have to do with your father renouncing your status as his heir?"

Zahir sighed and sat on the edge of the bed. He pulled off his shoes and tossed them to the side as he spoke. "She has a particular hatred for the Death Mages, Gods know why. For years, she has been taunting me about you and thinking that you're going to slaughter me in my sleep." When Mari halted in her walk to the bed, Zahir put his hands up in defense. "I don't believe those things. We've been corresponding for ten years and I feel like I kind of know you."

Mari smiled and sat beside Zahir. She put a hand on his knee and stared into his bright gold eyes. "I too feel like I know you. It feels weird meeting you after all these years of writing letters. Your voice isn't quite like I imagined."

"How did you imagine it?"

"Not as deep as it truly is. I thought maybe your words were stiff because you were a prince, but now I know that isn't true."

Mari realized that Zahir's face had drifted closer to hers as she spoke, his gold eyes fixed on her lips. Just as he started to lean closer, she quickly ducked her chin, causing him to stop short and pull back.

Zahir coughed and stood up. "I should sleep. I have to meet with Illan early tomorrow."

Mari nodded and watched her husband disappear into his dressing room to prepare for bed. Flopping back on the bed, she berated herself for not letting Zahir kiss her.

"What is wrong with me?"

Chapter Eight

Zahir

Zahir stood in the center of the concrete training room and took a long, deep breath. He ignited his hands in bright orange flames and pushed them out in front of him, sending cylinders of fire across the room. The flames climbed the gray concrete wall across the room and sputtered out against the protected ceiling. Zahir watched them spread out and sent more flying to either side of him. As those slid up the walls, he kicked his right foot up and down in an arc, sending a rainbow of flames up to the ceiling. His foot smacked the ground and he immediately put all of his weight on that foot, shooting another ball of flames from his left as he lifted it to the sky.

Zahir shed his shirt as sweat dripped down his back. He lifted a pair of twin blades from the wall and swung them around, slashing through the air, pushing a breeze around his ankles. From the end of the blades came two columns of flame that spun out as he moved through the room. He glanced at his feet, ensuring his footwork was light as he danced across the floor. He had spent hours working with Illan to perfect his skill. Zahir hit the blades together and brought them down toward the floor, sending a wall of flames towards the empty space in front of him.

When Zahir finally threw the swords to the wall, sinking down to the ground with his arms around his knees, panting, a voice echoed throughout the room. "You should treat those blades more carefully, Zahir."

"I am not in the mood, Uncle."

Heavy footsteps sounded as Illan made his way over to sit in front of him. He tucked his ankles beneath his knees and sat up straight, hands clasped over his extended stomach. "Do you wish to tell me what bothers you?"

"I fear that Anya is going to do something to Mari," Zahir said. "She's been more forward with her intentions for the crown. I worry that she will hurt or manipulate her into saying something she doesn't mean."

"What do you mean by that?" Illan asked, gesturing for Zahir to continue.

"If I were my sister, I would make Mari so uncomfortable and defensive that she could say or do something against Anya. I don't know that Mari would use her magic in a physical altercation, she has only used it against animals, and it doesn't seem to me like there is any non-lethal form of Death magic." Zahir remembered Mari's demonstration for him with the bird. He had been terrified that she could kill something on command.

If she could do that to a bird, he wondered how easy it was for her to kill a person. He wondered if she *would* kill someone.

"Death Mages are inherently peaceful after Morana." Zahir flinched at Illan's use of Morana's name. In Brahn, it was heavily frowned upon to speak it. "There is no need to be fearful, Zahir. She is long gone and will never return."

"It's still strange to hear you speak her name. Mari says it too and it's unsettling."

"The fear isn't real. You fear the name because you have been told to. Morana is gone," Illan said, his large brown eyes boring into Zahir's as he stared at him intensely.

"On that note, what if Mari and I have a child who ends up being like... Morana?" A chill ran down Zahir's spine as he spoke her name.

"Your fear is valid, Zahir. But I do not think you will raise a child so evil," Illan said. "You are one of the kindest men I have the pleasure of knowing. Your child will inherit your kindness, I'm sure of it. How are you and Mari getting along?"

"I think well," Zahir said as a coy smile spread across his lips. "Our conversations are easy. She is very sweet. It's strange because I feel like I knew so much about her, but in reality, I know nothing. It feels like we are fifteen steps ahead of where we should be in our relationship."

A smile crept its way onto Illan's lips. "I remember when Daria and I were first married." He looked away nostalgically, his smile fading just slightly. "We, too, had written letters for a few years. I learned about her siblings and her life down in the city. She learned about Ryker and my duties here at the palace. The first time we met, it was like we had known each other forever. When we held each other, it felt right. But at the same time, I didn't know what foods she liked to eat, or what she liked to do."

"How did you figure out those things while also trying to not rush through your relationship? I feel so close to Mari already, and I actually tried to kiss her last night, but she turned away." Zahir blushed with the embarrassment of talking about these things with his uncle.

"My father had an arranged marriage, too. He told me before I wed that it's more important to get to know who they are and what they like to do. You need to learn what foods they like to eat and what makes them happy. You should find out who she is before you pursue a romantic relationship. I know, it sounds backwards considering you have already married. But, trust me, it will be better in the long run." Illan offered Zahir a smile and reached forward to put a hand on his knee. "Daria and I only got along so well because we didn't stress about our romantic feelings, we wanted to be friends first and lovers second."

"Do you miss her?" Zahir asked, meeting his uncle's teary gaze.

"Every day, Zahir. There is not a day that goes by that I do not wish it was me, instead of her." Illan's voice cracked as he finished his sentence.

Sliding beside his uncle, he laid his head on his shoulder. Zahir had never been one for comforting words, but he and Illan didn't always need to speak. "I hope Mari and I can have a bond like you two."

Illan wrapped an arm around Zahir's shoulders and gave him a squeeze. "I have no doubt that you will."

Zahir straightened up and pushed his hair out of his eyes, tucking it behind his ears. "Are you ready to train?"

Illan shook his head. "I think you've done enough for today. Go spend time with Mari, there is plenty of time for training."

Zahir thanked his uncle for the advice and slowly made his way towards his chambers, thinking of ways to get to know Mari better.

Chapter Nine

Mari

M ari bent over, panting, and put her hands on her knees. Wisps of hair stuck to her forehead and neck and tightness building in her chest as her vision swirled. Bile rose in the back of her throat, but she bit her lip to keep it down.

"Are you all right?" Zahir asked, extending a hand.

"Yeah." Mari straightened, wiping the back of her hand across her forehead. She clenched her hands into fists in front of her face. "Let's go again."

"We can stop if you need to."

"Fight me, Zahir."

Zahir rushed forward, throwing himself at her. He reached out a hand to grab her arm, but Mari sidestepped just in time and turned around to see him already launching another attack. She tried to duck, but Zahir grabbed her wrists and pulled her to the ground, pressing her down.

Mari struggled under his weight as he pinned her arms, trying to remember what he had taught her. She bucked her hips up, sending Zahir face first into the ground, then whipped her arms down to her sides simultaneously, breaking his grip on her wrists. Quickly, she brought her hands together around Zahir's elbow and pulled it in, so he was leaning on his right forearm. She moved her left foot to the outside of his right and twisted her hips with all her might until Zahir rolled off her and she was straddling him. She pushed his hands to the ground and smiled.

"Finally." Mari sighed and slid off Zahir, lying beside him. She put an arm over her forehead and took in deep breaths.

"That was really good. I was worried that you broke my nose for a second." Zahir laughed and rubbed it.

Mari snapped her arm off her forehead. "I didn't though, right?"

Zahir laughed and turned to look at her. "No, I'm okay. Don't worry. I've taken worse hits."

"I'm so exhausted, Zahir. How do you do this all the time?" Her face was beet red and she had soaked her shirt through with sweat. Zahir looked like he hadn't even broken a sweat.

"I've been working on combat training for years now. I'm used to the exertion."

"If I had to do this every day for my entire life, I would probably be dead."

Zahir laughed. "Are you done for the day?"

"If you make me get up and defend myself one more Gods damned time, I will go back to Yu'güe." When Zahir laughed again, Mari added. "I'm not kidding."

"Sure, you will," Zahir's tone was a mix of sarcastic and playful. "Your punching needs more work."

"What do you mean? I hit you pretty hard. My hand hurts." Mari showed Zahir her red knuckles that still stung from when she punched his chest earlier.

"I barely even felt it, Mari. You need more force behind your punch." Mari frowned, so Zahir stood up and offered a hand to her. "I'll show you."

"You aren't going to hit me, are you? Then I'll really leave." Mari took his hand and stood.

Zahir shook his head and instructed Mari to plant her feet with her knees bent just a little. "The key to punching is using your whole upper body. Just using your arm isn't going to give you the power that you need. You need to utilize everything. Just the torque from your upper body can give you enough power to knock out an attacker. They can be on the ground so fast you won't even realize you hit them."

Mari squatted, balling her hands into fists on either side of her waist. She bent her knees and felt the burn start in her thighs. She twisted her torso from side to side and moved her hands a little in a small punching motion.

"Here," Zahir came up behind Mari, "can I position you?"

Mari nodded and he pushed her feet slightly further apart, lifting her knees out of their deep squat so that she was higher up. He placed his hand on top of her right and made a tight fist. When he put his left hand on her waist, Mari's face flushed red.

"So, we're going to take your right hand and punch. Instead of winding up straight back for your hit, we're going to just twist your whole torso back a little," Zahir pushed Mari's body back, moving with her, "and then we'll turn back around and throw the punch at the same time."

As Zahir twisted Mari back around, he helped her extend her arm so she could hit the imaginary target as her body began moving past center in the other direction, and then some.

"That didn't seem too hard." Mari's voice was quiet. She was very aware of Zahir's body pressed against her, heat radiating off his torso. She could feel his strong stomach through his shirt, and she coughed nervously as he tightened his grip on her waist.

Zahir released Mari and stepped back abruptly. "Uh, you want to punch through your target, not at them. And make sure your arm isn't completely extended; you could pull a muscle like that."

"Right, yes, that makes sense." Mari turned around to face Zahir, hoping her face wasn't as red as she thought. "Thank you. That was really helpful. But how am I ever going to remember that in a fight?"

"We will practice. It'll become second nature."

"Do we *have* to practice? Can't I just be good at it? I'm just naturally pretty good at magic." Mari groaned at the thought of having to sweat like a pig all the time to land a punch.

"What if someone gets too close? Or something happens and you can't use your magic. You know titanium can hinder the effectiveness of magic. What if you get too close to titanium?" Zahir was a practical man. Mari never planned for if-then scenarios; she didn't like to dwell on the future.

"Why do you have to use logic?" Mari sighed. "Have you ever practiced magic in the face of titanium?"

"Unfortunately, yes. We have a titanium gym in our dungeon for us to practice with. Gods forbid we get ambushed at the palace by rebels who use titanium to mitigate a mage's magic, we need to be prepared. If attackers get past our guards, we have to know how to defend ourselves in the worst-case scenarios."

"What does it feel like?"

Zahir seemed to shudder at the memory. "Cold. Really cold. As a Fire Mage, we're always warm. There's something akin to a hearth burning inside of us that keeps our flame going. When there's titanium all around, it takes so much energy to conjure up the tiniest of flames. A master mage can fight like a child, but your average mage can barely keep a flame lit."

"Oh, Gods, that's terrifying." Mari put her hands over her mouth.

"My father demanded Anya and I learn how to fight hand to hand, just in case. He was a commander in the army when my grandfather was king. There was a rebel attack on the palace when he was commander. They wore titanium armor and chained the guards up to the pillars. They cuffed my father's men in titanium, and him as well. No one could fight them with magic. They were completely helpless.

"That is, until my uncle came in and saved them. He was able to get the attacker closest to my father down in hand-to-hand combat. Once he freed my father, it was all over. Their power together was unyielding. They burned every single one of those intruders alive."

"They were burned alive," Mari repeated, shaking her head. "What an awful way to die."

Zahir nodded tersely. "It was the last time they fought together. Something broke inside them both. Killing tens of men, burning them alive, did something to them. They never fought side by side ever again. It's been thirty-five years since. I haven't even seen my uncle produce a single flame in my life."

Mari was floored. She couldn't imagine a high ranking official in Brahn not using his magic for over thirty years. She had never known it was even possible to not use magic. She had always felt an itch in the pit of her stomach if she went too long without using it.

"I can't believe that he wouldn't use his magic for that long. How does he protect himself?" Mari sat down on the floor to stretch out her legs.

"He doesn't need to. He retired from the army and has since been training my siblings and I in hand-to-hand combat. We train separately for three hours five days a week. I take the dawn slot, Anya in the late afternoon, and Roan at dusk. I'm sure he would be willing to train you with one of us if you'd like me to ask him."

Mari smiled. "I would really appreciate that. Not that you're not a good teacher, you are."

Zahir laughed. "Uncle Illan is better."

"I am excited to meet him," Mari said.

Zahir stretched his arms high above his head. "I must clean up; I have a meeting to attend shortly."

Mari nodded, and the pair of them set off to clean themselves up. The bath in the training washrooms was already full of steamy water when Mari approached it. She slid into the tub, the hot water instantly soothing her sore muscles and she sighed audibly before pushing her head under the water to scrub her face clean of grime. She had never felt so disgusting.

Scrubbing soap into her skin with a plush cloth that didn't hurt like the ones in Yu'güe did, it was even relaxing, rather than a chore. As Mari washed, she realized the water wasn't getting cold. It stayed the perfect soothing temperature that it had been when she'd entered the bath. Looking around, she saw a small perpetual flame beneath the tub reflecting in a mirror. It was then that she realized how good the Fire Mages had it. At this point in her bath back home, she would have already been cold and trying to wash her hair as quickly as possible to get out of the water. But here in Brahn, Mari took her time, enjoying the warmth that encased her body.

Once the pads of her fingers and toes were significantly pruned, Mari begrudgingly lifted herself out of the bath and dried herself off with another plush towel. After drying her hair, she slipped into a fresh set of training clothes and started to make her way in the direction of the kitchen. Her stomach had started growling loudly during her bath.

Mari followed the delicious smells down the hall to where ten people worked preparing a meal. She watched as they moved between each other, speaking instructions and commands. They were all oblivious to her as she walked to an open cabinet containing baskets of fruits. She quickly grabbed a long yellow fruit and scurried out of the room.

As she rounded a corner towards her room, she collided into someone, dropping her fruit with a gasp.

"Oh, King Ryker, I apologize. I should have been more aware of my surroundings." Mari said as she bowed deeply.

"Mari, what a splendid surprise. Please, there is no need for formalities; we are family, after all." Ryker pulled Mari out of her bow by a hand on her shoulder.

The king's hair was knotted and unruly and, although his glassy eyes seemed to see, they did not really register what was in front of him. There was something off about him, but Mari didn't know him well enough to make a proper judgement. She wished that Zahir was there with her.

"Right, of course. How should I refer to you?" she asked, looking down at her fruit on the floor instead of at him.

"Ryker is fine. Or Father, whichever is easiest for you."

Mari nodded as she brought her gaze back up to the king. "Thank you for your warmth. It is a great honor to be so welcomed into your family."

"Where are you headed?" Ryker asked, taking his eyes off Mari to scan the hallway over her shoulder.

"Back to my chambers. Zahir and I just finished a training session and I stopped by the kitchen to grab a snack." Mari gestured to the yellow fruit and slowly bent down to pick it up off the floor. "I accidentally dropped it when I bumped into you."

Ryker laughed. "Bananas are my favorite. Have you ever had one?"

"I can't say that I have."

"They come from Orcian. We have been there on diplomatic journeys. The last time was not a fun trip, I can tell you that, but Orcian is beautiful. Not as striking as Brahn, of course."

"Right, of course. No clan could match Brahn's beauty," Mari said, without missing a beat.

"Hmm. Not even Yu'güe?" Ryker asked, turning his gaze back to Mari.

Mari laughed nervously. "Definitely not. Yu'güe is nothing compared to Brahn." Guilt rose in the back of Mari's throat as she spoke ill of her home clan. She was not sure how Ryker expected her to answer, but she didn't think he would be opposed to a little flattery.

"Good answer." Ryker offered a tight-lipped smile. "I wouldn't want our future queen still feeling aligned with her old clan."

Mari felt like she was taking a test, that there was only one right answer here. "My allegiance is with my new family here in Brahn. I will do anything to better this clan." While she was going to be Brahn's next queen, she was still connected with Yu'güe. She would do anything to better Brahn, that much was true, but she would never do so if it meant hurting her home.

Ryker leaned in close and lowered his voice so even the flies on the walls wouldn't be able to hear. "I wouldn't have wanted to marry Zahir to someone who isn't fully invested in Brahn's affairs. He is a... special boy."

Mari blinked rapidly at Ryker. "What do you mean by that?"

Just as the king was about to speak, Maura rushed down the sun-streaked hallway toward them. "Ryker, sweetheart. You can't be wandering by yourself. Come, let's get you back to bed."

"Good night, Mari," Ryker said as Maura wrapped an arm around his waist. "It was lovely chatting with you."

"Thank you for finding him," Maura mouthed as she led him away.

Mari watched them disappear down the hallway before beginning the trek back to her room. The training clothes had started sticking to her body again, and Mari hadn't realized she had begun sweating. It was comforting to be out of a gown, however, even if the clothes were dirty. Living her whole life in pants had made it difficult for her to switch to fancy outfits that were hard to move in. At least in her training clothes, she could walk without tripping.

Zahir was already in their bedroom when Mari entered, with nothing but a towel wrapped around his waist. Her eyes trained on his chiseled chest, no matter how hard she tried to avert her gaze. Before she could stop herself, her eyes traveled lower to the muscles pointing towards his—

"Um, sorry," Mari squeaked, blushing and hurriedly going into her dressing room. She flattened her back against the door and slid down it, thoroughly embarrassed. Every time Zahir was without a shirt, she couldn't help but stare at him. She wondered what it would feel like to run her hands up and down his chest.

Mari shook her head, trying to get her obscene thoughts out of her head. There was a part of her that couldn't deny she wanted to be intimate with Zahir already.

She slid on a long green tunic and loose black pants that clasped around her ankles, cinching a belt around her waist and pulling her hair up into a knot. When she stepped back into the bedroom, she found Zahir had dressed in a tight white shirt that showed off the definition of the muscles in his back and black pants that clung to the meat of his thighs. She trailed her eyes down his chest and absentmindedly licked her lips.

"Do you want to go for a walk?" Zahir asked, holding out his arm for Mari to take.

Instead, she slid her hand into his, and he slowly lowered his arm to his side and led Mari through the palace and out to the gardens.

"My mother and I used to go for walks here all the time. We would sit by the pond and talk. We haven't done that since my father fell ill."

Mari hummed, unsure if she should mention her encounter with his father.

Zahir led her through the garden until they arrived at the shore of a small pond. Swimming in the pond were five swans, a mother and its babies. Zahir went to sit down by the edge of the water, but Mari froze, staring at the animals as she sat down with shaking breaths.

"Are you all right?" Zahir asked, stroking circles on the back of her hand with his thumb.

"I am actually terrified of birds," Mari said, her voice breathy.

"Do you want to sit somewhere else?" Zahir asked, moving to stand.

"Yes, please." Mari stood up immediately and walked backwards, never turning her back to the swans.

Zahir didn't let go of Mari's hand as he, too, moved backwards. Once they were far enough away that the swans were almost out of sight, she turned around and darted to the left.

"So why birds?" Zahir asked, letting a laugh escape his lips.

"It's not funny. I was almost killed by a water bird as a child. My brother didn't save me." Mari recounted the story about the water bird, eliciting a burst of laughter out of Zahir as he walked her through the garden.

"I'm sorry. I'm not laughing because it's funny you're terrified of birds. It's just a funny thing to picture." Zahir kissed Mari's hand lightly. "I promise to keep you safe from all birds."

"Let's sit here," Mari said, pointing to a large tree that had enough leaves to create a shady spot at its trunk.

Sliding down the trunk, she sat with her legs under her body. Zahir sat beside her, stretching his legs out in front of him and he pulled their clasped hands onto his thigh, rubbing circles on the back of her hand.

"Tell me about your brother," Zahir said softly.

Mari looked up at the sky as she took a deep breath and spoke. "Hanan was better than me at everything. He was six years older than I was, so it made sense. He was the kindest person. He often gave up food for me if I didn't have enough to eat. Hanan was everything to me. Did I ever tell you what happened?"

Zahir shook his head solemnly.

"He ran away. He was engaged to the princess of Orcian, but he was in love with another.... He refused to marry the Orcian girl. At the time, I thought it was really brave of him to stand up to our parents. The same night he ran away, he was killed."

"Gods, Mari. I am so sorry," Zahir whispered.

"If I could go back in time, I would tell him not to run. I'd tell him to plan his escape better."

Mari reflected upon her brother's departure. He had left in the middle of the night, leaving only a note saying what had happened and that he would write as soon as possible. Instead of her father bringing in a letter, he brought news of Hanan's death. He had buried the body at the boulders halfway up the main peak. Mari wept for hours that day, and her mother had to drag her away from the burial site.

"Anyway," Mari said, shifting her position so her knees were up against her chest and her arms wrapped around them, letting go of Zahir's hand. "I never got to hear if you had ever traveled out of Brahn. We were taken away from our tea before you could answer."

"I went to Orcian once with my father. He surpassed the council and went to discuss new trade routes with the Water Mages. It didn't go over well. They are creatures of habit."

"You went to Orcian? What was it like? Is it as beautiful as the books say?" Mari had only ever imagined the ice blue water and the towering sea green buildings.

"It's magnificent." Zahir smiled at his feet. "Waterfalls guard the entrance. The Water Mages will actually stop the water from falling to get in and out of the main city. Unlike Brahn, there are villages outside the city. People live in all different areas, with agriculture and ways of life spread out more than it is here.

Brahn has a very central community that doesn't spread beyond the city sectors.

"Inside the city is, dare I say it, even more breathtaking than Brahn. Every building is a pale blue or green, like sea glass. The city is right on the ocean and you can hear the waves crashing on the shore for miles. There are no streets, only canals that the mages either walk across or row boats. Any kind of walking path is made of packed brown sand that slides between your toes. No one wears shoes, which I wish I had known; I was getting sand out of mine for days afterwards. I long for the day I can go back there."

Zahir's smile never faltered and Mari realized this was the first time she had seen him so calm.

"Wow. That sounds incredible. Why didn't you take your shoes off when you started getting sand in them?"

"I tried, but my father made me put them back on. He was embarrassed to have me walking around in bare feet."

"I can imagine you as a kid walking around the sand in your bare feet," Mari said with a giggle. When Zahir didn't laugh, she held back a smile. "You weren't a child when this happened, were you?"

Redness flooded Zahir's face as he looked away. "I was nineteen..."

Mari clutched Zahir's thigh as she laughed. "You, the prince of Brahn, tried to walk around Orcian with no shoes on as an adult?"

"I didn't like the sand," Zahir said, putting a hand over his eyes. "The Water Mages were barefoot. I didn't see why *I* couldn't be."

"I would love to visit Orcian one day. I want to see all the clans," Mari said, with a longing sigh. Reading about the clans was one thing, but actually visiting would be a whole other experience.

"Maybe one day we can go. How are you enjoying Brahn so far?" Zahir asked, taking her hand again.

"There are so many different and new things here that I didn't think I would like. Your food, for example. It's so flavorful. Everything in Yu'güe is bland. I didn't know how I would feel about the vegetables, but I really enjoy them." Mari's stomach, as if on instinct, grumbled. "I think I'm getting hungry again."

Zahir chuckled. "I'm glad you like the food. Let's go get ourselves something to eat."

He stood, pulling Mari up beside him, but as she lurched to her feet, she felt one side of her body tilting. With a start, she grasped onto Zahir's shirt, steadying herself just in time for her not to topple over, and Zahir's warm arms wrapped tightly around her waist.

"Sorry," Mari said, her hands balled in the collar of his shirt as she looked up into his smiling face.

"You're not going anywhere." Zahir leaned down and pressed a kiss to Mari's cheek before taking her hand once more and leading her back towards the palace.

CHAPTER TEN

ZAHIR

Zahir's fingers thrummed one by one on the wooden table, tapping out the same monotonous note over and over. He nodded along as one of his advisors, Keir, droned on about persuading Lovíth to open up trade. Keir had been talking about this for the better part of an hour, and Zahir wanted nothing more than to put his head down on the table and take a nap. Just as his eyes were fluttering closed, Keir sat down and Illan posed a new topic of discussion.

"As we are all aware," Illan said, the legs of his chair scraping loudly against the tile floor. "King Ryker's memory has been fading more rapidly of late. Just this afternoon, he couldn't remember the latest rebel attack in the north city."

Zahir leaned forward in his chair, blood pounding in his ears. Last night, a group of rebels had climbed the city wall and slaughtered ten families. Bile burned the back of his throat as he remembered the bloody scene that he had awoken to when Illan had burst into his room, telling him to put on shoes. A chill went down Zahir's spine as he recalled the writing on the wall, red and dripping. *We are coming.* Zahir had set two guards outside his chambers to keep watch over Mari as she slept, and made sure they stayed with her all day, just in case.

Zahir must have missed part of what Illan said because suddenly, all eyes were on him. His cheeks burned red as he offered his uncle a tight smile. "I apologize, I didn't hear the last part of what you said, Uncle."

"I asked if you would be willing to take the throne from your father preemptively," Illan said, nodding his head almost imperceptibly.

Zahir opened his mouth to speak, but nothing came out. The idea of assuming the throne immediately both terrified and thrilled him. On the one hand, he had been training for this position for half his life. On the other, he still had a lot to learn. Zahir was unsure how to change, or write, laws. His knowledge on trade was questionable, at best. He had no new ideas on how to thwart the rebels, but it didn't seem like his father did either.

"If it is something that would benefit Brahn, it may be a good idea, but I wish to think about it before making a final decision," Zahir said, unsure if his answer was acceptable. The last time he chaired a meeting without his father, he nearly sent two thousand tons of iron to Orcian, rather than two thousand pounds, because of his poor penmanship. Illan had stayed calm during the ordeal, even though Brahn almost lost all of its iron stock.

"There isn't much time, Your Majesty," Patrice, an older woman who reminded Zahir of his grandmother, said. "King

Ryker is deteriorating every day. You need to start making some decisions."

"Yes, I do. But I want to make sure I am making the *right* decisions," Zahir said as he rubbed at his temples.

"You are ready, my prince," Illan said with a nod. "You have been training for this long enough. If your father were to die tonight, would you not take the throne?"

Zahir leaned back in his seat. If his father were to die, Zahir would have no choice but to become king. "In that case, I would."

"Then how is taking it by choice any different?" Keir countered, nodding to himself.

Zahir sighed. "It isn't. If in three days' time my father does not willingly step down, I will persuade him." Zahir slid his chair backward and rose quickly to his feet. "Please, enjoy your evenings, everyone."

Zahir walked slowly from the room, the soles of his shoes tapping loudly on the floor as he pulled his shoulders back and stared straight ahead at the doors that opened as he neared. He willed his hands to calm, so the room wouldn't see them shaking, but as soon as he turned the corner, Zahir bolted down the hall. If he wanted a quiet place in the palace, the library was the best place to hide.

Just as he reached the library doors, Illan's voice echoed throughout the hallway. "Let's talk, Zahir."

"I wish to be alone," Zahir said. He swung open the doors to the library and slinked inside, basking in the glow of the torch light.

"We both know that is a lie," Illan said as he followed. He grabbed a torch off the wall and held it up.

"I am unprepared to be king." Zahir walked toward one of the long, wooden tables lining the wall and slid onto one of the high-backed chairs, resting his chin on top of his folded arms.

"Why do you feel that way?" Illan asked, taking the chair to his right.

"I don't know the first thing about writing or changing laws. I have nearly messed up trade with Orcian before. I have never corresponded with Yu'güe. The one letter I sent Lovíth was met with an outright refusal. I wish my father would have let me actually *do* more instead of just watching him," Zahir explained. He blew a strand of hair off his face that immediately flopped back down over his nose.

"You do not have to rule alone, Zahir. You have an advisory council for a reason; they are hired to support and guide you. I believe that you are ready to rule Brahn. As someone who has watched you grow in this position, you are more than capable of being a king."

"I know I can be a king. I just want to be a good one." Zahir sighed and buried his face in his arms, his vision swimming and sending a wave of nausea through him.

"Do you think you will be a bad one?" Illan asked, his voice sliding up a note as he posed the question.

Zahir thought for a minute. "I am not sure. I don't agree with a lot of decisions my father made over the past few years regarding the rebels. But I also don't know if his choices were right in the end. A good king does everything for his people."

"Could you give up everything to save your people?"

"I'm not sure."

The idea of giving up his life of luxury was a strange thought. The one time Zahir had tried to cook for himself, he'd smoked out the kitchen so badly, the head chef had actually lost his temper. The first time he'd picked out his own clothing, the colors had clashed so much he'd had to give them away.

On the flip side, he could navigate the streets of the city with his eyes closed. He had walked those streets so many times, it was like walking through the palace. Zahir could get a manual labor job with all the working out he did. Lifting heavy objects was easy for him and he'd even helped out with a flour delivery once when one of the servants was ill.

"Could you give up Mari?"

Zahir shot straight up in his seat. "What?"

"These rebels are attacking because of your marriage. A pairing your father thought would bring peace."

"I don't want to give her up," Zahir said sharply.

Illan patted him on the shoulder. "That's the right answer. You clearly care for her."

"Of course, I do." Zahir smiled to himself, thinking of when she couldn't tear her eyes away from him when he emerged from his bath. "She's my wife. I should be going; she offered to help me dye my hair after the meeting ended." Zahir ran a hand through his hair where the dark brown roots of his natural hair color were starting to show. The dying of a prince or king's hair could be performed only by a parent or spouse. When Zahir had brought this up with Mari, she had exuberantly agreed to help, even if she didn't know what she was doing.

"Yes, it is looking a bit dingy," Illan teased, reaching over to ruffle Zahir's hair.

"Uncle." Zahir laughed, a wide smile spreading across his face. "I'm not a child anymore."

"I know you're not. But I can still treat you like one every now and again," Illan said as he pushed back from the table and led Zahir from the library. As the doors shut behind them, he pulled Zahir into an embrace.

He hadn't realized how much taller than Illan he'd grown. As his chin rested on top of his uncle's balding head, Zahir tried to remember the last time they'd hugged.

"Thank you for believing in me. I may not feel ready, but I have you to lean on," Zahir said, pulling away from Illan's embrace.

"Always, Zahir." Illan gave Zahir's shoulder a reassuring squeeze before heading down the hallway toward the gardens.

Turning on his heel, he began his walk to his chambers, where he was certain Mari was waiting for him. When she had pointed out his roots that morning, he had flushed with embarrassment; he hadn't meant to go so long without dying his hair, but he had a lot of things on his mind lately.

Just as he was turning the corner to his chambers, he smacked right into a guard. A loud 'oof' escaped the man's lips as he stumbled back a few steps and Zahir stepped back, startled. Zahir's eyes took in the black pants and jacket, signifying his royal guards before looking into a familiar pair of bright blue eyes.

"Oh, Trevor, I'm so sorry," Zahir said, reaching out to clasp the guard by his arms.

"Your Majesty, it is I who should be apologizing."

Zahir smiled at him, taking in his familiar pale face, his short black hair, cut right to his scalp and his lopsided smile. When Trevor looked back at Zahir, they both broke into laughter.

Zahir brushed the non-existent dirt from Trevor's chest as he spoke. "Must you insist on being so formal?"

Trevor dropped his voice to a whisper. "We have seen each other naked. I only insist on formalities to protect you."

Zahir's wide eyes darted over the guard's shoulder to the empty hallway. "Trevor, I asked you not to speak of this inside palace walls."

"You are married now. It doesn't matter what we did before this," Trevor said.

The night Zahir had spent wrapped in Trevor's arms in a small apartment down in the city flashed before his eyes. He still remembered the feel of Trevor's fingers drawing circles on his chest, and the thought made the hair on the back of his neck stand up. Guilt choked Zahir suddenly, and he shook his head.

"I'm married and I care very much for my wife."

"You never did like to play by the rules." Trevor winked at Zahir and reached out to lightly graze his hand.

Zahir smiled at the familiar contact, but pulled his hand away sharply. "Good night, Trevor."

Trevor nodded once. "Good night, Your Highness." Trevor offered Zahir a quick bow before striding down the hallway that Zahir came from.

He ran a hand through his hair and looked around, hoping no one was around to witness their risky conversation. In the three moon cycles after they'd had their evening together, Zahir had only spoken to Trevor in hushed conversations. The idea that someone would find out his secret terrified him. While he was unashamed, he did not wish to do anything to threaten his marriage to Mari. This pairing was his father's proudest decision and Zahir did not wish to disappoint.

Once Zahir had calmed his racing heart and assured himself that no one had seen him, he made his way through the door to his chambers where Mari sat on the floor, mixing a bowl at her feet. Her hair was pulled up on top of her head, cascading over her neck in a long bunch. She bit her lip in concentration as she huddled over the bowl of white dye.

"Ready?" Zahir asked, closing the door lightly behind him.

"Perfect timing," Mari said, getting to her feet. "I just finished mixing everything."

"Thank you for helping me with this. Let me change my clothing so I don't ruin these robes." Zahir looked down at the black robe he wore with the ever-burning candle stitched over his heart. It was his favorite thing to wear to meetings because the gold in the embroidery matched his eyes perfectly.

Sliding into a pair of loose black pants that cinched at his ankles, he met Mari in the bathroom, where a chair sat beside the bath. Zahir watched Mari's eyes trail down his chest and linger for just a second south of his abdomen before her cheeks flushed red and she turned quickly around. The coy smile that spread across Zahir's lips was hard to keep away; he liked that she found his body desirable.

Mari instructed Zahir to sit in the chair as she grabbed the bowl of dye and a brush to paint it on. "I have never dyed hair before, so please don't be mad if I mess this up."

Zahir let out a chuckle as he slid onto the chair Mari had set up. "I don't know that it is possible to mess it up. Just paint it onto the part of my hair that's the wrong color."

The brush tickled the top of Zahir's head as Mari dragged it across his roots. He suppressed a laugh when a glop of dye landed on his head and Mari apologized profusely for making a mess. When she sneezed and accidentally pushed the brush down onto his forehead, they both broke out into uncontrollable laughter. Zahir couldn't stop smiling when Mari tried to wipe it up onto his hair but ended up painting his entire forehead a bright white color.

When Mari moved from behind Zahir to in front, he couldn't help but look up at her face, eyes squinted in concentration and lips parted ever so slightly. Standing this close, he could smell the perfume she wore, one that reminded him of the lilies that bloomed in the wet season. When she cast her eyes downward for a second and met his gaze, Zahir sucked in a quiet breath. Her eyes shimmered in the low light of the room.

"I told you I was going to mess this up," Mari said with a sigh as she walked around the chair and placed the bowl on the floor behind Zahir. "You look like it rained hair dye."

Zahir spun around and straddled the chair, leaning his chin on the back. "It's fine, Mari. We're going to wash it out in a bit."

"Oh, that makes me feel a lot better," Mari said with a smile. She sat on the floor, curling her feet under her knees and leaning her elbows on her thighs. She pressed the palms of her hands into her chin and looked up at Zahir.

"Are you willing to dye my hair for the rest of our lives?" Zahir asked, tilting his head to the left.

"Hmm." Mari sighed. "If this turns out okay, then I will dye your hair whenever you want. If all your hair falls out because I did something wrong, then please ask someone else."

"Would you still like me if my hair fell out?" Zahir asked, trying to picture what he would look like without any hair.

"Only if you didn't have a lumpy head," Mari said with a laugh. Her laugh was contagious, always making Zahir smile. It bubbled up in her chest and escaped in little quiet bursts.

"Is that even possible?"

"Yes." Mari nodded. "Several of the elder council leaders on Yu'güe had gone bald in their old age and had bumpy heads. As a child, I couldn't stop looking at them."

Zahir let out a laugh that echoed off the walls. "I can't even imagine what a bumpy head would look like."

"Is it time to wash the dye out yet?" Mari asked.

"It's probably fine." Zahir stood up and leaned back to stretch out his back. The bones cracked and he let out a relieved sigh. He sat down in the bathtub, sliding down so his head was just beneath the faucet. "Just turn on the water and, if you don't mind, rub the dye away from my scalp."

"Are my hands going to get dyed?" Mari asked as she kneeled down behind Zahir. "Your pants are going to get wet."

"I was going to change them afterwards. Do you prefer I remove them?"

A bright blush crept on Mari's cheeks. "Whatever makes you comfortable?"

Zahir closed his eyes and let out a breathy laugh as he waited for the water to rush against his head.

Just as the warm water passed over his head, Zahir felt Mari thread her fingers through his hair and rub his scalp. He couldn't help but let out an involuntary moan as Mari pressed her fingers into his head.

"Did I hurt you?" Mari asked, pulling her hands away immediately.

"No. It felt good."

Zahir's stomach fluttered when Mari put her hands back into his hair. The feeling of her hands made butterflies fly in his chest; the pressure she put on his head was so relaxing that he wanted her to do this every day for the rest of his life. Every so often, he let out a soft moan, relishing in the massage.

When Mari shut the faucet off, Zahir almost complained; he never wanted her to stop. Mari handed him a plush white towel as he sat up and rubbed at his hair. Just as he was standing up, a bell sounded loudly, echoing off the walls and dropping a stone into his stomach. He threw the towel to the ground and leapt from the bathtub.

"What in the Gods' names is that?" Mari asked, her eyes wide as she covered her ears.

"Rebels."

CHAPTER ELEVEN

MARI

It took ten seconds for Mari and Zahir to rush from the room and down the hall. He grabbed his sword and slung it around his waist before gripping Mari's hand tightly, pulling her along behind him. The air was thick with smoke, and Mari coughed, trying not to vomit as they ran.

The doors to the palace were splintered, exposing the smoking city beyond, and men wearing black cloaks with a red circle insignia poured in through the holes, wielding chains, swords, and knives. Guards blocked the hall for Mari and Zahir, screaming at them to run. The sound of metal clanging together echoed loudly off the walls. Bloodied bodies littered the floor and Mari could see that several guards had already lost their lives.

Zahir grabbed Mari's hand and dragged her down the winding passages of the palace towards safety. Zahir had told her about a safe room in the catacombs but hadn't had a chance to show her. If only he had, she wouldn't have wondered how much further they had to run. Her heart thrummed hard in her chest like it was going to break her ribs.

Quickly glancing behind her as they ran, Mari saw cloaked figures gaining on them. "Zahir, they're coming!"

Zahir whipped his head around and narrowed his eyes as he threw a ball of fire in their direction, lighting up the hallway and buying them some time. "We have to move faster!"

"I can't keep up. This is as fast as I can run." Mari's voice broke with fear and tears rimmed her eyes.

"Dig deeper and run faster." Zahir gritted his teeth and continued tugging Mari along in his wake.

She pumped her legs and drove her free arm, but there was nothing she could do to move faster. The force of Zahir pulling her forward did nothing except remind her that she was only slowing him down.

As they neared the door to the catacomb entrance, white smoke filled the hallway, engulfing them and blocking their vision to the doors. Mari coughed, tightening her grip on Zahir's hand, and he pulled her to his chest, wrapping his free arm around her shoulders and pushing her into the wall to shield her with his body. He rested his chin on top of her head and squeezed her hand tightly as they waited for the room to clear.

"I'm scared." Mari's voice was barely even a whisper as she curled into his chest, his heart beating against her cheek.

"I'm not going to let them hurt you."

As the smoke cleared, Mari realized they were surrounded by men wielding weapons. She couldn't see their eyes, but each exhibited a devilish grin. It was then Mari knew exactly what she had to do. She pushed away from Zahir and took a deep breath. She clawed her hands upwards into the sky and called upon several souls to protect them. A pack of wolves made a half circle around the couple, facing the rebels with teeth bared, a web of ice forming on the ground as they moved into position. Mari noticed that as Zahir breathed, white puffs of air escaped his lips.

Zahir launched fire into the fight, igniting the clothes of some rebels. The men screamed, desperately trying to put the fires out before their skin burned. One man was not so lucky; the fire burned through his clothes and ignited his skin. It wasn't long before the acrid stench of burning flesh filled the room. Mari was immediately nauseated and gagged at the scent, throwing her hands to cover her nose and mouth.

Zahir broke out of the ghosts' protection and threw himself into the fight, bringing his foot up into an attacker's jaw, sending him sprawling onto the ground. He pounded another in the face, knocking him clean out. Mari stared in awe as Zahir delivered a swift kick to another man's side, putting him on his knees and then snapping the man's neck. The loud crack reverberated through the room and made Mari sick to her stomach as the man's lifeless body crumpled to the ground.

Three attackers broke their formation and rushed toward her, narrowly avoiding sliding on the ice. She breathed deeply as three spirits floated forward and passed through the men, freezing them on the spot. Their skin turned frosty and blue, their eyes the only things that could move. Mari pushed forward and kicked one man in the stomach, sending him sliding backwards and landing on his back with a loud crack. She punched another and was met with the realization that punching ice did, in fact, hurt. With a grunt, she kicked the man in the crotch, and as he unfroze, he fell to the ground with a bellow.

The third man moved before Mari could get to him and he swung his dagger at her chest, but she ducked quickly and fell hard onto the floor. Without a second thought, Mari raised her hand towards the man's chest and balled her hand into a fist. Everything happened too quickly for Mari to realize what she was doing. The silver soul leapt from the man's chest and floated beside the body that turned blue and collapsed to the floor. The electric burn down her spine made her scream out as the soul wrapped itself around her and dissipated.

It was only when the knife clattered to the ground beside Mari did she realize she had taken a person's life. She stared at the body, eyes wide and mouth agape. Her shaking breaths brought tears to her eyes. Her vision swirled as she leaned to her left and vomited all over the floor. Rising onto her hands and knees, she wasn't sure if she was coughing or sobbing.

Mari looked up just in time to see a knife hurtling toward her. She had enough time to slide out of the way, but not before the dagger sliced through her arm. Mari cried out, grabbing the wound with her other hand, but almost instantly, she realized that she had been cut with titanium—the one thing that could take away her magic. When she pulled her hand away from the injury, black smoke furled out of the wound and over her fingers. The fear that she could die hadn't hit her until that moment. Without her magic, she was completely defenseless.

119

Mari's body shook as she ducked under the man's knife, putting herself on her ass. When he brought it back down towards her face, she fell to the ground and scurried backwards. She tried desperately to call for her wolf spirits, but nothing came to her rescue. She looked wildly around to realize they were gone, and she was left completely defenseless. The man took her confusion to his advantage and launched himself on her, knocking her supine. Blood dripped from his nose onto Mari's cheeks as she thrashed under his weight, trying desperately to throw him off. The man put his hands around her throat and Mari tasted blood in her mouth as she struggled to breathe. Black stars danced at the edges of her vision as she tried to pry his hands away from her neck.

"Mari!" Zahir yelled, slamming his elbow into an attacker's face. "Remember what we practiced!"

Mari's vision began to blur as she racked her brain, trying to remember what Zahir taught her. She bucked her hips up, throwing the man face first into the ground. She threw her arms down to her sides simultaneously, loosening the man's grip on her throat. Quickly, she brought her hands together around his elbow and pulled it in, so he was leaning on his left forearm. She moved her right foot to the outside of his left and twisted her hips with all her might until the man rolled off of her and she was straddling him again. He never completely let go of her throat and was squeezing again when Mari drove her elbow into the man's stomach, causing him to cough blood onto her face. He lost his grip again and Mari ripped herself out of his grasp and rolled away from him.

When she stood, she delivered a swift kick to his face and spun around in search of Zahir. He was surrounded by three men, all trying to drive a sword through his torso. He had wielded his sword and beside him lay the headless corpses of two attackers. Zahir's face and chest were splattered with bright red blood as he stabbed and slashed at the rebels.

Mari ran over to him, just missing the blade of a sword as she ducked. As she stood, a blinding orange light lit up the hallway and the shattering of glass nearly burst her ear drums. Heat blew towards her, like the entire palace had been lit on fire. Mari shielded her eyes, squinting in the direction of the heat that had nearly burned her eyebrows off. She could just make out the edges of a blazing fire, out of which ran Anya and Taryn.

Anya's long black hair was flowing behind her as she ran, yelling at Taryn to run faster. Her white shirt was bloodied and torn, showing off a large cut across her abdomen. Taryn's braided hair bounced off her shoulder and her right pant leg was hanging by a thread just above the knee. Her face was splattered with blood, and she held one hand over her right eye.

"What's taking you so long?" Taryn yelled towards Mari and Zahir.

"We need help," Zahir said with a grunt, as he blocked an attack.

The two men were eye to eye just inches apart, but Zahir sliced his sword along the other rebel as a distraction, then kicked the man's legs out from underneath him. As the attacker slid to the ground, Zahir drove his sword into his chest.

Anya and Taryn both uncurled their fists to send a wall of fire towards Zahir; the bright orange flames spreading upward and outward as they came closer. Zahir pushed Mari perpendicularly away from the fire, causing her to lose her footing and crash to the ground. The screams of the rebels filled Mari's ears as the flames licked at their clothing and scorched their skin.

Mari doubled over and coughed, blood splattering the ground. She gasped, but couldn't seem to get a deep breath into her lungs. A pair of hands grabbed her shoulders and she immediately went on the defensive, bringing an elbow up to hit the attacker in the face.

"It's me," Zahir breathed into her ear.

Mari turned, and her eyes widened. Zahir's right eye was beginning to swell and his nose was crooked. "Oh Gods, Zahir. Are you okay?"

Zahir wiped some blood from his mouth. "Never better."

Mari looked around and realized all the attackers were unconscious or dead. "I can't access my magic. Someone cut me with a blade of titanium."

Zahir nodded and wrapped an arm around her. "We can tend to you when we're safe, but we need to keep moving."

His breaths were uneven and labored, and Mari snaked her arm around Zahir, helping him limp towards the catacomb entrance.

"Thank you," Zahir said as Anya fell into line beside him.

"You should have been able to handle them by yourself. You're weak," Anya spat, her voice quiet compared to the cacophony of the battle.

"Anya," Taryn warned, narrowing her eyes. "Not the time."

Anya whipped her head toward Taryn. "We took out double the rebels in half the time, Taryn. Zahir needs to use his magic more."

"I've been cut, Anya," Zahir said, breathlessly.

As they neared the catacomb entrance, the door was wide open and the three guards who were stationed there lay on the ground, daggers protruding from their chests.

"Fuck," Anya said angrily. "They found the safe room."

"Gods, Roan is down there." Zahir pulled Mari down the stairs into the darkness, his blood dripping on the steep stone steps. It felt like forever before they reached the bottom, where torches lit the way.

"We follow the light until the safe room." Zahir's voice was quiet, as if he didn't want anyone to hear. He readied a flame in his hand as he scanned the darkness for rebels.

Mari clutched Zahir's waist, her whole body feeling like it was on fire. Where she had been cut with the titanium was throbbing and the wound had yet to clot, blood still leaking down her bare arm. Her throat burned every time she swallowed, like she had eaten glass. When she breathed, the stench of blood assaulted her nose, but when she breathed through her mouth, her throat ached. The only sound that came out when she tried to tell Zahir she was scared was a wheeze.

The torches ended at a large metal door that was already wide open to reveal Anya and Taryn's side profiles. Their arms were wrapped in bright flames that illuminated Maura and Roan huddled in the corner. Maura pulled Roan's face to her chest and clamped a hand over his mouth.

"Mother," Zahir said as he and Mari passed the threshold into the room.

Mari's eyes immediately went to where Anya and Taryn were staring. Back against the wall stood five rebels, their titanium weapons glinting in the torchlight. In front of them, bound and gagged, was King Ryker. His unruly hair was caked with blood that ran from his forehead to his chin. Black smoke curled from his shoulders, where his robe had been sliced open and his eyes were locked on Maura's. It took Mari a second to notice the knife pressed against his throat.

Zahir whirled around and released his hold on Mari, stepping to his sister's side. Mari fell to the ground as he ignited his power, flames curling brightly around his forearms. He raised his arms like he was going to hurl fire at the rebels, but a voice made him stop.

"I wouldn't do that if I were you, princeling," the rebel holding the knife to Ryker's throat said. As he spoke, he made a small cut just under the king's chin and Zahir immediately paused.

"What do you want?" Zahir seethed, his shoulders rising and falling quickly with his rapid breaths.

"Give us the location of the Dual Mage."

Mari wasn't sure she'd heard the rebel right. There hadn't been a Dual Mage in thousands of years. She was intended to give birth to the first one.

"I don't know what you're talking about. Do you know?" Zahir asked his father. When Ryker nodded ever so slowly, Mari saw Zahir's shoulders deflate. "Tell them."

"He refuses," the rebel said with a laugh. "If you do not tell me what I want, I *will* kill your father."

"I don't have the information you want," Zahir bellowed. "There are no Dual Mages. Let him go right now or I swear to the Gods I will end you."

"Pity." The rebel slid the knife across Ryker's throat.

Simultaneously, three knives flew through the air, blade over hilt, and lodged themselves into Taryn's and Zahir's left shoulders, and Anya's right. They all staggered backward, hands flying to the hilts. Anya ripped hers out and launched herself toward the man who'd murdered her father, igniting him in flames. Anya's entire body was aglow as she took the assassin into her grasp. His screams were ear piercing but dulled into a gargling the longer Anya kept him ablaze. The acrid smoke filled the room, burning Mari's nostrils.

Mari stood quickly and rushed to Zahir's side. Instead of helping him, she raised her hands to the rebels as they moved closer to Anya. Quickly balling her fists, she pulled them back, hoping to take the souls of two of them. It was only then when she remembered the emptiness in her chest. Her magic had yet to return. She fell to a knee beside Zahir, clutching her chest. The gaping pit tore at her again, reminding her of the emptiness inside her.

Zahir grunted as he pulled the dagger from his shoulder, rushing to his father's side. Mari watched through swirling vision as he huddled over Ryker's body, moving his hands over his father's face. Mari saw Ryker's lips move slowly before his eyes went glassy and his chest stopped moving. Zahir banged his fist on the ground and screamed, tortuously loud. Anya bent down beside him and even through her blurred vision, Mari could make out Anya's tear-streaked face as she lay her head on her father's chest.

Taryn pulled the safe room door closed and set the lock in place before pulling Anya from Ryker's lifeless body. She wrapped Anya in her arms and led her to where Roan and Maura sobbed, silent tears streaking her cheeks. Anya sat beside her mother and leaned her head on Taryn's shoulder.

Mari barely registered Zahir coming beside her and pulling her next to him. Mari leaned her back against the wall, letting Zahir lay his head in her lap. She ran her fingers through his damp hair as they waited in stunned silence for help to arrive.

CHAPTER TWELVE

MARI

It was hours before a group of guards slid the door open. Immediately they ran for the king, shaking him and calling out to him, only to get no answer. It was then that three of the guards approached and gingerly lifted Zahir from his resting place on Mari's lap, helping him to his feet.

Maura was lifted by two men covered in cuts, bruises, and ash, and carefully led out of the room, followed by Anya and Taryn, who refused to stop holding hands. The fear in Taryn's eyes made Mari want to curl into a ball and hide. The last guard looked at Mari apologetically as he offered a hand to her. She took it graciously and was pulled from the floor, but she took only a single step before nearly collapsing. The guard scooped her into his arms, and she was so exhausted that she didn't even try to fight it.

Mari tried not to focus on the streaks of blood lining the walls and floors. She squeezed her eyes shut as she passed mangled bodies and charred corpses, shuddering at the sight of guards on the ground, limbs detached beside them. It took everything for her not to vomit at the scent of the charred flesh. Mari didn't understand how so much damage could be wrought in such a short amount of time.

The guard put Mari down on a bed, her head resting on a thin pillow. Mari took his hand as he went to walk away and squeezed it.

"Thank you. What is your name?" Mari said, her voice barely coming out as a whisper. With every word she spoke, she could feel her raw, aching throat.

"Lee, Your Highness," he said, his bright blue eyes shining in the sunlight streaming through her bedroom window.

Mari nodded and mouthed a silent, *thank you*, to the guard. She didn't want to risk speaking again and worsening the agonizing pain. Even as she breathed, her throat ached.

"I am just doing my job. I pray you have a speedy recovery." He nodded his head and backed from the room, the door falling shut behind him.

A squat older woman, with gray hair pulled back into a bun, wheeled a noisy wooden cart to Mari's side and perched on the bed beside her. The woman's cool hand pushed strands of hair from Mari's face and neck and placed a cool cloth on her forehead. Mari winced as the woman scraped a salve from a container and wiped it along the cuts on her arm. As a wet cloth was wiped across her face, the pain began to fade into a dull ache instead of a sharp stab. A cold compress was laid across

Mari's throat and she shivered at the temperature; the woman may as well have dunked her into a bath of ice.

Mari closed her eyes but was quickly shaken awake by the woman, who shook her head sternly and dribbled a few drops of a pink tonic into her mouth. It was then that the woman walked away and allowed her to rest. Mari turned her head to the side, realizing that Zahir was lying beside her. A man was holding his head steady as another woman pressed her finger's to Zahir's nose. She nodded and there was a loud crack as she moved Zahir's nose back into its original position. Zahir's groan ripped Mari's heart in half as it filled her ears. It ended abruptly and the man rolled Zahir's head to the side, eyes open but not really seeing. Mari reached out to grab Zahir's hand with her own, but her muscles were so sore, she could only move a few inches before a searing pain shot up to her shoulder. She sucked in a breath and instead opted to close her eyes until she fell into a fitful sleep.

Mari woke in a cold sweat as images of the attackers flooded her dreams, sending waves of terror through her. Her heart raced and she had trouble breathing when she woke to the woman who helped her earlier placing a new compress over her throat.

"Thank you," Mari whispered, the pain in her throat not any better than it had been before her nap.

"Shush." The woman placed a finger over her own lips. "You need to rest your throat. You have some bad bruising." The woman slid her hands along her own neck, demonstrating where Mari had bruises.

Mari grabbed the woman's hand and tapped in the universal code all clans shared. She remembered very little of the code, except for the words she had learned as a young child in her schooling. She recalled only certain words and phrases related to feelings and basic questions. She couldn't use it in everyday life, but was hoping she knew enough to communicate with now. Mari tapped the words *sleep* and *help*.

The woman nodded, seeming to understand, and plucked a small vial from her apron and helped Mari take a couple sips. The liquid scorched her throat, but Mari forced it down, tears pricking at the corners of her eyes.

"This should help. Rest now, my lady." The woman brushed the hair out of Mari's face and left as quietly as she had come.

Mari's eyes drifted over to Zahir, who was still not awake. In the faint light from the torches, Mari could see that his face was no longer covered in blood, but he had a cloth covering his right eye. His hands were bandaged around the knuckles and there was a strip of fabric across Zahir's nose and a dark red bandage was wrapped around his shoulder and upper arm. Mari noticed Zahir's hand twitch off his bare stomach before the closest torch blinked out, casting dark shadows over them.

Mari didn't remember falling asleep, but she felt the unbearable pain across her body. Her throat felt like it was bleeding, and her head hurt like she had been hit by a tree. The cuts on her face and arms burned like nothing she had ever felt before. It took every effort for her to open her eyes and pull her hands to her face, inspecting her red, swollen knuckles. Her ring had been taken off and the finger was bandaged to her middle one; she couldn't even remember having her hands bandaged.

She groaned as she put her hands down and turned her head to check on Zahir, only to see him already awake to meet her gaze. His nose and both eyes were swollen, and blood had soaked through the bandages on his hands. Mari gave a smile that was more of a grimace, and wiggled her fingers in a slight wave.

"How are you feeling?" Zahir asked, his voice raspy.

Mari shrugged and pointed to her throat, and then her head. She mouthed the word *hurts*.

"You have a full handprint around your neck. It's going to take some time for that to heal. I didn't think he gripped you that hard."

Mari raised a hand to her throat but felt nothing different from before. The compress had gone warm in the time she'd been asleep. Mari tapped on the back of Zahir's hand the word *you* and furrowed her eyebrows as if she were asking a question.

"I was given a numbing salve to help the pain; I don't feel too bad. My nose is broken; I can't breathe through it. They tried to snap it back in place, but I don't think it did the right thing," Zahir said. Mari noticed that his voice was more nasally than normal. "My father is ... dead."

Mari reached out to grab Zahir's hand, but it fell just short. Zahir extended his fingers and the tips brushed the tips of Mari's. It was comforting to know that he was there with her.

"Everything is going to change," Zahir said, wiping a tear off his cheek with the back of his hand. "I have to assume the throne."

Mari nodded her head. In the hours they'd sat in the safe room, Zahir had mumbled about being a king while he faded in and out of consciousness. Mari's thoughts had originally gone to her and Zahir's injuries, not their future, because at the time that was the most pressing thing. But as they sat there in the dark, waiting for rescue, she'd begun to think about how her life, while already drastically different than it had been just weeks prior, was going to change once again. From huntress, to princess, to queen, Mari didn't know what her new role in Brahn would consist of.

"Our lives will be scrutinized even more than they were before. We will be expected to have an heir immediately." Zahir ran a hand over his face and knotted his fingers in his blood-caked hair.

Mari tapped out the word *no* on the back of Zahir's hand with her thumb. Her mind was miles away from thinking about children. Before that, they had to heal, be crowned, and have a relationship. The idea of being intimate with Zahir both thrilled and terrified her. She couldn't help how she stared at the muscles on Zahir's torso, or the way his hands made everything he held look small. But the thought of being completely bared to him exposed her to a vulnerability she wasn't ready to show.

"If we don't produce an heir, we won't have a succession for the throne. The crown would go to Anya, maybe Roan, if Illan could convince the council. I can't sit here and know Anya is only one step away from the throne, Mari, I can't."

Mari furrowed her brow and thought of how she could possibly respond to this using the universal code. There was no way for her to ask if they could change the law to put Roan next in line, regardless of the council's opinions.

Taking a deep breath, Mari spoke in a hoarse voice. "Would Brahn accept a Fire and Death Mage as their ruler?" Hearing herself talk almost brought tears to her eyes. She sounded so weak and fragile, like she would break under the pressure of a thumb. Mari coughed and she could have sworn it felt like someone had shaved her throat with a knife.

Zahir was silent for a long time before he answered. "If my father thought it would work, then I believe it would too."

"But Morana," Mari rasped.

"There used to be Dual Mages when the clans weren't separated."

"But the clans *did* separate. If we are the ones to break that for the first time in many years, who knows how people would react."

"Mari, we have to produce an heir. There is no way around that, especially now that I am to be king. Do you understand what that means?"

Mari did realize what it meant, but she didn't have to like it. There were repercussions to birthing the first Dual Mage in millennia. For ten years, she had sat in silent fear as this day approached. She'd smiled and said she was so excited to bring Yu'güe's culture outside the island and share her magic with the Fire Mages. She'd agreed that it would be a blessing from the

Gods. But no one had seen that the smile never reached her eyes.

Zahir muttered something unintelligible under his breath as the bathing room door opened to reveal Mari's caretaker. She carried a saturated cloth, splattered with blood over to the balcony and hung it on the railing. Her white apron was covered in dark red blood and Mari didn't know how long she'd been walking around like that. Mari gave a forced smile to the older lady as she unwrapped Mari's knuckles and applied some salve that burned as it touched her skin. The woman changed the cloth around Mari's throat and her eyes widened as she saw the bruising.

"No speaking." The medic shot a pointed glare at Zahir, as if she knew he had riled her up. "Do not encourage her to speak."

Zahir nodded. "Do not worry Amí; I'll make sure she follows your instructions."

Amí scoffed and pointed a finger at Zahir. "No more talk of children. I was merely one room away and could hear you stressing your wife out. She needs to heal before that happens." Amí shook her head at Zahir and gave Mari a smile. "If you do have children, I would be honored to deliver them. But *only* if you stop talking."

Mari smiled at Amí's kind words. She mouthed the words, thank you, and Amí smiled, putting her hand on Mari's shoulder to give a little squeeze. Amí left Mari and Zahir alone once again. Only this time, there was nothing but silence between the pair.

Mari turned her head to him again and saw Zahir staring up at the ceiling, his chest rising and falling quickly. Mari flung her hand out to get Zahir's attention and he eventually turned his head to the side, his less swollen eye gazing at her.

Although she and Zahir were still figuring out their relationship and boundaries, it was strange for her to have their first fight before their first actual kiss. Mari hoped that as time went on, they would spend time together, just the two of them, without injuries and coronations looming over their heads.

She tapped on the back of Zahir's hand. Two short taps for *I* and five quick staccato notes for *scared*.

"You're scared?" Zahir asked, his eyes softening. When Mari nodded, he sighed. "Me, too. This was extremely unprecedented. I don't know how the rebels have gained so much support, or where they got their weapons."

Mari tapped out another sequence: *What do?*

Zahir took a long time before answering. "I. . . I simply don't know. I need to speak with Illan. We could retaliate. Fight back so they don't have the upper hand. We can talk to them, find out why they believe a Dual Mage is already living."

Want do?

Zahir smiled. "You really don't know much code, do you?" Mari shook her head and let out an embarrassed sigh. "My father would tell me to fight back and kill every single one of them. Burn their camp to the ground. But... I don't know that I like that idea. He fought everything with violence, and it didn't end well for him. I am sorry that this happened. I never thought this would be something we would need to fear. I could go for a glass of whiskey at this point."

S.C. MUIR

Mari had to stifle a laugh and she nodded, knowing a glass of wine would make this all easier to process.

"You are not following my instructions, my prince," Amí's voice was loud as she kneeled beside Mari and replaced the compress yet again. "I walk away for one minute and I come back and hear you talking about rebel plans from down the hall."

Zahir raised his hands in defeat. "She has not said one word, Amí! I swear it." He put a hand over his heart.

"I did not know I would have to be so explicit. No talk of babies. Or of attacks. No politics or planning. And especially no talk of alcohol. We could all use a drink and hearing about it only makes it harder. You need to heal, both of you." Amí sent a pointed look to Zahir and shook her head. "You may be king, but you still have to listen to me. *And* your wife."

Zahir laughed. "Okay, Amí. I do apologize. What may I talk to my wife about?"

A sly smile appeared on Amí's lips as she spoke, "Ducks."

"Ducks?"

"Ducks." Amí's laugh was light and airy. "And horses." With that, Amí gave Mari a tonic to ease her pain and left the room, the warm compress thrown over her shoulder.

"So, where do you stand on ducks?" Zahir rolled his eyes, wincing in pain as he did so.

Mari let out a huff and tapped out *scary* on his hand.

The laugh that escaped from Zahir's chest was full and brought a huge smile to Mari's face. "See, this is why I didn't want to talk about ducks. Now, what about horses?"

When Mari responded with *don't know*, Zahir laughed.

136

"Have you ever ridden a horse?"

Never.

"We are going to change that once you are better. I think you'll like them. My horse, his name is Xander, is a beautiful black stallion. He's in the prime of his life and loves to gallop through the forest. I try to take him out every week myself, but it has gotten more difficult the more I've had to step in for my father. I will introduce you to Xander soon, I swear it," Zahir said, placing a hand over his heart.

Mari smiled and shook her head, sighing. A part of her couldn't believe that Zahir knew her most embarrassing truth, and she didn't know his. It was then that the pain relief kicked in and Mari burst out laughing. Her head spun with the medicine and she felt embarrassment flush through her cheeks. She wished she could speak, if only to ask what Zahir was afraid of.

Chapter Thirteen

Zahir

Zahir hated council meetings. His ten advisors, instead of helping him make his own decisions, were convinced they were collectively the king. For hours, Zahir had to listen to them tell him what he should do, without getting a single word in. Five of his advisors wanted him to slaughter every single rebel who set foot inside the city walls. The other half thought he should discuss peace negotiations so they wouldn't retaliate even harder.

Illan gave Zahir an apologetic look every time he tried to stop the fighting, but nothing changed. Zahir had gotten annoyed at his uncle several times over the past hour, because he, too, thought Zahir should retaliate. Zahir didn't know what he wanted to do.

If he retaliated, he would be serving justice that was deserved. These rebels invaded his home, hurt his wife, and killed his father. They slaughtered innocent people throughout the city.

They killed his guards, who answered their call to action with their lives. Every time he looked at Mari and watched her wince with tears in her eyes while she drank soup and tea, he wanted to burn those rebels alive. When he thought about the light leaving his father's eyes in the 'safest place in the palace', he wanted to watch the life drain out of those rebels' faces.

But when he thought about his father's cruel regime, Zahir didn't have any desire to slaughter. Memories of people being killed in the streets, terrified that one day they, too, might be slaughtered by their own king's guards, bubbled to the surface. The mother and daughter Zahir had rescued were the same ones his father ordered to their deaths. The children who wandered the streets because their parents had been murdered for allegedly being rebel sympathizers pulled on Zahir's heart.

"Are you even listening to us, Your Majesty?" Demi asked, arms crossed over their chest and dark eyes glaring at Zahir.

"Yes, of course." Zahir sat forward in his seat, hoping no one knew that he was lying through his teeth.

"What do you want to do?" Avery leaned forward in her seat, her hands folded to match Zahir's posture, as she looked directly into his eyes.

Zahir held her gaze as he answered, "I don't know."

"Your Highness," Demi said, rolling their eyes, "You have to make a decision."

"You can't just sit here and wait for the rebels to attack again," Avery said, shaking her head.

"Negotiating with them may lead to better results," said Malek, an older man with salt and pepper hair. "King Ryker, rest his heart, fought every threat with violence and it did not end well."

"Do not speak about our late king in such a way," Yair snapped, his hand slamming down on the table. The veins in his forearms protruded as he leaned forward. "He did what he thought was right for our city."

As the bickering started up again, Zahir leaned back in his chair, fighting the urge to rub his temples. After only two days of healing, Zahir desperately wanted to take a nap. While the bruising on his face had gone down and his nose felt remarkably better, the pain from his knife wound was a throbbing ache. Each time he moved his arm, he swallowed the need to groan. He wasn't sure why his face had begun to heal so quickly while Mari's cuts and bruises seemed to only be getting worse. Zahir wanted to help her, but he didn't know how. The healing salves were working, just slowly.

Zahir reminisced about earlier that morning, when they had been woken up by Amí as she thrust the curtains open. She had sat them up, fluffed their pillows, and given them breakfast in bed. When Zahir told her that there were plenty of maids who could have done that for her, Amí insisted she wanted to take care of her best patients. Zahir's protein-filled breakfast was much more filling than Mari's hot broth, tea, and mashed vegetables. She was clearly disappointed that her food was so boring and soft compared to Zahir's pork and eggs. When Amí turned her back, he offered Mari a bite of his eggs. But it seemed Amí had eyes in the back of her head, because she chided Zahir for being so careless. Mari seemed to suppress a giggle, and Zahir had to force himself not to smile at the memory of her. Then his advisors would *really* know he wasn't paying attention.

"Prince Zahir," Illan said, his voice snapping Zahir out of his daydream. "A decision needs to be made."

Zahir nodded his head slowly. "I think we should take a break. I would like to think about things without you all present." Zahir moved to stand, but Demi put a hand up, stopping him in a weird squat that made his thighs burn.

"While you take all the time you want, there are people in this city, terrified that they will be next. If the palace isn't safe, then no home is." Their voice was even, and Zahir thought there may have even been a little bit of fear.

"We will reconvene in two hours' time," Zahir said, guilt rising in his throat at the thought of his people being terrified.

Zahir strode from the room, head high and breaths even. As the heavy metal doors slammed shut behind him, he kept his chin up as he walked to his chambers, where he hoped Mari would be resting. He wanted her opinion about what he should do. Seeing as she was the most removed from the situation, she would be unbiased. The country she had lived in her whole life was not under attack, and her family hadn't been hurt.

Mari was sitting in bed reading a dusty book when Zahir entered the room. Her eyes lit up and she gave him a little wave as she marked her place and set the book down beside her. Zahir drank in the calm of her face and the chestnut color of the hair that fell over her shoulders. Her bright green eyes shone with happiness and her thin lips curled into a smile. Zahir smiled at her as he shrugged off his robes and sat beside her on the bed.

"How are you feeling?" Zahir asked, reaching for her hand. Every time he touched her, it was like he had been struck by lightning. When she nodded and said better, he felt himself relax just a bit. Her voice was still hoarse and quiet, and she still winced when she talked, but it was nice to hear her speak.

"I wanted to ask you something. My advisors are giving advice on what I should do about the rebels and I want to know what you would do. The first option is to retaliate and kill all of them. The second is to talk to them and figure out what they want and why they think there is a Dual Mage. I am completely torn. Both methods have merit. I don't want to be my father and jump right into violence, but I don't want to look weak in front of my people." Zahir sighed. It was relaxing to finally say his thoughts out loud, instead of having them bouncing around in his brain.

Mari held up two fingers and mouthed the word *peace*. Zahir remembered reading a passage about Yu'güe one late night in the library several weeks ago. He had been tossing and turning for hours, worrying about whether he and Mari would get along. He had traipsed to the library and found a book on Yu'güe's culture in the hopes of figuring out what her temperament might be. In it, he learned that Death Mages were inherently peaceful. While every mage was terrified of their magic, they never wanted to use it to harm others, only for necessity. Zahir had wondered if Mari would be peaceful like the rest of her clan, or ruthless like Morana. When he'd finally fallen back asleep that night, his nightmares had been all consuming. A faceless woman had stood over him and brought him to the brink of death, and back, over and over again. He'd woken in a cold sweat, heart pounding, and breaths shallow. He hadn't let himself think about his future bride for days afterwards.

Zahir should have known she would opt for peace. "I *want* to negotiate. I want peace. But I worry it will make me look weak. All I want is to ensure the safety of my people. If I make bad choices so early on, will they renounce me? I want to be different from my father. He made questionable decisions for a lot of his reign and was not well received. Is it worth it for me to risk that?

"If I don't retaliate and they attack again, I will look weak because I could have stopped it. If I could have squashed the rebellion before it escalated even higher and I don't, will my people hate me? I just... don't want to make the wrong decision." Zahir sighed, tears coming to his eyes at the thought of his father. He bit down and forced them to recede. Now was not the time to grieve.

Mari shrugged and put a hand on Zahir's arm, rubbing up and down. "Peace isn't weakness," she whispered, speaking each word slowly and deliberately.

Zahir sighed. "I know it's not. It just feels that way." Zahir stood abruptly, knocking Mari's hand onto the bed. "I need to get some exercise. It will help me think more clearly. Are you okay? I can stay if you would like."

Mari shook her head and shooed him away with the flick of her hand. Zahir didn't want to leave, but he knew that if he didn't, he would never settle the battle going on in his mind.

The walk to the training room was long and quiet. He forced himself to ignore the thoughts in his head for just a few minutes. All he wanted was a little peace and quiet. Thankfully, over the past few days, the corpses had been dragged away, and the blood had been scrubbed from the floors and walls. Zahir breathed a sigh of relief as he passed the clean walls, the reminder of the dead no longer right in front of him.

The concrete training room was freezing cold when Zahir walked in. The windows let in beautiful bright light that should have warmed the room, but Zahir thought that if it were just a few degrees colder, he could see his breath. Zahir breathed into his hands, rubbing them together before walking to the center of the room and taking several long, deep breaths.

Raising his hands up to the ceiling, he shot out two straight, bright columns of flame. He watched as they smacked against the ceiling, furling outwards in every direction. As they moved, they slowly dimmed until they were extinguished. Zahir stepped forward and kicked his left leg out, sending a flaming blast out of the bottom of his foot. He evened his weight out and made a ball of flame in front of his chest that grew as he pulled his hands apart and shrunk as he brought them closer together. Zahir threw the ball forward and watched as it expanded into an entire wall of flames.

As Zahir practiced, he let his mind wander. From the rebels to food, he let every thought wash over him. His thoughts came in one ear and were sent out the other. He didn't dwell on a single one; they were gone as soon as they appeared.

That was until a memory of his father came to light. Zahir was twelve years old again, looking up at Ryker with wide eyes. His father had taken him for a horse ride through the forest and Zahir could remember the wind in his hair, blowing it back over his shoulders. He rode behind the king, whose hair blew backwards majestically and Zahir could only hope he looked just as magnificent when he was older. Ryker looked over his shoulder and asked if he wanted to stop. Zahir, stomach growling, and legs screaming, said yes and pulled to the side where a small river cut through the forest. The white rapids crashed into rocks as it flowed.

Ryker offered Zahir an apple and some nuts. Zahir ate greedily, as if he were never going to eat again.

"Don't make yourself sick, my boy," Ryker said, sitting down and dipping his bare toes in the river.

Zahir sat beside his father and swung his legs over the edge. There was a two foot drop between the ground and the water and Zahir's legs were just too short to reach.

"When will I be tall like you?" Zahir asked, watching as his father kicked water around with his feet.

"Soon. You will be a man soon."

"But how will I know that I'm a man?" Zahir asked, unsure what the difference was between a man and a boy. Looking between them, Zahir could tell he was just a boy. He was short and lanky. He didn't fill out his clothing, and his voice cracked with every other sentence. Ryker was tall and could wrangle a misbehaving horse as if it were nothing. Zahir wanted to know

145

when he would stop being small and be able to fill out his clothing fully.

"You will be a man when you grow taller," Ryker said as he ruffled Zahir's hair. Zahir had just started growing out his hair and it had just passed his chin. It was an awkward length and he kept it pulled back all the time.

Now that Zahir was taller, he knew he looked like a man. He was almost as tall as his father was. He could heft the broadswords as if they were nothing. His clothes were no longer baggy on his body. His long hair made him look regal, not awkward.

But he didn't feel like an adult. He was unsure of himself and his position. He questioned his decisions and his ability to rule. He didn't live up to what his father was.

His father told him to be a man. To be strong.

His father told him to not let people walk all over him. To stand his ground.

His father told him to never let his chin drop when he was unsure. To always stand tall.

His father told him to be brave. To not fear death or any man.

His father told him that these were the traits of a good king.

But Zahir didn't feel strong. He wanted to negotiate with the people who killed his father. He wanted to hide and ignore the problems going on outside these walls. He wanted someone to tell him what to do. He didn't want to make the wrong decision. And both decisions felt wrong to him.

As Zahir punched flames at the walls, he just wanted his father to make this decision. If Ryker chose violence, at least Zahir would feel no guilt for playing a part in someone's death. If Ryker chose peace, Zahir wasn't the one who ignored the threats.

You will get nowhere if you let others walk all over you.

Zahir sent a wall of flame out in front of him. He kneeled to the ground and sprayed flames in every direction as he spun around and shifted his weight, so he finished on the opposite knee.

A good king fights for his people.

Zahir flipped backwards, shooting an arc of flames out from his feet.

A man never backs down from a fight.

Zahir stopped suddenly as the tears fell. He dropped to his knees and slammed his fists on the ground, a scream ripping through his chest. He let himself cry and curse Brahn. He allowed himself to grieve, for the first time, for his father.

And Zahir was not going to let his father's death be in vain.

Chapter Fourteen

Mari

Mari sat on the steps of the palace, a cup of hot tea in her hand, anxiously waiting for Zahir to return. As she sipped, she realized her throat felt better, to the point that she didn't want to cry with every swallow. She shook her leg up and down impatiently, making the flesh on her thigh jiggle underneath her dress. The hot sun burned into the skin on Mari's face and back, but she refused to move inside. The wind blew into her every so often, relieving some of the heat from the sun. Beside her stood two guards, armed to the teeth in full black armor; Mari wondered if they were completely drenched in sweat under there. She had to persuade the guards to let her sit outside; three days after the rebel attack, everyone in the palace was still on edge.

The only sounds that filled Mari's ears were the hooves of guards on horses trotting around the grounds every five minutes. Since the attack, there had been patrols every hour of the day, ensuring the safety of the royal family. Mari didn't feel secure, even with the increased measures; there was always a feeling that made her look over her shoulder.

Mari leaned her chin in her palm as she willed her eyes to stay open. She hadn't gotten a good night's sleep in days. Mari had woken several times throughout the night with a gasp, shooting up in bed, her nightgown drenched in cold sweat, and her hands shaking violently as she ran them through her hair.

Her repeated nightmares gave her no reprieve. As soon as she had calmed her speeding heart and fallen back asleep, the dreams came back, and the cycle repeated itself. In every dream, she relived the attacks, replaying the scene where she stole the souls of several rebels. She could do nothing as their bodies froze in place and their souls flew towards her. Just thinking about it again made her shudder.

Whenever Mari looked down at her hands, she could have sworn they were covered in blood. She had put her hands on many of them, making them bleed and taking their lives. No matter the cost, the Death Mages had sworn never to use their magic against another mage. Mari was terrified that if anyone from her home found out, she would never be allowed back. Yu'güe had a hard law that if a Death Mage killed a mage, they would be ostracized from the clan, never to return.

Mari wondered why that law hadn't applied to her own father when he had killed his own son.

She pushed thoughts of her brother from her head as the smells of spiced foods drifted through the air from the palace kitchens. The palace cooks were preparing for Ryker's funeral and were creating dishes that the king had enjoyed the most. In Brahn, funerals were celebrations of life. The people cooked the foods the deceased loved and sat around talking about their life. The body was set ablaze on a pyre and a prayer was sent to Brahn to welcome the deceased into the afterlife.

The fanfare was different from what Mari was used to. Back home, Mari had been at many funerals that consisted simply of bringing a body to the mountains and laying it to rest there, saying a prayer for Yu'güe to use the body of the deceased in the way she needed most. Death wasn't a sad thing in Mari's clan, but Hanan's was the only one that had made her cry.

Mari wiped the sweat from her brow and shifted her legs on the bumpy concrete stairs before finishing the last of her tea. The floral taste was foreign on her tongue, but it was refreshing under the baking sun. Mari held the cup close to her body as she looked out on the city. The slanted roofs of homes and businesses of the upper circle reflected the light from the sun, and the warm colors made it look like the city was ablaze. The buildings rose high from the ground, windows letting in all the natural light. It was a view Mari knew she would never tire of.

She hadn't been able to take in the view from this height during her wedding. The expansive city seemed to go on for miles and her eyes scanned the streets to see blurs of mages hustling around. It was hard to pick out the sounds that rose from the city aside from horse hooves, but she knew that there were many things happening down there. She wondered if she would ever be allowed out of the palace again with the threat of the rebels.

150

Loud cheers erupted suddenly from the streets below and Mari leapt to her feet, dropping her cup on the stairs. It shattered into ceramic pieces around her feet, but she barely noticed as the screams grew louder and a group of soldiers came into view. Zahir rode a black stallion at the front of the group, a sword raised high. Mari could see blood dried on the blade and Zahir wove it around above his head. A crowd of people followed behind Zahir, and Mari could hear the cheers increase as they neared the palace.

Mari's heart sank as she stared at the sword Zahir held. After their conversation, she was hoping that he was going to talk to the rebels, not slaughter them. Disappointment rose in her chest. Peace was always the best option; it was why Yu'güe had isolated themselves. Ryker had fought violence with violence and was murdered. Mari did not wish to sit by and watch Zahir make the same choices his father did.

Mari slowly descended the palace steps, narrowly avoiding the shards of ceramic, and met Zahir at the bottom. She looked at him, trying to hide the disappointment in her eyes, as he sheathed his sword and swung off his horse. His long hair fell elegantly around his shoulders and stuck only a little to the sides of his neck. He rushed to Mari and took her in his arms, lifting her up. Mari forced a smile onto her face for the people, but wanted nothing more than to scream.

"May I kiss you when I put you down?" Zahir whispered as he slowed his spinning pace.

"Yes." Mari was breathless when Zahir settled her on the ground. He looked deep into her eyes and put a hand on the back of her neck, pulling her to his lips. His other hand fell on the small of her back and Mari put her hands on either side of Zahir's waist. A loud whistle filled her ears, drowning out the sound of her heartbeat.

When Zahir pulled away, Mari was certain she was flushed red. He turned away to raise a fist in the air towards the crowd that had gathered in front of the palace. "We have defeated the rebels!" Cries erupted at Zahir's announcement, and people instantly began hugging one another and celebrating. "I could not have done this without my fellow soldiers, to whom I owe our success." Zahir waved a hand at the men who were dismounting their horses and graciously accepting Zahir's kind words.

"Prince Zahir," a woman's voice rose from the group of people, and she waved her hand back and forth. When Zahir acknowledged her, she yelled a question at him. "How did you do it?"

"We scouted the city for their camp. There were over fifty men there boasting about how they took down the High King Ryker of Brahn. They made horrid remarks about our clan and my family. They said crass things about my wife, mother, and sister. We waited along the tree line, biding our time until we could attack. It was several hours before we made our move. I do not know if these men would say the same, but it was barely even a fight. It was not long before we had every man on the ground begging for his life.

"We slew every man who took away the life of a guard, a chef, a friend, a king." Zahir paused to take a deep breath. "We no longer need to fear the rebels. They pose a threat to us no longer. Brahn can live in peace without fear of these insurgents."

Zahir raised his sword once again to even louder cheers. Mari smiled at the celebration and leaned into Zahir, looking up at his face. In less than a day, the swelling around his eyes had decreased significantly and the minor scrapes along his face and neck had already faded to light lines. Mari was shocked at how well the salves worked for him, but not as well for her.

"Princess Mari?" Another mage raised a hand, and Mari nodded at him to proceed. "How does it feel to be here for a military victory?"

Mari smiled up at Zahir, bile rising in her throat. He met her gaze and smiled right back at her, unaware of her true feelings. "I have so much pride for our clan and I am enthralled to know that my husband, our future king, saved us from further pain and heartache by slaying these rebels. It is amazing to be here, celebrating with our people. I know that High King Ryker would have been proud," Mari said, knowing that every word was a complete lie.

She hated what Zahir did. He should have talked to them, not slaughtered them. If he hadn't killed them all, she wondered if they would come back ten times stronger, with even more hatred in their hearts.

"Thank you, Princess Mari, for such kind words. We must go back inside to continue preparations for my father's funeral. I encourage you all to attend this evening at the palace steps, at dusk." Zahir waved goodbye to the crowd and wrapped an arm around Mari's shoulders, guiding her back up the stairs.

Mari's dress swayed at her ankles, the smooth silk rubbing along her skin. Mari slid her arm around Zahir's waist and leaned into him. "Did you really defeat *all* the rebels?"

"I'm sure of it," Zahir whispered, keeping his eyes straight ahead, to the top of the stairs.

"I thought you were going to negotiate with them," Mari said, lowering her voice to a whisper.

"I had to avenge my father. These rebels murdered him in cold blood. They had to pay for that," Zahir said, his tone darkening.

Mari furrowed her eyebrows. "Violence isn't always the answer, Zahir."

"Mari." Zahir stopped walking and held a hand up. "It is done. I made my decision, and I am *proud* of what I did. We must prepare for my father's funeral."

"What do we need to do?" Mari asked, her eyebrows slanting inwards. She wasn't anywhere close to being done talking to Zahir about his choices. If he didn't want her opinion, then why did he even ask?

Zahir laughed and ran a hand over his face. "We must bathe, dress, and write a passage to say about my father. And we only have a few hours of daylight left before dusk is upon us. I can help you figure out what to say. But first"—Zahir swung open the door to their bedroom and it slammed against the wall with a loud bang—"a bath."

Zahir released Mari and dropped his gear on the floor of their bedroom before wandering over to the washroom, closing the door behind him. Mari took a breath before sitting herself down at the desk and putting her head down on her folded arms. Anger ran through her now that she was alone.

Mari was absolutely furious that Zahir had asked for her opinion and then completely ignored her. He hadn't even told her what he had decided before he left. For all she knew, he had gone out there to walk into his death.

"Are you all right?" Zahir's voice filled the room as the door to the washroom opened.

Mari turned in her seat, pulling her feet up onto the chair. Her eyes traced down Zahir's bare chest and her cheeks flared red. She was mad at herself for feeling so attracted to him, even when she was so mad. "Just tired."

A light knock rapped at the door before it slowly opened and Roan popped his head in, his mop of hair falling over his forehead and obscuring his left eye. He blew a puff of air up towards his eyebrows, sending it floating up before flopping immediately down over his forehead again.

"Can I come in?" he asked, his voice barely above a whisper.

"Of course, little man." Zahir walked over and opened the door wider for Roan to enter.

Immediately, the little boy dashed into the room and climbed onto the bed, swinging his feet off the side. "I don't want to go to our father's funeral." Roan crossed his arms over his chest, sticking his bottom lip out.

"Let me put some pants on, and then we can talk about it, okay?" Zahir asked, gesturing to the towel wrapped around his waist.

Roan nodded, and when Zahir left the room, he patted the spot on the bed next to him. "Will you sit next to me?" His wide eyes bore into Mari's and she nodded.

"Sure, Roan." Mari stood up, wiping her hands on the skirt of her dress. She softly placed herself on the edge of the bed beside him.

"I don't want to go." Roan sighed, leaning his head on Mari's arm.

Mari swallowed, feeling her heart pound. "I understand. It will be over soon."

"I want it to be over now. I miss him."

"I know you do. When I was your age, I lost someone really important to me, too. I didn't know what to do about it. But, eventually, I learned I wasn't saying goodbye to him, just 'see you later'. We aren't really *gone*. You will see your father again, I think." Mari's voice shook as she spoke, not entirely sure how to comfort a young boy who lost his father so suddenly.

"How do you know that?" Roan asked, looking at Mari, his eyes wide and brimming with tears. He wiped the back of his hand across his nose, smearing snot onto his face.

"I just do," Mari said, hoping it was enough. While she wasn't sure what Brahn's views on death were, she didn't believe anyone was truly gone. "It's going to be okay. You have so many people who love you and who will help you with this."

"Including you?"

Mari put an arm around Roan's shoulders and pulled him into her side. "Of course. We're family, you and me. I'm your new big sister. You let me know if you ever need anything, okay?"

"Okay." Roan held out his pinkie finger. "Promise?"

Mari smiled and linked her pinkie finger with Roan's, shaking their hands up and down a couple of times. "I promise."

Zahir cleared his throat and Mari looked up to see him leaning against the door of his dressing room, now fully clothed. His hair was pulled back into a bun at the back of his head. Several strands fell loose onto his shoulders as he walked over and took a seat on the other side of Roan.

"You're so strong, little man. I don't know how you do it." Zahir clapped Roan on the back, bringing a smile to the young boy's face.

Roan puffed out his chest. "It's because I'm going to be a warrior. I have to be strong!" Roan lifted his arms and flexed his muscles.

"Woah!" Zahir put his hands up in mock surrender. "You've gotten so strong! You might just be able to beat me in a fight."

Roan leapt to his feet and put his fists up to guard his face. "Oh, I definitely can!"

Zahir let out a roaring laugh, clutching at his stomach. He stood up slowly, towering over his little brother, and put his own fists up to guard his face. "Give me everything you have, kid."

Roan lunged forward, striking out at Zahir's stomach with his fist. Zahir side stepped, bringing his hands down to protect his stomach as Roan launched at him again, aiming for Zahir's side. Zahir grabbed Roan by the armpits and pulled him off the ground, bringing him to eye level.

"Hey, that's not fair!" Roan yelled, laughing. "Put me back on the ground!"

Zahir smiled as he put his brother back down, allowing him to regain a fighting stance. Roan took a deep breath before faking a punch with his left hand and actually swinging at Zahir's stomach with his right hand. Zahir fell for the fake move and gasped as Roan's fist connected with the side of his stomach.

"Oof," Zahir groaned, falling to a knee and clutching his side.

Roan took this time to pounce on Zahir, throwing all of his body weight into Zahir's chest. Zahir caught Roan and fell backwards, allowing his brother to sit on his stomach, fists raised.

"Do you yield, brother?" Roan asked, panting. Sweat ran down his face and a big smile was plastered on his lips.

Zahir put his hands in front of his face and sighed. "I yield. You are quite the fighter, my brother. You will make a fine warrior when you are grown."

Roan raised his hands in the air and cackled. "I won, I am the champion, and I will be king."

Mari smiled at the two boys, seeing the love for Roan in Zahir's soft expression. She clapped for Roan and gave a little holler of encouragement. Roan pushed himself off Zahir and ran a lap around the room, his hands raised and his hair smacking his forehead.

Zahir stood slowly and made his way beside Mari, sitting on the spot beside her. "I let him win," he whispered to Mari as Roan reached the opposite side of the room.

"I'm sure you did." Mari laughed, shaking her head teasingly at Zahir. "You definitely did *not* lose a fight to a nine-year-old."

Zahir put a hand to his chest and leaned back. "You have no faith in me."

"That's not true." Mari smiled. "I just believe that Roan is an excellent fighter."

"Yes, I am!" Roan stopped his jog in front of Mari and Zahir, panting and eyes wild.

"I think you need some rest, little man. We have a long day ahead of us." Zahir smiled before scooping Roan up into his arms and plopping him at the top of the bed.

"I'm not tired," Roan whined, squirming out of Zahir's grasp.

"How about you lie down, and I sing for you? Just like when you were little." Zahir nestled Roan into the pillows and tucked him in underneath a blanket.

Roan gasped and clapped his hands together. "But if I don't fall asleep, is that okay?"

"Of course. But my songs always put you right to sleep. Do you not remember?" Roan nodded his head and stared at Zahir expectantly.

Zahir sat on the edge of the bed next to Roan's knees and Mari waited with bated breath to hear Zahir sing. A deep melody escaped Zahir's lips as he began a song. The sound was like honey, rich and lovely. Mari couldn't recognize the words, but found herself swaying along to the melody, drinking in the rich sound of Zahir's voice.

Mari closed her own eyes and focused only on her husband's singing. Waves of peace flooded her mind and body, giving her a moment to think about nothing. To be calm and relaxed, for the first time in a long while. She couldn't remember a time when she had felt this tranquil.

Mari snapped out of her trance as soon as Zahir's song ended and only silence filled the room. She opened her eyes slowly, nearly lulled to sleep herself, and saw Zahir lean down to brush the hair from Roan's face and pull the blanket up to his neck. When Zahir turned around to see Mari smiling at him, he pointed to the balcony. The two of them silently stood and made their way outside, careful to make as little noise as possible.

"You have such a beautiful voice," Mari complimented once the door was closed behind them. The wind whipped at her face, sending her hair flying.

"Thank you. I used to sing for Roan when he was a baby. He never wanted to sleep, but one song and he would be out for the night." Zahir smiled, looking out at the gardens as he leaned against the railing.

"What language were you singing in? I didn't recognize any of it."

"It's the ancient language of Brahn. It's what we spoke before the mages, apparently. Most of our traditional songs are in the ancient language."

"Do you know what you were singing?"

"Not a word." Zahir laughed. "I could be singing him wildly inappropriate songs for all I know."

Mari snickered, trying to keep her voice low. "So, you could be singing about murder or sex, and he would have no idea?"

"Absolutely none." Zahir looked at Mari and nodded. "You are really good with him."

Mari shrugged. "I was so nervous. I don't know the first thing about children."

"You are a natural. He was so relaxed around you. I was listening as I put new clothing on. He has really taken a liking to you."

"He is an easy child. I can empathize with him. I remember losing my brother, Hanan, at that age; it's really hard to understand." Mari sighed. "Is he going to be okay?"

"I am sure he will be. He is a strong boy, stronger than I was at his age. I cried if I squished a bug."

Mari giggled. "I cried whenever I saw a drawing of a bird, so I think we are even."

"They are harmless, Mari." Zahir smiled, taking a step closer.

Mari huffed, pointing a finger in his direction. "It is not funny, Zahir. You have to be scared of something. What do you fear?"

"Not birds, that is for certain." Mari narrowed her eyes at Zahir, and he put his palms out in surrender. "I am scared of failure."

Mari rolled her eyes. "That is something you can avoid, though."

"Not really." Zahir sighed. "I am terrified of failing as a king. Of not being able to protect Brahn or Roan... or you. I watched my father die..." he trailed off, grief beginning to catch up with him. He cleared his throat and seemed to push the sadness away. "I am scared of letting those I love down."

Mari blushed wildly at Zahir's mention of not being able to protect her. Suddenly, what he had chosen to do made sense. While she didn't like his choice, she could understand why he killed all those rebels. He wanted to protect those he loved.

Mari couldn't help but think about Hanan. If the roles had been reversed and Mari had actually *watched* Hanan's death, would she not have wanted revenge? Hadn't Mari wanted her father to pay for killing her brother? She'd had dreams where her father was exiled from the clan because the elders found out what he did. She'd had several nightmares where she killed him with her magic and watched the life drain from his face. Those dreams sent her into a panic because they had felt so real. If Hanan was the one who'd been killed by rebels, Mari realized she, too, would have done anything to avenge his death.

"Zahir?" Mari reached out to put a hand on his arm. "I apologize. You are going to be a great king. You are kind and thoughtful. You have put my feelings and comfort level above your own in these few weeks I've known you." Mari realized that, as she was speaking, affection had taken root in her heart.

There was a sudden change in Zahir as he leaned against the balcony railing and stared out at the gardens. His eyes settled on the trees waving in the breeze and Mari tried to follow his line of sight but couldn't see anything particularly interesting about the green trees.

"I just... I can't believe my father is gone." Zahir sighed, wiping a hand across his cheek to chase away the tears. "We didn't have the best relationship. But now I will never even have the chance to fix it."

Mari rubbed a hand up and down his arm in what she hoped was a comforting gesture. The feelings from when her brother left Yu'güe were still fresh in her mind and she could only imagine how much worse Zahir was feeling. As much as she resented her father, she would have been shocked if he passed so suddenly and violently.

"Can I do anything for you?" Mari asked.

Zahir pulled his hair out of its bun and let it curl around his shoulders as he pulled his shoulders back. "Let me run my eulogy by you. Once I write it, that is. If Roan stirs, can you occupy him?"

Mari nodded and gave Zahir a soft smile as he swung open the doors and trudged over to the desk, his head hanging low. Leaning on the balcony, she took in the gardens—the leaves rustling in the same warm breeze that kept the sweat from forming on her brow. Mari put her weight on her wrists as she leaned forward to get a better look around the corner. Two rabbits ran through the trees in what looked like a game of chase and a patch of bright yellow flowers was swaying in the breeze.

Mari could just see the edge of the city from her perch on their balcony. The slanted black roofs reflected the heat from the sun, distorting the view beyond. The slight breeze that whipped at Mari's cheeks was refreshing enough that she didn't notice the heat. Noise from a couple of carriages floated around the corners of the palace and horses' hooves clipped on the cobble-stone streets. The one thing Mari loved most about Brahn was that there was always white noise. In Yu'güe, the only prevalent sound was the occasional crunching of snow beneath boots as someone walked beside her home.

Mari turned to see Zahir writing frantically at his desk. As he rested his cheek in his palm and crossed something out angrily, she went inside, shutting the doors quietly behind her. Sitting on the floor beside the bed, she placed a blank piece of paper in front of her, wondering how she was going to write a eulogy for a man she barely even knew.

Chapter Fifteen

Zahir

Zahir had practiced the eulogy only a handful of times before stepping up to read it in front of his entire clan. He pulled the folded pieces of paper from his pocket and tried to press out the wrinkles. Why he had kept them in his pocket, he had no idea. Zahir had written and rewritten his father's eulogy too many times to count before settling on a final draft. The words just never seemed to feel right.

It had broken Zahir's heart to recite a rehearsed speech without crying. His grief came in waves, pulling him under only when he was alone. His father always told him crying was a weakness, thus he had learned to hide his pain when around others. But as soon as he was alone, he broke down like a child. He couldn't keep himself from letting tears fall in front of Mari, but he felt strangely more comfortable around her than people he had known his entire life.

Zahir took a deep breath as he walked to the edge of the stairs and looked into the eyes of his people, who had all come to pay respect to his father. "Thank you all for attending King Ryker's funeral this evening. I know he is with us in spirit and would have been moved to know his people loved him so much.

"My father was the bravest man I knew. He walked into every situation with his head held high, confident we would come out victorious. Sometimes we did, and others we didn't. But he was always confident we would 'get them next time'. He taught me how to be brave. I try to walk into every situation, thinking we will win. I try to not fear what could happen if we lose, just like he didn't fear it. It's going to be hard without him here." Zahir's throat burned as he held back the tears that were threatening to fall.

"My father always made decisions that benefitted Brahn. I remember him telling me that the best decisions were those made when thinking about the clan. Because in the end, everything we do affects us all. You were all my father's main priority; he did nothing without considering the effects on you. That is the best lesson I learned from him. I want to be just like him, making these decisions for *you*." Zahir tried not to make eye contact with anyone as he spoke about wanting to be like his father. While he didn't want to be exactly like Ryker, he wanted to help his people. Zahir didn't want to talk about his father as king because he didn't agree with a lot of his decisions. But that was how Brahn knew him, as their king.

Zahir smiled to himself as he began his favorite part of the eulogy. "You didn't know my father as anything other than a king. So, I'm here to tell you what he was like. He had the biggest appetite of anyone I knew; he could eat an entire cow and ask for another." Laugher erupted from the crowd and pride swelled in Zahir's chest, happy that his joke was well received. "He was always willing to help us. If Prince Roan needed help with his studies, my father was the first to sit with him and help. If Princess Anya was practicing her magic and he watched, he always told her that she was doing a wonderful job and that he was proud of her. Whenever I had questions about how laws and rulings worked, my father would sit and answer every single question I had. He always made time for us, and for that, I am beyond grateful. I will miss my father, as I'm sure we all will, but I know he is with our Gods. And we will see him again."

Zahir held his breath as he stepped back in line with his family, trying not to choke on the smoke furling off Ryker's funeral pyre as it was ignited. The foul stench of burning flesh filled his nostrils and it took everything in his power not to flinch. The smell reminded him of the rebel bodies he had burned; he could still see their distorted faces in his mind. Except there was something worse about his own father's body charring. Atop the steps of the palace, the wood platform with Ryker's body burned bright orange, illuminating the dark sky. The sun had barely set before the funeral, as was customary in Brahn. Zahir stole a glance towards the people lining the stairs, eyes burning into Zahir and his family, paying silent respects to their dead king.

When Mari's hand slipped into Zahir's, he squeezed it and wrapped her fingers between his, but kept his eyes fixed on the funeral pyre. After she had tried, and failed, to write a eulogy, Zahir had decided to try to write one that was enough for both of them.

Anya stood beside Zahir, hands clasped behind her back and her gaze unmoving from the flames. Taryn had her hand on Anya's shoulder, her hair in a tight braid down her back and her gaze on Anya. Maura had a cloth wrapped in her hands that she kept dabbing to her eyes every few minutes, while Roan clutched his mother's skirts, tears freely flowing down his cheeks and leaving wet spots on his gray tunic. Illan stood beside them, his head held high and hands in front of his stomach, eyes fixed on the flames. Zahir thought for half a second that Illan was glaring at Ryker's pyre, but his expression softened seconds later.

Once the body had burned for longer than Zahir wished to watch, he spoke to the crowd, thanking them for attending. He said a final prayer for his father's soul, asking Brahn to provide solace for his father, knowing he served his clan well as king. As Zahir spoke those words, he had a moment where he asked himself whether his father truly did lead well. While Zahir judged a lot of his last decisions, some others were good. He had increased trade with Orcian and tried constantly to open communication with Lovíth. While he'd terrorized his citizens in his last few moon cycles, he had reason. The rebels had really confused his decision making.

Zahir led his family back into the palace, where a large meal had been prepared. He took his father's seat at the head of the table and Mari slid into place to his right. Illan took the seat to his left, followed by Maura. Roan sat beside Mari, his chin leaning on the table, and Anya put a hand on his shoulder as she slid out the chair beside her little brother.

Zahir cleared his throat and raised a glass filled with wine. "Ryker will be missed. Brahn has gained a faithful soul in the afterlife."

Everyone raised their goblets, repeating Ryker's name, before sipping the dark red wine. The alcohol scratched at his already painful throat; holding back tears had always forced a large burning lump in his throat that only got worse the longer he kept himself from crying.

"He would have loved this meal. All of his favorites in one sitting." Maura smiled, cutting into her fish.

"He would have eaten everything." Anya laughed, salting her pork. "Father was always so excited about solstice dinners. That's when Chef made the salted cod."

Illan laughed. "He always ate too much of that growing up. Every solstice, I would listen to him get ill as the sun went down."

Zahir felt a wave of grief wash over him as he spoke. "Father was a complex man, and I wish I had spent more time with him. But he sure knew how to throw a party."

"I think our twenty-fifth anniversary was the best one, with the fire dancers." Maura smiled, finishing her glass of wine and gesturing for a servant to pour her another.

"That was quite the party." Anya smiled. "That was the first time Taryn joined us for something like that."

"That was a great day!" Taryn chimed in, from where she was seated beside Anya, giving her a warm smile. "I really liked the dancing, but I absolutely adored the desserts. There were so many. And they were all so colorful. I remember there was this little chocolate, flakey, creamy dessert that just melted on my tongue."

"It got its name, snuff, because it was served after our spiciest dishes. The chef said it was supposed to put out the burning on your tongue," Roan's voice piped up and Zahir smiled at his brother, proud.

Every day Roan impressed him. Zahir knew that if Roan were his son, there would be no question that he would be the next king.

"You are just a walking textbook; did you know that?" Taryn said, reaching across Anya to ruffle Roan's hair. "I remember when you were just a little boy and would ask questions about everything. The color of the sky, the reasons it rains, why it is always so warm. You wanted to learn everything. It seems like you did. You are very impressive, Roan."

"He's going to be a scholar one day." Illan pointed his fork at Roan and gave him a wink.

"No," Roan protested, crossing his arms. "I am going to be a warrior."

"You can be whatever you want to be, little man." Zahir smiled warmly at his brother and finished his second goblet of wine. After not eating for several hours, the wine was causing a light-headedness in Zahir that he welcomed with open arms.

"I will be a warrior. I beat you in a fight already!"

Eyes flew to Zahir, and he put his hands up defensively. "He won fair and square." Zahir winked at Illan when Roan looked at Anya boastfully.

"It's true, I was there," Mari said with a laugh.

Taryn reached over suddenly and pushed the collar of Anya's robes down. "Your collar is sticking up, like always." Taryn folded the corners down so they were no longer askew. "What would you do without me?"

Anya gave Taryn a smile. "I honestly don't know."

"Well, your collar would always be out of place, for one." Taryn giggled, shaking her head. "And you wouldn't know how to dress yourself. When we first met, you were always wearing clashing colors and your outfits didn't compliment your figure. It was only after we went shopping for the first time that you found something that showcased your beauty."

Before Anya had a chance to respond, Roan's little voice piped up. "Taryn, do you love Anya?"

The table fell silent as Taryn widened her eyes. "Of course, I love her, Roan. She's my twin flame. Besides that, she is my best friend. There is no one I love more."

"But do you *love* her?"

"All right, that's enough Roan," Anya snapped.

As Illan filled the uncomfortable silence that followed with a story about Ryker, Zahir watched Anya lean over and whisper something to Taryn. When Taryn turned her head to meet Anya's gaze, Zahir could see the pleading look on Anya's face. It was clear that Anya loved Taryn, but those feelings were not reciprocated. It finally clicked why Anya had refused to marry:

she liked women. For the first time in his life, Zahir felt like he had something in common with his sister—love for the same sex.

As the night progressed, the room filled with stories about Ryker and memories that made everyone chuckle. Goblets were emptied time and time again, and the stories became more outlandish and less formal.

"The first date your father brought me on was a complete failure, according to him," Maura said, finishing another glass of wine. "He planned a whole picnic for us to eat in the gardens of the palace. What he didn't know, though, was that I didn't eat meat at the time. Almost all the food he brought was some kind of animal and I had to, very uncomfortably, tell him I couldn't eat any of it. He felt so bad and apologized profusely, but I didn't mind. Instead, we went to the kitchens and snacked on chocolate cake. That was when I knew he was the one for me."

"That doesn't sound like a complete failure," Taryn said with a smile. "It sounds like it was a happy accident."

"That's what I think, too," Maura said, her smile faltering just enough to show her sadness.

"When I first started my mage training, I burned Father's eyebrows off," Anya said, stifling a laugh.

Zahir burst out laughing. "That was *your* fault? I have never heard this story."

"At least I could produce a flame before I was ten, unlike *some people*," Anya said, narrowing her eyes at him. "Anyway, I was trying to just make a simple ball of flame, but it got out of control.

I hit him right in the face. He's lucky he put it out before I burned all his hair off."

"I thought your magic couldn't burn you," Mari said.

Zahir had almost forgotten she was there; she had barely said a thing since they sat down for dinner.

"It can burn our hair, but not our skin," Zahir explained. "I remember the mess Father and I made when we dyed my hair for the first time."

Zahir toyed with the ends of his hair, suddenly ten years old again, looking up at his father with wide eyes. He had just been named heir and his father had taken him aside the next day and helped him acquire the silver hair dye. Zahir had been nervous about dying his own hair, but Ryker had offered to do it for him. Ryker got the dye all over Zahir's face and neck and it stained his skin for hours. Ryker was upset with himself, but Zahir was just happy that he'd had a bonding moment with his father. He'd always seen Ryker as stoic and selfish, but that was the first time he'd realized his father was more complex than he'd originally thought.

Several hours and too many glasses of wine later, Mari and Zahir trudged back to their room, leaning into the wall and stumbling over their feet. Mari had stopped to slip off her heels before she tripped and broke an ankle and the torches lining the halls did not provide enough light, which meant Zahir had nearly smacked face first into several servants, apologizing profusely and telling them to take the rest of the night off.

"Are you sure you're able to make it back?" Mari asked, her words slurring together as she put a hand on Zahir's arm, squeezing lightly. Zahir felt a blush creep up on his cheeks; every time Mari touched him; his heart stopped for a moment. When she ran her fingers along his arm, it took everything in his power not to press her against the wall and pull her into a kiss.

"I'm fine," Zahir said.

Every time he looked at her, he couldn't help but feel guilty. The bruising around her neck had gotten a little lighter, but she still winced when she ate solid foods. Every time he watched her struggle to speak, he couldn't help the anger that washed over him. He was so furious with himself that he'd failed to protect her. If he couldn't protect her, how was he going to protect her *and* a child?

Zahir felt guilty that his injuries were healing much faster than Mari's. He didn't understand why his bruising was so minimal and his nose had started to feel better already. He could almost take a full breath out of his nose while her voice was still very hoarse.

He burst through the door to their bedroom and nearly collapsed onto the bed. His feet hung off the end and his arms fell to his sides. Mari kneeled on the bed in front of him, a fit of giggles taking over.

"Come on, Zahir. You can't sleep like this," Mari protested as she grabbed Zahir's forearms and tried to yank him higher on the bed. Zahir didn't move an inch, but Mari fell backwards into the pillows, laughter erupting from her lips. "Come here, you big lump."

Zahir adored the sound of her laugh; it always made his heart flutter.

"Lump?" Zahir picked his head up, cocking an eyebrow before breaking out into a fit of laughter.

"An accurate description." Mari smiled before nestling into the pillows, a noise of contentment escaping her lips.

She shimmied out of her dress, leaving only her under garments before sliding beneath the blanket and closing her eyes. Zahir averted his gaze even though all he wanted to do was see what her body looked like undressed.

"I had a great time tonight. I really feel like a part of the family now."

"You are a part of my family; you're to be the queen," Zahir said, sliding into place beside Mari.

"I know that." Mari opened her eyes and rolled them at Zahir. "But I *feel* like I belong now. Like everything is falling into place."

Zahir couldn't remember falling asleep, but he remembered the pounding headache that woke him up several hours later. He groaned, putting a hand to his head, trying to stop the pain. He heard Mari stir and her hand lightly grazed against his forearm.

"I could use some of that tea," Mari whispered.

"I can get you your tea." When Zahir spoke, his voice was different than he had ever heard it. It was gravelly and barely audible to even his own ears.

Zahir rolled himself out of bed, landing on his feet with a soft thud. He moaned as he stood up straight, reaching his arms over his head to stretch his back out. Ever since he had fallen off his horse when he was seven, his back hurt every morning; it made him think he was getting old. Zahir found the cart in the center of the room that sported a teapot and two cups. He was so blessed to have people who knew exactly what he needed. Since he was young, the same three servants had worked with him and always made sure he had tea when he woke up after a night of drinking. Zahir poured both himself and Mari a cup before walking over to her. He placed the cups down on the nightstand and helped Mari sit up before letting her take the drink from him.

Within minutes of sipping the piping hot liquid, Zahir's headache was already starting to fade. This was the only tea he did, in fact, have a strong opinion about. It tasted like dirt, but it worked. Zahir watched Mari take small, slow sips of her tea. Her eyes were nearly closed as she squinted at the bright sunlight that streaked into the room.

As Zahir looked at Mari, that same anger rose in his chest at the bruising around her neck. Zahir wanted to turn around, but he forced himself to look at Mari, making a promise to himself that he would never let her get hurt like that ever again.

"Are you all right?" Mari asked, setting her cup down on the nightstand beside her.

Zahir nodded his head and moved to sit on the edge of the bed by Mari's knees. He took her hand in his and sighed.

"I am so sorry you got hurt," Zahir said, squeezing Mari's hand lightly. "I promise to never let that happen again."

"It isn't your fault," Mari said, her voice still gravelly.

"It is." When Mari opened her mouth to protest, Zahir put a hand up. "It is completely my fault. I should have been able to protect you. I should have gotten us to the safe room faster. I promise I will work harder, and I will let no one hurt you like that ever again."

"Zahir," Mari whispered. He met her gaze to see the sheen of tears in her eyes. "It isn't your fault. I'm okay."

"What happens when we have a child, and I can't protect both of you?" Zahir looked down at his hand, intertwined with Mari's. "If anything happened to you..." Zahir trailed off, not sure how to finish his sentence. *If anything happened to you, I would lose my Gods-damned mind. I would burn every person alive who hurt you. I would never forgive myself.*

"I know." Mari rubbed circles on the back of Zahir's hand with her thumb, as if she already knew what he was thinking. "Do you have a free day today?"

Zahir sighed, sinking his shoulders lower than they already were. "I wish I did."

"That's okay. I can find something to do."

Zahir's words came out of his mouth before they even went through his brain. "I will change my schedule for you. We should do something today."

CHAPTER SIXTEEN

MARI

True to his word, Zahir rearranged his schedule for Mari. It had only taken him an hour and an argument with his advisors. Mari stood outside the advisor chamber doors while Zahir convinced his advisors to postpone their meetings another day so he could spend time with Mari. The one thing Mari noticed was that none of the advisors seemed to think Zahir's opinions were valid. She didn't like the way they talked to him, like he was a child with no experience. She hated that they told him he was doing the wrong thing and to reconsider. She was angered when one of them said spending time with her was 'a waste of time'.

Zahir came out of the advisor chambers with his hair out of the perfect bun he had put it up in earlier. His face was blank, devoid of any emotion, and Mari now understood why he hated council meetings; his advisors refused to take him seriously.

"Are you sure you want to spend the day together?" Mari asked as he approached her, sliding his hand into hers.

"Absolutely," Zahir said, pulling her forward down the hallway. His hand was slick with a layer of sweat, but Mari refused to let go. Even if she wanted to, she knew Zahir needed the contact. "It is worth every tongue lashing from my council."

Mari laughed. "What did you have in mind for today?"

The more she spoke, the more pain her throat was in. She could get through several sentences without a problem, but at a certain point, she wanted to stop talking. She had taken a pain relief tonic just before they went to the council, but it had only just started to kick in. Mari hoped that as time went on, she would be able to actually speak with Zahir.

"I convinced a couple of guards to take us out into the city," Zahir said, turning to face her.

Mari's eyes widened and she moved her head forward just an inch. "Are you sure it's safe?"

"I am certain. We took out all of the rebels. If you feel more comfortable, we can stay here, though."

"No," Mari said, steeling her nerves. "Let's go."

Mari didn't particularly feel comfortable heading into the city so soon after the attacks, despite their group being wiped out. Her nightmares played in her head, taunting her with ideas of rebels invading once again. But that was impossible; Zahir had seen to that.

Zahir led Mari down the steep palace staircase and into the bustling streets below. The first thing Mari noticed about Brahn as they walked through the streets, was how few people were around. All of the shops had their doors shut tight, ushering customers in to escape the brutal heat. Mari fanned herself as they walked through the streets towards a store Zahir insisted they visit.

More than once, they were stopped by citizens who ogled over them, excited to have met the soon to be king and queen. Mari blushed every time one of the girls told her how pretty she was and Zahir's chest puffed out each time one of them tried to flirt with him. He was a good sport, always being kind to the girls, but ultimately grabbing Mari's hand before the end of the interaction.

Zahir took Mari into a store that was lined with all kinds of beautiful jewelry and clothing. Mari was never much for fanciful items back in Yu'güe, but the craftsmanship of the jewels in Brahn was exquisite. She tried on nearly everything: earrings that sparkled in the light, bracelets of every color of the rainbow, and rings that pulled attention away from her wedding band. Zahir made her choose something to buy and she settled on a silver necklace with a ruby dangling from its end. He paid a handsome price for it, and Mari was floored by the generous gift to her and his help of circulating coin to his people. It fell right above the dip in her chest, drawing Zahir's eyes there when he looked. Mari blushed every time she caught him looking, but if Zahir noticed, he didn't mention it.

After visiting a few more shops, picking up clothing for the both of them, Zahir pulled Mari into a quaint restaurant that was empty except for them. The six guards who accompanied them escorted them to a private room in the back of the restaurant, three guarding the door from the outside and three inside with them. Mari had to admit that they hadn't gotten in the way of the day as she thought they might have. She was thankful for their presence; it made her feel more secure.

"What kind of food do they have here?" Mari asked, wondering why no one had come with a list of dishes.

"Only the traditional dishes of Brahn. They're going to bring a little of everything so you can try it. They always know what to bring out." Zahir smiled, looking around the room. The walls were just windows that you could only see out of. Zahir had explained that they were made of some sort of glass that prevented people from looking inside, which is why he said it was his favorite place to go.

Soon enough, platters of aromatic foods were splayed on the table in front of them. Mari took small scoops of fish, vegetables, squirrel, potatoes, and rice onto her plate. Every mouthful of food was better than the last. Mari moaned as she tried the squirrel, apprehensive at first. All the flavors pricked her tongue, leaving behind the spices. She was gulping down water by the time she was done with her plate, causing Zahir to laugh.

"I can't believe how much spice you can eat before you need water." Zahir smiled.

"It's just so good I don't want to stop!" Mari exclaimed, taking a breath of air. "Besides, you barely drink anything when you eat."

"I grew up with these spices. You didn't have them in Yu'güe."

Once they finished their meal, Zahir dragged Mari off to another one of his favorite places in the city, Square Park. The little park was a four-block square in the middle of the city which housed a pond with a bridge over it, a small play area for children, and a white gazebo at one end of the bridge.

"Come on." Zahir took Mari's hand and led her to the apex of the bridge, leaning over the railing where they were shaded by large trees. "Look at the fish."

Mari leaned over the bridge and saw rainbow fish swimming in circles beneath the bridge. They swam in groups, looking like they were playing, and Mari was amazed at their beauty; the sun reflected beautiful color combinations off their scales, creating rainbows under the surface.

"What are they?"

"Rainfish. They get the name because they look like the colors of the sky after it rains. It doesn't often rain here, but when it does it is absolutely beautiful afterwards." Zahir leaned on the railing, his elbows pressing against Mari's. He turned his head to look at her as she watched the fish.

"They're beautiful."

"I know," Zahir's voice was quiet.

Mari turned her head and saw that Zahir was staring at her, not the fish. A blush crept onto her cheeks as she met his eyes. "Are you talking about me or the fish?" Mari asked, although she already knew the answer. Her heart raced and she glanced at Zahir's lips, silently begging him to kiss her.

Zahir placed a finger under her chin and pulled her head forward as he leaned in. "You," he said. "Always you."

As he moved to close the gap between them, Mari turned her face down, suddenly shy. She stared at the fish swimming beneath the bridge. The affection that had taken root in her heart made her want nothing more than to pull Zahir into a deep kiss; however, she had no interest in doing that in a public setting. All of their kisses had been surrounded by people; she wanted just one where there was no one around to see them.

"It's getting a little warm, would you mind if we headed back to the palace?" Mari asked, fanning her red face with her hand. The heat of the day was brutal, and she still hadn't gotten used to it. Mari's hair stuck to the sweat on her neck, but whenever she peeled it off, even more would stick there.

"Of course," Zahir said, a hint of disappointment clear in his voice as he wrapped an arm around Mari's shoulders.

As they walked back to the palace, Mari snaked her arm around Zahir's waist and rested her fingertips right about his hip bone. She absentmindedly grazed her fingertips along his warm skin and Zahir kept glancing at her from the corner of his eyes. She noticed that as she moved her fingers, his breath hitched.

The walk back was filled with a pleasant silence. Every time Zahir looked down at her, she would gaze up at him with adoration on her face. Mari took in the shops and she pointed out to Zahir which ones she wanted to visit on a subsequent trip. Most notably, there was a bookshop that Mari knew she had to visit. She would have made Zahir stop if there hadn't been a sign in the window saying it was closed for lunch.

As they climbed the palace steps, Mari was surprised to see Illan standing there, hands resting on his stomach, his fingers drumming a pattern. When she looked up at Zahir, she could tell he was just as confused as she was. Zahir stopped them at the top of the steps, ushering his uncle inside before saying a word.

"Is there a problem?" Zahir asked. Mari could hear the thickness of concern in his voice.

"Two things. First, you two are to be crowned tomorrow." Mari watched as the color drained from Zahir's face. "Second, the one rebel we took captive has given us some valuable information. They told us the rebels are searching for a Dual Mage who they believe to have fire magic. They are uncertain as to the other type."

It took Zahir several seconds to respond. "We have defeated the rebels; why does this information matter?"

"There is a Dual Mage in our city, Zahir," Illan said. "We have to find them."

"That is impossible." Zahir released his hold on Mari's shoulders and she slid away from him but remained close, surprise hitting her in the chest. "How could a Dual Mage be alive if there are only Fire Mages in Brahn?"

"My guess? A child of a sailor who went to another clan to trade."

"We only trade with Orcian. Unless it happened the one time that we traded with Lovíth for medicine. Do you think this Dual Mage, should they exist, is a Fire and Water Mage?" Zahir asked, eyes nearly bugging out of his head.

"Wouldn't their magic lead them to be like Morana?" Mari asked. Morana's combination of Life and Death magic was what people believed led her to insanity.

"It is absolutely a possibility," Illan said. "We need to take this claim seriously."

"Absolutely not," Zahir's voice was commanding and Mari had never heard such authority from him. "There is no Dual Mage. If there were, we would know."

"What if this person doesn't even know themselves?" Mari asked. "If their parents didn't tell them, they would have no idea."

"I think if someone could harness two magics, they would know," Zahir scoffed. "If I could magically heal myself, I would be aware of it."

"At least consider the possibility, Zahir," Mari said, trying to encourage Zahir to be open minded. "There are a lot of things we don't know. If it was an accident, it is absolutely possible someone could have given birth to a Dual Mage."

"She is right, Zahir. You should think about the possibility."

Mari was glad he was siding with her. The possibility of a Dual Mage running amuck in the city both excited and terrified her. The idea of a Dual Mage not connected to the throne made her feel better about what she and Zahir had been married to do. On the other hand, the idea that there was someone with immense power that no one knew about was horrifying. It gave them the advantage of surprise along with the incredible power.

"Aside from the fact I don't believe this is possible, we defeated the rebels. They can't find someone when they're all dead," Zahir said, crossing his arms over his chest.

"Why won't you just consider the possibility?" Mari asked, putting her hands on her hips.

Zahir ran a hand down his face. "It isn't possible. I am done talking about this."

He stormed away, leaving Mari confused and aggravated.

"Is he always this stubborn?" Mari asked Illan, who was shaking his head.

"Unfortunately, yes. I'm going to see if I can talk to him," Illan said as he walked after Zahir.

Mari stood in the hall not sure where to go. She had been inundated with so much information in so few minutes that she wasn't sure how to process it all. In less than one day, she would become a queen. Zahir's coronation was tomorrow, which meant that they would be the official rulers of Brahn tomorrow. A shiver ran up Mari's spine at that thought. She had learned nothing about Brahn since arriving and didn't think she was ready to become its queen.

Being the princess had been little work on her part; she had been focused on getting to know Zahir and his family. She had protected her new family during the attacks. She had helped fight the rebels. But those were things she had done without feeling like she'd had to; she'd acted on instinct in those instances. Now that she was going to be a queen, she didn't know what her new duties would be. She knew supporting Zahir was the biggest one. But what else? No one had prepared her for the next part of her journey in Brahn, and she hadn't asked anyone. It seemed like Zahir did most, if not all, of the decision making. For the most part, Mari was fine with that. She didn't think she should make decisions about Brahn, a clan she didn't know a lot about.

But she did want to be included. When Zahir had made the decision to slaughter the rebels, her feelings had been hurt. He'd asked her opinion, only to disregard it completely. In Yu'güe, her parents had asked her opinions and occasionally taken her suggestions. When they hadn't, her father would sit her down and tell her why. He didn't leave anything to the imagination. He'd always told her he was training her to be a leader. But if Mari wasn't helping Zahir, then what was her role? She wasn't content with raising children and being a pretty face. She wanted to *do* something. And she would be damned if anyone was going to let her sit on the sidelines. With that, Mari set off towards the library, determined to learn anything she could about Dual Mages.

CHAPTER SEVENTEEN

MARI

When Mari was twelve, her instructor had required her to show her classmates how to move souls around on command. For six days straight, Mari had practiced her magic day and night, needing it to be perfect for her presentation. She'd barely eaten or slept for nearly a week, lying awake in her bed imagining every scenario of how it could go wrong: she could fall, not summon anything at all, or move the wrong thing at the wrong time. Then all of her classmates would laugh at her—the useless daughter of Yu'güe's leaders.

The day it came time for her to showcase her magic, she stood at the front of the class, hands shaking and palms sweating. Her instructor had told her to relax, but all Mari could hear was the pounding of blood in her ears. Instead of summoning her souls, the contents of her stomach had come flying out. She'd panicked and fainted, crashing her head onto the cold ground.

Now, eight years later, she made sure to not eat anything before stepping under the makeshift stage set up at the bottom of the palace steps. A circular hole loomed above her, where she and Zahir would appear as the metal platform they stood on rose. Mari wiped her sweaty palms on her dress skirts and took several deep breaths.

"Are you all right?" Zahir asked, taking Mari's hand.

Mari felt that the gesture was out of place since she and Zahir hadn't spoken since their argument the previous afternoon. Mari hadn't spoken to Zahir when she'd returned from the library at the end of the day, stacks of books in her arms. She'd found him already asleep and, by the time she woke this morning, he was already gone.

Mari shook her head. "Nervous."

She looked straight ahead, worried about vomiting on Zahir seconds before his coronation.

Zahir rubbed his thumb across the back of Mari's hand. "It's going to be fine. You don't even have to do anything. Do you get nervous in front of crowds?"

"Extremely." Mari barely trusted herself enough to respond with single words to Zahir's questions.

"Hey," Zahir paused and Mari turned to glance at him, her head spinning. "You are going to be fine. Just smile and it will be over before you know it. All you have to do is kneel there and then watch me speak. That's it. Everyone will be looking at me, not you."

Mari nodded and rested her forehead on Zahir's shoulder. "This is embarrassing. You know my biggest fears, and you don't seem to have any."

"I told you, failure."

"That's not embarrassing."

Zahir was silent for several seconds before he took a deep breath, whispering into Mari's ear so the guards wouldn't overhear. "Thunderstorms. I can't sleep if there's thunder and lightning outside. It's really embarrassing."

"That *is* embarrassing." Mari smiled, shaking her head. "Does it thunder often in Brahn?"

"Our rainy season is coming up. Just wait. If you like storms, it's wonderful. If you can't stand them, it is an absolute nightmare."

Just then, the metal platform the couple stood on rose quickly, nearly knocking Mari off her feet at the sudden jolt of movement. Zahir pulled her against his body and made sure she was steady before leaning just far enough away that she looked comfortable on her own. Mari took in a deep breath of fresh air as she saw the entirety of Brahn standing in front of the stage. The sea of people cheered, their arms raised and clapping for them. Mari squinted as the sun hit her eyes and she had to fight the urge to shield her eyes.

Zahir raised his hand to wave to the crowd and Mari did the same, tightening her grip on his hand. She forced a smile, but even she knew it wasn't convincing. Her heart pounded in her chest and she couldn't tell what was louder: the blood pounding in her ears or the raucous cheering. Zahir's smile was as vibrant as ever as he greeted his people. Anya, Taryn, and Maura sat on the side of the stage in the center of all the royal advisors. Anya's face was stony, and her pursed lips and furrowed eyebrows made Mari want to cower, but she remained composed, conscious of the many faces looking up at them. Maura and Taryn were smiling brightly at the pair while Roan stood next to his mother, his eyes sparkling and his hands clapping wildly. His hair was tousled, a stark contrast to his perfectly pressed clothes.

Illan ushered Mari and Zahir to the center of the stage, having both of them kneel side by side on plush red cushions. Mari was thankful her dress was long, so she didn't have to worry about showing everyone her undergarments as she kneeled. The dress she wore was blood red and hugged her hips, the heavy fabric weighing her shoulders down so she had to fight to keep her back straight. Sweat already pooled on her body from the burning sun. After several weeks in Brahn, Mari had noticed the light brown freckles that brushed her shoulders and nose. Even with the layers of sun protection, the light tan on her face made her look healthier. Why this was done in the heat of the day was beyond Mari's comprehension.

Zahir was wearing long ceremonial robes that flew in the wind as he moved. The gold crown sat on top of his head, newly shined, and his voluminous hair curled around his arms with every gust of the wind. Mari could only hope that her hair was as beautiful as Zahir's. Her auburn hair fell in thick curls over her shoulders; she had stared at her hair for a long time before the coronation. It felt much more like her than the stiff updo she had been forced to wear for her wedding. This was the first time Mari had been styled and thought everything was genuinely beautiful.

"Today," Illan spoke loudly as he put a hand on Zahir's shoulder, "we celebrate an ever-joyous occasion. On this day, we coronate our next High King, Zahir. While we still mourn the loss of King Ryker, we know that he is still with us and his reign will go down in history. But, on this day, we welcome a new king's reign. On this day, we bless our next king."

Maura stood to walk over and stand behind Zahir, placing one hand on his left shoulder and the other gripping a new gold crown shimmering with red stones, holding it out for the people to see. "Today we crown my son, High Prince Zahir. I place this crown on his brow as a symbol of my trust in him to lead Brahn to greatness." Maura removed Zahir's current crown and lowered the new one onto his head until it sat snugly. Zahir rose and faced his people, his eyes shining bright.

Zahir turned and took a tiara from a stout man who had scurried up with it as he stood. He took a place behind Mari and thrust the tiara into the air. The silver diadem glinted in the sun, the diamonds shimmering. "I place this crown on my wife's head to symbolize her oath to you. Princess Mari has pledged her service to the people of Brahn, despite being born and raised in Yu'güe. She cares for Brahn and its people deeply and has suffered with you at the loss of King Ryker. Princess Mari will be our next High Queen of Brahn." Zahir settled the tiara just behind Mari's hairline and she rose, taking his hand in hers.

"All rise for High King Zahir and Queen Mari of Brahn," Illan's voice rang out, echoing loudly. He lifted his hands to Mari and Zahir, who stood gripping hands as the sound of applause deafened them. "Let us bow to our High King and Queen!" he cried and immediately swept into a low bow.

Mari looked out at the sea of people and saw them simultaneously dip into bows. Not a single person refused, and her breath hitched as the world swam before her eyes.

Zahir squeezed reassuringly before letting go of Mari's hand and walked over to Illan, stopping beside him. Once everyone had their eyes trained on him, he began to speak. "My beloved citizens of Brahn. I am deeply honored to be crowned as your king. I will strive to do right by you and make decisions for the best of Brahn and its loyal citizens. I vow that I will always put your interests first and help make Brahn the best it can be.

"I would like to address the attack that occurred on the palace several days ago. The rebel groups that have been invading the mage clans struck here, in Brahn. Queen Mari and I nearly lost our lives to the rebels. It was only through our training and skill that we were able to survive. My father was slayed by one of those rebels and High Princess Anya took his life. Because of her, and because of Queen Mari, the rest of us survived. I vowed to you all that I would take revenge, and along with the team of soldiers who accompanied me to their camp, I fought and killed every last rebel we could find. There is no more reason to fear the rebels, for they have been defeated!"

Zahir stepped back from the edge of the stairs and walked back to Mari as the audience hollered and cheered. Mari clapped her hands, amazed at how incredible Zahir was at public speaking. She wished that she was as poised before crowds.

Unfortunately, she didn't think she would ever be able to speak like Zahir, no matter how much she practiced.

Mari took Zahir's outstretched arm as they were led back into the palace, the cheers from the city below fading as they moved into the building. The cool air inside washed over Mari as the doors closed and they were finally out of the brutal heat.

"I'm so proud of you Zahir," Maura said, walking in front of her son and giving him a tight squeeze. "High King Zahir of Brahn."

Zahir smiled brightly at his mother as they broke their embrace. "Thank you, Mother."

"King," Roan said, wrapping his arms around Zahir's legs. "That's weird."

Zahir and Mari both broke out into laughter. He reached down to ruffle Roan's hair and spoke with a smile. "It will definitely take some getting used to."

"It won't be long until you're no longer king," Anya said, leaning against the wall and glancing at her fingernails. "Once the rebels usurp the throne, Brahn will burn to the ground."

"Anya," Maura snapped, thrusting a finger in her direction. "That is enough."

Anya shrugged. "I'm not saying anything that isn't true. Or that our people aren't already thinking." She waltzed away, her hips swaying as she did.

"I'm going to speak with your sister," Maura said. She placed a hand on Zahir's arm. "Your father would have been so proud of you."

As Maura walked away, Zahir took a deep breath and looked at the ceiling. Mari could tell he was trying to blink away tears and she wrapped an arm around his waist, pulling him into a hug. He slowly put his arms around her shoulders and leaned his chin on her head, behind the tiara.

"Your speech was very elegant. You are wonderful at public speaking," Mari said, trapped against Zahir's chest in a way she honestly didn't mind.

"Thank you." Zahir's voice was quiet. "I have had a lot of practice. It's something I have no choice but to be good at."

"Well, you did a great job."

"That means a lot," Zahir said. Mari could tell that he was smiling. "How about we have dinner, just the two of us? I'm really sorry about lashing out yesterday. I was really stressed."

"I appreciate the apology. I went to the library yesterday and found out a bit of information about Dual Mages. Maybe we can talk about it, soon?" Mari asked, hopeful. She was eager to share what she'd learned with Zahir as soon as possible.

"Absolutely. Let's have dinner and then tomorrow I want to hear about everything you read," Zahir said, offering Mari a small smile.

He laced his fingers with hers and led her through the palace towards their rooms. On the way, he paused outside the ballroom and pulled Mari inside. She gawked at the ballroom where she and Zahir had danced, decorated now with long tables, velvet chairs, and floral arrangements. Black and gold banners fell from the ceiling, painted with scenes from her wedding. Her first kiss with Zahir, their first dance, walking from the reception arm in arm. Mari and Zahir both looked radiant. Neither of them looked uncomfortable, but Mari knew that they both had been.

She wondered what other lies the paintings around the palace told.

"Wow," Mari breathed. "Those paintings are beautiful."

"They did a wonderful job. I saw these this morning; I wanted to show you." The bright smile on his face brought a smile to hers, too.

"Thank you for showing me," Mari said. As she looked at Zahir, her stomach let out a loud rumble and she broke into a giggle as she said, "Maybe we should go have that dinner."

Returning to their room to change, Mari picked out a pair of loose-fitting black pants and a tight dark green shirt that hugged her curves and cropped just above the waistband of her pants, showing off an inch of her midriff. She kept her hair in loose curls but placed the tiara on a shelf; there was no sense wearing a crown to dinner, and she wondered if she'd ever get used to its weight.

Mari emerged to see Zahir wearing a black tunic and pants that he was still straightening out. She watched as the deep vee of his abdomen was suddenly covered by his shirt, and turned away to see that a table had been set up on the balcony.

"How did that get set up so fast?" Mari asked, turning back to Zahir.

"I requested this earlier. I wanted to have a quiet evening to ourselves after the events of the day," Zahir said, motioning for Mari to follow him.

He led her outside and pulled out a chair. She sat down and he pushed her seat in gently and took the chair across from her, pouring each of them a glass of brown whiskey.

Zahir raised his glass. "To our first dinner as king and queen." He smiled at Mari, who clinked her glass against his before drinking the caramel liquor. Mari had never tasted whiskey before, but she was excited for it, nonetheless. The whiskey burned her throat, and she coughed a few times.

"How do you drink that?" Mari asked, coughing violently. Aside from the usual pain she felt, the alcohol stung her sore throat.

Zahir swirled the liquid in his glass and Mari noticed that it was not empty. "You're not supposed to drink it all at once. Just sip it."

Mari felt a blush creep up on her cheeks and she pursed her lips. "Oh. That would make more sense..." Mari placed her empty glass gingerly on the table. "It's still disgusting, though." She laughed, reaching for the unopened bottle of red wine instead. "This is more my style." She poured herself a full glass and offered Zahir some before he shook his head and topped off his glass with more whiskey.

"Do you drink alcohol in Yu'güe?" Zahir asked as he opened the lids of the food platters, exposing a warm white paste speck-led with green, sliced pink fish that smelled like it was cooked in butter, and brown rice mixed with varying shades of red.

"Only for special occasions: weddings, funerals, birthdays, things of the sort." Mari scooped a little of everything onto her plate. She prodded the white paste with the end of her fork and brought it to her nose. She inhaled deeply, the scent of butter and herbs assaulting her nostrils. The smell was overwhelming. "What is this?"

Zahir laughed as he served himself large helpings of everything. "You've never eaten mashed potatoes?"

"Is that different from any other type of potato?" Mari asked, taking a small bite. Her eyes lit up and she shoveled several forkfuls into her mouth.

"Uh, no. It's just potatoes that you... mash?" Zahir's eyebrows knitted together as he spoke.

"Well, this is embarrassing." Mari rubbed her temples with her left hand, cheeks ablaze. Although it shouldn't have been expected that she knew everything about Brahn's cuisine, her heart pounded every time she remembered her knowledge was extremely limited.

"What's your favorite color?" Zahir asked, taking a long sip of his whiskey.

Mari looked at his hand wrapped around the glass, and she thought about those hands wrapped around her waist.

She coughed and straightened up to answer his question. "Orange. But not a bright orange, more like the sunrise. What's yours?"

"Red. Like the fire I burn." As if on cue, Zahir lit the candles lining the edge of the balcony with a shot of fire from his fingertips.

"That was really impressive." Mari gaped at Zahir, who somehow managed not to burn either of them.

He blew on the tips of his fingers as if to cool them down. "I aim to please. I was never a natural, though."

"It took me a little longer than most to learn my magic," Mari refilled her wine glass as she spoke. "It was hard for me, at first, to kill animals. I didn't like the idea of doing it. But once my mother taught me how to hunt, I started to understand it was our lifeline." Mari looked down at her plate, remembering the men she had killed the night of the invasion. Their faces were burned into her memory and she wasn't sure if she would ever be able to forget them.

"Is everything okay?" Zahir asked, leaning forward on the table.

"Fine," Mari said as she plastered a smile on her face. The last thing she wanted was to ruin her date because of her foul mood. "Tell me a story about learning your magic."

Zahir put his hands up as if he were hanging up a painting. "Anya and I were showing our father what we had learned. She cartwheeled around the room, flames spurting out of her hands. She could even use fire breath. Then there was me. I tried to jump and push some flames from my feet. I fell right on my ass and lit my father's hair on fire. He was *not* happy."

Mari burst out laughing, spraying wine from her mouth and onto the table. She covered her lips with her hand and tears welled in her eyes. "Oh Gods, that must have been embarrassing."

Zahir tilted his head back and roared with laughter, the sound echoing off the walls. "Wow. I don't think I'll ever be able to do that again."

Mari wiped her face off and dabbed at the tablecloth. "I don't know if this is going to come out."

"It's fine, we have plenty," Zahir said, still laughing.

Mari couldn't help the laugh that bubbled out of her. "Okay, you know my darkest fear. You've seen me spit wine all over the table. Clearly, I'm not fit to be a queen."

"And I'm afraid of thunderstorms," Zahir said. "Maybe we are both just a mess."

"A perfect match," Mari said, reaching forward to clink her glass to Zahir's. She swallowed the last of her wine and filled her glass for a third time. The alcohol was beginning to spread warmth throughout her body and soothe her aching throat. The more she drank, the less pain she felt while speaking. She knew, though, that she would regret all this talking in the morning.

"So, I've been wanting to ask..." Zahir said, refilling his whiskey glass. "Have you ever been... intimate with someone?"

"Um, no," Mari said, a blush creeping up on her cheeks.

"You don't sound too certain."

"There was one boy, Fahran." Mari nodded her head and gulped down her wine. "We got fake married when we were nine. It was very romantic. You might need to fight him since our marriage was never annulled."

"Seriously." Zahir laughed, shaking his head. "Was there someone back home?"

Mari didn't answer for a long time. She was trying to figure out exactly how to explain. "There really was a boy named Fahran. And we really did get fake married when we were nine. After that we were inseparable. I know it sounds silly, but it's how we became friends. He would help me with my work at school and he was the son of my mother's best friend. Fahran was one of the few people I was allowed to spend any time with.

"When we were teenagers, we kissed a few times, but it never went past that. We had an understanding that I was to be married to someone of my father's choice. As much as we wanted to be together, we knew it would never be."

"That is so sad." Zahir reached across the table to grab Mari's hand, rubbing his thumb over the back in soothing circles.

"Did you have any romantic interests?" Mari asked, wanting desperately to change the spotlight. If she spoke about Fahran, she would have told Zahir that he was the reason she hadn't lost her Gods damned mind after Hanan died. That he had been the only reason she was able to get out of bed every morning, because he'd been the person to distract her and make her laugh.

"Two. Although, neither of them were *romantic*..." Zahir slowly cut off the end of his sentence.

"What does that mean?" she asked. Mari knew the answer was sex, but she wanted to hear it from him. She didn't know why she cared, but somehow knowing felt better than not knowing.

"I was with Taryn for a while. It was never romantic, just stress relief and familiarity."

"Is she the only girl you've ever been intimate with?"

"Yes, she is the only woman I've been with."

The way Zahir's voice trailed off at the end had Mari guessing there may be more to the story. "Are you sure?"

Zahir took a deep breath and took a large swig of his whiskey. "A few years ago, when I was eighteen, there was a palace guard. It wasn't really anything. He," Zahir paused, lifting his eyes to meet Mari's intrigued expression, "is the only man I have been with." Zahir kept his gaze on Mari's face as he finished speaking, and she thought he was trying to read her mind. The volume of his voice was barely audible over the breeze rustling the leaves.

"I can understand. It's really none of my business who you slept with. I was just being curious."

Zahir blinked, leaning back in his seat. "Really? I thought most women might feel weird about it. No one knows except my uncle. He promised to keep my secret."

"I don't care, Zahir." Mari offered him a shy smile.

Zahir leaned back in his seat, swirling the whiskey in his glass. "I am so glad to *finally* tell someone other than my uncle. He didn't quite know what to say, but he was there for me." Zahir sighed as he reached his hand across the table and clasped Mari's hand tightly. "Thank you."

Mari dripped wine on the table as she poured herself another glass. "Was it just experimenting, or do you feel about men the way you do women?"

Zahir looked up at the starry sky. "I find men attractive, especially those who are more muscular and taller than I am, but I don't think I would want to marry a man. I think I would like to be the dominant one in a relationship."

Mari snorted. "If you haven't realized yet, I'm not quite the submissive type." As soon as Mari said it, she realized it wasn't quite true. She had always bent to her father's whim, preparing to be everything he wanted in a daughter. Though she was now out of his home, the realization hit her that she was still doing everything he wanted of her.

"I haven't gotten you into bed yet." Zahir smirked as Mari widened her eyes. "That could change."

Mari nearly choked on her wine. She burst out laughing, but not because she felt uncomfortable, but because it sounded so out of character for Zahir. He had seemed so nervous whenever he was flirting with her. She wondered if the whiskey was going to his head the way the wine was making her hold back giggles.

Zahir leaned forward in his seat, leaning his forearms on the table, the veins in his hands distended as he flexed his hands. "Have I made you uncomfortable?"

"No, I just didn't expect that." Mari couldn't take her eyes from his large hands. Her face flushed red as her breath audibly hitched. She immediately snapped her gaze back up to Zahir's face, which she saw held a coy smile.

Mari went to pour herself another glass of wine but realized she had completely emptied the bottle. When she looked out toward the gardens, the sun had set, and her vision swirled. She thought the whole world was turning on its side.

"Would you like to go for a walk?" Zahir asked

"Now? It's the middle of the night." Mari glanced at the rising moon's position. "My mother always said you could tell the time by the position of the sun and moon. I think she was full of shit because I can't tell what time it is."

"It's barely past sundown. We just started eating." Zahir gestured to the food, which had gone cold. "Or not."

"Let's go for a walk." Mari stood and slid her hand into Zahir's. His palm was rough with calluses, and standing this close to him, she could see the moonlight glinting in his golden eyes. He looked radiant.

Mari let Zahir lead her through the halls of the castle, one hand holding a flame to light their way, the other gripping hers. Zahir pointed out little things as they went. The first curtain he burned as a child, the hideaway he slid into when playing hide and seek with Roan, the table that he split his head open on when he was nine. Zahir pulled his hair back and Mari could just make out the smallest scar on his hairline in the dim light of his fire.

Zahir slid his arm around Mari's waist and pulled her into his body, scanning her face. "You are so beautiful, Mari."

Mari bent her head and looked away, hiding the blush creeping on her cheeks. "Thank you, Zahir."

He lightly took her chin with his fingertips and pulled her gaze back to his. Wisps of his hair had broken free of his ponytail and fell across his cheeks. As Zahir leaned his face closer to Mari's, she moved her chin up and let his lips brush against hers. She sighed and let Zahir press her into the wall with his body. He kept one hand on her chin and gripped her waist tight with the other. She snaked her arms around his neck and pulled on the hair in his ponytail, eliciting a soft groan from Zahir's mouth.

Zahir pulled away, not dropping his hands from their positions. "I have been dying to do that for days."

"Do it again," Mari said, breathless.

Mari noticed that Zahir's lips were warm and tasted like whiskey when he kissed her. Zahir dropped his hand from her chin and gripped Mari's waist with both hands. She was electric with excitement. The desire to kiss Zahir had been building the more time they spent together and, in this moment, nothing else existed. There were no rebels. No Dual Mage. No royal duties. There was nothing but the feel of his lips on hers and the sound of their breathing as they kissed.

Zahir pulled away and leaned his forehead on Mari's. His chest rose and fell quickly as they looked into each other's eyes. "How about that walk?"

Mari nodded and they uncurled their bodies to continue down the hall. She ran her hands through her hair and held it up off her neck to get it out of the sweat that was building there. "Is it always so hot in here?"

"I think that might be from the wine." Zahir laughed, pulling the band out of his hair and holding it out to Mari. "Here, you can use this."

When Mari looked up, she nearly sighed at the sight of Zahir's hair falling around his shoulders and framing his sharp jaw. The men in Yu'güe kept their hair short, but there was something about Zahir's long hair that Mari found exquisitely beautiful.

"Thank you, that is very kind." She gulped as she took the band, sweeping her hair up into a bun on the top of her head. "How do I look?" Mari giggled, knowing her hair looked like a greasy mess.

"May I?" Zahir gestured to her hair and she nodded and turned around. He pulled the band out, letting her hair fall back over her shoulders before sweeping it off her neck. A shiver ran its way down Mari's back as Zahir's fingers lightly grazed her skin and she desperately hoped he didn't notice. Once her hair was bound, Zahir spun her around and inspected it. Mari smiled at his quizzical expression. "Now it's perfect."

Mari held her hand out for Zahir and he took it happily, dragging her down the corridor to the kitchens. The vast kitchens were completely empty at the hour, letting Mari's eyes fall on the large chocolate cake sitting on the counter with a couple of slices cut out of it.

"Is this for a special occasion?" Mari asked, her mouth beginning to water as she released Zahir's hand and walked towards the cake.

"Oh, no. Taryn loves cake, so they make sure to always have one baked for her." Zahir said, opening a drawer and moving some things around. "She is happy to share."

He approached Mari's side with utensils and dishes and lightly nudged her out of the way with his hip to cut two large pieces for them. Pushing himself onto the counter, he let his legs swing against the cabinets as he took a bite of the cake.

Mari jumped up across from him onto a wooden preparation table and sank her fork into the soft dessert. The chocolate danced on her tongue as she moaned in delight. "This is the best thing I have ever eaten."

Zahir laughed as Mari moaned with every bite. "I am so glad you enjoy our food."

"'Enjoy' is absolutely an understatement." Mari licked her lips after every bite, not wanting to waste a single fleck of cake. "What is your favorite dish?"

Zahir thought for a moment before he answered, pointing his fork at Mari. "Does whiskey count?" Mari laughed and shook her head. "Well, then I would have to say our salted salmon is delicious. It's the fish we had tonight."

"Oh, yes that is amazing. I think my favorite, so far, are those smashed potatoes."

"Mashed." Zahir smiled.

"What's the difference?" Mari laughed, hopping down from the table and taking a few steps to the cake. "Can I have more?"

"You're queen; you can do anything you would like."

Mari cut herself another large slice, and one for Zahir as well, before reclaiming her spot. "Can I tell you something?" Mari was suddenly confident. She felt the desire to tell Zahir about Hanan. She wanted him to know the most terrifying truth of her life.

"Anything," Zahir said, leveling his gaze with Mari's.

Mari took a deep breath and began to speak quickly. "I said I was okay with you being interested in men, and that is the truth. But what I didn't tell you is that so was my brother. He was in love with a man from Yu'güe. That was the real reason he refused to marry the Princess of Orcian. He wanted to marry the man he had been with for years. Our father screamed at him for *hours*. I was ten. I hid in my room until Hanan decided that he was going to run away.

"After Hanan came to say goodbye, I thought I would see him again. My father was so angry with him, I believe he followed and... killed him. He never explicitly told me, but he has hinted at it. He always threatened me by saying 'I wouldn't want to end up like Hanan' whenever I tried to disobey him. I was furious for so long. I couldn't wait to get out of his home."

It was as if a weight lifted off Mari's shoulders. She had finally... *finally* told someone her deepest truth.

"Oh Gods, Mari..." Zahir jumped down from his place on the counter and stepped between Mari's legs. He put his hands on her thighs and looked deep into her eyes. "That is so horrible. I... How did you survive there for so long?"

"I had to. I knew that our marriage was my way to get out. I am so angry at my father. He had no right to tell Hanan who he could love. I loved Hanan so much and my father took him away from me before I was old enough to have a real relationship with him." Mari couldn't help the tears that fell as she spoke. As the words poured from her mouth, the sense of relief that she felt was overwhelming.

"Gods... I can't imagine what you went through. I am so sorry that happened to you."

"Thank you," Mari said but grimaced, suddenly overcome with nausea.

Zahir caught Mari's forearm in his hand. "Are you well?"

"I think the wine is catching up to me," Mari said, putting a hand to her stomach.

"Let's go back. Do you need me to carry you?" Zahir asked, sliding an arm around Mari's waist and holding one of her hands in his at shoulder height.

"No, I can walk. I just need to lie down."

Mari and Zahir stumbled through the halls, their shoes making loud echoes through the palace. Zahir tried to distract her with stories of him as a child, but she was entirely focused on not throwing up all over him. If she could just lie down, she could fall asleep before she was ill.

After an excruciatingly long amount of time, Zahir flung open the door to their bedroom and led Mari to their bed. She flopped onto it with her feet hanging off the end. Zahir scooped her feet up and removed her shoes before placing her legs gently on the bed. He pulled the blanket up to her shoulders and swept the hair off her face.

Mari made a noise that was supposed to be a thank you but came out like a whimper. She felt Zahir's weight shift the bed as he slid beneath the blanket beside her. After a moment, he rubbed soothing circles on her shoulders. As she closed her eyes, she could hear Zahir's voice sing a soft melody. The quiet song helped Mari drift to sleep, the churning in her stomach calming as he sang to her.

CHAPTER EIGHTEEN

ZAHIR

While Zahir waited for Mari to wake, he sat on the balcony, skimming through the old and dusty leatherbound book Mari had brought back from the library. He had noticed it sitting on the desk and knew it wasn't one he had grabbed, so he took it to the balcony and tried to find whatever information Mari wanted to tell him. He knew she wouldn't be feeling well once she woke up, and he had to meet with Illan by noon to discuss the threats of a Dual Mage.

Zahir didn't believe that a Dual Mage could possibly be alive. The idea was so ludicrous that he had almost completely discounted it. He didn't know how it could have happened, other than a child of a sailor. They were the only ones who had contact with the other clans, but even then, the chances were slim. He didn't think it was viable. But then again, Illan and Mari were fully convinced the rebels' claim was true. He had no idea why they were blindly believing the word of a rebel and he was wary about accepting this truth from someone out to destroy him.

Zahir found a page whose corner had been folded down. He assumed this was Mari's doing so he read the page in front of him.

The last Dual Mage after Noire to walk the clans was Haru, a Life and Fire Mage. He lived for one hundred and twelve years before he died, never passing on his magic. After Noire, he was "too afraid to pass on his ability". Years later, it was seen that the secondary magic was bred out until it was non-existent. If a Life and Fire Mage were to mate with a Life Mage, the Life magic was twice as strong as the Fire. This continued through generations before the Dual Mages had passed and their descendants could only use one type of magic.

Dual Mages had extraordinary abilities. Their life spans were generally longer, and they could use their magic in new and creative ways. Haru was able to create living beings out of flame and use them in his fight against Noire. He was able to heal injuries with flame, and instead of just destroying things, he was a healer for his part of the city.

It had been seen, however, that Dual Mages who were unable to train one of their magics died by the time they were thirty. Ignoring one magic to focus on another not only made that one weaker, but actually harmed the mage. It was seen that these mages became physically ill just one moon cycle before their death.

Zahir pulled his nose out of the book and stared down at the page. Dual Mages could die if they denied half of their magic. A shiver ran down Zahir's spine as he thought about that. If the Dual Mage existed and didn't know, they were in even more danger than Zahir thought. The rebels would be after them, yes, but they might be coming close to their death. If they did know, however, they were the most powerful mage in Brahn. And that absolutely terrified Zahir. He was king and if there was someone more powerful, they could take over the throne.

Zahir still didn't know if he believed the rumors, but he was certain he had to at least try and find this Dual Mage, if only to protect his title, and his family. He didn't know if this person would harm those he loved, but he wasn't going to take that chance again. Watching Mari nearly be strangled to death still weighed heavy on his heart. Every time he looked at her, all he wanted to do was wrap her in his arms and never let go. When Zahir had held his father while he died, something had broken inside him. His father had let out two words before he died that Zahir was still replaying over and over in his head.

'It's you.'

"What was me?" Zahir asked himself.

Several options ran through his head. He was the only hope. He was the king. He was his father's favorite child. Zahir had no idea what his father meant by those words. But if anyone would have the answer, it was probably Illan.

Zahir slid his chair back and it squealed against the wooden balcony. He cringed, hoping he hadn't woken Mari. When he stepped back through the doors into their room, however, he saw she was still sound asleep, her hair a wild mess and an arm over her eyes. Mari's mouth was wide open, and he could see just the smallest stream of drool down her cheek. He suppressed a laugh and opened the drawer of his desk to write a note.

My dearest, Mari,

I went to speak with Illan. I hope to be back before you wake, If I'm not, please help yourself to some tea and pastries. They are delicious and I think you'll like the chocolate one.

-Zahir

Zahir placed the letter on Mari's bedside table and slipped out of the room and into the hallway, closing the door as silently as he could. When it closed, he walked down the hall, still trying to keep his steps quiet. Sometimes they echoed in the empty halls and he knew Mari needed her sleep.

As he rounded the corner to the entryway, Zahir nearly collided with Anya. She put her hands out to stop him in his tracks, but he stopped himself in time. Whenever she put her hands on him, it never ended well. The last time, she had nearly burned down one of the paintings of their family.

"Good morning, Anya," Zahir said, side stepping her and trying to continue on his walk.

Anya snatched Zahir's wrist as he walked by. She jerked him back, so they were face to face. "I wanted to say, great choice going to kill the rebels. You did the right thing."

"You do?" For some reason, this made Zahir's heart pound.

"I would have done the same thing. It's a choice Father would have made. Maybe I was wrong... You may be a fine king after all."

Zahir didn't like the smirk that toyed at the corners of her mouth. Anya had a way of getting under his skin that looked like a compliment if anyone else heard it. The idea that she would have made the same choice unsettled Zahir. He didn't like that he made a choice that Anya approved of, mostly because he thought she would destroy the clan if she held any power.

"Thank you, Anya," he said, trying to hide the waver in his voice. "I appreciate your support."

"Father would be proud of the choice you made. It's a pity that you kept that one alive. They did give some valuable information, though."

Zahir's hands shook as he shoved them in the pockets of his pants. "What do you know about that?"

"These walls talk, Zahir. I know you have a prisoner in the dungeons and that there's a Dual Mage in Brahn."

"No, there isn't. It's a false claim by the rebels to deter us." Zahir actually believed what he said. If he were busy searching for someone who may or may not exist, his attention would be away from the crown. While he had defeated the rebels, there was still unrest in the city where his marriage was concerned. He wondered how many people in the city were rebel sympathizers who agreed that he was unfit to rule.

"I don't know," Anya began. "What if it's true? If there truly is a Dual Mage in Brahn, then your crown may be in danger. If you're asking for my advice, I think you should find them."

"I'm not asking for your opinion. I do not need it. I have a council for a reason."

"Pity," Anya said, beginning to walk away. "Because last I heard, you couldn't make a single decision in that room."

"Stop," Zahir commanded, taking several deep breaths. "Who told you these things?"

Anya looked over her shoulder with a sly smile. "You're not the only one who speaks with the advisors." With that, she rounded the corner to her room and left Zahir standing alone in the hallway.

His advisors were talking with Anya. How many, he didn't know. But there was at least one who was divulging information to Anya that she shouldn't have. White hot anger ripped through Zahir as he clenched his fists and sparks danced across his knuckles. He needed to find Illan, and quickly.

Zahir stormed through the halls, nearly knocking a guard flat on his ass. Zahir was barely able to mutter an apology as he raced through the palace towards the training room. Every morning, Illan practiced his swordsmanship alone and Zahir had a habit of interrupting him.

Sure enough, Zahir broke through the doors to see Illan slicing through the air with a two-handed sword in his hands. His red, puffy face was shining with sweat and he stopped the blade mid-air as Zahir approached.

"What do I owe this pleasure, *King* Zahir?" Illan asked with a smile.

Zahir would have returned his Uncle's warm smile if it weren't for his anger towards his sister. "Advisors are feeding Anya information."

Illan walked to put the blade back on its hook before responding to Zahir's claim. "How do you know?"

"She knows what the prisoner said about the Dual Mage. She was told that I couldn't make a decision about the rebels during the last meeting. She would only know that if someone told her," Zahir said, releasing his fists only to curl his fingers back in.

Illan towel dried his face and lifted a large glass of water off the floor. "What is the downside to her knowing these things? She is your sister after all."

Zahir thought for a moment. "Having information that only I have kept her close to the crown. I hate that she is so close to it. If I were to die unexpectedly, she would be queen."

"Then isn't it a good thing she has this information?" Illan asked, stretching his arms high over his head.

"If she were to be queen, Brahn would burn to the ground."

"I know you dislike Anya—"

"I hate her. She torments me every chance she gets. She only told me she knew this information to rile me up. She knows I want her nowhere near the crown," Zahir said, huffing out short breaths.

"Do you know which advisor leaked this information?" Illan asked.

"No. I think if it was anyone, it would be Demi. They hated that I was so indecisive. It could have been a moment of annoyance, and I don't want them dismissed. But I want to tell the council they had no right sharing information with Anya."

"You have every right to do that. They are here to serve *you*, not Anya."

"Anya also said I did the right thing killing all those rebels," Zahir said, looking down at his feet.

"Is that a bad thing? Do you regret your decision?" Illan asked.

"I didn't until she said it was a choice she, too, would have made. I want to rule differently than my father. I really hated how violent he was with his own people. I want to break that cycle, but clearly I'm not doing a very good job." Zahir's lips pressed tightly into a grimace. He had disappointed himself in acting like his father instead of the king he really wanted to be. "I want to be kind and forgiving. I want to understand our people. I want to give them a sense of safety and peace."

"And you will. Give yourself a break, Zahir. Your father died so suddenly and violently. It is only natural to desire to avenge his death. If it makes you feel any better, I think you did the right thing too." Illan put a hand on Zahir's shoulder. "You are doing a good job. There are so many factors at play and you've only been king for a day. Give yourself time. You can't be perfect all the time."

Zahir sighed and closed his eyes. He knew Illan was right. Between the rebels, his marriage, and his father's death, Zahir had a lot to think about. While he had been training to be king, he actually had no practice. He wasn't going to be perfect right away, and that was difficult for Zahir to accept.

"On the subject of my father," Zahir started. "His last words to me were 'it's you'. Do you have any idea what he was referring to?"

Illan looked at Zahir with furrowed brows. "I have no idea what he could have been saying. His memory was fading; he may not have even known what he was saying to you."

Zahir sighed. "I can't figure it out. I wish he had told me more. I wish he was still here."

"Me, too," Illan said, pulling Zahir into a tight embrace.

He collapsed against his uncle, realizing, not for the first time, that Illan was more like a father than an uncle.

Chapter Nineteen

Mari

Mari stared in awe as she watched Anya and Taryn practice their magic. They moved in sync, dancing through their steps. As they parted, their flames moved away and as they came back together, they surrounded them, swirling up to the ceiling. Mari was mesmerized by the smooth transition from offensive to defensive movements.

Once Zahir had returned from his adventure earlier that day, he'd sat with Mari as she ate her breakfast, and he ate his second meal of the day. They'd talked about what they had both read in the book about Dual Mages. Mari was still worried that Zahir wasn't taking the threat seriously, but at least he wasn't flat out denying it anymore. He was beginning to admit that there may be *some* truth to the rumor. She could only hope that he would choose to actually do something about it.

Anya and Taryn put their hands up towards each other before spinning halfway around and shooting mirror images of flames towards either wall. Mari had to dive to the floor to avoid being hit. She saw Anya's smirk as she spun back towards Taryn, whose hair was coming loose from its braid. The two of them kneeled down and reached for each other, locking hands. They thrust their free hands forward, and out came a rising wall of flame. It encircled them and spiraled up to the ceiling.

"Beautiful work, ladies," Illan said, clapping his hands. "Let's move into a more offensive practice before we end."

Anya and Taryn stood and smirked at each other. They each took a few steps backwards before immediately throwing fists of flame at each other. Mari watched in horror as they shot flames in every direction. While they were dueling, their movements were still in sync. Every time Anya hurled an attack at Taryn, she sidestepped it like she was prepared. Anya dodged every bit of fire that Taryn let out of her hands.

As the fight went on, their power seemed to grow tenfold. The more intense their fight, the greater their power. Anya screamed something unintelligible as she hurled a cone of flames towards Taryn, who stepped through as if it weren't even there. She sent a wall of flame towards Anya and it smacked her right in the face. Anya stumbled backwards and fell to a knee before launching herself at Taryn.

Mari watched in shock as Taryn grabbed Anya's wrist and the two of them shot flames to the ceiling and down the walls. Taryn kicked out at Anya, flames erupting from her heel and landing on Anya's stomach, sending her flying backwards. Their wall of fire dissipated as Anya crashed to the ground. It was then that

Illan stepped into the conflict, wrapping his arms around Taryn and pulling her away.

"Illan, put me down right this instant!" Taryn screeched, clawing at Illan's arms. "I am going to *kill* her."

"Not if I kill you first," Anya seethed, staggering to her feet. "How dare you intervene, Illan."

"We are done for today," Illan said, setting Taryn back down and stepping between the pair. "You both need to calm down. Anya, leave the room. Taryn, stay here until Anya is far enough away."

Anya stormed from the room, her dark hair swaying around her shoulders and her clothes clinging to her body from the exertion. Mari watched as the doors slammed shut. It was only then that Illan let Taryn leave. She walked slowly out of the room, as if trying to keep as much distance between herself and Anya as she could manage.

Once Taryn was gone, Mari let herself speak. "They are terrifying when they fight."

Illan couldn't help but laugh. "Twin flames, while incredible, are scary when they get angered. You weren't hurt, were you?"

Mari looked down at her exposed arms and legs to make sure she hadn't been burned. "I am fine. I'm ready to get to our lesson."

Illan gave Mari a smile. "I had the thought to practice in the titanium gym. Does that sound okay to you?"

Panic washed over Mari. "That sounds terrifying. I'm not sure that I am ready for that." The idea of being completely surrounded by titanium horrified Mari. After being cut with the titanium blade, she still had dreams where she couldn't access her magic. That empty feeling made her heart drop whenever she thought about it.

"I know it's scary, but it is worth it to train down there. If you get cut with titanium again, I don't want you to freeze from fear," Illan said, his voice soothing Mari's nerves.

When she finally agreed, Illan led her down a staircase in the back left corner of the training gym. At the bottom of the seemingly never ending staircase, Illan swung open a door and the overwhelming cold hit Mari like a ton of bricks as she stepped into the training arena lined with titanium. She shivered involuntarily at the nearly undeniable urge to claw out the gaping emptiness in her chest. Wrapping her arms around her stomach nervously, she walked further into the room, the emptiness only growing deeper.

"Does it always feel this way?" Mari asked, attempting to hide the shake in her voice. She scratched at her chest, as if she would be able to cut out the ache in her body. Being in a room completely lined with titanium was much worse than being cut with a single blade. It felt like her entire body was going to implode.

"Yes," Illan said, scratching at his chest too. "Zahir says that the feeling doesn't get any worse, even as time goes on."

"What kind of training do we do in here?" Mari asked as she walked toward the wall with swords and chains hanging on hooks. "Swordsmanship?"

"Yes, but not with those." Illan pulled two wooden swords from a closet on the far side of the room and presented one to

Mari. She took it and swung it around. "We can work on your footwork first. Footwork is more important than anything when fighting with a sword."

Mari nodded and watched as Illan moved forward and back, side to side, in little circles, and pivoted. He was extremely graceful as he showed her the basic movements that would keep her centered. "Why is footwork so important?"

"The goal is that it gives you a balanced center from which you can lunge, retreat, attack, whatever you want to do. You have to assess how close your opponent is and thus how close you'll have to be to hit him, or just how far out of reach you need to be to avoid being hit." Illan led Mari in a series of lunges and retreats. "You don't want to give your opponent the opportunity to react. If your opponent sucks you in a little closer whenever he advances or retreats, you'll be within range and never see an attack coming."

Mari nearly fell three times when trying to pivot too quickly. "How do you get power in your strike?"

"Pushing your body weight forward with the attack will help you get maximum power. Stepping, lunging, or rushing forward as you're landing the attack will give you the most power you can muster. Like hand-to-hand combat, it's easier to land a successful hit if you use all of your body." Illan demonstrated an attack with his fake sword. He lunged forward, slicing from side to side as he moved. He then showed Mari what the attack would look like if he didn't move at all. Mari noted that movement was just as important as landing the actual blow.

Mari swung her sword, but nearly tripped as the emptiness caved her chest in. She was struggling to breathe, and her head was pounding. The discomfort seemed to only get worse the longer she was in the room. She wondered if it would get better over time or if she would feel ill every time she came down here. Her vision swirled in front of her eyes as she tried again to hit Illan with her sword.

"How are you feeling?" Illan asked as he lightly tapped Mari's shoulder with his wooden sword.

Nausea rolled in Mari's stomach as she lifted her gaze to Illan's. "I'm fine. Let's keep going."

Illan immediately took a step back and held his sword loosely in his left hand by his side. "It is most important to take care of your body before you learn something new. I think we should go back upstairs."

"One more time, and then we can go upstairs," Mari said, determined not to fail. She needed to overcome the fear and be able to fight against titanium.

"One more, and that's it," Illan agreed and waited for Mari to launch an attack.

Mari began swinging her sword at Illan, trying to land a hit, but he dodged or blocked every swing, moving like a snake avoiding capture. Illan swung his sword at Mari, hitting her lightly on the side and ending their sparring session.

The overwhelming urge to rip open her chest prevailed as she waited for Illan to put the practice swords back. The sweat running down her back wasn't hot and sticky, but ice cold. She shivered and crossed her arms over her chest in hope of

224

warming herself up. As she waited, her thoughts lingered on the rebel attacks.

That initial fear of losing her magic was ripe. She could still remember the emptiness in her body and the relief she'd felt once it returned. It had flooded back into her body, all at once, finally allowing her to take a deep breath without her lungs burning in protest. Mari tried to conjure a soul as she waited for Illan, but nothing came out of her fingers. Her one protection was gone and her ability to fight for herself was lacking. While she'd fared well enough during the rebel attacks, she still was terrified that she would completely freeze again if she lost her magic.

Mari was relieved when Illan led her out of the titanium gym and back upstairs to the normal training area. She instantly took a deep breath, feeling the gaping hole in her chest shrink until it was filled. The sense of her magic returning to her body was something she never wanted to feel again outside of a training scenario.

"It feels so good to have my magic back." Mari flexed her fingers out in front of her and wiggled her shoulders back and forth. She immediately called a rabbit's soul to her feet and was glad to watch it hop around her ankles. It only lasted for a minute before it dissipated. "What happened?"

"It will take some time for your magic to return to its full strength. You may only be able to do small amounts of magic for a few hours," Illan said, sitting on the ground and gesturing for Mari to sit across from him.

Mari sat in the same position with her legs crossed so her feet were under her knees. "I really don't like training in the titanium gym."

"No one does, Mari. But it is something you have to do. You need to know how to protect yourself in the worst-case situations." Illan put his hands on his knees. "We are going to do a bit of meditation to end our training. You presumably have a lot of nervous energy and I want to make sure you relax."

Mari closed her eyes and breathed slowly in and out, following Illan's instructions. His calm voice was soothing as she counted in for five and out for six. She let her thoughts come like waves, washing over her and dissipating as soon as they arrived.

She thought about the rebel attack and pictured the rebels surrounding her and Zahir. She imagined running through the halls to get to the safe room, the blur of colors that flew past her eyes as she sprinted. She could still see Ryker's body lying there, lifeless and cold.

But as soon as these thoughts came, Mari forced them from her mind. She let every thought run its course before it was kicked from her mind. She told herself it was okay to think about those things, so long as she didn't dwell on them.

After a few silent minutes, Mari's body was heavy, and she was ready for a nap. Her stomach growled loudly, telling her it was time for another meal and her dry lips alerted her to their desperate need for water. Once Illan let her leave, she made an immediate beeline for her rooms, stopping only to ask the kitchen staff to send a meal up when they had a minute to spare. When they called her 'Your Majesty', she had to keep herself from flinching; the name was still strange to her and she wasn't sure that she would ever get used to the title.

Mari washed and changed out of her sweaty training clothing into a nightgown with a brown fuzzy robe over it. She didn't care that someone might walk in on her in pajamas; she was Queen, after all.

Just a minute after she emerged from her dressing room, a servant brought in several plates of food and set them down on the balcony. A bottle of wine was opened, and a crystal glass was filled with the dark red liquid. Mari smiled to herself as she grabbed a book and slid onto the chair on the balcony. Zahir kept a small stack of books on his desk and Mari figured he wouldn't mind her borrowing a small fictional one.

Mari sipped her wine as she opened to the first page of the book. The opening line was captivating, and she dove right in, nearly forgetting about her dinner for several pages. By the time she remembered, the steaming food was lukewarm, but she didn't mind. The salted cod was delicious, and the dark green vegetables were coated in so much butter that it didn't matter how cold they were.

Mari wasn't sure how much time passed between her eating, drinking, and reading before Zahir walked into the room as the sun began to set. She didn't register his presence until she saw him leaning against the door frame out of the corner of her eye. Mari smiled as she marked her page in the book and set it down on the table.

"How long have you been standing there?" Mari asked, stretching her arms out over her head.

"Just a second. How was your training today?" Zahir asked before putting a hand to his mouth to yawn.

"Exhausting," Mari said before erupting into a yawn as well. "I feel like I got buried by a thousand bricks. Illan took me to the titanium gym. I did not enjoy the experience very much."

"I didn't expect you to," Zahir said with a laugh. "I hate it there."

"My whole body is weak," Mari said, realizing for the first time just how run down she was. Her eyes burned and her head pounded. Her arms ached and her legs screamed. The ache in her chest was gone, but the memory of it weighed heavily on her mind. "I think I'm going to take a nap."

"I think I might join you. I spent the whole day in the library doing research on Dual Mages. My eyes feel like they're going to pop right out of my head," Zahir said, rubbing at his eyes with the heels of his hands.

Mari stood, leaving the empty plates on the balcony, but taking the book with her. She had gotten halfway through it and was dying to know what happened to the characters. She rested the book on her bedside table before sliding off her robe. Slipping under the covers, she pulled the blanket up to her shoulders and wrapped her arms around her pillow. Zahir slid into bed beside her and when Mari looked over her shoulder, she could see him cocooned in the blanket.

Mari didn't know how long she slept before the shifting of the bed beneath her woke her. She opened her eyes a smidge to see Zahir fully dressed and opening the balcony doors. He shut them quietly, but Mari heard the metal furniture scraping on the wooden balcony. She slid from the bed and slowly opened the balcony doors, poking her head out. Zahir wasn't there. Looking around, she spotted his shoe disappearing up onto the edge of the roof.

"What is he doing?" Mari whispered to herself before hoisting herself up onto the railing and peering over the edge. Her muscles screamed, still incredibly sore from her training. Zahir walked up the roof towards the peak on his toes, silent like a cat.

Mari reached and pulled herself up, swinging her left leg up and hoisting herself onto her knees on the edge of the roof. Silently, she followed after Zahir. At the apex of the roof, she saw him crouched down near the edge, his hands resting beside his feet. He was looking out at the city, bright lights shining for miles. The city was busy with life.

"What are you doing up here?" Mari asked, walking towards Zahir and crouching down beside him.

Zahir jumped in surprise but caught himself before he teetered off balance. "I come up here whenever I need to think."

Mari nodded and wrapped her hands around her knees. "Do you want to talk about it?"

Zahir was silent for a few minutes before answering. "Do you promise not to say anything to anyone?" Mari nodded fervently. "I keep reliving the attack."

"What do you mean?"

"Every time I close my eyes, I see those rebels. I see the corpses of guards. I picture you being choked by that man. I imagine how many men I killed with my bare hands and hear the crack of their bones. I see the knife sliding across my father's throat." Zahir sighed. "I watched my father die, Mari. That's not something I'm ever going to forget."

Mari reached her hand over and ran her thumb over Zahir's hand. "I'm so sorry. Is there anything I can do for you?"

"No. I just need time. We both nearly died. So many good soldiers died."

"Did you know any of the guards who died? Personally, I mean."

Zahir nodded solemnly. "Several. Many were guards who died when the rebels busted down the door. They didn't even have a chance." Zahir's breaths were shaky as he finished speaking.

"Zahir, I'm so sorry. I had no idea you were grieving for people other than your father. They are all with the Gods."

He nodded. "I know they are. I know they are okay, and I will see them again. But that doesn't make it any easier." Tears spilled out of Zahir's eyes and down his cheeks.

Mari's heart broke as she listened. "I can't imagine what you are going through. I pray that you will find healing soon. But until then, I am here for you. You can lean on me as much as you need."

"Thank you, Mari. I am beyond blessed by the Gods that our fathers struck whatever deal they did to allow me the honor of being your husband."

"I am lucky, too, Zahir. I couldn't have asked for a better man to be my husband." Mari leaned her head on Zahir's shoulders, closing her eyes.

"Your words are too kind, Mari. You are so sweet, and beautiful. I was terrified I would be married to Taryn. She's nice, don't get me wrong, but she is *way* too upbeat. Besides, she is so close with Anya and we both know how awful my sister can be." Zahir laughed.

"Did you ever want to marry Taryn?" Mari asked, genuinely curious.

"No. I didn't want Anya anywhere near the crown and if Taryn was my wife, my worst fears would come true. I know Anya would be as awful a leader as my father and I couldn't sit by and let her be close to the throne. Taryn gives her that pathway."

Mari nodded. "Why does Anya want the throne so much?"

"She believes she is the rightful heir because she is older. My father chooses who takes the throne and he decided that I would rule. Anya hasn't accepted this fact because throughout Brahn's history, the eldest child has always become king or queen. This is the first time the oldest child won't become the next leader."

"That makes a lot of sense now. Even if it is tradition, why is she so upset with you? It wasn't your decision."

"I think she's just jealous. She's always better than me at everything and this is the first time I will have something she does not." Zahir shook his head in annoyance.

"Anya probably would be just as, if not more, ruthless than your father." Mari wasn't sure if she was saying the right things but wanted to support Zahir dealing with everything.

"Illan agrees with me, and with you. He is overjoyed that my father passed the honor onto me." After a long pause, Zahir changed the subject. "Since you came up here, would you like to join me in something a little crazy?"

Mari laughed. "Of all the things I was expecting you to say, never in a million years could I have guessed that. What do you have in mind?"

It was thirty minutes later when Mari and Zahir dressed in dark clothing and covered their hair with scarves and hats. Zahir helped Mari braid her hair down her back so she could shove it up into a head covering.

"Where are we going?" Mari asked as she followed Zahir out onto the balcony.

"You'll see. You won't be disappointed, I promise." Zahir stepped up onto the railing of the balcony and pulled himself up onto the roof above. He offered her a hand to pull her the rest of the way up, but Mari refused, swinging her leg up like she had before. Once on top of the roof, Zahir led Mari across to the back of the palace as quickly and quietly as possible.

"Why did we go all the way down to get re-dressed, just to come back up here?"

Zahir laughed. "Don't ruin the surprise for yourself. Come on, we have to jump."

"I'm sorry, we have to do *what?*" Mari looked at Zahir, her eyes wide at the realization that they were sneaking out of the palace without any guards.

"There's a six-foot gap between this part of the roof and the servant's quarters. From there, we can climb the fence and get out into the city." Zahir smiled and leaped off the roof, landing with a roll onto the roof that sat seven feet below them. "Come on." Zahir's voice was a whisper, but it was loud enough in the silent night.

Mari looked down and it felt like with every second she was getting further from the roof. "It's okay, I'll just sit here. You have fun, though."

"You're going to be fine. Don't worry. I've done this a hundred times; you're not going to get hurt." Zahir waved for Mari to follow him.

Mari took another look down and shook her head vigorously. "I think I'm scared of heights."

Zahir laughed. "Didn't you ever hike the mountains in Yu'güe?"

"That is so different. I'm not jumping *off* the mountains."

"Just jump. I promise you'll be okay." Zahir waved for her to jump again.

Mari took a deep breath and stood up slowly, her legs shaking. She took a couple steps back before running off the edge of the roof, launching herself into the air. Her legs continued to make running motions as she fell through the sky and she landed with a soft thud on the roof, rolling onto her back as she hit the ground. Her breaths were shaky and uneven, but she realized that she didn't die a horrible death.

"I am never doing that again," Mari warned, standing up with a grunt.

"That was very entertaining to watch." Zahir chuckled, leading Mari across the roof and over to the fence that stood between them and freedom. "Just follow me. It's not that bad."

Zahir expertly scaled the fence, as if he'd done it a thousand times. He slinked up and over, placing his feet in footholds Mari couldn't see, and landing with a soft thud on the ground beyond.

"Not that bad my ass," Mari grumbled, throwing herself at the fence. It clanked loudly and shifted under her weight. She had a hard time pulling herself up, her fingers in pain when she linked them through the holes. Soon enough, she swung her left leg over and propelled herself over. She let out a yelp as she fell and landed on the ground with a hard crash.

"Are you okay?" Zahir asked, trying not to laugh.

"Don't ever make me do that again," Mari groaned, rolling onto her side. Zahir extended an arm and helped her to her feet. She dusted off her shirt and pants as she stood. "Why are there no guards?"

Zahir led Mari through the streets toward the city. "They take five minutes to ride around the palace walls; we had a very small window to leave."

"Are you sure this is safe? We haven't been allowed out without guards in the entire time I've been here," Mari said, wrapping her shawl tighter around her shoulders. The air had chilled greatly since the morning and suddenly the thin clothes she wore weren't enough to keep the cool temperature off her neck.

"I do this every moon cycle. I will protect you, should you need it," Zahir said, pulling his scarf tighter around his hair.

As they neared the city, Mari felt even more in awe than she had on the roof. The lights were brighter up close and there were people bustling through the streets, as if everyone was needed somewhere important. Young adults were giggling in the street, drinking iced drinks or snacking on something. People led their friends through shops for clothes or household items. Others were drinking in bars or eating meals with their families at the various restaurants. Everyone Mari passed looked happy to be doing whatever they were fixated on.

Zahir grabbed Mari's hand as she fell a few steps behind, pulling her into his chest as they walked through the city. She felt a blush creep up on her cheeks as they walked hand and hand through the streets. Mari couldn't keep her eyes off the windows, noticing that there were intricate designs painted on the glass.

"What is that pattern for? I keep seeing it." Mari pointed to one of the residential homes that had what looked like an incomplete star surrounded by a thick circle. She thought it also could have been the letter A. In some windows it was large and obvious, but in others it was small, in the corner. Mari saw one dripping red paint down a wall that looked brand new.

"I honestly don't know," Zahir said, after a long pause.

"So, where are we going?" Mari asked, turning her eyes back to Zahir.

"On the third day of every moon cycle, my friends and I meet at a small tavern on the edge of the city. We have been doing this for three years and only the cycle before our marriage did anyone miss the evening." The smile that lit up Zahir's face made Mari smile back.

"And people at this tavern just accept that the prince, now king, drinks there?" Mari asked, eyebrows furrowed at the thought.

"There are very few people there. The bartender promised to be discreet, closing his doors to other patrons every cycle, and he has kept his word so far."

"How did you start doing this?" Mari asked.

"I was under a lot of stress as my father's memory faded. Illan started putting pressure on me to get more involved in decision making. Two of my friends are guards inside the palace, and they invited me to come to this tavern. We started doing it consistently and then one brought his fiancée and the other, his brother. Our group got a little bigger over the years, but we try to come out every moon cycle," Zahir explained. Mari could see the joy in his face as he talked about his friends.

"That sounds lovely," Mari said.

After winding through alleyways and busy streets, Zahir pulled Mari into a small building that wouldn't have caught Mari's eye if she hadn't been dragged towards it. It was a squat black structure with a dark metal door and it looked out of place amongst the bright lights as it hid in the shadows of the streetlamps.

Mari was surprised to see a small room with various tables and a single person waiting by the counter, tapping their fingers on the wood. They chatted with a large man behind the counter who filled a glass to the brim with dark red wine. Loud music played that Mari didn't recognize, the heavy sound resonating in her ribs. Her shoes stuck to the floor as she walked behind Zahir, as if it hadn't ever been washed. The dark room was barely illuminated, save for a small fireplace in the back and a lantern on every table, all of which were empty except one in the back left corner. Mari could feel the warmth from the fire, a welcome comfort from the cold air outside.

As they approached the table in the back left, Zahir ripped his scarf from his head and shook out his hair, prompting Mari to do the same. Her braid thudded lightly against her left shoulder as it fell from the thin scarf. Mari watched as two people laughed and clinked glasses of dark amber liquid together.

"Z!" the one closest to them said with a smile. One of his front teeth was missing and his dark brown hair was cut short, showing off his flushed face and neck.

"How are you, Raf?" Zahir asked, taking a seat next to him. Mari tentatively sat between Zahir and a woman who gave her a huge smile.

"Not bad; can't complain. Is this your lovely bride?" the man with the missing tooth asked, eyeing Mari.

"Lo and behold the Queen of Brahn," Zahir said proudly, gesturing to Mari who flushed a bright shade of red. She wiggled her fingers in a shy greeting.

"It's a pleasure, Your Royal Highness," Raf said, making a ridiculous bowing motion.

"Knock it off, Raf." The girl rolled her eyes. "I'm Reina, it's great to meet you."

She stuck out her hand for Mari to shake. Her dark brown eyes matched her smooth umber brown skin, and her long, luscious hair framed her face perfectly, accentuating her beauty.

"You as well." Mari shook Reina's hand and noticed it was heavily calloused.

"Where are Kiernan and Rodrick?" Zahir asked Reina, leaning forward on the table.

"Your guess is as good as mine. Rick said he would be here tonight. I guess he and Kiernan had duties to attend to," Reina said before finishing the last of her drink.

Zahir turned to Mari to explain. "Rodrick and Kiernan are royal guards. They both work inside the palace. With the increased security, they must have gotten stuck there. Raf is a blacksmith in town. Reina is Rodrick's fiancée, and joined our group last year."

"It's great to meet you both." Mari smiled tentatively. She desperately wanted to make a good impression on Zahir's friends and wished she had gotten time to prepare.

"What're you drinking tonight?" Reina asked her, holding up her empty glass to a passing waitress to get her attention.

"I don't drink much, but I guess wine?" Mari shrugged. She knew she didn't like whiskey, but wine was the only other alcoholic beverage she'd ever tried.

"Oh, no. Absolutely not." Reina smiled at the waitress as she came over. "I'll take a gin and lemon. And so will she." Reina nodded at Mari who just nodded sheepishly when the waitress confirmed her order.

"Let's get eight shots of vodka." Raf smiled at the waitress, adding a 'please' as she nodded.

"How is the palace treating you?" Reina asked Mari, leaning both elbows on the table.

"It's definitely different from Yu'güe. But I think I might actually like it better. Don't ever let my family hear me say that, though." Mari laughed, getting a small chuckle out of the group.

"And how's my princeling treating you?" Raf asked, throwing an arm around Zahir's shoulders. Zahir picked up Raf's arm and placed it gently on the table, patting his hand.

Mari blushed. "He's great. He kicked my ass in training, though. I've never been trained in hand-to-hand combat."

"Zahir, don't you know you can't hit your wife?" Reina shook her head at Zahir jokingly.

Zahir put his hands up in defense. "Hey, she asked me to."

"It's true, I did," Mari said, looking at Zahir and earning a laugh from his friends.

It was then that the waitress returned with their drinks, placing them all in the center of the table. Mari and Reina took theirs while the men shot their vodka back-to-back. Mari took a tentative sip of her drink and was overwhelmed with the sweetness. It tasted nothing like alcohol.

"What's in this?" Mari asked, her eyes wide with happiness.

Reina laughed heartily. "Gin, water, lemon juice, and sugar. I guess you're enjoying it?"

"It's delicious," Mari said. Sweet alcohol was a new experience for her, and she was not disappointed. "So, what kind of stories can you tell me about Zahir?"

"Let me tell you the time I first met Zahir," Reina started, a smirk pulling the left corner of her mouth up.

Zahir folded his arms and put his head on the table. "Gods, not this story."

Mari looked at Zahir, hiding like a child, and laughed. He looked ridiculous with his hair falling over the table and into his now empty glass of vodka.

"It was maybe three moon cycles after Rick and I started dating. I had been asking to meet his friends forever because he spoke so highly of them. I had no idea that one of these friends was the high prince. I was so shocked, I had no idea how to act. Well, it turns out Zahir had already drunk way too many shots of vodka. He was slurring his words and could barely walk straight. I was so uncomfortable. Knowing that this person," Reina gestured to Zahir, "was going to be the next king absolutely terrified me. The man could barely string a sentence together."

"In my defense," Zahir said, sitting up, "I didn't know Rodrick was bringing you. I thought he was coming alone. This was also the day Illan suggested I take over for my father as soon as possible."

"Well, I know that *now*." Reina rolled her eyes and looked back at Mari. "When I tell you that I was a little scared that Zahir would have the crown, I'm not lying. I genuinely thought our whole clan would go to shit. The next time I came with Rodrick, he asked Zahir to refrain from drinking so he could actually remember meeting me. That's when I realized how nice he was. I was still hesitant to know he would be our king, but after all this time, I can see he is going to do a great job."

"Thank you, Reina. I'm glad you gave me a second chance," Zahir said, laughing.

"This one time," Raf started, leaning forward onto his elbows. "Zahir tried to climb a tree."

"Raf, when is your new boyfriend getting here?" Zahir asked suddenly, his tone urgent. Mari laughed, wanting to know the tree climbing story.

Raf sat up straight in his seat and looked around for someone. His eyes lit up and he raised an arm, waving. Mari turned around in her seat to see what Raf's boyfriend looked like and her heart dropped out of her stomach. She dropped her drink on the floor, the glass shattering around her feet.

"Mari are you okay?" Zahir asked, putting a hand on her shoulder.

She shook her head and whispered, "Hanan?"

CHAPTER TWENTY

MARI

Mari stared in disbelief as she put her hands on Hanan's chest. She pressed hard against him, almost shoving him back because there was absolutely no way he was real. His tight black shirt showed off black ink running down his arms in intricate designs and his light brown hair fell haphazardly over his forehead, obscuring his dark brown eyes. He looked the same as Mari remembered, except the rest of his baby fat had left his now tanned face and his jawline had sharpened and squared out. Mari had tried over the years to picture what Hanan might look like as she aged, but she could never get it right.

"I thought you were dead," Mari breathed. Her legs were wobbly as she grabbed Hanan's shoulder to steady herself. She fell into her brother's open arms and let out ten years' worth of tears.

Hanan's hug was the most secure thing Mari had ever felt. His arms tight around her shoulders kept her pinned against his chest, and the way his chin rested on top of her head reminded her of days when Hanan would give her a hug before they went to bed every night. The softness of his shirt brought up a memory of when Hanan would read to her, sitting beside her in the bed until she fell asleep on his shoulder. His hug was home.

"Why would you think that?" Hanan asked. The strain in his voice sounded like he was about to break down crying, too.

"Our father told everyone you died." Mari reeled back from Hanan and looked up into his face. "Is it really you?"

"I'm here, Mari. This is real." He released Mari and she stepped back, not really wanting to break the embrace. "Father told you I was dead?"

"He... insinuated that *he* killed you," Mari said, her voice barely a whisper.

Hanan's eyes went wide and his hands balled into fists at his side. "I'm going to kill *him*."

"Where have you been hiding?" Mari asked, not even trying to stop the tears that cascaded down her cheeks. She wiped at them with the heel of her hand. Relieved didn't even begin to cover her emotions. Confusion spun her brain around in circles while relief crashed over her like waves in the ocean. Anger bubbled in her chest.

"I trekked through the mountains until I reached the coast. It was then that I took a ship over to Lovíth. I stayed there for a few moon cycles, trying to make money any way I could. I helped out on some of the fishing boats, putting worms on lines and bailing out the boats. I eventually got a job descaling the fish. Once I had enough money to buy passage on a ship, I came here to Brahn. I figured this was the last place anyone would look for me. The clan is huge and there are too many people for one person to make a difference.

"Here, I found quick work on a farm. Raf's family's farm, actually." Hanan paused and looked over at the table where everyone was trying, and failing, to not stare at the two of them. "I helped clean the stables and kill the cattle. They gave me housing and food; it was a good job. Raf was the first person I told the story of what really happened. He accidentally let it slip to his parents, but they couldn't care less; a pair of hands on the farm was a pair of hands. It didn't matter where they came from. I've been living with them ever since."

"Why didn't you write?" Mari choked out the words. She had thought he was dead. But if he were alive, there was no reason why he couldn't have written to her over the years.

Hanan sighed and ran a hand through his hair. "Father was going to exile me if I refused to marry the Princess of Orcian. He threatened to send me into the mountains alone, with nothing. If I wrote to you and he found out where I was... I thought he would hunt me down."

Mari nodded, finally understanding. He wasn't safe. Mari didn't know if he ever would be truly safe from their father. If he wanted to find Hanan, he could; it would just take a long time and too many resources for it to be worth it. Besides, her father had made a connection with an outside clan, arguably a better one than if Hanan had married the Orcian princess.

"Did he hurt you?" Hanan asked suddenly, putting a hand on Mari's shoulder.

"What?" Mari asked, shaking her head.

"Did our father hurt you?"

"He never laid a hand on me," Mari said. She looked down at her feet and suddenly everything made so much more sense. "He hit you, didn't he?"

"You didn't know?" Hanan asked, tears glistening in his eyes.

Mari shook her head again. "I think I was too young to realize. What else did he do to you?" Terror pulled her into darkness and her happiness was the only thing that kept her in the light. If she ever saw her father again, she would barely be able to contain her fury.

"He threatened to leave me in the mountains with nothing if I didn't marry who he wanted. He locked me outside our home one night, as if trying to give me a taste of what it would be like. I broke into our schoolhouse and slept there. When that failed, he tried to beat my feelings out of me."

"I'm going to kill him," Mari said, balling her fists at her side. She breathed rapidly, chest rising and falling quicker.

"You're going to have to get in line, kid," Hanan said, wiping a tear from his left eye as he let out a breathy laugh.

"After you left," Mari said, trying to get used to replacing '*died*' with '*left*', "he called you a disgrace and never spoke your name again. He told us he buried you at a big boulder a quarter way up one of the peaks. Every time I went hunting, I stopped there on the way back. I went to tell you that you weren't a disgrace. Because you aren't."

The tears that fell down Hanan's cheeks caused more salty streaks on Mari's face. The bone crushing hug that he pulled her into just made them both cry harder. They stood there, locked in an embrace for several long minutes, bodies shaking with sobs.

"I saw you on your wedding day," Hanan said into Mari's hair.

"As I passed through the town? I thought I saw you, too. I guess I did," Mari said. Finally, the knowledge that her brother was there on her wedding day gave her peace.

Mari and Hanan stood in their embrace for a long time, holding onto each other and never wanting to let go. The silence that passed between them filled ten long years of separation and lies. Mari's mind kept going back to her father, who had lied to her for her whole life. He'd pretended to kill Hanan to control her. He wanted nothing more than a perfect child who abided by his every command. He had never wanted a child, he wanted a piece in his political game.

Only when Raf came over did Mari and Hanan break apart. Hanan wiped his face dry of tears and gave Raf a hug and kiss before the three of them walked back to the table.

"So, this is your husband," Hanan said, looking Zahir up and down. "Father chose a good one."

He stuck his hand out to Hanan. "Welcome back from the dead."

Zahir smiled as Hanan clasped his hand and Mari let out a loud laugh that just released all the tension she had built up in her chest. Tears welled in her eyes from laughter and she clutched her stomach as it began to hurt. For some reason, Zahir's joke hit her just right in this tense moment.

"You may be king, but I will not hesitate to kill you if you hurt my sister," Hanan was smiling to make sure Zahir understood this was a figure of speech.

Zahir laughed. "I think she would kill me herself."

"I'm actually surprised you two are out tonight," Raf said as he called over the waitress to order another round of drinks for everyone.

Zahir shook his head, eyebrows scrunched inward. "Why is that?"

Mari leaned forward on the table, heart beginning to beat a little harder.

"With so many people openly in rebellion, I didn't expect you to show up," Raf said, leaning back in his chair. By his casual shrug, this didn't seem like a surprise to him.

"Rebellion?" Zahir asked, sitting up straighter. "Who is in rebellion?"

"You don't know?" Reina asked, tilting her head to the side. When Zahir shook his head, she continued. "Did you see the signs in the windows? The little 'A' surrounded by a circle. It's a symbol that people display to signify they are openly dissenting."

"For what reason?" Zahir asked.

Mari closed her eyes and leaned back, fear settling in over her heart like a dark storm cloud.

"People are furious that you went to slaughter the rebels without finding out what they wanted. You made the same decision your father would have made, and people hated that," Raf said, bluntly.

"I did know what they wanted. My advisors put pressure on me to find them and kill them. I did it to save the city from future attacks. They killed my father. Does that not mean anything? They assassinated the king," Zahir said, his voice rising. He flexed his hands in and out of fists as he spoke, and Mari resisted the urge to reach out and hold his hand.

"You weren't transparent," Reina said, speaking quietly. "That's the problem many had with King Ryker."

Zahir put his palms flat on the table. "There wasn't time for transparency. I had to act before they planned to assassinate me or anyone else."

"You did consider talking to them," Mari said. As soon as she said the words, she wished she could take them back. The anger in Zahir's eyes nearly made her recoil, but she spoke again. "You asked what I would do. I told you I would talk to them and you outright ignored my advice."

"I didn't ignore it," Zahir said, defensively. "I made the decision to attack them to protect our city."

"No," Raf said, shaking his head. "You wanted revenge."

"I don't need to hear this," Zahir said. He pushed his chair back and it scraped loudly against the wood floor. "We're leaving."

"No," Mari said. She looked up at Zahir who's eyes were nearly burning. "You can't not listen to your friends because you don't like their opinion, or mine for that matter. Your friends are telling you that your people are openly dissenting, and your response is to defend your actions and then leave. That's not putting your people first."

"We are leaving," Zahir's low, rumbling voice was more terrifying than a yell ever could have been.

Mari mustered all the courage she could and stood, looking up into Zahir's eyes. She pointed a finger into his chest as she spoke. "Sit. Down." Zahir glared at her as he complied. Mari turned back to Reina. "What does the symbol mean?"

Reina and Raf exchanged a nervous glance. "It means they want Anya on the throne, in place of Zahir," Reina said, in a voice nearly a whisper.

The silence that followed was gut wrenching. It went on for several long minutes as Zahir stared into his folded hands. Mari slowly sat back down and put a hand over Zahir's. She knew how much that must hurt him to know his people want his sister to rule them. Zahir's biggest fear was staring him right in the face and Mari wondered if it was too late to stop the rebellion.

The waitress brought over a fresh round of drinks but they went untouched until Zahir took a long sip of his whiskey, the ice clinking against the side of the glass.

"I... I had no idea," Zahir said. "Why did no one tell me?"

"Rodrick said he told the captain of the guard. He's the one who found out what it meant," Raf said, reaching to hold Hanan's hand.

"But why did no one tell *me?*" Zahir took another long sip of his drink and ran a hand through his long hair.

"I don't know," Raf said, shaking his head.

Zahir wrapped his hands around Mari's. "I need to stop this. How do I stop the rebellion?"

"You need to speak with your advisors and with Illan," Mari suggested.

"No advisors," Zahir snapped. "They are clearly keeping information from me and leaking information to Anya... and who knows who else. I can't trust any of them. Illan is the only one who holds my full trust."

"Zahir," Mari said, trying desperately to keep her voice calm. "You can't discount every one of your advisors. They are not all bad."

Zahir let out a tense sigh and sagged his shoulders. "If I don't know who to trust, then I can't trust any of them."

Mari slid her chair back and tried to lift Zahir out of his chair. "We should go. You need to talk to Illan."

Once Mari and Zahir had bundled their hair back up, they bid a good night to Zahir's friends. Mari gave Hanan a long hug, letting him know how relieved she was to know he was okay. She promised to see him soon and invite him to the palace one day. She told him that Raf was wonderful and that she could see how happy they were together. She needed to make sure Hanan understood that she loved him unconditionally.

CHAPTER TWENTY-ONE

ZAHIR

Zahir sat on top of the palace stairs, watching the sun creep over the horizon as it lit the sky in bright pinks and oranges. He lay on his back, his head turned so his right cheek rested on his shoulder, his right hand elevating his head a few inches from the ground. The breeze had begun to turn from a soft chill to a comforting warmth as he lay there, waiting for the sun to rise. He watched as the rays cast a light orange glow over the city, illuminating the roofs and streets. He could see that the peaks of the mountains were also just starting to bask in the sun's light. Zahir could smell the fresh eggs and breakfast meats cooking in the kitchen the longer he lay there. The only thing that would have made the morning better was if the two guards that stood watch over him were inside. The comfort of solitude was something Zahir longed for as he waited for Illan to wake, despite the protests from his guards.

When he and Mari had arrived home after the bar, Illan had already been asleep. While Mari was able to fall asleep quickly, Zahir had lain in bed staring at the ceiling, his thoughts racing. He wanted to know why his people wanted Anya as their queen. He desperately needed to know how to fix his mistakes. If only they knew he didn't want to be like his father, maybe they would understand his motives. Zahir tossed and turned for a while before deciding it was pointless and he wasn't getting any sleep. So, while Mari slept, Zahir crept out to the staircase to watch the stars twinkle before they disappeared, and the sun took their place.

A carriage rolling through the streets caught Zahir's eye and he sat up suddenly, blood rushing to his head. He swayed, the edges of his vision blurring slightly. As he watched the horse drawn carriage paraded through the streets, white parchment flew from the windows. Zahir could just barely make out the sheets as they flitted to the ground. He watched it pass the palace, papers landing at the bottom of the stairs as they drove past. Immediately, Zahir stood and rushed down the stairs, his heart racing.

His hands shook as he bent to pick up one of the papers, and when his eyes finally settled on the words, his heart dropped straight from his chest onto the ground. Five lines of text made Zahir crumple the paper and throw it as far away as he could.

Do you want another Dictator Ryker on the throne?

King Zahir is hiding information about a Dual Mage living in Brahn from the public.

A Fire Mage bred another to make the strongest mage in millennia.

We do not accept you, King Zahir.

Queen Anya would never hide this from us.

Zahir began to scoop up as many papers as he could from the bottom of the palace steps. He yelled for guards to collect them as quickly as they could, scrambling to pick up the papers before anyone else could see them. But as the sun rose higher in the sky and Zahir's arms became fuller, he realized his quest was futile. Soon, everyone in Brahn would know that there was a Dual Mage in their midst. While Zahir was still doubting the legitimacy of this claim, the whole city would believe that he knew this information was true.

"Stop," Zahir commanded. Immediately, the guards around him dropped their fliers and stood straight up to face Zahir. "Resume your duties."

Zahir lifted his head high as he jogged up the palace steps two at a time. Sweat beaded on his neck as his unbound hair bounced against his shoulders. He blew strands from his face as he ran, needing it out of his face. As soon as Zahir was up the stairs, he rushed to Illan's chambers. There was no letting him sleep now, Illan needed to be awake and helping Zahir figure out what to do.

Zahir pounded a fist on Illan's wooden door. "Uncle, there is an emergency." Zahir didn't stop his knocking until Illan swung open the door, half clothed.

Illan scratched his bare stomach with one hand while he rubbed his left eye with the other. "Who is dead?"

"No one is dead, but—"

"Zahir," Illan said with a sigh, "If no one is dead then why did you wake me before sunrise?"

Zahir thrust a flier through the door to Illan. "These are littering the city."

Illan took the flier from Zahir and walked back to his bed, motioning for Zahir to follow. Illan sat on the foot of the bed before bringing the flier closer to his face to read. As his eyes scanned the page, Zahir could see the lines of worry creasing his uncle's forehead.

When Illan looked up from the paper, Zahir could see the panic in his eyes. "The rebels have not been defeated."

"And they want Anya on the throne," Zahir said. He could feel the panic in his chest, making it hard to breathe, and wondered if Illan could tell. "People are displaying 'A' symbols in their windows to publicly show their dissent."

"Dissent to what? What could you have possibly done to anger the whole clan?" Illan asked, scratching his head.

"Apparently, slaughtering the rebels. One of the guards told the captain the information about the symbol, but it never reached us."

"Ren wouldn't keep that from us. They are dedicated. We need to talk to them. And we need to address this, publicly, before it gets any worse," Illan said, standing up and going to his dressing room.

Zahir sighed and put his hands in his hair, giving the slightest tug. "There is no way there is a Dual Mage."

"You can't ignore this anymore, Zahir. The whole city will know within a few hours. If you want people to take you seriously, you need to be transparent," Illan's voice was slightly muffled through the door.

"But it's not possible," Zahir said, looking around the room.

Illan's chambers hadn't changed for as long as Zahir could remember. The large four poster bed had a dark wood night table on either side. On one sat a painting of Illan's late wife, Daria. On the other sat a bottle of perfume, that Zahir had always assumed was his aunt's. On the desk sat several framed paintings of Daria and their child, Megara. The sickness that had caused their death was extremely contagious and Illan hadn't been allowed around either of them as they died.

"Zahir," Illan said, stepping out of his dressing room in a pair of flowing black pants that cinched at his ankles and a short-sleeved shirt that may have been a hair too small. "Ignoring this will not make it go away. As your uncle and your advisor, you *must* do something about this."

"I want to tell the people what I believe, not what I think they want to hear. Isn't that the right thing?" Zahir asked.

"Sometimes it is best to lie," Illan said, putting a hand on Zahir's shoulder. "Being a good leader is more than honesty; it's knowing how to deal with crises. And sometimes, that means lying."

"I don't want to be like my father. He lied so often to the public to control them. I don't want to do that," Zahir said, sighing. "I just... I want to be good."

"You are good, Zahir. Would you like to get other opinions before you say something? We can have the council here shortly."

Zahir shook his head rapidly. "Absolutely not. Someone is feeding information to Anya. She knows about things that we have discussed in meetings."

"She probably listened at the door. Your advisors are sworn to serve you and only you," Illan said.

"She told me outright that they have been leaking information to her," Zahir said, clenching his hands into fists. "I can't trust any of them right now. Only you."

"Zahir, do you know what that means? It means you have no council, no sounding board. The only opinion is mine, and Mari's should you ask her. What does she think of this?"

"I... don't know. She knows someone is leaking information. She said I should come talk to you," Zahir said.

"Do you want to address the Dual Mage first, or figure out who you think could be betraying you?" Illan asked, removing his hand from Zahir's shoulder.

"Advisors first. If I find nothing in one day, I will make a statement to the public."

"I am making it known I disagree, but I support you in your decision," Illan said.

"This is what I feel I have to do," Zahir said, putting a fist over his heart. He splayed out his fingers over his chest.

Zahir spun on his heel and walked from the room, slightly aggravated that Illan wasn't on his side. For once, he was making a decision that he felt was right. While the last decision he made didn't go in his favor, he had felt it was right at that moment.

He was going to make mistakes, and it was something he was going to have to live with. But making mistakes could cost him everything he had worked so hard for.

As Zahir paced around the palace, his mind ran in a million directions. His first thought was to confront his advisors directly. But all that would do is stir up confusion and anger. If there really was someone feeding information to Anya, the last thing he wanted to do was push them closer to her. Or worse, push others to her side. Having his people against him was one thing, but his advisors were a whole other situation. If he had no one to help him make good decisions, then he was truly alone in a position he was already terrified to be in.

Zahir couldn't help the sparks that flung out of his fingers as he traipsed the halls. The surge of panic and anger forced them from his hands. His eyes scanned the ceiling, desperately searching for a plan forward. The next option rose quickly in Zahir's mind: kill the problem at the source. Which meant having Anya tell him directly who she was working with.

He wondered if Anya would actually tell him. All the signs pointed to no, but if he were able to say just the right things then maybe she would. Zahir didn't know what he would do to the person who had betrayed him, but he knew the aftermath would be brutal.

"What the hell are you doing?" Anya asked, her voice reminding Zahir of the scraping of nails on a rough surface.

"I was about to come find you, actually," Zahir said, immediately stopping his pacing and standing to face Anya. The permanent smirk on her face was present and Zahir wanted nothing more than to slap it off her face.

"To come ask me to take the crown? Gladly," Anya said, her tone sickeningly sweet. She reached out, as if to actually take something from Zahir.

"You will have to pry it out of my cold, dead hands," Zahir sneered. "Who on my council is giving you information?"

Anya's laugh nearly made Zahir's ears bleed. "You're still harping on about that? The question you should be asking is who told the rebels where the safe room was."

Zahir's heart nearly stopped in his chest. In the entire time since the rebel attack, not once had it crossed his mind how the rebels found the safe room. He hadn't given himself time to think about it, his mind continuously occupied since that dreadful night. Had someone given them its location?

"Do you know if someone did?" Zahir asked, his heart pounding. He could have sworn Anya was able to hear the drum in his chest.

Anya twirled a strand of hair around her pointer finger. "What would I know? I'm just a *princess*." She nearly spat out the last word.

"Anya," Zahir growled, sparks shooting out of his fingertips. "If you know something and aren't telling me, I swear to the Gods you will regret it."

"Don't you think if I knew something I would be out there, hunting down whoever did it? They killed our father, Zahir. Someone *must* pay for that," Anya seethed, her hands clenching into fists at her side.

He took a step towards his sister. "I swear to the Gods... If you had *anything* to do with this, you will regret it." Zahir's voice was a low rumble in his chest. He wouldn't put it past Anya to stoop to a level so low. If the rebels had gone in with the intention to kill Zahir, instead of his father, Anya's path to the throne would be clear.

Anya stepped even closer to minimize the gap between them. She put a hand on Zahir's chest and pushed, sending Zahir backwards onto his left foot. She took another step closer and pushed again, nearly knocking Zahir to the ground. He quickly regained his footing and braced himself for Anya's next hit.

"If you think for one second that *I* am the reason for our father's death you are sorely mistaken." Anya swung her leg up and kicked Zahir's chest with the bottom of her foot. He stumbled backward, but not before gripping Anya's ankle and pulling. She slid forward, yelping as Zahir yanked on her leg.

"Whoever is responsible will regret their decisions. While I find this person, stay the hell out of my way. Don't you dare talk to my advisors or, so help me, I will kill you," Zahir said, dropping Anya's foot to the floor.

Anya landed in a low lunge, her hands on either side of her extended leg to support her. She slid her other leg forward and stood to face him. Zahir could see the fire in her eyes as a satisfied smirk grew on his face. He had finally, after all these years of her tormenting him, gotten under her skin.

Zahir spun on his heel and strode from his sister, towards the guards' quarters. If anyone would know how the rebels got into the palace, it would be the guards. He could hear raucous laughter and the clinking of glasses as he approached. The guards lived all the way across the palace from the royal family. Living in the palace meant they sacrificed time with their families to serve Zahir and his family. While most had spouses and children down in the city, they only saw their loved ones on special occasions. Zahir's ideal life for them would be having their families live in houses around the palace so they could visit more often and watch their children grow up.

Behind the open wooden doors was a celebration that seemed to have been going for many hours. Guards in their casual clothing laughed, danced, and drank in their shared space. Lining the walls were bunk beds that were neatly made up with blankets. In the center of the long, rectangular room was a table, atop which sat a cake with bright blue frosting like the color of the sea. Wine and whiskey glasses were filled and emptied immediately. Zahir leaned against the open door frame, watching his guards relax, even though it was early morning.

"Your Majesty," Ren, the captain of the guard, said, sweeping into a low bow.

Zahir watched as the rest of his guards paused and bowed to him. "Please, don't stop your party. What are you celebrating?"

"My wife just had a baby boy," Elise, the newest of the guards, said happily. Her eyes were glistening with tears as she swayed on her feet.

"You should be with her. Go, you are relieved of duties for a moon cycle. I will find someone to replace you for the time," Zahir said, smiling at Elise. "Congratulations."

Elise dropped her wine glass on the ground, and it shattered loudly, spilling dark red wine over the wood floor. "Really?" She looked at Zahir with hopeful, wide eyes.

"Yes. You should be with her," Zahir said, smiling.

Elise ran to Zahir and hugged him suddenly. Zahir laughed as he wrapped his arms around Elise's shoulders, lightly. "Thank you so much." She backed up, seemingly realizing she'd hugged the King of Brahn. "I'm so—"

Zahir held a hand up to silence her. "There is no need to apologize. Enjoy your time off. Does your son have a name yet?"

Elise nodded enthusiastically. "Zoan. We combined your name and Prince Roan's."

"I am honored." Zahir put a hand to his chest, shocked that someone named their child after him.

Elise nearly pranced from the room after saying goodbye to her comrades and gathering her things. Zahir watched as she ran down the hall, away to her wife and newborn son. His heart was full when he turned back to Ren.

"Can I speak with you for a minute?" Zahir asked.

"Of course," Ren said. They instructed everyone to return to their party and to drink an extra glass for Elise.

Zahir slowly closed the door behind Ren and walked them down the hall until they were slightly out of earshot of the party. Ren pushed their short hair out of their eyes before putting their arms behind their back and spreading their legs shoulder width apart.

"Did Rodrick come to you with information about the rebel insignia showing up across the city?" Zahir asked, looking over his shoulder nervously as if someone were listening in.

Ren blinked their eyes and furrowed their brow. "No, he hasn't shown up for his round in two days."

"Two days?" Zahir asked, shaking his head. "His fiancée told me he's been busy here."

Ren shook their head, sending their hair back into their eyes. "No, sir. He has not been here. What is this insignia you mention?"

"It's an 'A' in a circle. I saw it in a few windows across the city the other night. I was later informed that Rodrick knew it was a sign for open dissent," Zahir said. "So, then you haven't seen this sign?"

"I have not. This is the first I have heard of it." Ren looked away from Zahir, as if collecting their thoughts. "I can ask my guards, if you would like. I can see if anyone has noticed this signal. Don't worry, Your Majesty, those rebels will *never* penetrate this palace again."

"Do you know how they got in?" Zahir asked, cringing as he remembered the broken-down door and bloodied corpses beneath it.

"They took a battering ram to the door. It was one hell of a ram because they knocked the door down easily," Ren said. "I keep playing that night over in my head and there are so many things that went wrong. Including them finding the safe room. I am still unsure how they found it."

Zahir looked around before he lowered his voice. "I think we have someone on the inside helping the rebels."

Ren lurched back, their eyes wide and searching Zahir's hardened expression. "Surely that isn't true."

"I don't know for sure. If you, or anyone, sees something out of the ordinary can you alert me?" Zahir asked. If anyone was going to notice something awry, it would be the people who were paid to do so.

"Of course. We will do everything we can," Ren said. They reached a hand towards Zahir. When Zahir grasped their hand in his, they spoke again. "You have my word. You and your family will be perfectly safe."

"Thank you, Ren. I know I can always count on your loyalty."

Zahir watched as Ren disappeared into the room. The sounds of the party flitted out to meet Zahir and he wished, just for a minute, that he could join them. His guards worked so closely together that he watched them interact like family. He would see them joke around during their off hours and laugh over dinner. He watched them clasp each other in an embrace when something exciting happened. He saw them console others when someone died. Zahir knew those bonds were unbreakable.

As Zahir walked away, he felt a hand around his wrist. Zahir wrenched his body around, fist raised and ready to attack whoever held him. When he took in Trevor's face, he relaxed and put his arm back to his side.

"Gods, Trevor. You scared me," Zahir said, breathless.

Trevor's bright blue eyes reflected the low torchlight and as his grip on Zahir's wrist changed from a vice to a light feathery touch, it reminded Zahir of those nights they had spent alone together.

"I'm sorry," Trevor said, his voice just barely a whisper. Zahir could smell the wine on his breath. "I just had to know what was going on."

Zahir paused, not sure if he should tell Trevor the truth. On one hand, Trevor was one of his guards and Ren would probably tell him, anyway. But on the other... Zahir's trust was lacking.

Trevor took a step back and shook his head. "I can't believe you would think so low of me."

"Wait," Zahir said as Trevor began to turn around. "It's not that I don't trust you..."

"Then what is it?"

Zahir opened his mouth to speak but closed it after a few seconds. He didn't know what exactly it was. Trevor was someone who kept his deepest secret close to his heart and hadn't told a soul. Zahir had absolutely no reason not to trust him. But something in the back of his mind convinced him to tell no one what was going on. Especially because Rodrick, one of his closest friends, was suddenly missing after discovering the rebel symbol. He didn't want to risk Trevor's life.

"I can't tell you," Zahir said, sighing. "Please, you just have to trust me."

Trevor shook his head and walked back to the party. Before he opened the door, he turned to look at Zahir. "I have never broken your trust."

With that, he disappeared into the room, the sound from inside becoming loud for only a second while the door was opened.

Zahir leaned his back against the wall and closed his eyes. His heart pounded in his chest and his thoughts swirled around his mind like the wind around the branches of a tree. Zahir put a hand to his forehead, suddenly regretting his decisions. He banged the back of his head on the wall, annoyed with himself. Trevor was one person he never planned on pushing away.

Zahir's stomach grumbled loudly and he reluctantly pushed himself from the wall in search of something to eat. His stomach churned; he hadn't eaten since last night. As he walked towards the kitchen, he passed servants scuttling around with laundry or cleaning supplies. When he bid them all good morning, some bowed, others bid him a good morning as well, and some said nothing. He had never been met with silence and it unnerved him. He wondered if there were servants in the palace who were rebels.

All of the servants knew where every safe room was, in case of a rebel attack. All except for one. Only a handful of people knew the one the royal family used, including the kitchen staff. The entrance was so close to the kitchens that they were told where it was, in case they needed a place to hide immediately. The servants knew every other inch of the palace like the back of their hands. They knew the entrances and exits, the guard rotations, where there were less guards. There was no reason why a servant couldn't be betraying him.

When Zahir walked into the kitchen, he saw a group of three standing in the corner, speaking in hushed voices. They didn't notice Zahir as he stood there, watching them talk. He couldn't hear what they were saying but caught single words from their conversation. Tired. Safe. Rebels.

"Good morning," Zahir said as he made his way towards the dry food cabinet.

The servants nearly jumped out of their skin. One looked at him with wide eyes that Zahir thought could have been out of fear. The group bowed to him before turning back to their conversation. When Zahir caught the words *safe room*, he nearly dropped the dried beef he was holding.

"Please get out," Zahir said, as calmly as he could.

The eldest of the group turned to Zahir and nodded. "Of course, Your Majesty."

As they made to leave the room, Zahir stopped them. "Out of the palace."

"But my king, this is our livelihood," the woman sounded like she was on the verge of tears.

"I hear you speaking of rebels and safe rooms. I want you *out* of my home immediately." Zahir narrowed his eyes at the group who all stared at him in stunned silence. When they didn't move, he spoke again. "Now."

"Yes, Your Majesty," the woman said, bitterness in her tone. As they left, Zahir ripped off a chunk of his dried beef and ate it hurriedly.

If he'd made a mistake in firing them, so be it. It was easier than having traitors in his midst.

266

Chapter Twenty-Two

Mari

When Mari heard what Zahir had done, she nearly slapped him. He'd fired three of the best servants for simply discussing the rebels. While she was on a stroll towards the gardens, she'd seen them walking out with tear-stained faces. When she'd asked what happened, they'd simply told her that Zahir had overheard them talking about the rebel attack and fired them. Mari was fuming; Zahir was supposed to figure out which of his advisors were betraying him, not his staff.

Mari found Zahir outside in the gardens, his back against a tree and his knees tucked up to his chest. He rested his chin on his knees and stared blankly at the grass beneath his feet. Mari stormed up to him and blocked the bright sun that had been shining on his face as she put her hands on her hips.

"Why did you fire those servants?" Mari asked, trying to control her anger.

"They were betraying us," Zahir said, not turning his head to look at Mari. "I heard them talking about the rebels and the safe rooms."

"I spoke to them on their way out; they were talking about it because they are *scared*, Zahir. They nearly lost their lives and were trying to prepare for if it ever happened again." She had apologized profusely to the servants and had asked them to stay, but they refused, saying they had to listen to the king.

Zahir wordlessly stood up until he was towering over Mari and she had to crane her neck to look up into his eyes. "It won't happen again because there are no more rebels in our home."

Mari widened her eyes. "You were supposed to find out which of your advisors were betraying you, not who of your staff. What happened?"

"I spoke with Anya, who made me realize there had to be someone on the inside to tell the rebels where our safe room was," Zahir said, crossing his arms over his chest.

"So, you fired these people because *Anya*, who you've been warning me about since day one, convinced you to change who you were looking for?" Mari asked. None of this made any sense; Zahir never would have listened to Anya if he were in a good headspace.

"I can finally see things clearly, Mari. The people who work in the palace know everything about us and our home. They are the most likely culprits."

"What about the advisor who is feeding information to Anya? Do you no longer care about that?"

"I plan on speaking with each of my advisors once I finish vetting our servants and guards."

"Zahir," Mari said, trying to keep her voice as calm as possible. "There are hundreds of people who work here. That could take several moon cycles."

"Then we will do it," Zahir said. "I don't fear hard work."

"Please, Zahir, just think about what you're doing," Mari nearly begged. She could almost see Zahir slipping through her fingers. If he continued down this path, he would lose sight of everything else: his advisors, the Dual Mage, their relationship. She knew she had to convince him to stop and think for a second, but didn't know how.

"I have thought about it, Mari. Why can't you trust me?" Zahir's eyes searched her face, as if actually looking for her trust.

"Because I don't think this is a good idea," Mari said. She was nearly pleading with Zahir. She could see just how scared he was, but she also could tell he wasn't thinking rationally.

"*You* are not the ruler of Brahn, Mari. I am trying to protect my family. I'm trying to protect you." He ran a hand through his hair and shook his head. "I need a break."

Zahir turned his back to Mari and walked further into the gardens. Mari watched him go, his head down and his strides slow. She could have caught up to him but didn't want to have a conversation that just went in circles. Twice now Zahir had refused to listen to her opinion and it was beginning to frustrate her.

Mari turned on her heel and strode back into the palace. If this were Yu'güe and she were the leader, she knew exactly how she would handle this situation. First, she would look for and discover the Dual Mage. Then, she would help them hide while she figured out how to quell a rebellion. That was the trickier thing. Mari didn't know how to deal with a rebellion. The one point of contention Mari remembered in Yu'güe was regarding food allocation.

One winter, when food stores were very low, the council had been allocating the same amount of food to families of five as to single people. While the singles had plenty to eat, the families were often rationing their food and giving more to the children. When the issue was brought to the council, they immediately reworked the system so that each person was allotted the same amount of food, rather than each household. When that became too difficult to manage, they eventually changed it so that each family was required to store their own food, but the council would have a backup storage in case there wasn't enough for a household. In these situations, Mari remembered the council listening to the issues and making a plan to fix it. But here in Brahn, Mari watched Zahir make decisions without truly thinking how they could impact people.

As Mari thought about the different ways decisions were made in Yu'güe, she realized she had a small sample to look at. If she were going to have a clear picture, she needed to speak with someone who had seen a lot of both Brahn and Yu'güe. That person was Hanan. He had lived in Yu'güe for his entire adolescence and Brahn for most of his adult life.

Mari found a guard who was walking towards her down the hall. She requested the guard to bring Hanan to the palace.

Before she had left the bar the previous night, she'd made sure to get Hanan's address so she could see him again. Mari hadn't intended on seeing him less than a day later, but she told the guard his address and they set off to find him.

Mari waited by the front entrance to the palace for her brother, pacing back and forth. She watched as a large painting of Zahir was hung beside a portrait of Ryker. Zahir's long flowing white hair framed his strong jaw, highlighting the angles of his face. His bright golden eyes looked absolutely radiant in the painting. The royal armor he wore was black and his hair was a stark contrast that looked stunning.

Looking around the rest of the entryway, Mari saw that all the portraits were nearly the same. Between Zahir and Ryker, she deduced that the rest of the portraits were Brahn's kings. They all had the same long white hair, the strong, sharp jaw, and radiant eyes. While the color changed between the men, the shape was extremely similar. Seeing the portraits side by side, Mari saw just how much Zahir looked like Ryker. She hadn't noticed it when Ryker was alive, but they had the exact same face shape. With the hair, they nearly looked identical, save for Ryker's dark brown eyes.

Just as Mari began to look closer at Zahir's grandfather and great-grandfather, the palace doors opened and Hanan walked in beside the guard Mari had sent to retrieve him. His eyes were wide as he took in the extravagant entryway and crystal chandelier hanging above Mari's head. He didn't even seem to register that Mari was standing right there. He looked exactly the same as he had the night before, his tight short sleeved shirt showing off the black ink on his arms and his light brown hair falling haphazardly over his forehead. Mari took in her brother, still in shock that he was truly alive and well.

"Hanan," Mari said, smiling ear to ear. "Thank you for coming."

"Well, when the queen herself requests an audience with me, I can't exactly say no," Hanan said.

Mari laughed as she hugged her brother. She led Hanan through the palace, briefly showing him the library, the training room and titanium gym, and the kitchens on the way to her room. At the titanium gym, Hanan had nearly fainted, feeling weak from the effect. Even Mari had felt that same want to claw out the emptiness in her chest. She hadn't even gone inside, but it still reached her from outside the door.

Finally back in her room, Mari and Hanan settled on the floor, leaning against the bed, with a cup of warm tea in their hands. Mari remembered being six, Hanan twelve, and they would sit against one of their beds after a long hunting trip to warm up with their dinner. Their mother never cared that they ate in their rooms, unless they spilled. Mari felt tears brim her eyes as she remembered those nights with Hanan, laughing until she couldn't breathe.

"What did you want to talk about?" Hanan asked. He sipped his tea and tilted his head at Mari.

Mari took a deep breath and leaned her head against the bed. "I need your opinion on something. You have seen both Brahn and Yu'güe. You've watched Ryker make decisions and you watched our father lead the council. The way our clans do things is so different. I think Zahir is making a bad choice. He

272

is convinced that there is someone inside the palace feeding information to the rebels and that is how they got in here. He fired three servants this morning simply because he overheard them talking about the safe rooms. I think it was reckless of him because he didn't know why they were discussing it. When I asked them, they told me it was because they were scared."

"First things first, Mari, Brahn and Yu'güe are so different. Brahn has thousands of people living in the city, and even more living outside its walls. Yu'güe only has a few hundred, if that. You can't compare the decision-making process of clans that different."

"Why not?" Mari asked. "The same skills would transfer, no matter the size."

"Absolutely not," Hanan said with a laugh. "With hundreds of people, they can know each other. You can see who is struggling and who is well off. With thousands, there is no way that you can know everyone. In Yu'güe, the council structure works because everyone knows everyone. If they had thousands of people, they couldn't possibly listen to every person. Here in Brahn, there are too many people to make decisions that impact everyone the same way."

Mari nodded, understanding what Hanan was trying to say. "Right, but you can still talk to people before relieving them of their duties instead of assuming you know what they are talking about."

"Not necessarily. If you had to choose between a stranger and someone you loved, who would you choose?"

Mari didn't want to answer. The answer was someone she loved. There was no doubt in her mind that she would put those she cared for above those that she didn't know. But she felt horrible to admit it. She was supposed to be selfless and put others above herself; that was the duty of a ruler.

"The person I love," Mari said finally, looking away from Hanan. She could see him nod out of the corner of her eye.

"Zahir was doing what he thought was right to protect his family. You shouldn't fault him for that. Did he make a rash decision? Maybe. But he thought it was the right one. You don't have to agree on every choice."

"Father used to tell me that I was going to be the first person to bring Yu'güe out of its borders in millennia. But the longer I'm here, I don't know how true that is. I tried to convince Zahir to negotiate with the rebels and he slaughtered them instead, which led to dissent. I told him that firing those servants was the wrong decision. But both of his decisions were made because of emotion, not logic. Yu'güe always made decisions based on logic," Mari said.

"You can still make logical decisions, Mari. That isn't going away. One of Yu'güe's faults is that decisions were always made so that everything was fair for everyone. You can't do that in Brahn; you would drive yourself mad," Hanan said. "Listen, I watched Ryker make decisions. I watched him make bad decisions, and good ones too. The one thing I can say is that Brahn's leadership seems to make choices based on what they think is good for the clan as a whole. While not everyone will be happy with that, you can't please everyone."

Mari nodded her head slowly, finally understanding. She had been trying to bring Yu'güe to Brahn. Instead of uprooting their entire system, like she had been suggesting, she had to blend Yu'güe into Brahn. Her job was not to make Brahn like Yu'güe; it was to impart her knowledge, but not force a new political structure.

"I finally understand," Mari said. "Father made me believe that I had to turn Brahn into Yu'güe. But clearly, that isn't going to work."

"Should Zahir have killed all those rebels? Maybe not. But I don't know that negotiating with them would have done anything either," Hanan said, running a hand through his hair.

Just as Mari was about to speak, a knock rapped on the door. When Mari told them to enter, she saw a young servant with a note in his hand. He scurried over to Mari and handed it to her. Once he was out of the room, Mari unfolded the single piece of parchment and read it silently to herself.

Mari,

I hope you are finding life in Brahn to be pleasant. Yu'güe misses your bright spirit and mind. We have heard tales of rebel attacks and assassinations. We hope you are well, despite all that has happened. Please write to us soon, we would like to know you are safe.

The letter wasn't signed, but Mari knew her father's handwriting. The letter wasn't particularly kind or loving, but her father was not known for his kindness. Seeing her father's handwriting ignited anger in Mari. For years, he had made her believe he was a murderous monster. When instead, he was a manipulative one.

He had manipulated every decision for years simply because he made Mari think Hanan had been killed by his own hand. But now, holding this letter in her hands beside Hanan, she wanted nothing more than to destroy it. Mari crumpled the parchment and threw it across the room with all her might. It bounced off the wall and fell to the floor beside the door.

"Wow, someone made you mad," Hanan said, his tone suggesting jest.

"It's from our father," Mari said as she huffed out a breath. "I am absolutely furious. He made me think you were dead, Hanan. He doesn't deserve to know that I'm safe."

"No, he doesn't. Our father is not a good man, Mari. It's the reason I left."

Mari nodded. "I know. And I'm glad you did. I'm so glad you have the life you deserve."

"Me, too," Hanan said, a smile creeping onto his lips.

"Why didn't you come see me after Zahir and I got married?" Mari asked. "You were here in the city."

"Honestly," Hanan began after a pause, "I thought you were going to be mad at me. I thought you would be upset that I left and never looked back."

"I could never be angry with you for that. You needed to leave," Mari said. But she wondered how she would have felt if she hadn't been told he was dead. She wondered if she would have been furious with him for not writing to let her know he was okay. "I'm angry with our father. If I were to purposefully kill someone, it would be him."

Hanan cocked his head. "How do you accidentally kill some-one?"

Mari tore her gaze from Hanan, shame ripping a hole in her chest. "I killed one of the rebels during the invasion. I didn't mean to. I was scared and he was about to kill me. I didn't think I just... reacted."

Hanan was quiet for a long time. He stared at Mari and she refused to look at him. She kept her eyes trained on the cup she had put at her feet like it was the most interesting thing in the world. "I'm glad you're alive."

Mari slowly turned to face Hanan and searched his face for a lie. "I killed someone, Hanan. I will never be allowed back into Yu'güe if they knew."

Hanan nodded his head solemnly. "Do you even want to go back?"

Mari thought about that for a minute. She asked herself what waited for her back in Yu'güe. A manipulative father. A hunting ground in the mountains. Fresh snow on the ground that crunched under her boots. There were no friends who would welcome her home. Her brother was beside her in Brahn. The one person she would want to see was Fahran, the boy she had spent her childhood enamored with. But other than that, there was nothing back home for her.

"No," Mari said. "I don't think I do."

"Well then, it doesn't really matter. You saved your own life, maybe even Zahir's. I think *that* is what matters," Hanan said. "It doesn't change how I see you."

"Thank you," Mari said. Relief washed over her like a tidal wave. She hadn't realized just how anxious she had been about Hanan thinking less of her for breaking the Death Mage's cardinal rule.

The door to Mari's bedroom opened quickly and Zahir walked through, eyes trained on the floor. Mari noticed that his hair was knotted, and his eyes had dark bags beneath them. She could see how his shoulders sagged as he walked and how his feet didn't quite come off the floor.

"Zahir?" Mari asked, standing up quickly.

Zahir lifted his gaze to Mari, but it didn't quite look like he truly saw her. "Hi, Mari. Oh, Hanan, what a nice surprise."

Hanan stood beside Mari and nodded to Zahir. "It's nice to see you again. I should be going." He reached over and hugged Mari. "Good luck."

Hanan shook Zahir's hand on the way out and Mari watched the door shut behind Zahir. As they locked eyes again, they both spoke at the exact same time.

"I'm sorry," they both said.

Mari walked over to Zahir and put her hands on either side of his face.

"Zahir, when was the last time you slept?" Mari asked, more aware of the glassy look in his eyes now that she was closer.

"Not since the night before last," Zahir said, after a brief pause. "I'm not tired."

"Zahir, you need to sleep. Come on, let me get you into bed." Mari reached for Zahir's wrist but only brushed her fingertips along his hand before he jerked back. Mari blinked rapidly at Zahir, confused why he didn't want her touch.

"I am too busy to sleep. I have a meeting with my advisors shortly to discuss my plan for vetting palace employees. You may join me if you wish, but if you're just going to convince me this is a bad idea, then please leave me alone." He ran a hand through his disheveled hair and Mari could see just how stressed he looked.

"If I come with you, will you sleep after this meeting?" Mari asked, hoping to get him to rest. He was going to make no progress if he ran himself into the ground.

"Okay," Zahir said, closing his eyes briefly. "Maybe I do need to rest before investigating further."

"Thank you," Mari said, taking a step closer to Zahir. "May I hug you?"

Zahir pulled Mari into an embrace, resting his chin on top of her head. When Mari snaked her arms around his waist, she could feel him relax into her. His weight shifted so she was almost supporting him as they stood there, wrapped in each other's arms.

"Thank you," Zahir whispered into Mari's hair.

"For what?" Mari asked.

"Taking care of me. I find that sometimes I get so lost in my work that I forget how to live," Zahir said.

"I will always be here to help take care of you," Mari said, a small smile rising on her lips. "I'm on your side, I promise. I just want you to think about your decisions before you make them."

Zahir didn't answer, but Mari could sense his relief in the way he pulled away and kissed Mari's forehead lightly. When he smiled softly at her, she brought her hands up to the sides of his face and pulled him down to her for a light kiss. An electric buzz shot through her body as their lips met and Zahir put a hand on Mari's waist, trailing his fingertips under the hem of her shirt.

Mari blushed wildly and pulled away slowly, suddenly shy from the touch. She didn't want to let go of him, but she desperately wanted to change out of her casual shirt and pants if she was going to a council meeting.

Chapter Twenty-Three

Mari

M ari loved the way Zahir looked in his royal black armor that reflected the bright torch light. The crown on his head pushed wisps of his hair onto his forehead. His dark brown roots were just beginning to show, but not enough to warrant dying his hair again. Mari had stepped into a sweeping red gown that hugged her torso and sprayed out at her hips until it reached the ground. Her tiara rested on top of her head and she used several pins to keep it in place. When she wore her hair down, she realized it moved around too much if she didn't pin it.

"Are you ready for your first council meeting?" Zahir asked, grabbing her hand.

"I think so. What should I be expecting?" Mari squeezed Zahir's fingers as they walked down the halls.

"Arguing and annoyance. I find myself zoned out in a lot of these meetings. They really like to argue," Zahir said with a breathy laugh.

Mari raised her eyebrows. "I take it you don't pay attention, then."

Zahir shrugged, a sly smile pulling up the corners of his mouth. "Sometimes I have my beautiful wife on my mind."

Heat rose in Mari's cheeks when Zahir winked at her. She wanted to laugh; he looked silly when he winked, but she didn't want to offend him. "I didn't realize I was so *distracting*," Mari teased, finally letting the laugh come from her mouth.

"Darling," Zahir said, lowering his voice. "Sometimes—"

Zahir was immediately cut off when they rounded the corner and nearly walked right into Illan. He stood outside the advisor chambers, waiting by the open door. He smiled at Zahir and Mari, waving them closer.

"Mari, I'm glad you could join us," Illan said. "I think you will enjoy your first council meeting."

"I already told her how horrible they are," Zahir said, lowering his voice so no one inside the room could hear.

Illan burst out laughing. "They really are horrible, aren't they?" Illan looked back to Mari as he spoke. "You may never want to come back after this. Our council is a little on edge today."

"Let's get this over with," Zahir said.

The large circular room was bare except for a round table that took up most of the space. Around it, sat nine people in flowing shirts and pants of varying shades of red and gold. Zahir's advisors ranged in genders and ages and reminded Mari of the council back in Yu'güe. There, they had an equal representation of genders and ages to ensure everyone had an advocate on the council. Mari liked that Brahn's council was representative of its people and hoped that Zahir, too, realized that it was a good thing.

Zahir and Mari took their seats at the farthest part of the table, facing the door. Once they were seated in their high-backed wooden chairs, the rest of the room took their own seats. Mari saw a small placard in front of each advisor with their name. She took a minute to read through them as Zahir began their meeting.

"We have a full agenda today. First and foremost, I believe there to be a rebel living or working in our palace. The rebels found our safe room too quickly for it to be a coincidence. I would like us to devise a plan for vetting our personnel.

"Second, there is a rebel sign popping up around the city. It is an 'A' in a circle, and it means two things. One, that people are openly in dissent. Two, they wish Anya to be on the throne. I would like to discuss methods to quell a rebellion in Brahn.

"Lastly, one of you is feeding information to Anya. It needs to stop, *immediately*. You serve me, not my sister. I am your king. Any information that is spoken in this room is confidential. If it happens again, I can guarantee you will not like the outcome," Zahir said, keeping an even tone the whole time.

Mari noticed that when Zahir spoke about the rebel symbol, there were varying reactions. Some seemed surprised, like they had never heard of this before. Others nodded their heads, seemingly aware of the situation. Mari wondered why, if they knew, they hadn't brought the information to Zahir.

One advisor, Demi, stood up. Their short black hair showed off the sharp angles of their face and their dark brown eyes.

"Your Majesty, it would take too long to question every person in this palace. Hundreds of people live or work here."

Zahir nodded his head. "I understand that. However, my family's safety is my top priority. My wife was severely injured during the rebel attack. My father was murdered. Both Princess Anya and Taryn were injured during the fight. I will *not* put their lives in danger again. If that means questioning every single person here, then that is what we will do."

"Sir." An older advisor named Malek stood up, scratching at his salt and pepper hair. "If you want to do this, I suggest starting with certain groups and then narrowing it down based on their answers."

"What about the Dual Mage?" Avery, a young woman with flowing blonde hair, asked as she stood. "We have done nothing to find them and keep them safe from the rebels."

"We are not discussing that today, Avery," Zahir said with a sigh. "We will have a separate meeting to discuss the Dual Mage."

Mari watched as Zahir ran a hand down his face. She could feel his frustration; his advisors were already questioning him, and it hadn't even been five minutes since the start of the meeting.

"What if we split up the interviewing load between the ten of us?" A young man, Yair, stood. "If we divide the work, it will go quicker."

"That is a great idea, Yair." Zahir nodded. "We will gather a list of our personnel and assign each of you a certain number. On to the second task, the rebel symbol. Were any of you aware of the symbol before I mentioned it?"

Two advisors, Marjorie and Dustin, raised their hands shyly. Marjorie's bright red face and wide blue eyes made Mari think that she was embarrassed to admit it. Dustin's blank stare made Mari wonder if he didn't care about the rebels, or even sympathized with them. She wondered why he didn't feel shame for keeping the information from Zahir.

"Why was I not informed?" Zahir asked, leaning forward in his seat to lean his elbows on the table.

"Your Highness," Dustin said as he stood. His voice was smooth, and it drawled out of his mouth in a carefree way. "I do sincerely apologize for not telling you. I thought the guard who told me would inform you."

"Who did you speak to?" Zahir asked, scrunching his eyebrows in.

As the man took a breath to speak once again, the doors to the meeting hall burst open, hitting the walls with a loud bang. Zahir immediately jumped out of his seat, conjuring a flame in the palm of his hand as Mari's eyes landed on the group of men who entered the room, hoods obscuring their eyes and blades in their hands. Mari nearly jumped out of her skin when she realized that the rebels had entered the palace, again.

"Guards!" Zahir screamed, pulling Mari to her feet.

"There's no use princeling," one of the men spoke, his voice rough like sand. "We have your guards otherwise occupied."

"What do you want?" Illan demanded, pulling a sword from his waist that Mari hadn't noticed before.

A loud crack of thunder shook the palace, and Mari felt Zahir tense beside her.

"Him." The man pointed his blade towards Zahir, level with his chest. "We want him."

Zahir launched a ball of fire towards the invaders, spraying flames in every direction once it hit the ground. Fire engulfed the dark curtains lining the walls, illuminating the room to new levels. Mari's heart thrummed in her chest as the heat smacked her in the face. The invaders dodged expertly, the twelve men scattering. The advisors stood, lighting their hands and arms in flames to fight.

Mari wobbled on her feet as she watched the rebels wield titanium weapons that glinted in the torch light. The familiar panic of being around titanium made her legs weak as she raised her hands to call spirits to her aid. She pulled out the largest animals in her arsenal: two elk, and a bear. Mari swept her hand out in front of her, moving her wrist in tight circles to control the souls' movements. They charged towards the rebels, who were frozen for a second in what Mari hoped was fear.

Lightning flashed through the windows as thunder rumbled overhead. The elk soul ran through one of the invaders, turning his body to an icy blue while one of the advisors surged forward and tackled them to the ground, igniting their body in flames.

Mari again raised her arms, calling another set of souls to her aid. She had to close her eyes as her heart dropped from her chest when the rebel that she killed in the invasion manifested in the room. She couldn't watch as he ran forward to attack his comrades. The decision to kill that rebel still weighed heavy on her heart; seeing his face again made the guilt rise in her chest all over again.

Another crack of lightning illuminated the room and Mari saw Zahir shut his eyes momentarily. Mari squeezed his arm, knowing how much more terrifying this had become for him. He opened his eyes again and raised the walls of fire around them.

Peering through the flames, Mari scanned the room, hoping to find someone who had lost their dagger to the fight. While no one had lost a weapon, three men had lost their lives, blood pooling on the floor around them.

"Call off the ring of fire."

Zahir looked at her sideways. "It's protecting us from the rebels."

"Just do it!" Mari demanded. While she was still shaky with her swordsmanship, she no longer would be afraid. These rebels were nothing compared to her and Zahir's magic. They were able to escape alive the last time and Mari was determined to have the same fate this time.

Zahir ended his concentration on the protective circle around them and Mari scrambled over the table, racing forward. She struggled in her dress and planned to cut some room in the skirt as soon as she had a weapon. She jumped off the table and was immediately met by a rebel who swiped his sword at her head. Mari heard Zahir yell her name as she dodged, the blade narrowly missing her throat.

Mari landed a punch to the man's groin, causing him to double over, and she stood and brought her knee up, connecting with his face, the crack resonating throughout the room. The man fell to a knee and swiped the blade at Mari's ankles, but she had already moved around him. She needed to get a blade, and quickly.

As Mari reached down to unbuckle a dagger from one of the older man's belts, she was pulled up by her hair and lost her grip on the blade. It clattered to the ground as her head was yanked backwards and she saw the face of an invader, smiling wickedly at her. Mari felt an arm wrap around her chest, pinning her arms above the elbow, and another swipe a knife against her throat lightly. She immediately stopped moving as the knife came to a stop. A hollowness began to fill her chest and black smoke furled up in front of her face. She silently cursed; her magic was gone, and she was defenseless. She watched as the souls dissipated, vanishing into thin air. Mari couldn't feel them come back into her, and she hoped they would be there again.

"Mari!" Zahir and Illan both screamed, making a run for her.

The assailant pressed the knife into Mari's throat, drawing a little bit of blood. "I wouldn't get any closer if I were you."

Zahir and Illan came to a stop, eyes darting between Mari and the cloaked man. Zahir brought one hand back, igniting it in flames. The other held a small ball of fire hovering just above the heel of his hand. Illan wielded his sword diagonally across his body in a defensive position.

"Let her go," Zahir growled, his voice deep.

The assailant laughed. "I don't think I will." He pulled Mari closer to his body and she let out a little squeak in fear.

Mari's heart raced and she began to panic. The cut on her throat dripped blood down the front of her dress, soaking the skin beneath. She didn't know how deep the cut was, but she could tell it was more than just a scratch. The pain was becoming increasingly sharp.

"What do you want from me?" There was a hint of panic in Zahir's voice. He kept his eyes locked with Mari's.

"We want you to turn over the Dual Mage," the man seethed, his words dripping like acid.

"I don't know who they are!" Zahir yelled. "I have no information on the Dual Mage's location."

The man's grip tightened on Mari as she tried to step on his foot. He slid his foot away expertly and sliced a cut down Mari's cheek before plunging the dagger into her shoulder. Mari cursed in pain as the man trapped her foot behind his own.

"Mari!" Zahir screamed and ignited his entire body in flames. "If you don't let her go, I swear you will regret it." His voice was a low growl, and his eyes were burning with anger.

"You know more than you are letting us in on. You *must* know of the Dual Mage running amuck in your own city, disrupting the lives of your people."

"If there were someone disrupting the livelihood of my people, they would have been dealt with."

The man laughed. "You didn't deal with us. You didn't even consider us a credible threat. I think your little wife here would call us a threat, wouldn't you, darling?"

Mari nodded slowly, letting the man believe whatever he wanted. She hoped that if she complied, he would let go of her.

"Fine. You want me? Take me," Zahir said, quelling the flames in his hands and putting them down by his side. "Just let her go."

"No!" The animalistic scream ripped through Mari's throat. "Zahir, you can't do this."

The assailant laughed. "The lengths a man will go to for love. I think this one will make a good pet." He dragged his fingertips down Mari's cheek, and she ground her teeth to keep from jerking away.

"Take me. I will give myself up if you just let her go."

"Zahir, you can't." Mari was in tears at the thought of Zahir being taken by these men.

"Commander, lower your sword." The hooded man stared at Illan who, after a minute, lowered his sword to his waist.

Two men came behind Illan and Zahir, binding their wrists behind their backs with titanium chains. Zahir winced as the chain ripped into his skin, hindering his magic. Illan seemed unfazed by the chains; his eyes were locked on Zahir as he was thrust to his knees. The men were pushed face down onto the ground, their ankles bound together as well.

"We will bring her back when you give us some *useful* information." The man pulled Mari backwards, the knife still touching her throat.

"No! Mari!" Zahir screamed, lifting his head just enough to see Mari being dragged from the room.

As soon as Mari lost sight of Zahir and Illan, she was gagged, blindfolded, and dragged out of the castle by two people holding her wrists and ankles. She tried to thrash but was met with kicks to her sides when her movements hindered their walking. Before Mari was tossed into the back of a carriage, metal chains were wrapped around her wrists and the dagger was pulled out of her shoulder. Mari sucked in a breath, trying to hold back a cry of pain as the wound was opened.

As the carriage drove off, all Mari knew was that she was heading away from the palace at an ungodly speed. Mari sent a prayer up to the Gods, asking for her and Zahir's safety in this mess. The smooth road of the city soon turned into the bumpy road of the countryside. As the carriage bumped over rocks, Mari rolled all over the place, unable to steady herself with her wrists bound. The pain in her shoulder was unbearable. Every time Mari was jostled around, she let out a whimper. She could feel the blood on her shoulder from the dampness she felt growing on her gown.

As she became nauseous, the carriage came to a halt and Mari was dragged outside through grass that swept around her ankles. Her gown was heavy as she was marched across the grass and warm air brushed across her face, pulling a few strands of hair off her sweating face. She could hear the sounds of metal clanking and horses whinnying, but she couldn't hear any of the usual noises of the city, like the carriages riding on the cobblestone streets.

Mari heard the unmistakable sound of a door creaking open, then she was forced inside, tripping over the entryway, where she crashed to the ground. She couldn't put her bound arms out in front of her to break her fall, so her head slammed into the ground. Nausea ripped through her as the blinding pain made her head swim. The wound in her shoulder screamed in pain as Mari rolled onto her side, and a heavy pair of boots walked up beside her. She let out a scream as one of those boots slammed down onto her left hand. The unmistakable sound of cracking bone resonated loudly in Mari's ears and pain shot through her hand and up her arm.

Two hands lifted her up under her arms and led her further from the door. She was thrown haphazardly down to the ground and the loud slam of a door made Mari think she was alone. She lay on her stomach and used her elbows to push herself up onto her knees. Scooting over to the wall, she rubbed her face along it, shifting the blindfold up onto her forehead. Next, she pulled her hands up to her face and tugged the gag down around her neck with her unbroken right hand. When she looked at her left, she cringed, seeing for the first time the way her fingers sat at obscure angles and bones protruded from her thumb. Hot tears fell down her face and she could taste the blood they mixed with on the way down.

The room she was in was completely bare, save for a bowl of water and a single piece of bread. Mari shifted so that she was sitting with her legs out in front of her, hands in her lap, and head back against the wall. She stared at the closed door, willing it to open. When it stayed shut, her tears continued to fall freely down her cheeks. The hope that Zahir would find her was dissipating. She didn't know how he could possibly find her when she had been carried out of the city in the middle of a storm.

Chapter Twenty-Four

Zahir

Zahir stared at the table in front of him, watching his fingers drum on the wood. He sat back in his chair in the advisor chambers, blocking out the surrounding arguments. It had been a week since Mari had been taken. Every night, Zahir lay awake, watching the ceiling and hoping to the Gods that Mari was okay. He hadn't slept for more than a few hours each night and was sick with worry about what they might be doing to her.

Every day, Zahir looked at maps for potential hiding spots. He had taken soldiers out with him to scour the area outside the city walls and had searched high and low for where the rebels may have been hiding her. But he hadn't found her... yet. There was nothing, *nothing*, that would have him stop searching for her.

While he sat and listened to his advisors scream at each other, and at him, to address the public about the Dual Mage concerns, Zahir thought about Mari. He thought about the fear on her face when she was cut with her assailant's blade. He heard her screams as she was dragged out of his sight. These were the things that he saw late into the night when he closed his eyes.

"Your Majesty," Alex, one of Zahir's most influential advisors, raised her voice. "Are you even paying attention to us?"

He slowly sat forward in his seat and leaned his elbows on the table. "No, I am not. While you sit here discussing what we should do about a Dual Mage, who I'm not sure even exists, I am worrying about *my wife*, your queen, who is in the clutches of the Rebels. If you truthfully think that I should be more concerned about another person who I am not *in love with*, then by all means, keep fucking talking." Zahir's words came out in a growl, the anger and fear he had been dealing with silently for the past week finally boiling over.

Zahir was met with silence. He stood up abruptly, the chair scraping loudly against the floor, and stormed from the room. He heard Illan stand up and run behind him but Zahir knew if he didn't get out of there, he would have said things he truthfully regretted.

"Zahir," Illan said breathlessly as he caught up. "Where are you going?"

"To find Mari." Zahir rushed forward, needing to get to his horse immediately. He wasn't going to delay any longer. He would find her.

Illan grabbed Zahir's elbow, spinning him around. He placed his hands on either of Zahir's shoulders to look him in the eyes. "Not without me. Let's go rally your troops."

Zahir felt tears prick the corners of his eyes. "Thank you, Uncle."

Illan and Zahir ran through the halls of the palace to find their soldiers. They burst into their quarters, pulling them from their card game and asking if they were ready to rescue the queen. Without hesitation, every single soldier stood and suited up in shining black armor, swords hanging from their hips. Zahir had never been so thankful to have such loyal soldiers at his disposal.

Illan pulled out a map as they walked towards the stables, marking with circles any places they had yet to look. One location, at the base of the mountains far to the east, was where Illan wanted to go. He thought the mountains would provide shelter and there was rumor that there were caves beneath them, which would be perfect for hiding. Zahir had doubts about these caves. He did not believe that getting lost in a labyrinth would be the best method for finding Mari. He didn't want to waste another day with a poor search.

Zahir pointed to a section on the map to the south of the city. There were no natural barriers: no sea, no mountains. It would not be the best place to hide. However, if Zahir were trying to hide, he would go where no one would think of. No one in their right mind would think the Gladina Rebels were hiding in plain sight, but after a week of worry and no sleep, there was a low chance that Zahir was thinking straight. So, he listened to his gut. To the south was where they would search.

As Zahir mounted his horse, he had the overwhelming urge to throw up. Instead, he swallowed the feeling and surged forward. His nerves had gotten the better of him before, but there would be nothing that would stand in his way now. So, he locked his anxiety in the deepest part of his chest and threw the key away.

Nothing would stop him from finding Mari.

Zahir's soldiers followed behind and the deafening sound of hooves on the cobblestone street filled his ears. People whipped their heads to watch as he flew past, his hair blowing wildly in the wind. Some of his citizens waved and cheered, thanking him for searching for their queen and for being such a loyal king. Guilt washed over Zahir as he realized that he was being selfish. He wasn't being a loyal king. He was not doing his duty to his people. Instead of searching for a Dual Mage, who may or may not exist, he was rescuing his wife. If he were truly doing his duty to his people, he would have someone searching for this Dual Mage.

Zahir ignored his citizens as he raced through the streets, the windows of shops blurring together as he passed. The clop of his horse's hooves on the stone soothed his aching heart. The crisp warm breeze blew his hair back over his shoulders, leaving it flying behind him. His dark brown roots were showing at the top of his head. When Zahir had tried to dye them, he thought only of Mari's fingers in his hair. He had dropped the dye on the ground as he pictured her, not running her fingers through his hair, but broken and bloody at the hands of the rebels. He didn't know what they were doing to her, but he prayed to the Gods she was alive.

The wind quelled the sweat running on his forehead, washing him with a coolness he ached for. The grass outside the city's walls was a bright green, the same color as Mari's eyes.

He pictured those beautiful eyes, wide with terror as she was manhandled by the rebels. Zahir closed his eyes, trying to push the image away and instead thought of her shining smile that crinkled the skin at the corners of her eyes after they kissed. He remembered the anger in her eyes every time they disagreed; he would take that wrath any day over the sheer terror.

Zahir raced through the trees, not bothering to wait for the soldiers who followed him. Stealing a glance over his shoulder, he saw they were at least a quarter mile behind, and drifting even further back. Instead of slowing his pace, Zahir kicked at the sides of his horse, willing her to move quicker. His horse responded with a snort and pushed her legs faster, sending Zahir to his feet. He crouched over his stallion, thighs burning, as he weaved through the bright orange trees.

It was Zahir's favorite time of year, the leaves on the trees beginning to shift to varying shades of orange and red. As a child, Zahir had loved to step on the leaves that fell to the ground, hearing their loud crunch beneath his toes. But now, as his horse crunched the leaves beneath her hooves, all Zahir could hear was the breaking of bones... Mari's bones.

Zahir clenched his jaw, the need to find his wife overwhelming him. As he rode his horse further away from the city, the loud noises he was so accustomed to petered out to an eerie silence. While he normally treasured the silence, at this moment he was only wanting to hear the noises of the Gladina Rebels. He focused on the noises between the howling of the wind: the croaking of frogs, the chirping of birds and hooting of large owls, and the monotone buzzing of insects that swarmed his face.

Usually, he would have swatted the bugs away, but he let them buzz around his face like he was a flower, drawing them in.

Suddenly, a hardy laugh made Zahir tug on the reins of his horse. His mare came to a sharp stop, nearly throwing Zahir over her head. He brushed her mane softly to soothe her as he listened for the sound again. The rustling leaves were just quiet enough for a voice to come through the trees. Zahir snapped his head to the right where he had heard the sound and dismounted. After tying his horse to a tree, he crept along the tree line and into the forest in search of that voice. Clasping his hand around the silver hilt of his sword to keep the blade from clanging against his leg, he walked deeper into the forest.

Just as Zahir ducked behind a tree, he saw a clearing. Peeking out from his hiding spot, he saw fifty men around a small cottage. He was shocked to realize they hadn't heard him on the horse when he could hear them so clearly. They wore the hoods of the rebels and carried weapons at their waists. They walked around, completing various tasks like building fires or skinning animals, or just sitting around talking. Laughter and conversations floated up to where Zahir perched, boiling the anger in his blood even more. These men were *enjoying themselves* while Mari was suffering.

Zahir's eyes landed on the cottage. The windows were all dark and it looked like it couldn't be inhabited by all the men. It was very small, probably only occupying their leader. Zahir's heart stopped, hoping Mari was somewhere in that house.

"Are those the rebels?" Illan asked as he crouched beside Zahir, his hand gripping the dark brown bark of the tree. Zahir wasn't sure how Illan had caught up so quickly and wondered just how long he had been crouching there.

"Yes," Zahir breathed, not taking his eyes off the cottage.

"What would you like to do?" Illan looked behind him and gestured for the rest of the soldiers to come over quietly.

As Zahir's men silently took up positions behind various trees, looking to their leader, Zahir took several long slow breaths. "We attack." Zahir stood and slowly crept along the tree line. There was approximately one hundred yards between where he walked, and the cottage and his twenty men were outnumbered by more than two to one. If he and Mari could take down several of these rebels, then his twenty soldiers could manage fifty.

Zahir's foot landed on a twig, snapping it in half, the sound loud in his ears. The rebels immediately stopped what they were doing and turned their heads in Zahir's direction. He cursed loudly and stepped out from behind the trees. He slowly let the anger course through his veins and ignited every inch of his body. As he staggered through the grass, leaving a blazing fire in his wake, several of the rebels took a hesitant step back.

"Where the hell is she?" Zahir roared as he clapped his hands together and sent a cone of fire at the rebels. Some were quick enough to dodge the fire, but two rebels got caught in the flames, their screams loud in the silent clearing. "Where is my wife?"

If there had ever been any room for negotiations, it was long gone. The rebels wielded their titanium chains and daggers as they charged at Zahir. Just as they surged forward, Zahir's men revealed themselves, igniting their bodies in flame. The rebels' steps faltered for just a second before they continued on, screams rippling through their chests.

Zahir's soldiers lined up beside him before all twenty of them, simultaneously, raised their arms and slammed them down, sending a tidal wave of bright orange flame at their attackers. Rebels dove every which way, trying to avoid the burning attack. As some of them got caught in it, their cries of pain bore into Zahir's eardrums. Zahir shut out their sobs as he marched forward, grabbing hold of whatever piece of a rebel he could get and turning them into a human torch. Their skin charred under his fingers, but he refused to let go, even when they swung at him with their blades. He didn't care if they were mortals and weak in comparison; they were his enemies who deserved their deaths for what they had done to his family.

A blade sliced at his hair and Zahir watched as a few strands of his white hair fell to the ground. Eyes ablaze, Zahir whipped around and tackled his assailant to the ground, their blade scattering. Just as he was about to choke his attacker, Illan thrust a blade into the man's throat, blood spurting onto Zahir's face. Illan pulled Zahir off the man and pushed him forward towards the cottage, yelling at him to find Mari.

Zahir lurched forward and slowly fought his way to the cottage. As he burned man after man, the guilt in his chest ripped open and he couldn't contain the white-hot tears that forced their way down his face. The scent of charring flesh was so strong that Zahir gagged with every breath he took. Looking over his shoulder, he saw black smoke furling into the sky, obscuring the tree line.

The door to the cottage was wide open when he got there. Zahir raced in, feet slamming on the wooden floor. Immediately to his left was a small kitchen that was uninhabited, but plates of cooked meat sat untouched on the table. Half-drunk mugs of wine were standing alone on the table next to yellow stained napkins. To his left, Zahir saw a small room with nothing but a fireplace and several chairs. In the center of the floor was a large dark red stain that had to be blood. Bile rose in Zahir's throat as he realized that could be Mari's blood on the floor.

Just as Zahir was going to surge forward, a familiar face walked out from a side room, clad in armor. Zahir sucked in a breath as he was met by Rodrick, his longtime friend and palace guard who had gone missing. Rodrick's eyes burned with anger as he stared down Zahir.

"Rodrick, what are you doing here?" Zahir asked, shaking his head. He couldn't believe that Rodrick could have betrayed him this way.

Rodrick brought flames to his palms. "Leave, Zahir. We need information on the Dual Mage."

"It was you," Zahir said, his voice dropping low. He didn't hesitate before throwing a ball of flames.

Rodrick dodged them expertly and unsheathed his sword. He surged forward, but Zahir was able to side-step in time to draw his own blade. Without a second thought, Zahir stabbed Rodrick in the back of his leg, piercing his entire thigh. Rodrick screamed in pain as he fell to his knees.

"I don't want to do this," Zahir said, pulling his sword from Rodrick's leg and walking around to face him.

"Do it, you coward," Rodrick spat.

Zahir leveled his sword with Rodrick's neck and hesitated for just a second before thrusting his sword through Rodrick's throat. When Zahir pulled it out, he watched Rodrick fall forward, clutching his neck. Zahir let the tears of guilt fall from his eyes, knowing the repercussions of what he had just done. Above all, Zahir was incredibly hurt that Rodrick would ever have betrayed him like that. There was no way Rodrick could have worked alone, though. He wouldn't have known they were having a council meeting if he wasn't in the palace. So, there was still at least one person left who was responsible for this.

At the end of the hallway was a single door that had a light shining through the crack above the ground. Zahir reached his hand out and grasped the handle just to realize it was locked. He took a couple of steps back before kicking as hard as he could at the corner of the door. It splintered where it sat against the wall and swung slowly open. On the floor of the small, empty room was Mari.

Zahir's heart lurched in his chest as he surged toward her. It was then he saw how bloody and bruised she was. The bones protruding out of her hands were covered in dried blood. Her hands were so swollen they were nearly unrecognizable. Bruises lined her face in varying shades of blue and purple and her shoulder was caked in dark red blood from the dagger wound. Zahir bent down on one knee and put his hand on Mari's face.

"What did they do to you?" Zahir whispered, running his fingers along her cheek and neck. He traced the large bruises lightly with his fingertips.

Mari's eyes opened to slits and stared at Zahir, as if she didn't even recognize him. Her plea to not hurt her was barely audible over the thrumming of Zahir's heart. He slowly slid his arms under her and scooped her up, one hand beneath her knees and the other pulling her torso into his chest. The bodice of her dress shifted around Mari's body slightly as he carried her, and he wondered how much weight she could have lost in just a few days. She must have been starving.

"Are you here to save me?" Mari asked with a small smile on her lips.

"Yes, darling. I will always save you."

"It's like I'm a princess," Mari said.

As Zahir carried her over the threshold of the cottage and back onto the battlefield, he realized the sounds of fighting had stopped. The only noise was the roaring of the fire that was still burning through the grass.

Zahir felt a ripple of energy run through him as a vibrant green light encased his hands. He nearly dropped Mari to the ground as her body, too, was covered by the light. Zahir recognized the familiar feeling of magic coursing through his arms, electrocuting him, and sending shivers down his spine. His heart raced and he nearly stopped breathing as the green light flooded Mari's body and her pale face regained its pinkness. He watched as the bones in her hand were shifted to a normal angle until they no longer protruded from the skin.

As Illan locked eyes with Zahir, the horrifying truth washed over him: *he was the Dual Mage.*

CHAPTER TWENTY-FIVE

ZAHIR

Z ahir rocked back and forth on his heels, watching Mari sleep. In the three days since he had found her, he had refused to leave her side. The stubble growing on his chin was so itchy that he'd almost left to shave but didn't want Mari to be alone when she woke. His hair was heavy with grease and he had kept it in a bun at the back of his head for over a day now. Servants brought him meals, but he was barely able to pick at the meat and bread they brought. His stomach churned with anxiety as he waited for his wife to wake up.

When he'd brought her to the medical wing of the palace, Amí couldn't find anything wrong with her, other than the fact she had not been well nourished. She had inspected Mari for bruises, breaks, and scrapes, but came up with nothing. Zahir wrung his hands together and paced back and forth, knowing that *he* was the reason why Mari wasn't broken.

Even as he stood there, watching her sleep, he still pictured her with blood and bones protruding from her skin. He saw her near-lifeless form on the floor of that house, shivering and delirious. She hadn't even realized it was he who rescued her. He wondered what she thought happened, or if she even remembered any of it. While he couldn't get the vision of her out of his mind, he prayed to the Gods that she had no memory of her kidnapping. He prayed that she would be okay, physically and mentally, because he never would be okay again. He would see her on death's door every time he closed his eyes. It was half the reason he had barely slept.

The other reason was because of the horrifying truth. He was a Fire and Life Mage. He was the one the rebels were looking for. He was the reason Mari was kidnapped. He truly believed it was his fault that Mari had been taken. If only he had known...

Zahir rubbed his eyes with the heels of his palms and stars danced across his vision. His eyelids were heavy, beginning to droop the longer he stood in the room. He had kept Mari in the medical wing so she had access to anything she may need when she woke. When Zahir pulled his hands away from his eyes, he saw his mother walking into the room with a folded piece of parchment in her hands.

"How is Mari doing?" Maura asked. Her sad eyes went to Mari and she sighed.

"What are you doing here?" Zahir asked. He hadn't seen his mother since he'd found out the truth about his magic and wanted nothing to do with her at the moment. As much as he blamed himself, he blamed his parents tenfold.

"I wanted to give you this," she said, holding out the parchment. "It's a letter from your father. I was supposed to give it to you on your coronation day, but you had enough going on that you didn't need the added stress."

Zahir reached out and took the letter from his mother. It was an old and yellowed piece of parchment that curled at the edges. He looked down at it, folded in thirds, and wanted to rip it in half. He didn't want a letter from his father. He wanted an explanation.

"Why didn't you tell me what I was?" Zahir asked, nearly spitting out the words.

"Read the letter," Maura said. "It will explain everything."

Maura turned to leave and Zahir watched her go, the door shutting silently behind her. He took a deep breath before sitting down in a chair, unfolding the letter slowly. The parchment crackled as he moved it and he was suddenly afraid it would rip in his hands.

Happy Coronation Day, King Zahir.

If you are reading this, I have presumably passed on. But knowing how my memory has been lately, maybe I am still here. You will have to let me know.

Before you were born, your mother and I prayed for a boy. Anya was a handful, and we wondered if a boy would be easier. In fact, you were worse than even she was. But we loved you all the same.

You were born not to Maura, but to another woman, Zena, from Lovíth. I wanted a son who would be a powerful king. I wanted a son who would break the divides between the clans.

Our lives have been separated for too long. We live in fear of Morana, someone who ruined the Dual Mage legacy. The first King of Brahn was a Fire and Life Mage; we wanted you to be like him. We wanted you to break the divide.

We tell you this on your coronation day so you can begin your reign on a clean slate. So, you know the truths behind me and my rule. To rule, you need to learn from your past kings.

You, the first Dual Mage in millennia, will break down walls and forge new alliances. You will help create a new world and new beginnings. And I wish I could be there to see it.

We tell you this now because Dual Mages, if they have not mastered their magic, by the time they turn thirty, will die. I tell you this, not to scare you, but to motivate you to learn to use the Life Magic that runs in your blood. The Life Mages are expecting you before your thirtieth birthday. I write this letter while you are twenty-two. I hope this gets to you in time. Otherwise, I would have given it to you in four years' time from now.

Remember Zahir, you are strong. You are wise. You are a Dual Mage.

-Father

Zahir didn't realize he had been crying. He wasn't sure when it had started, but now that the hot tears were dotting the page in his hands, he pulled it away from his face. Zahir put a hand over his eyes and let the sobs come. There were so many reasons that he was crying: he missed his father, he was angry that no one had told him what he was, and he was sad that this burden fell on his shoulders. If he had gotten this letter on his coronation day, the trouble with the rebels would have been over and done with.

It would have been over with because he would have easily given his life if it meant saving those he loved.

Zahir desperately needed to know why his mother had waited to give him this letter. She had known about the rebels and their goals. If only she had given it to him earlier...

Zahir wasn't sure whether he was angrier at his father, for not telling him sooner, or his mother, for not giving him this letter when she was supposed to. He would have given *anything* to have gotten this letter on his coronation day. It would have changed so many things. If he had known even before the first rebel attack, he could have saved his father. But saving his father meant dying in his place.

If Zahir had died in his father's place, he never would have gotten to know Mari like he had. His heart dropped to the floor, thinking about the pain it would have caused Mari if he'd died. Or the pain it would have caused Roan and Illan. Even his mother and father. Zahir wondered if his father would have felt as guilty as Zahir did, knowing something could have been done.

CHAPTER TWENTY-SIX

MARI

M ari fell in and out of consciousness for hours. Noises would wake her up, but a steady silence would push her back into a dreamless sleep. The sounds of metal clanging woke her with a start, but it was only seconds before she was pulled back into unconsciousness. She imagined Zahir sitting beside her. She could hear his voice in her mind, telling her she was going to be okay. He would whisper that he was there and that she was safe. But she knew it was all a dream for she was trapped in titanium chains on the floor. She didn't realize that the pain in her back was gone and that she could move her fingers.

The only thing that woke Mari after four days, was Zahir rubbing his thumb across the back of her hand. She groaned and rolled over, her head pounding.

"Mari?" Zahir's voice was quiet, as if he were unsure if she were awake.

"Not now Zahir," Mari grumbled, throwing a hand over her eyes. As soon as her hand splayed across her face, she realized that she was not laying in a ball on the floor but was in a bed under a blanket. Mari immediately shot up her eyes landing on a very worried looking Zahir. "Zahir! Oh, my Gods."

A huge smile spread across his lips. "How are you feeling, darling?"

"Nauseous." Mari put a hand to her mouth. "Zahir I need something to throw up into."

Zahir immediately passed her a bucket, just in time for her to empty the contents of her stomach. Nothing besides water landed in the bucket, but Mari felt instantly better. Zahir had a wet cloth already on her knee to wipe her face with and she lifted it to her mouth and gingerly wiped it clean.

"I apologize that you had to see that."

"That's nothing. You threw up in my lap on the ride through the city."

Mari gawked at Zahir. "No, I didn't."

Zahir nodded his head slowly. "You did. Right on my crotch. I had to burn the whole outfit."

"Gods, I'm so sorry." Mari laid her head back down on the pillow, casting the bucket to the floor. "My head hurts."

"You haven't had any food in a week, maybe longer. They've been injecting sugar water, and regular water, into your system to keep you from dying. You were out for a long time, Mari."

"How long was I gone?" She wasn't entirely sure she wanted to know the answer, but she had to ask.

Zahir looked away before answering, as if he were ashamed. "Seven days."

The impact hit her like an avalanche. Seven days. She had been held captive for seven days.

"Wow."

"Do you remember anything?"

Mari shook her head. "Not much after the first couple of days. I just remember being cold. I was always so cold."

"Did they feed you?"

"I think I had bread and water. But not often. I was always so hungry." Mari looked up at the ceiling. "Can I have something to eat?"

"I'll get Amí." Zahir stood from the bed and walked to the door, running his hands through his hair.

Mari tried to sit up on her own but felt immediately dizzy, so she settled into the pillows, breathing through her mouth so she wouldn't throw up again. Her head swam and her stomach growled loudly. She racked her brain, trying to remember what had happened to her, but no memories came to the surface.

A few minutes passed before Zahir led Amí through the door. Mari was glad to see the old woman who had cared for her after the first rebel attack.

"Hello, my Queen." Amí dipped into a shallow bow. "How are you feeling?"

"Hungry. And dizzy." Mari forced out a smile, but she figured it came out more like a grimace.

"Do you want to try a little bit of bread?"

Mari nodded eagerly. "Please. And maybe some tea?"

"No. Bread and water. We can try tea later on if you keep this down." Amí retrieved a tray from outside that held a single slice of bread and a large cup of water. She placed it on the bed before helping Mari sit up with her back against the headboard.

Placing the tray on her lap, Amí instructed Mari to nibble on the bread and take small sips of the water until it was done. She warned Mari that if she ate too fast, she would feel ill again.

Mari took several small nibbles, and sips of water, waiting for it to settle in her stomach before trying again. It took her longer than it ever had to finish a single piece of bread and a cup of water. When she was done, all she wanted was more food.

"I will bring you more." Amí turned to Zahir and pointed a finger at him. "Don't let her eat it for an hour. I don't care if you are king; if you let her eat it, I *will* scold you."

Zahir held his hands up in defeat. "You know I will always listen to you, Amí."

"Maybe not when you have such a beautiful woman in your bed." Ami gave him an offhanded wave as she left the room with the tray.

Zahir made his way over to the bed and sat beside Mari, grabbing her hand in his. "I was so worried about you."

"What happened while I was gone?" Mari asked. "What happened when you found me?"

Zahir took in a deep breath as he began explaining everything she had missed. "Once they took you, every rebel in the castle scattered, leaving carnage in their wake. So many people died, Mari. It took several guards to break Illan and me free of the titanium chains. We tried to follow the carriage they took you away in, but you were too far gone. So Illan and I scoured the city, trying to find any information we could about where you had gone. We even reached out to Hanan and Raf to see if either of them knew anything.

"Once we exhausted all the possibilities in the city, we started looking at the maps of the towns around us. We knew they wouldn't have taken you far because they would want to watch any movement from the palace. So, we looked into any breaks in the mountains and rivers. We searched the woods with the guards for any sign of the rebels. Most days, we came home empty handed."

"Most days?" Mari asked. Her heart was racing as she listened to the story. While Zahir was looking for her, she had been on the brink of death, barely even trying to cling to life.

Zahir took a deep breath before he told her what happened when he found the rebels who took her. How he nearly endangered his soldiers up by stepping on a twig. How he had to hurt the men who took her.

"What did you do to them?" Mari whispered, grabbing Zahir's hands.

Zahir was quiet for a long time. He looked at his thighs as he took deep breaths. "I burned them all."

Mari recoiled, pressing a hand to her mouth as bile rose in the back of her throat. "You burned them alive?"

"Mari," Zahir locked his gaze on Mari's pale face, "I would ignite the world if it meant saving you."

She leaned her head on Zahir's shoulder, picturing the bodies of men burning into the ground by his hand. She could see him,

313

encased in flame, eyes wild, running to her, igniting every man he passed in bright orange flames. Anger rose in her chest, but guilt flooded her throat. Burning to death was a terrible way to die, but she was thankful for Zahir's rescue.

"Then what happened?" Mari squeezed her eyes shut, shutting out the image of Zahir as a vicious murderer.

"I kicked the door down to get to you."

The vague memory of Zahir opening the door came to her mind. "When you picked me up, it felt like everything was better. I actually felt the pain leaving my back and knees. I must've finally stretched out instead of being in a ball."

"Good."

Mari furrowed her eyebrows and pulled her head from Zahir's shoulder, unsure why he was so quiet. "Is there something you're not telling me?"

"We found out who the Dual Mage was when we invaded their hideout."

Mari gasped, her hands flying to her mouth. "How did you find out? Were they part of the rebel group?"

Zahir shook his head. He met Mari's eyes as his head turned to hers. "It's me, Mari. I am the Fire and Life Mage."

Mari stared at Zahir in disbelief, unblinking. "*You* are the Dual Mage?" She laughed. "No, really, who is it?"

Zahir didn't crack a smile. "It really is me, Mari. I'm a Fire and Life Mage."

"How is that even possible?" Mari asked, her eyes starting to go wide.

"My mother is a woman in Lovíth, named Zena. My father wanted me to break the divide between the clans," Zahir said,

"How did you figure this out?"

"When I carried you from the house, my whole body was encased in a green light. It traveled down to your back and knees, where my hands were. I don't know if you remember this, but you seemed to feel better when that happened."

Mari thought back to that day, her memory still hazy. "I vaguely remember seeing some green light, but I thought I was hallucinating."

"It was no hallucination. I think I healed your injuries or took away your pain. I'm honestly not even sure how it works or what happened."

"Zahir, I can't believe you've been alive for twenty-five years and you didn't know." Mari gasped. "We were meant to make a Triad, then."

"Yes, that seems to be the case. I believe my father wanted to create a Triad between all but water magic."

"The Life and Death magics are opposites, though. Couldn't that be dangerous?" Mari asked, her head still not completely comprehending all this information.

"Extremely. A Triad has never been created, at least to our knowledge."

Mari put a hand to her lips. "I just can't believe it. All this time we were fighting against the rebels, they were searching for *you*. Are you going to tell Brahn?"

Zahir shook his head violently. "Absolutely not. I can't risk them knowing."

"Half the army knows, what if this gets out? How will you handle that?"

"I don't know," Zahir said, with a sigh.

"We can handle it with the advisors, then," Mari said.

Sudden sobs overcame Mari and she felt Zahir snake his arms around her waist, pulling her to him. She cried onto his chest for the people who had died. She sobbed for the pain she'd gone through. She wept with the knowledge that she was never truly safe in the palace.

"Zahir," Mari said between sobs, "I was so scared. I don't remember much, but I remember being so godsdamned terrified."

Zahir pulled Mari tighter to his body and kissed her forehead. "It's okay. You're safe now. I'm here and I will *never* let anything like that happen to you ever again."

"We were attacked *twice* in the palace. We aren't safe here. How did the rebels get in?" Mari sniffled and wiped tears from her cheeks.

Zahir was quiet for a long time before he answered. "Rodrick, Reina's fiancé. He betrayed me."

"Why would he do that?"

"I never got an answer." Zahir took a deep breath and cupped Mari's cheek in his hand. "Take all the time you need to digest it all. I can leave you alone, if you wish."

Zahir shifted his weight to stand, but Mari reached out and wrapped a hand around his wrist. "Stay with me."

Zahir slid closer to Mari and pulled her against his chest as he lounged beside her. She leaned her head in the crook of his shoulder snaking an arm around his waist. "I'll always stay with you."

Mari kissed Zahir's hand that was resting on the front of her shoulder. "What are you going to do? Are you going to train with a Life Mage?"

"I can't unless I want the whole world to know I am a Dual Mage." Zahir shook his head, a smile playing at the corners of his mouth.

"Is that really such a bad thing? I mean, you are, realistically, the most powerful mage in our world. You have a connection with two of the Gods who made the world." Mari slid her fingers between Zahir's and played with them distractedly. "I think that would be celebrated."

"The mages of Brahn could question my right to rule, as could those of Lovíth," Zahir said.

"Or they would *worship* you. I don't think they will cast you out because you're different. Because in reality, you have always been different," Mari said, eyes sparkling.

Zahir brushed his lips lightly across the crown of Mari's head. "You might be right. But I can't help but be concerned about what if you're wrong."

"We're going to talk to the council about it. It's all we can really do at this point."

"How can you be so calm about this?"

Mari laughed. "I think I have some pain tonic in my system so I *might* be high."

Zahir laughed uproariously as Illan walked through the door to the infirmary and smiled at the couple.

"How are you feeling, Mari?" he asked, sliding into the room. His white beard had been shaved off and Mari had to blink a few times before she recognized him.

"Your beard is gone!" Mari exclaimed.

Illan let out a laugh. "That it is. This is what happens when you get your magic back after many years and accidentally burn half of it off."

Both Mari and Zahir's eyes went wide as Zahir spoke. "You can use your magic again?"

Illan smiled and brought his hand up to his chest. A small flame erupted in his palm and the biggest smile spread across Zahir's face. "I can hardly believe it either. It has been so long since I could do this."

"I am so happy for you, Illan." Zahir instructed Illan to take a seat. "Do you need something?"

"I want to speak with you both, actually. I was doing some reading on Dual Mages from the old days. There is a lot of great information in our library, which I shouldn't have been surprised about. But I digress. Dual Mages were extremely common back before the clans split. Almost half of the mages in our world had blended magic. They were some of the most powerful mages to exist, able to use both magics at the same time. Life and Fire Mages were able to create living beings from flames. They could use these flame creatures to kill men or hunt for them. It was absolutely incredible."

"Why do you tell me this, Illan? I do not wish to be that powerful. I am terrified of that, actually." Zahir pulled at the hair on the crown of his head, like he did whenever he was nervous.

"I was about to get to my point. There are other stories that are not as... glamorous. There were several mages who didn't know they had immense power until they were alive for many years. As they got older, their magic began to fizzle out. They began to barely be able to do the simplest of magic. It is said that if the secondary ability is left dormant, a mage will lose both magics."

Zahir closed his eyes and hit his head against the wall behind him. "I know."

"What?" Illan asked, shaking his head.

"My father wrote me a letter. He said that if I don't use my Life Magic within the next few years, I will die."

Mari grasped Zahir's hand tightly in hers. "You have to train with the Life Mages."

"How is that going to work?" Zahir opened his eyes and stared at Illan. "I can't leave for Lovíth, and we can't have a Life Mage come live in the palace with the idea of there being someone here who is betraying us."

"We cannot risk you dying, Zahir. You are *King*," Illan said as he rubbed at his forehead. "You know I do not usually give you explicit instructions, but you need to train your life magic."

"I can't." Zahir locked eyes with Illan. "Do you know what that would mean? I would have to leave Brahn. I cannot leave our people."

"If you don't leave now, you will die. And you will leave Brahn *forever*," Mari said, the volume of her voice rising.

Zahir shifted his gaze to Mari. "I am not leaving you here, alone. Not when we don't know if we can trust our staff." When

Illan asked, Zahir explained their theory. "Mari, I can't leave you."

Mari offered him a reassuring smile. "Do you not understand? You could leave me *forever.*"

"No. I will *not* change my mind on this. We cannot risk me leaving when there are so many things up in the air right now." When Mari and Illan began to protest. "Stop. This is the end of the discussion."

"Gods, Zahir! Why are you so stubborn?" Mari yelled just as Roan's head popped into view. Mari immediately covered her mouth with her hands and Illan burst out into raucous laughter.

"Roan!" Zahir's voice was strained as he welcomed his brother. "Come on in, little man."

"Is Mari better yet?" Roan asked, walking closer to the bed. He had on royal armor that matched Zahir's perfectly and a little crown sat on top of his head. His curly hair had grown longer in the past couple of weeks and Mari offered him a smile.

"I am much better, Roan. Come," Mari patted the bed next to her, "sit with us."

Roan excitedly climbed into bed and snuggled up next to Mari, putting his head in her lap. Mari laughed as the crown slid off his head between her legs. "I wanted to tell you about all the new things I learned while you were healing."

"Maybe not right..." Zahir began but Mari cut him off by holding up a finger.

"What did you learn, Roan?" Mari gave Roan a look that encouraged him to speak.

"When I found out that Zahir was special, I started reading some books. I wanted to learn about what he was and what new magic he had. He is the first Fire and Life Mage in ten thousand and thirteen years. He is the first royal family member of Brahn to be a Dual Mage since the first king.

"I read a lot about what will happen if he doesn't use his life magic and I got really scared. If he only uses his fire, he will die. He will die soon and leave me all alone. I know he would never do that, but I just got really scared. So, I read some more. If he uses his life magic, he could extend his life for another hundred years. Dual Mages usually had shorter life spans because of the double levels of magic in their blood, but a Dual Mage with life magic could outlive anyone." Roan kicked his feet in the air as he repeated everything he learned.

"I would never leave you, little man. You can't get rid of me that easily." Zahir reached over and ruffled Roan's hair.

Mari could see the strained expression that now occupied Zahir's face. "Zahir is going to be alive for a long time, Roan. You have nothing to worry about." Even as Mari said the words, she had a hard time believing them. She had no idea that Zahir could die if he lost his magic. She wondered if Zahir had known because his calm expression had confused her.

"I missed you, Mari. I am glad you're home," Roan said. He wrapped his little arms around her knees.

Mari put a hand on Roan's shoulder. "I missed you, too. I'm staying here, don't worry. I won't leave again any time soon."

CHAPTER TWENTY-SEVEN

MARI

I t was the third time in a week that Mari had woken from her sleep, screams ripping from her throat and sweat matting her hair to her neck. Zahir bolted awake each time, ready to fight an intruder threatening their lives. When he realized it was a nightmare, he would wrap her in his arms, tell her it was just a dream and that she was safe. He would wipe the back of her neck and face with a cloth, clearing away the sweat. He would kiss her head and whisper that he was going to protect her, that he would never let them take her again.

But this nightmare wasn't reliving the seven days she'd spent with the rebels. Mari dreamed that it had never ended. That she was still there, dying because of the lack of food and bitter cold. Barely surviving on bread and water, then nothing at all.

That there was no Zahir to rescue her.

That her kidnappers had broken even more bones than the ones in her hands.

That she was going to die alone in that room, curled up on the floor.

But Mari didn't tell Zahir any of this. She let him hold her against his chest until his breathing was even and a snore tumbled from him. Then, she lay awake in his arms, staring into the darkness, hoping that the nightmares would stop assaulting her.

Once she knew Zahir was in a deep sleep, she rolled out of his arms and slid out of bed, pushing her feet into a pair of slippers. She padded silently across the room to the door and opened it slowly, keeping the wood from creaking. Once out of the room, the door shut, and with Zahir none the wiser, Mari crept down the hall and picked up one of the torches from the wall to guide her through the maze of the palace.

Mari wasn't sure where she was going, but every time Zahir fell back asleep after one of her nightmares, she snuck out. There was something stifling about sitting in the dark to deal with her trauma. So, Mari walked. Some nights she got something to eat from the kitchens. Others, she just wandered until the torch light burned her eyes. On this night, Mari knew where she wanted to go.

The torches that lined the wall burned bright, casting eerie shadows around every corner of the halls. Mari's heart would stop for a second every time one of the shadows looked like a man. Often, it was just a trick of the light. Other times, it was a servant scurrying past to finish their duties overnight. Mari was surprised at the number of servants who wandered the halls at night. She had never run into the same pair twice, save for once in the kitchens when she went to have a slice of cake and look at the stars from the gardens.

Mari set the torch on a holder near the palace doors before she pushed them open, the cool night air whipping across her face. She pulled her night clothes tighter around her body with her arms and she made her way down onto the damp grass. She plopped down beneath a tree, pulling her knees up and resting her forearms there. Her fingers caressed her chin as she tilted her head up to look at the stars above. The clear sky showcased thousands of twinkling stars and the moon shone full and bright.

Mari named aloud the constellations she could recognize: The Hunter, the Maiden, Arrow, and Flame. She counted until she reached fifteen. Her eyes scanned the night sky, searching for the one constellation she could never seem to pick out: The Eternal Flame. It was the only constellation named for Brahn and the Fire Mages. Three stars in a vertical line with six at the top, in a shaky oval.

The legend of the Eternal Flame came from the story that Brahn gave his mages a flame that never went out. When he first blessed the mages with their magic, there was famine because the mages had trouble controlling their magic; their food had burned easily. So, Brahn gave them the eternal flame at the peak of their mountain ranges. It is said that the stars aligned to commemorate the glorious event that ended the famine by providing the mages a way to control the way they cooked their food. The mages were able to cook their meat atop the mountains and feed their people. Legend has it that the constellation lies above the peak of that mountain. But no matter how long Mari scanned the peaks, she could never find where the eternal flame was in the sky.

"Are you cold?" A female voice floated to Mari's ears as a blanket was placed around her shoulders.

Mari turned her head to see Maura standing behind her, a smile on her face and two cups of tea in her hands. "Yes, thank you." Mari wrapped the blanket tight around her shoulders, not realizing she was shivering.

"What are you doing out here?" Maura asked as she sat down and heated the cups of tea until they were steaming. She held one out to Mari, who took it graciously.

"I couldn't sleep." Mari sighed as she sipped the warm jasmine tea. "What are you doing awake?"

"I couldn't sleep, either." Maura sipped her drink and pulled her plush robe around her. "I saw you sitting out here and thought you might need a companion."

"You are too kind, Maura." Mari smiled at her mother-in-law and turned her gaze back to the sky. "Can you point out the Eternal Flame to me?"

Maura let out a chuckle and raised her finger towards a mountain range in the East. "The Rana Mountains housed the eternal flame in the days of old. Above the third peak from the left is where the flame was placed." Maura dragged her finger upwards and Mari tried to follow the direction. "Right there you can see the three stars that make up the candle and then directly above are the rest of the stars. Do you see it?"

Mari squinted her eyes and tilted her body to match Maura's. She could barely see the mountain range in the dark, but she could just barely make out a couple of stars above the peak. She saw two stars in a vertical line and a few in an oval above it. To her, the stars making up the constellation were exceptionally dull. "It is very difficult to see."

"They say only Fire Mages can see the constellation in its true glory. These are the brightest stars in the sky. I can see them as soon as the sun sets, and all throughout the night. What do they look like to you?"

"They are not bright," Mari admitted, sheepishly. "I can barely see them."

"Maybe one day Brahn will allow you to see it in all of its glory." Maura lowered her hand and took a long sip of her tea. "Do you wish to speak about what troubles you?"

Mari took a quick sip of her tea and turned her body to face Maura. "I worry for Zahir."

Maura let out a deep sigh. "I, too, worry. He has never been good at dealing with stressful events."

Mari's laugh was breathy. "It is ironic he is king then, is it not?"

"I guess it is." Maura let out a little giggle.

"I should get back to bed. It is very late after all." Maura stood, pulling her robe tightly around her chest and holding her hand out for Mari's cup. "Goodnight." Mari placed the cup in Maura's hand as she turned away and walked back into the castle.

Mari waited until the door closed behind Maura before she, too, stood and wandered back inside. The night air whipped her hair and as Mari pushed it from her face, the flashback of being pulled by her hair made her pause. She remembered the man who yanked her back, pressing a knife into her throat. She remembered the panic that rose in her throat as she fought to get out of his grasp. She would never forget the blood that ran down her throat.

Without a second thought, Mari ran to the kitchens in search of shears. She was determined to never let her hair become a liability ever again. She found the shears in one of the many cabinets and she grabbed them quickly before she could change her mind. On the way back to her room, she considered what she was going to do, but pushed the worry from her mind. Zahir was still sleeping in their bedroom, none the wiser of what she was planning.

Once Mari locked herself in the bathing room, she stepped up to the mirror, pulling her hair in front of her chest. Tears streamed down her face as she cut at her hair, watching it fall to the floor in large clumps. Mari grunted as she tore through her locks, letting it pile up around her feet. She kicked it away angrily, her foot only just missing the mirror itself.

When she looked in the mirror again, she realized what she had done. Her hair rested at the length of her chin, uneven and tattered. The shears clanged to the ground as she raised a hand to the ends of her hair, playing with the now short strands. No longer would her hair be a liability.

"Hello, sister," Anya purred, the torches illuminating the coy smile on her lips. She had slinked into the bathing room without Mari even noticing.

"What are you doing here Anya? Zahir is sleeping," Mari said.

"What the hell did you do to yourself?" Anya asked, gliding closer and reaching a hand out to touch Mari's hair.

Mari raised a protective hand and swatted Anya's away. "I wanted a change."

"It looks like you lost your Gods-damned mind." Anya let out a low laugh. "I'm sure Zahir is going to *love* your new look."

It took everything in Mari's power not to roll her eyes. "What are you doing here, Anya?"

"I saw you running back here with those shears. I wasn't going to miss it if you were stabbing Zahir," Anya said, letting out a little laugh. When Mari didn't respond, Anya continued. "I just wanted to have a little chat with my sister. To see how you were doing."

"I'm doing fine, thank you for asking."

Anya laughed devilishly. "You know, I can hear your screams from my room. I could tell that scream anywhere now." Mari knew that Anya was just taunting her. "It sounds like someone is being tortured in here every night. Is Zahir *that* bad in bed?"

"You very well know that is not the reason."

"Oh, lighten up Mari. It's a joke. You can laugh." Anya paused, waiting for Mari to laugh but Mari refused to give Anya any reaction she wanted. "You and I both know that Zahir may not be my father's son."

"I don't know what you're talking about, Anya."

"Oh, please." Anya slid her feet from the table and leaned forward on her elbows. "If Zahir isn't a legitimate heir, he loses the throne. Then what happens to you? Do you get shipped back to Yu'güe?"

"He is your father's son." Mari was surprised that Anya had been thinking these things. She must not have known that Ryker gave Zahir the letter explaining his parentage.

"I'm going to be honest. Zahir never took after our father. He was never cutthroat. It is extremely plausible that he is a bastard son. I'm going to find out."

"Anya don't dig into it. Zahir was appointed heir and you weren't. I understand how much that must hurt. But you have to let it go," Mari said. "Ryker is his father. He told Zahir in a letter."

Anya laughed hysterically, wiping a tear from her eye for dramatic effect. "Mari, you and I both know I am not going to let this go. Zahir is a bastard," she spat the word, "I'm going to make sure all of Brahn knows it. It goes against the royal decrees. He can't be the king if he's illegitimate. I *will* make sure of it."

Anya turned and began to slink towards the door, but Mari caught her wrist, stopping her in her tracks. "If you do that, Anya, you will lose any chance of a reconciliation with Zahir."

"There was never going to be a reconciliation." Anya ripped her wrist from Mari's grasp and grimaced before walking out the door, leaving it open so Mari could watch her shoot a look of disgust towards Zahir.

When the door slammed shut, Zahir woke with a start, whipping his head around, looking for Mari. She stepped out from the bathing room, hoping Zahir couldn't quite see her hair.

"What are you doing up?" Zahir asked.

"I couldn't sleep," Mari said, coming closer. "I did something."

Mari approached Zahir and when she sat on the bed, she noticed Zahir staring at her hair. "Are you okay?"

"Yes. I couldn't keep my hair long with the memory of that man who took me. He pulled my hair. I couldn't take it being a liability anymore," Mari said, feeling tears prick her eyes.

"I understand. If it makes you happy, then I'm happy," Zahir said. He sat up and pulled Mari closer to him to kiss her softly. He raised his hands to cup her cheeks and Mari covered his hands with her own.

Mari only pulled away because there was a knock on the door. Every time she and Zahir kissed, it seemed like there was an interruption. All she wanted was some peace to kiss her husband. Mari groaned as she got up to answer the door. Behind it, stood Illan, a letter in his hand.

"I love your hair," Illan said, offering Mari a smile. "I am terribly sorry to disturb you, but I have something for Zahir."

Illan bustled into the room, holding the parchment out for Zahir. When he approached the bed, Zahir scooted to the end and took the paper from his uncle.

"What is this?" Zahir asked.

"Please don't be angry with me," Illan said. "I sent word to Lovíth about you being a Dual Mage to ask if they would come here to train you."

"What?" Zahir nearly growled. "Illan, I told you I didn't want this."

"Zahir, I let you make decisions all the time for yourself. You could die, Zahir. You *need* to train your Life Magic," Illan said, waving his hands to accentuate his point.

"How could you do this without asking me first?" Zahir asked, ripping open the letter. His eyes scanned the page rapidly and he looked back up at Illan, eyes narrowed. "They can't come here. Life Magic is connected to the land in Lovíth. They only train new mages there. They need me to come for eight moon cycles, at minimum."

"Then, you will go," Illan said, as if there were no other options.

"Illan," Zahir said, standing up. "I can't leave Brahn. I can't leave Mari. She has been through enough and I will *not* leave her here alone."

"Do I get a say in this?" Mari asked, stepping forward to be in Zahir's line of sight. "If it were up to me, you would go."

"Mari," Zahir said, walking to her and taking her face in his hands. "I can't leave you. I just can't. I need to know that you are safe."

Mari put her hands on Zahir's waist and spoke slowly. "If you don't go, you will die. And then you will leave me *forever*. Do you understand what that means? I will be alone, and you will be gone." Mari felt tears brim her eyes.

"Eight moon cycles is a long time, Mari. A lot can change in that time," Zahir said. "I don't want to leave you. I want to experience this life with you."

"That is why you must go," Mari said. "You need to train so we can grow old and gray together. Otherwise, I'll be here, alone, cursing myself because you didn't go to Lovíth. There is no life for us if you don't go."

Zahir was quiet for a long time. He held Mari, eyes scanning her face. Mari could almost see the thoughts swirling in his mind. She could almost see the pieces falling into place in his mind.

"I don't want to leave you," Zahir said, his voice just a whisper.

"We will write. I promise it will be okay. You need to do this," Mari said, squeezing Zahir's waist.

Zahir pulled Mari into his chest. "I will go so we can have a life together. I don't want to miss any of it."

Mari almost cried in relief. The thought of Zahir dying in just four years made her panic. If he died... she wouldn't be able to live with herself, knowing she could have prevented it.

When Zahir let her go, he turned to Illan. "We must call the council here. We have much to do and little time to do it. Lovíth asked me to be there in one week."

Mari watched Zahir and Illan leave before she fell backwards onto the bed, her heart heavy and her eyes full of tears.

Chapter Twenty-Eight

Mari

Mari hadn't realized she was sleeping until she felt Zahir pulling her against him and planting a light kiss along her lips. Her eyes fluttered open as he moved away. The light was just streaming into the windows as they lay tangled in each other's arms. They stayed like that, even when the servants came to escort them to a meal; refusing to get up from bed. With just a few fleeting days left, all that was left was spending time together and preparing the country for their king's absence.

As Zahir's fingers massaged Mari's head, she found herself listening to the sound of his pulse. Her head rested in the crook of his shoulder and she could hear the steady pounding of his heart. Looking close enough, she could see his neck pulsate in time with the beats. Mari nestled into Zahir, pulling herself closer to him, snaking a leg over his and pulling his body closer.

Zahir let out a laugh when Mari failed to bring him any closer. "I am going to miss you."

She looked up at him and gave him a sad smile. "And I, you."

Zahir pressed his lips to Mari's forehead for a long moment and only pulled away to rest his cheek on her head. "Do you want to sneak out one last time before I leave?"

Mari pulled her head back and laughed. "You are a king and yet you want to sneak out like a young boy."

"I may be a king, but I am still young."

Mari rolled her eyes but gave a toothy grin. "Let's go. Did you have somewhere in mind? Are we going back to that bar with your friends?"

"I thought we could go somewhere alone. We will begin preparations tomorrow, and I fear we will not have another night like this before I leave." Zahir blinked back tears as he looked away from Mari. But she saw the pain in his expression.

Mari lifted her head to press her lips to Zahir's cheek. "I would like that."

"Before we go, how about a picnic?" Zahir asked, sliding out of the bed. He picked up from the floor beside him a brown wicker basket filled with various foods.

Mari sat up in bed, excited. "Oh, how lovely. This was so sweet of you, Zahir."

Zahir and Mari slipped into loose clothing that would give them the ability to climb onto the roof. They tied their light scarves around their necks to hide their hair once they finished eating. Zahir scooped the basket into his arms, hopped up onto the railing and hoisted himself up onto the roof. Mari watched his feet disappear and looked at the edge of the roof, mouth wide, as Zahir popped his head back out, silver hair falling down over his face. He had still yet to dye it, no matter how many times Mari had offered to help.

"Step onto the railing, I will pull you up," Zahir said. He reached his arms down, waiting for Mari to follow his instructions.

Mari smiled as she stepped from the chair to the railing, gripping onto the edge of the roof for dear life. She slowly wrapped her hands one by one around Zahir's toned forearms as he gripped hers. She felt herself be pulled from the railing and up towards Zahir's face.

"Please don't drop me," Mari whispered as her head came over the edge of the roof.

"Swing your leg up." Zahir's voice was strained as he pulled back on Mari's arms. She obliged and swung her left leg up until her knee was resting on the roof. It was then that she was able to use some of her strength to hoist herself up and get her other knee up. By the time she was fully kneeling on the roof, her shoulder throbbed, and her heart hammered in her chest. "That wasn't so bad, was it?" Zahir's breathy laughter rang out.

Mari slowly stood and made her way to Zahir who was beginning to lay out a large cloth towards the top of the roof. She grabbed the other end of it and helped Zahir flatten it. Zahir immediately sat down, not wanting it to blow away in the breeze that was sending their hair flying. Out of the basket came various small meats, bread, and spreads. Mari's stomach grumbled on cue as Zahir passed her the food.

"What is it with you and the roof?" Mari asked, taking a bite of her snack. She moaned in delight. "What is this?" She had piled a thin slice of red meat onto a small slice of brown bread.

"Elk. We have a few that run around here. It's a specialty since we don't get them very often." Zahir moaned at his own mouthful of food.

"It's delicious. I ate elk all the time growing up, but it never tasted this good." Mari took another slice and ate it without any supplement, sucking the juices off her fingers. "So, the roof?"

Zahir held up a finger as he finished chewing. "It was the only place in this palace that no one would find me. No one thought to check the roof when I went missing. It was always my bedroom, the library, or the training rooms. Besides, it was the one place Anya couldn't get up onto. She is terrified of heights."

"Understandable. I am not a huge *fan* of heights, but I wouldn't say I'm scared of them." Mari shrugged and dipped some bread in a jar of purple jelly. It wiggled when she touched it, but it was the sweetest thing she had eaten in a long time. "What is this?" Mari asked, pointing to the jelly.

"Blackberry preserve. When I was a child, I ate it on *every-thing*. There wasn't a meal where I didn't eat blackberry preserve." Zahir shook his head and laughed. "What were you like when you were young?"

Mari looked out at the city for the first time since they sat down. She couldn't see or hear anything coming from the city, but she could imagine the people rushing around, getting their own meals. She thought of all the delicious smells coming from the restaurants down there as Zahir pulled her through the streets. She thought about kids playing in the streets, laughing and running in circles, their parents glad they were busying themselves.

"Before Hanan left," Mari began, "I was really outgoing and energetic. I would always be playing with the neighbor kids, or with Hanan. We would throw an animal skull around or chase each other. Sometimes, if it had just snowed, we would build a fort and hide in it until our parents called us for dinner. It didn't matter that he was six years older, he would always play with me."

Mari described the time her brother caused a snow fight with the neighboring kids. He had been aiming the ball for Mari's back, but she ducked just in time. The ball hit their mean neighbor, Iza, in the face. She was so mad that she tackled Hanan right into a snow drift. The rest of the kids watching took sides, flinging snow into the other kids' faces. Mari ended up putting snow down Iza's shirt and she pushed Mari into the same drift as Hanan. The snow went down her pants, making Mari yelp in surprise. It was then that Hanan tackled Iza himself, burying her beneath the snow.

Zahir was smiling brightly as Mari told him the story of the snow fight. "That sounds like so much fun. I would have loved to do that."

Mari stuffed another piece of bread in her mouth with a red jam. "What's this?" She asked through her bread.

Zahir cracked a smile. "Fire jelly. It's a little spicy, even for me. How much did you have?"

It was then that Mari's eyes began to water. The spice from the jelly had hit her right in the back of her throat as she swallowed, making her feel like she was choking. She instantly stuck her tongue out and fanned it frantically with her hand.

"Do you have water?" Mari panted, desperately in need of relief.

Zahir pulled a glass vase of water out of the basket and poured some into a small cup for Mari. She snatched the cup from Zahir and doused the fire on her tongue. When the water cooled off the spice, Mari sighed and put the cup back in the basket.

"That was a little too spicy for me. The flavor was good, though." Mari touched a finger to her lips, which she could have sworn were swollen.

Mari stared out to the mountains as she and Zahir finished their meal. They sat in a comfortable silence, realizing sadly that this was one of the last meals they would share together before Zahir left.

"Before we get too sad about my departure, let's go on our adventure," Zahir said, smiling at Mari.

By the time Zahir packed up the empty food containers and brought the basket back into their room, Mari had covered her now short hair with the thin scarf. Her hair was still a mess, but she really wanted someone to fix it. The look wasn't exactly *flattering* for a queen.

Once Zahir was back on the roof, he led Mari across the jump between roofs and helped her scale the fence on the other side. Once he had helped her back to the ground, he laced his fingers with her and set off to the east. Mari took one look at the city behind them, lights blinding, and street noise floating through the silent trees and wondered where Zahir could be taking her outside of the city. The forest before them was dense with trees and the looming unknown made Mari cling tightly to Zahir's hand.

Zahir slowed his pace. "Do you wish to go back?"

"No!" Mari shook her head violently. "We are two strong mages; we should be able to handle ourselves."

Mari's nerves made her jump each time an owl hooted, or a deer ruffled the bushes near them. Her heart gave a little start whenever she stepped on a stick and the echoing snap resonated through the trees. When a squirrel jumped from a tree and landed in their path, Mari nearly screamed with fright. It wasn't that she was scared of the forest; it was that she didn't want to be blindsided by an attack.

Dark thoughts ran through her mind that the rebels would find and kill them. Visions of watching Zahir be tortured and put to death made her nearly ask to turn around. But, as this was the last adventure they would have for a long time, she went on, blindly following Zahir through the thick forest.

Zahir's gaze never wandered from the path in front of them. All he did was stare ahead, occasionally scanning to the left and right. He spoke infrequently, only to ask Mari if she was okay or if she needed a break. It was several miles before the incline of their walk changed sharply. Mari felt her breathing become more like pants as they climbed the incline. The trees were still too dense for Mari to see, but she had a feeling that it was a mountain they were climbing.

After a long stretch of time, Mari had to stop and sit on a stump to catch her breath. She wiped sweat from her face with the scarf around her head. She flapped the collar of her shirt, pulling the cool night air over her chest. The chill in the air made the sweat on her stomach frigid. When Zahir went to wrap an arm around Mari to keep her warm, she pushed him away, panting that she was too warm to be touched.

Zahir leaned casually against the tree beside Mari, barely breaking a sweat. "Do you wish to go back?"

"How much longer is this walk?" Mari asked, swiping the back of her hand across her forehead. "And how are you not exhausted?"

"About a mile. Do you think you can make it? I promise it is worth it. I used to come here after my father first started losing his memory. Sometimes the roof wasn't enough." Zahir unwrapped the scarf from his own head and wiped the sweat from the back of Mari's neck.

"Yes, I can make it. I just need another minute." Mari put her hands on top of her head. "I used to be able to do this all the time in Yu'güe. What happened to me?"

"You had some serious trauma."

Mari willed herself to stand. The burning of her thighs as she stood made her bite her lip to hold back a groan. Mari stretched out her calf muscles before looking towards the top of the mountain. "I can do this."

Zahir chuckled as he walked beside Mari as she continued to walk up. Breathing never became easier and her legs screamed as they walked further and further away from the city. As they climbed, the trees became thinner and Mari was able to see bits of light from the city behind them. She constantly looked over her shoulder, taking in the shrinking glow in all of its beauty. The stars and moon began to light up their way as the thick leaves parted. Mari was able to see the rocky path beneath her feet without Zahir shining his flame directly at her feet. She glanced up at the sky and saw the two stars from the Eternal Flame shining above her. Even up close, the constellation still wasn't breathtaking.

When Zahir finally pulled off to the side and sat down on a large boulder, Mari nearly collapsed into him. She sat beside him, leaning her head on his shoulder while she caught her breath. Her heart pounded from the exertion and her hands shook with exhaustion. It was only then that she realized they hadn't brought any food or water with them.

"Open your eyes, darling." Zahir's voice was a husky whisper in her ears.

Mari hadn't even realized she had closed her eyes until she opened them, gasping when she looked out on the entirety of Brahn. The city looked like its own sky of twinkling lights. The silence from the peak of the mountain was more serene than the roof had ever been.

"This is... breathtaking." As if to prove her point, Mari inhaled a shaking breath.

Zahir lifted his hand just past the top of the city. "If you look close enough, you can see the ocean from here."

Mari followed Zahir's finger and could just barely make out where the sky met the ground in a wavy line.

"I want to sail. I took a boat from Yu'güe to Brahn, but I want to see the ocean when I'm not wracked with nerves. I want to know what being on a boat is like when I don't already want to throw up," Mari said.

"You wanted to throw up on your way to our wedding?" Zahir's eyebrows pointed down.

"From the nerves, Zahir! I didn't want to throw up because of *you*. It was more the thought of my entire life changing, moving halfway across the world to marry someone I had never met. It's weird to think that a year ago, I didn't know who you were or even what you looked like. But now..." Mari trailed off, thinking about how close she had felt to Zahir after just a few moon cycles.

"But now it seems weird that we may never have met?" Zahir took the words right out of her mouth.

A year ago, Mari had no idea what Zahir was like. While they wrote letters, she didn't know how much of his words were him versus his obligation to her. Never in a million lifetimes would she have thought she would marry a prince who would turn out to be the first Dual Mage in millennia. And now, she couldn't imagine spending every day with anyone else.

"Thank you for saving me from the rebels. I owe you a life debt." Mari leaned her head on Zahir's shoulder.

Zahir wrapped an arm around her and scratched his nails up and down the small of Mari's back. "I think marrying me is as good a life debt as any."

Mari felt Zahir's chest heave with laughter. "Give yourself a little credit, Zahir. I think you are a little more likable than you believe yourself to be."

"I never thought I would marry someone so kind and thoughtful. I didn't know who my father would choose. I am very lucky it is you." Zahir leaned his cheek on Mari's head, trapping her head on his shoulder.

"Can you believe it's been just a few moon cycles since we met? It feels as if I have known you for years."

"I agree. I know about your fear of birds and your hatred of whiskey. I've learned about your sympathetic nature and how you eat cake in large bites, like it might disappear." Zahir paused and pulled his head from Mari's and lifted her chin with his fingertips to meet his gaze. "I never imagined knowing those things about someone, but now I can't imagine not knowing them about you."

Mari leaned up to press her lips to Zahir's and pulled his hair out of its bun with her fingertips. It fell around his shoulders and tickled Mari's cheeks. She leaned away from the kiss and ran her fingers through the ends of his soft silky hair.

"I like your hair better down."

As Mari went to kiss Zahir again, he pulled her upward suddenly until she was wrapped in his embrace. His hands rested on the small of her back and hers were wrapped around his neck. She leaned her head on his shoulder, closing her eyes and taking in his scent. Zahir began to slowly sway back and forth, spinning her slowly around, a soft hum escaping him.

Mari leaned into the swaying and listened to Zahir hum a strangely familiar song. She listened to the notes drifting into the night as she tried to place where she had heard that song before. It was not the song that he sang to Roan as he slept. Several minutes later, Mari realized where she recognized the song from.

"This is the song we danced to at our wedding." Mari's voice was a whisper as she smiled to herself.

"Indeed, it is."

Mari tilted her head up to meet Zahir's lips, settling into his arms, but as one hand snaked up her back to grasp the back of her neck the kiss went from soft to forceful. Zahir's insistent mouth parted Mari's lips as giddiness rose in her chest and she kissed him back just as fervently. She laced her fingers into the hair at the back of his head and gave a light tug. Zahir sighed into Mari's mouth as he dragged his nails across her back.

Mari lifted his shirt off over his head, exposing his muscled chest, and she ran her hands down his muscles, raking her nails across his skin. He gripped her waist hard when she did this and toyed with the bottom of her shirt until he pulled it off, exposing her to him for the first time. Mari tried to cover her stomach with her arms, but Zahir pulled them away, trailing his eyes up and down her body.

"You are radiant, Mari." He pressed kisses down her jawline and neck to her collarbone. He nipped at the sensitive skin there, eliciting a soft moan from her. He trailed his lips lower down her chest as she let out soft gasps. Mari wasn't sure what came over her as she unbuckled Zahir's trousers and pushed them down. All she knew was that she wanted to have every inch of him pressed against her.

Zahir kicked off his trousers so they landed in a heap beside him and pressed his body against Mari's. He slowly pushed her backwards until her back was against the rock face of the mountain. Zahir aided Mari in stepping out of her pants before he lowered her to the ground. He hovered over her, his hair falling to frame his face and she writhed beneath him as he settled his weight on her, lining himself up with her. Mari felt like she was going to fly out of her skin. She moaned as he skimmed his fingernails up her thigh, tracing over—

Mari wrapped a hand around him as she arched her back and his whole body shuddered. Zahir crashed his lips into hers, quieting the sounds coming from both their mouths. When there was a second of silence for a breath, Zahir trailed kisses down Mari's throat and onto her chest.

"Do you want to—"

"*Don't stop.*"

Zahir forced himself up, looking Mari in the eyes. "Are you sure?"

"Yes, Zahir. I want to."

Mari's heart rate increased as she spoke, and Zahir pulled off her undergarments until she was completely naked beneath him.

"Tell me if you want me to stop."

Zahir slid into her, slow and deep, and she kissed his shoulder as he stilled, making sure she was adjusted. As Mari lifted her lips to Zahir's, he began to move, the two of them moaning into a kiss. Beneath the starry sky, it felt like there was nothing other than this moment.

No rebels.

No leaving for Lovíth.

Nothing except the sound of the breeze and the presence of the other.

Chapter Twenty-Nine

Mari

Two days later, a conference was called. The same area was set up yet again at the base of the palace steps and Zahir's speech was so elegant it moved some of the members of the crowd to tears. Even Mari held back tears, despite helping Zahir rehearse it several times. His voice was so persuasive that she could see the understanding in the eyes of their citizens. Zahir spoke so highly of Mari, wiping away any trepidation of ruling Brahn with Illan's aid by calling her "regal, intelligent, and innovating". She was surprised when he choked back tears as he spoke about leaving her for nearly a year.

Mari worried that the people would absolutely riot about Zahir being a Dual Mage. So, they thought of a lie to use in the meantime until he conquered his life magic:he was traveling to Lovíth to expand his knowledge of the other clans and to build a connection with the other mages. He had expressed previously that he wanted to open trade, but this was the first time he had put out a plan to achieve that. Mari could see the confused expressions in the crowd, but she hoped those would diminish with time, as trade with Lovíth could actually open up.

But when he turned around and made his way over to her, she knew they were real tears. She knew he was truly going to miss her and leaving was ripping his heart in two, just as it was her own. He kissed her cheek and grasped her hand as Illan stepped forward to lead a prayer, asking Brahn to guide Zahir on his journey and make it worthwhile.

The crowd stood and raised their hands to the sky, flames dancing on their fingertips. Zahir's mouth dropped open slightly and his eyes widened, then he, too, raised his hand and sent flames swirling in the air above him and Mari.

"It's a warrior's sendoff. It's a tradition here when we send our commanders into battle." Zahir whispered in Mari's ear. "It is the highest honor of any soldier."

"You deserve it. You are putting the world above yourself." Mari smiled. "I am lucky to have you as my husband."

"It is I, who has been blessed."

When the flames died away, thunderous applause filled the air and Mari spotted Hanan standing in the front row, pride in his eyes. He was proud of her. Mari's heart swelled at the thought .

As the couple was led to the docks by their advisors and a swarm of guards, Mari heard Zahir's name being called. No title, just Zahir. The pair turned their heads to see the group of Zahir's friends pushing their way towards them.

"Guards, give us a minute." Zahir waved them through and soon Raf was crashing into him, wrapping his arms around his waist.

"I can't believe you're leaving." Raf wrenched himself from the hug and punched Zahir hard in the shoulder.

"Ow! What the hell was that for?" Zahir rubbed his arm, a smile forming on his lips.

"You didn't tell us you were leaving," he said.

Mari watched Reina approach tentatively. "I'm going to miss you, Zahir."

"I'll miss you, too. How are you—"

"Fine," Reina said, sticking her hand out for Zahir to shake. "You will be great."

Mari could see the tension between the two. Illan had Reina questioned as soon as Zahir told him Rodrick betrayed the royal family. Despite Zahir's protests, she was kept in the palace for several days until she was allowed to go home. Zahir had yet to reach out to her with an apology, even though he'd told Mari he wanted to.

"Who am I going to drink whiskey with now?" Raf asked, throwing his hands up into the air. "You are my whiskey boy."

Zahir laughed as he answered. "You're just going to have to teach Mari to like whiskey."

"Oh, no." Mari put her hands up defensively. "Do *not* drag me into this."

Zahir stepped back and reached out a hand to Hanan. "I hope when I come back, we can spend more time together. I would like to get to know you more, brother."

Hanan shook Zahir's hand and gave him a warm smile. "I would like that very much."

Mari's heart swelled at the sight of Zahir talking with his friends. He promised them he would write and swore that the night he came back he would meet them at the bar. He told them that Mari would sit in his spot at the table if she were able to get away from the palace.

Once the guards demanded they depart, Mari and Zahir were led to the docks. A large boat sat in the water, high above the dock, a crew loading supplies and weapons onto the deck. About twenty men carried crates and yelled directions to load everything in time for departure. Mari could see the sweat running down the men's faces as they approached.

Her breath hitched. She did not want to say goodbye to Zahir. It seemed that he noticed and asked the guards for a moment alone before he boarded. They begrudgingly obliged, letting Zahir drag Mari fifteen feet away.

He wrapped his arms around her shoulders and she snaked hers around his waist, gripping him tightly. The tears flowed from her eyes onto the fabric of his shirt, surely leaving wet spots. Mari felt his chest rising and falling unevenly and she knew that he had tears as well.

"Promise me you'll write," Mari said, her voice wavering.

Zahir laughed. "Of course, I'll write. Don't burn the clan to the ground."

"How could I do that? I'm not a Fire Mage!" Mari laughed, hiccupping.

Zahir pulled away from Mari and wrapped her in a deep kiss. Mari pulled him closer, so that every inch of their bodies was touching, so that there was no space between them.

"I will miss you." Zahir wiped tears from his eyes.

"I will miss you. Go be the mage you were born to be."

Mari led Zahir back towards the guards and inevitably to the ship. Zahir embraced her one last time before giving Illan a hug and thanking him for everything he had done. Zahir sighed, turning away, and walked to the ship's ladder. Maura stood at the bottom, waiting to say her goodbyes. She embraced her son tightly and gave him a kiss on his forehead. She seemed to whisper something meaningful, for Zahir was once again wiping tears from his eyes.

Once he broke from his conversation with his mother, Zahir greeted the captain with a handshake and followed him up the ladder. Halfway up, he turned his head and met Mari's gaze. She smiled and gave a small wave before blowing him a kiss. Zahir pretended to catch it and put it into his heart.

Once every man was aboard the ship, it launched through the water, the sails waving in the wind. It rushed through the water, creating a wake in its path and it wasn't until Zahir was out of sight and the sails were fading over the horizon that Mari let her smile drop.

Instead of crying, Mari straightened and turned to Illan. "We have much work to do." She projected her voice, hoping she sounded secure in the decision.

"We can begin tomorrow, my Queen. Today has been long and you should rest." Illan gave her a knowing smile. "We will meet at dawn tomorrow."

Mari nodded. "Very well. Let us go home."

Mari took one last look over her shoulder and saw one last flap of Brahn's flag before it disappeared over the horizon. She sighed and kept walking, praying that Zahir would find everything he was looking for.

Epilogue

A group of fifty men sat around a table, their hoods pulled over their eyes and titanium weapons sitting on their laps. The room was dark save for a single oil lamp at the front of the room. The seat at the front was empty, waiting for someone to take its place. Every man was silent except for the occasional loud exhale that turned every head in the room.

A set of footsteps echoed around the concrete room until they stopped at the empty chair. The scratch of the wooden legs on the ground was ear splitting. A woman in a black cloak slid onto the seat, her hood covering her eyes. She laid his weapon in front of her, folding her hands over the hilt of the sword.

"My people." Her voice sounded like gravel as it echoed around the room. "We now know the identity of the Dual Mage whom we seek. King Zahir of Brahn is a Fire and Life Mage. He and his armies slaughtered our people. He has just departed for Lovíth. It is only a matter of time until he can harness his full abilities. Once he does, he and the other mages will be unstoppable. If he can live, others may begin to mate with mages from other clans.

"This reign must come to an end. We must stop the tyranny of the mages before it is too late. We have two options. We either infiltrate Lovíth and assassinate King Zahir or we invade Brahn again, a much harder task, and bring harm to Queen Mari. We must assess our options carefully and ensure we are making the right decision."

A voice broke a beat of silence. "I believe that an assassination attempt may force us to sacrifice some of our members. And we are dwindling due to the slaughter."

"You may be right, Klaus." The woman at the head of the table pulled a dagger from her waist and flung it at the man who spoke. A choking sound escaped Klaus' lips as the dagger struck him in the throat and he collapsed onto the table. "However, this is not a democracy."

ACKNOWLEDGEMENTS

I can't even begin to express the feels. This book has been a work in progress for many years and seeing it on the page is just *squeals*. I am so grateful for everyone who encouraged me to finish this story and just get the words on the page.

First, I must thank my editors, Claire and Darby, from Second Pass Editing. You two saw this manuscript in a rough condition and since then this has blossomed into something I am so proud of. Thank you for pushing me through the doubts I had with your positive comments, your LOLs to my (obviously hilarious) dialogue, and your love for my characters. Every suggestion you made was extremely helpful and I will never be able to thank you enough for working with me for so many months.

Thank you to Stef from Seventh Star Art for designing my stunning cover! I gave you a vibe and you delivered in a way that I could never have dreamt of. I can't wait to work with you again.

Thank you to my alpha readers, who read my ~~horrible~~ first draft and encouraged me to edit this thing. Tamar and Dan, you guys are the best. Tamar, your immediate love for my story is the reason I kept writing. Those like ten texts you sent me at 3am because you couldn't put down the book made me cry. And that meant the world to me. Dan, you sat down and helped me plan out my book after I totally pantsed my first draft and let me talk about this story for hours on end, no matter what. Thank you so much.

My beta readers: Jackie, Lea, Tamar (again), Jess, Rachel, Sarosh, Becca, and Sue... thank you. All of you gave me such AMAZING feedback and love that really helped shape this novel. Thank you first of all for reading it, and also for giving me all of the of feedback. I really appreciate everything you did to help. And thank you for loving my characters like I love them.

Mom and Dad, thank you for your years of encouragement. From my first novel ten-plus years ago to this one now, you have always been rooting for me. And I can't even express how much that truly means to me. Your support has always been something I could rely on and I am eternally grateful for that. I love you both so much. Thank you for everything.

To my fiancé Dan, you have been so amazing. Thank you for loving me in my insanity while I did this. Thank you for spending three hours planning my story arc with me. Thank you for giving me so many ideas and lines of witty dialogue. Just thank you. I couldn't have done this without you.

To you, dear reader, for picking up an indie author's debut. I really hope you enjoyed the beginning of Mari and Zahir's journey.

ABOUT AUTHOR

S. C. Muir is a queer debut author from New York living with her fiancé. S. C. is a research scientist with a B.S. Chemistry from Binghamton University and is pursuing her M.S. Chemistry. When she can tear herself away from a book, S. C. enjoys hiking, traveling, and watching Survivor or Our Flag Means Death. To keep tabs on her writing she can be found on **Instagram and Tiktok: @scmuir.author.** You can sign up for S. C. Muir's newsletter on www.scmuirauthor.com to stay up to date and get exclusive information!

Made in the USA
Middletown, DE
27 October 2023

41342473R00217